"Ten seconds to impact."

"Battle screen maximum," WarAvocat ordered.

In the exterior view the Guardship vanished behind an oily shimmer.

"Five seconds to impact. Three. Two. One."

Both views died in a storm of light.

Then in the exterior view the Guardship ploughed through the nuclear fury. The great terror had not so much as shivered.

WarAvocat chuckled. "For a second, there, they were cheering over yonder." His humor vanished. "Let's take it before they purge the data banks."

"Are we taking prisoners?"

"I see no point, beyond SOP for interrogation. Deified?"

The Deified held their tongues. Thumbs down for the heroes of V. Rothica.

VII Gemina launched the assault battalion, then turned and followed other assault craft already headed for Merod Schene.

# THE DRAGON NEVER SLEEPS

Other books by Glen Cook

# THE DRAGON NEVER SLEEPS

# GLEN COOK

**NIGHT SHADE BOOKS**
SAN FRANCISCO

*The Dragon Never Sleeps* © 1988 by Glen Cook
This edition of *The Dragon Never Sleeps* © 2009 by
Night Shade Books

Cover art by John Berkey

Cover design by Claudia Noble
Interior layout and design by Jeremy Lassen

ISBN 978-1-59780-148-5

**Night Shade Books**
Please visit us on the web at
http://www.nightshadebooks.com

*He lies ever upon his hoard,*

*his heart jealous and mean.*

*Never believe he has nodded*

*because his eyes have closed.*

*The dragon never sleeps.*

— Kez Maefele,

speaking to the Dire Radiant

# - 1 -

**Guardship:** *VII Gemina*
**On rest station in trojan L5 off P. Jaksonica 3**
**11/23 shipsyear 3681; year 43 of the Deified**
**Kole Marmigus**
**Dictats: The Deified Ansehl Ronygos, dct. 12**
       **WarAvocat Hanaver Strate, dct. 1**
**Alert status: Green Three**
       **WarCrew sleeping [.03 duty section]**
**Surveillance Mode: Passive**

All was quiet in Hall of the Watchers. The whisper of electronics was soporific. Watchers struggled to stay awake. Third WatchMaster roamed silently, tapping shoulders with an ivory baton.

His admonitions were not vigorous. WarAvocat had not yet left his quarters. He might not. He was preoccupied with a new dalliance.

None of the Deified observed from their screens.

It had been this quiet for a shipsyear.

A *ping!* wakened everyone. Third WatchMaster tried to stroll toward the sound's source. His legs betrayed him.

It was that kind of time. Any trivial break in routine caused quickened breathing.

The Deified Thalygos Mundt came onscreen, his expression malign as always. Third WatchMaster asked, "What do we have, Break Detect?"

"Traveler breaking off the Web, WatchMaster."

Third WatchMaster looked to the head of the Hall. The

appropriate displays were up. The routine challenge had pulsed out. He glanced up. The Deified Thalygos Mundt had gone.

What was it like, being a living part of the ship? It was a vagrant curiosity. He was young yet. Only the old entertained ambitions toward immortality.

The backfeed from the breakaway appeared on the wall, downsped pulse content running from right to left: Glorious Spent, *House Cholot, bound from V. Rothica to D. Vawnii via P. Jaksonica: general cargo and passengers. Cargo and passenger transhipments scheduled at P. Jaksonica 3B, data follows.*

Routine. A passenger list, in case one was wanted and stupid enough to travel without changing identity.

"WatchMaster! I have an emergency signal!"

"Bring it up audial. Alert, Yellow Three." All over the Guardship green lights went yellow, blinking.

The message: "... *Gemina,* we've had an unauthorized discharge of an emergency escape pod...."

Third WatchMaster snapped, "Alert, Yellow One! Page WarAvocat. Relay the incoming to appropriate divisions."

"... not yet know if anyone was aboard...."

"Search. Find that pod."

"We have it, WatchMaster."

"Lock on. Track and Probe." Conscious of the screens overhead, he barked, "Get the data on the wall. I want everything up when WarAvocat arrives."

Throughout *VII Gemina* the shift prepared for whatever demands might be placed on the Guardship.

"WatchMaster. We have Lock and Track. That pod is under control. Trajectory indicates a surface destination near Cholot Varagona."

Was there another city on P. Jaksonica 3? "Probe data?"

"None yet, WatchMaster."

"Feed the target data to WarCentral. Pulse Canon Garrison Varagona. Prepare to intercept illegal downbound."

Half the overhead screens were live now but the Deified remained silent. Still, he felt compelled to demonstrate his grip. "Probe? How long is it going to take?"

"First approximation is due up, WatchMaster.... Here it comes. One biological lifeform. Artifact or nonhuman."

Third WatchMaster hesitated. He did not want the disapprobation that would follow an order to waken the whole Guardship. "Alert, Red Three." He slapped his baton into his palm, repeated it more forcefully.

Alarms snarled. Decks and bulkheads shivered. The air whispered and murmured and became cooler as inertial sectors locking-in distressed peacetime flow patterns. Already dim lighting faded as power shunted to battle screen generators. Sound levels rose as normally silent Watchers ran verbal checks with their neighbors.

Then came a bone-vibrating grumble as starspace drives went on line and Web tractor wells lit off.

Third WatchMaster sighed, ran a hand through brown hair, adjusted his khaki OpsCrew uniform. He had reached the limit of his authority.

The wall began running information from the Cholot Traveler's report of conditions on the Web. The data proclaimed a routine passage.

WarAvocat Hanaver Strate, Dictat, immaculate in WarCrew black and silver, entered Hall of the Watchers.

## - 2 -

Lady Midnight drifted through the perpetual twilight of Merod Schene DownTown, tall, brittle as leaf gold beaten translucent. Her lavender eyes darted from one nest of gloom to the next. Her slim, pale, fragile face was dewed with sweat. Her thin white hands fluttered like panicky hummingbirds. She started at a rustle from a shadow's heart, clutched her hands to her breast, wrapped her shivering wings more tightly around her. The last hints of their usual silken glimmer faded to shades of lead.

It was hot and damp and musty down there, decayed and slimy, dark and deadly, with sudden patches of fetid air, like an old jungle battleground. Small things scuttled away.

Midnight was afraid.

Fear was a new feeling. Fear was not part of her design. She had been made for the salons and bedrooms of high society. Fear had had to be learned.

Lady Midnight savored new things. But this fear she did not like. It stole the color from her wings. It gnawed her innards like cancer. It took away sleep and robbed her of appetite. It was an assassin that butchered the rhythm of her dance-in-flight. It knotted her muscles till they ached.

"Fool," she murmured in an angel's voice. "You're Immune." She swished clothing of pastel panels as thin as imagination. "You can't be touched." The fear did not subside.

Merod Schene DownTown reeked of insanity. The madness was spreading. Immunity could lose its value any minute.

Scraping, clicking sounds came from the deeper darknesses. Things were following her. Crazy things, evil things, the worst discards and mistakes, that till recently had confined their predations to the deepest hours of the night. She felt their mad eyes measuring her.

They grew bolder all the time.

She paused outside the breezeway leading to her destination. The silence in there was more intimidating than the clicks and slithers growing louder behind her. She did not want to go ahead. But they were working themselves up back there.

Something moved in the breezeway.

Terror yanked a melodic whimper from Midnight's throat.

Dark dread rolled over her, filled her hollow bones with

liquid nitrogen. Then warmth swamped her as she recognized the shadow. "Amber Soul!"

The shadow shifted shape, becoming something out of nightmare, rushed past. Clicks, squeaks, scrabblings, whines, the hiss of scales on decomposed pavement moved away hurriedly. Lady Midnight rushed along the dank passage, through a doorway, into a brightly lighted room, where she fell trembling into Turtle's arms.

Only after her heartbeat slackened and her shaking stopped was she smitten by the incongruity of being held and comforted by a creature so much shorter.

Strange as she was, Midnight was human. Turtle was not.

Turtle stood 1.75 meters tall and 1 meter wide. He massed 125 kilos, not a gram of it fat. He had skin the color and texture of a snake's belly. His features vaguely resembled a turtle's. But there was nothing slow or lumbering about him. He moved like a cat.

Amber Soul drifted inside, now wearing human form, draped in apparent golden brocade. Half a meter taller than Midnight, she seemed regal. Her psionic menace had gone silent. *They grow bolder.*

"It's the madness," Midnight piped. "It's spreading. It's into UpTown and even the High City feels its breath." Turtle had said that last time. She did not think of things like that herself.

"They got their messenger out?" Turtle asked.

"Yes. Aboard a Cholot Traveler. Disguised as the child of a High City lord from F. M'Cartica 5."

"So the infection bounds from world to world. They are fools. Where was the Traveler bound?"

"P. Jaksonica."

Turtle settled into a chair, for all his lethal mass a weary little creature. He picked at a button on his homemade shirt. "Yes. The thing will be fool enough to try it. P. Jaksonica 3.

Still under the Ban."

Turtle always knew so much. He amazed everyone. How could he know, trapped here in Merod Schene DownTown?

He looked Midnight in the eye. "The cure will not be long coming if it tries to reach Cholot Varagona." He closed his reptilian eyes briefly, which was no closing at all, for he had only nictating membranes. "Bless the Concord. There is no saving fools. Ladies, it is time we saw to our own welfare."

*Is there no chance for the Concord?* Amber Soul asked. Just the edge of that thought was enough to make Midnight's head buzz. Amber Soul almost never communicated with anyone. When she did she knocked you down.

"None," Turtle said. "The thing is one of those jackstraw rebellions that come along every human generation. I have seen a hundred. They don't last. The *Enherrenraat* did not last a year and it was five hundred in the shaping." He paused, then asked rhetorically, "How old are the Guardships? They were old when I was young. Sometimes it seems the stars themselves are younger and the Guardships were created old and wily and deadly and there was never a moment when they were not invincible."

No one knew Turtle's true age. Turtle would not say. They joked that DownTown had been built around him.

Turtle seldom talked about Turtle. Whence had he come? What was he? The last indigene of V. Rothica 4? There were ruins in the deserts. Unlikely that he was of the precursor race, though. Nobody was that old.

An artifact, then? Like Lady Midnight? Created in a laboratory for some inscrutable purpose even he had forgotten? The warrens of DownTown festered with artifacts who had outlived the usefulness of their designs. And it was thick with mistakes. The hobby life designers seldom destroyed their mistakes. They just turned them out. And some were terrible.

And some bred true.

If not an artifact, might Turtle be an alien, lost, stranded, planetbound far from home?

That was the popular theory.

Turtle told nothing about himself directly, but Turtle told stories, only to the very young, on the streets of DownTown. He mirrored childhood dreams, singing interstellar songs, spinning epics of great ships clambering the Web. He told tales of warmer worlds and far suns, of races no DownTowner would ever see, of great fires searing the deep between the stars as warships met in battles of unimaginable fury. Perhaps he spoke of the destruction of the *Enherrenraat*. Or perhaps he spoke of another struggle more remote in space and time. He sang his songs of far wars in shades of emotion that said he had seen them himself, that he might have been among those who had gained only shattered dreams.

Turtle broke a long silence. "If it does try to carry its message to Cholot Varagona it will be taken. Canon garrison will pulse P. Jaksonica station. Every Traveler out will carry a call for the Guardships. The first to arrive will pick the thing's brain to the last synapse. Then it will come sniffing up the creature's backtrail. First stop: Merod Schene."

Lady Midnight trilled, "Will they be that terrible?"

"Huh! Worse than you imagine. A Cholot Traveler picks up a shapeshifting illegal of a race supposedly eradicated from a Merod world and delivers it to a Cholot world under the Ban. They will be thorough. We must assure our own safety. Precautions never taken are the only sort that leave one with regrets."

Amber Soul paced. She radiated a harsh, almost angry concurrence backed by emotions dark and deep and so powerful Lady Midnight cringed away from her.

"We may be in for interesting times," Turtle observed. "I

suppose it had to happen."

# - 3 -

WarAvocat was a lean old man whose dark uniform accentuated the pallor of his face. Deathshead. Crawling with colors and shadows from the displays. Hard, dark eyes. Thin, tight lips that had forgotten how to smile a thousand years ago. Sound seemed to fade as he approached, the air to grow more chill.

WarAvocat took in the wall display in one devouring glance. "Satisfactory, WatchMaster."

"Grace, WarAvocat."

"Most satisfactory." Hanaver Strate moved toward the Probe team.

A Probe spokeswoman said, "The second approximation is up, WatchMaster. The lifeform in that pod is both alien and engineered."

Third WatchMaster's dispassion cracked. He did not need *Gemina*'s ID. "A krekelen! No known alien could have gotten near a Traveler's escape pods. The ship's own programmes would have prevented it."

"*Gemina* concurs, sir."

WarAvocat almost smiled. It had been a long time without action. "Access, all crews." A shimmer hovering behind him leapt his shoulder. "Alert, Red One." Alarms screamed. "All ready batteries commence firing. Intercept and Pursuit, commence launch. ConCom. Assemble an I and I team for transfer to P. Jaksonica station."

Third WatchMaster observed, "The pod is in the outer atmosphere already, WarAvocat."

Meaning the batteries' beams would lose coherency, that projectiles would be inaccurate, that the fighters would be wasted because they could not go down into atmosphere.

"Missiles? No. Too late." They accelerated so swiftly they would hit atmosphere like hitting a wall. "Perfectly timed. The thing is crafty."

"Hellspinners?"

"Probably too late for those, too. But they'll make an exemplary display." WarAvocat spoke to the shimmer. "Access, Weapons. Hellspinners, loose. Access, Hall of the Soldiers. Soldiers, warm one battalion of heavy infantry data-prepped for a search-and-kill in Cholot Varagona."

The air murmured, "Have you a unit preference, WarAvocat?"

"Whichever is up." WarAvocat's busy eye noted those from the off shifts who were tardy reaching stations. Second WatchMaster was among the latest. He wilted under WarAvocat's glare. "Access, Communications. Pulse to Station P. Jaksonica 3B. Total quarantine incoming Cholot Traveler *Glorious Spent*. Responsibility: STASIS. WarAvocat, Guardship *VII Gemina*."

WarAvocat recalled his interceptors and sent his pursuit fighters to escort the Traveler to dock. "WatchMaster. Efficiency deserves opportunity. I'm sending you to station as prize officer. Empowered to direct and employ I and I and STASIS."

Third WatchMaster flushed. Such an opportunity, unplanned, unscheduled, could make his career. Could get him nominated to WarCrew. Could get him elected if he did his job well. Or could shatter his chances forever if he fouled up. "Grace, WarAvocat."

"The I and I team will leave soon. You'll have to hurry. Second WatchMaster!"

Second arrived briskly, face red. "WarAvocat?"

"Relieve Third. You'll stand his shifts in addition to your own."

Second WatchMaster swallowed. "Grace, WarAvocat."

"Get going," WarAvocat told Third. "Don't embarrass me."

The Twist Masters loosed their unpredictable vortices. The furies ripped across space and clawed at the atmosphere of P. Jaksonica 3, scrawling fire upon the skies of that world, birthing auroras that would persist for days.

They rattled and scaled and scarred the falling pod but they did not stop it. At three thousand meters the krekelen bailed out. At twenty-five hundred, Canon garrison took the pod under fire.

They reported the illegal destroyed.

In Hall of the Watchers they knew better. Track followed the krekelen to the surface and into the city.

## - 4 -

Gloom was a fourth presence there with the three Immunes. Midnight said, "I don't want to go out there now. The Darkness has become the tyrant of the night."

Turtle replied, "Then don't go. Unless you have to dance tonight? Amber Soul and I could see you to the lift."

Midnight was a cloud dancer, engineered for that and exotic erotic usage in House Banat-Marath. Her owner of record, a House Director's whelp on *wanderjahr*, had become bored with his pretty toy and had discarded her, without documentation, her only assets those designed into her fragile body.

She had survived.

"No. Not tonight. There's little demand for me now."

"Funny. I'd think just the opposite. Eat, drink, and make merry. Maybe trouble will go away."

Midnight lived in the High City usually, drifting from sponsor to sponsor. If she fell out of fashion there, she worked the merchant baronets of UpTown, who strove to emulate the decadence of their overlords. But DownTown was her spiritual home, as it was for all the outcast, the discarded, the ignored, the ordinary, and the abhorred. Princes of lost and vanquished races languished there, hip by thigh with pimps and murderers and worse.

"What do they know in the High City?" Turtle asked. "What do they feel? What do they fear? What do they think?" Midnight was eyes and ears for the Immunes. The Canon lords did not guard their tongues around her. She was a nothing, invisible.

"They know there's unrest. But they vie at demonstrating their indifference. They're amused by the idea of rebellion. But the UpTown merchants are concerned. An uprising would be bad for business."

"Commerce will go to hell when that Guardship breaks off the Web. It will nail this rock down tighter than a marble in a sealed canister."

*Will one come? Sure?* Amber Soul remained unconvinced.

She could not comprehend humanity. The personas she projected functioned adequately, but even to Turtle she seemed insubstantial, like a shadow cast from another dimension. There was no fathoming her in her natural state.

She was an incredible rarity. How she had come to be stranded on V. Rothica 4 was a mystery. Even she did not remember.

She had been around almost as long as Turtle. When he thought about it, he could recall when she was not there but not when she had arrived. He knew more about her than anyone, but what he knew was minute.

Amber Soul was a force in DownTown, an anima, feared by all, best ignored.

"They will come," Turtle assured her. "Sure as the darkness weaves the night from afternoon. The breath of death is less certain than the vigilance of the Guardships. Pray that the Concord does nothing stupid before the Guardship arrives.

Its appearance will bank their ardor." He reflected a moment. "This krekelen business has an odor. I suspect a manipulation by some House."

"They wouldn't stir rebellion against themselves, would they?" Midnight protested. She remained as naive as Amber Soul remained mysterious.

"They would, and they have done. The *Enherrenraat* was born from a greed-fever dream in Cholot and Merod. The dream grew up to become a nightmare. Cholot and Merod are paying still. The fury of the Guardships was so exemplary that it has not been challenged since, but the universe spawns fools and insects in numbers beyond all reason."

Something tickled the outside walls; something tested the door. An odor hovered on the brink of perception, like the electric promise before a storm. There were rustlings and what could have been whispers, a harassment that had begun after Midnight's arrival. It had grown worse as darkness flowed like slime between the ten thousand legs supporting DownTown. It was pure night out now. The creatures of darkness were on the hunt.

One wall groaned and bowed as something huge pressed against it. A network of lines spread upon the bulge. They widened, overflowed one another, turned the brown of paper too near a flame.

Something oozed through, trickled down. It was the color of blood.

"That is quite enough!" Turtle snapped, exasperated.

Amber Soul rested spidery fingers upon the bulge. A psionic darkness filled the room, a ghost of menace that hammered through the wall. There were muted cries. Then silence.

"They are playing intimidation games. In their insanity, they will pass beyond games soon. We will confer with the others tomorrow. Steps must be taken."

There were eleven Immunes in Merod Schene. None

supported the Concord.

Turtle turned to Midnight. "How is Lord Askenasry?"

"He's still alive. He grows weaker, though his will remains steel. He won't be with us much longer. I dance for him once a week. He no longer makes other demands."

"Will you dance for him again soon?"

"Tomorrow night."

"Does he remember me?"

"He asks about you sometimes."

"Ask if he will see me. Tell him I'm ready to collect."

"If we survive the night." A timorous creature, she was shaking.

"We will survive this night and many more," Turtle promised. "We will outlive the Concord. *I* must. I have much to do before I go."

## - 5 -

Whine dying. An exclamatory *ping!* Jo Klass drew a frigid breath of medicine and machine, opened her eyes. She felt eager, curious, a touch of trepidation. What would it be? Warming was like wakening to a day guaranteed to be exciting.

How long had she slept?

Not that it mattered. Nothing changed.

As always there was a moth flutter of panic as the air grew hot and humid. The cell walls pressed in. Its lid opaqued with moisture. She scrawled an obscenity in the condensation.

The lid opened. Beyond lay the familiar white overhead of the warming room. How many times had she wakened thus, staring up at that sky of pipe and cable? Too often to recall.

Air swirled in, chilled her.

What was it? Another *Enherrenraat?* Fear stroked her. She had died that time. It haunted her, though the bud had detoured her around it.

Sometimes she thought she dreamed about dying while she was in the cell, but she remembered no dreams once she wakened.

A face drifted into view. "Off and on, soldier." No relief at finding her alive instead of a shriveled blue-black mummy. No expression at all. Just on to the next cell and next check.

Jo bounced out as filled with vitality as anyone in perfect health could be. Her squad tumbled out of neighboring cells, as naked as she. Shaigon eyed her, thoughts obvious. "Watch it, soldier."

"I am, Sarge. I am." He lifted one shaggy eyebrow.

"Later. Maybe. If you're a good boy." She counted ears and divided by two. All present. "Let's move." Their cells had returned to stowage. The team followed her, mouthing the usual gibes and wisecracks. Clary and Squat grabbed hands. A sleep in the ice had not changed their relationship. Eyes roved old comrades, seeking remembered scars. Unmarked skin could say a lot about last time out.

They dressed in loose black shipboards and retrieved personals. Clad and inspected, Jo led them toward the briefing center. News of the day drifted back from earlier squads.

"Hanaver Strate is WarAvocat now."

"Wasn't he Chief of Staff? What year is it?"

"Year forty-three of the Deified Kole Marmigus. Strate got elected Dictat, too."

"One of the *living*? I thought the first requirement was you had to be Deified."

Colorless laughter.

Marmigus Deified? It *had* been a long time. He'd just become OpsAvocat last time they were out. "Must have been slow times."

"Bet it's a routine cleanup, Sarge. Ain't nobody in a hurry."

"Ship is Red One, Hake."

"Ain't breaking out nobody but infantry. Somebody dropped a condiment tray."

Jo paused at the theater hatchway. "Can it, troops."

They entered a space where thirty thousand could be seated. They nodded to soldiers they knew, found seats, stared at their officers, waited. Above the stage, in large but unpretentious letters, was the motto "I Am A Soldier." It was posted over every exit from WarCrew country. It emblazoned a patch worn by WarCrew, encircling a numeral VII superimposed upon a caricature of the tutelary, a naked woman running that did not seem warlike to Jo.

How about a wide, muscular thug like her, short, ratty hair and a bloody ax in hand? Be more like the truth.

People did not shy away when Jo Klass walked past, but she could not be convinced that she was not unattractive.

The lander grounded. Jo trudged out into P. Jaksonica 3's reddish daylight. Hake had it right. They were cleaning up a spill. A krekelen shapechanger, for Tawn's sake!

She glared at Cholot Varagona. It looked like every out-port city on every House-dominated world in Canon. The houses were so damned conservative they would not stray from one standard prefab design. If you wanted something different, you had to hunt up a non-House world.

The High City floated a thousand meters up, connected to UpTown by a flexible tube containing passenger and freight lifts. The proconsuls of the House, the very rich and their hangers-on, remained safely isolated there.

The legs of UpTown lifted it, too, above the perils of a world poorly tamed and, especially, above the taint of the tamers. Administrators and functionaries; Canon garrison if there was one; House dependent, cadet, and allied merchants; contract operators; these lived UpTown.

DownTown was the base of the social pyramid. Its own

gradient declined toward the deepest shadow beneath the belly of UpTown.

Some were big, some were small, but that basic structure formed the capital on ten thousand worlds.

Jo activated her suit and bounced to her right. Her squad followed. Sensors systems came up, displaying in color on the sensitized inner surface of her faceplate, defining her surroundings. She could breathe the air. It was not too cold out there. But the info she cared about was that there were no unfriendly weapons nearby.

Data from *VII Gemina,* relayed from the lander, interrupted once a minute for five seconds, mapping the city as Probe saw it. The krekelen remained stationary near the heart of DownTown.

City work. Jo hated it. Cities were treacherous. You never knew who would hit you with what from where. The system was not great at detecting non-energy weapons.

Linkup. Circle complete. Nothing would get out. Came the order to advance.

Jo glanced up at the High City, at the flaming star of *VII Gemina*, which seemed tangled among fairy spires. How frightened they must be, those Cholot lordlings, wondering if the landing party had come to end the Ban by toppling UpTown and killing the High City's gravs.

There was no resistance. The few beings Jo saw stood rigidly immobile, staring with terrified eyes. Seldom had she seen so many sports, discards, and bizarre aliens. And this world had been allowed no outside contact for centuries. The creepy-crawlies were taking over.

The target did not move till the circle was under a kilometer in diameter. Jo's faceplate began displaying *Gemina* track in five-second alternates with suit local. Up on battalion net, for all officers and NCOs: "A reminder from up top, people. We *will* take it alive." No commentary, of course. That was there only in tone.

I Am A Soldier.

Corollary: I Obey.

On platoon net: "It's headed our way, people."

Jo matched *Gemina*-feed with a suit-local heat trace a hundred meters out. She outlocked *Gemina*, fixed the track, switched on squad tac. "Coming right down our throats, guys."

"Why can't we see it? You see it, Sarge? Anybody see it?"

No one did. But it ought to be visible. It was on top of them.

Top! She looked up, adjusted to max enhancement. There. Something scuttling along a beam.

Her bolt edged it perfectly. It went into nerve lock, clung to a stress lattice branching from a pylon, slowly changed into what looked like a black plastic film. Jo switched to platoon tac. "Platoon, Second Squad. We got it."

## - 6 -

The chamber was a perfect globe a thousand meters across. A great mass floated near its heart, slightly upward as gravity was oriented. Lightning leaped from the curved walls to the mass. Tin-sheet thunder beat its chest and howled around the cavity. Gouts of red, gaseous flame exploded across the darkness. Self-congratulatory devil's laughter pranced between the valleys of the thunder.

A woman stood in the mouth of a corridor ending at the wall of the chamber. "He's in a dramatic mood today." Her companion was a youth who looked seventeen. She looked twenty-one. He was. She was not. She was much older and more cruel. The sorrow of the torturer looked out through her pale blue eyes.

"When will we kill him?" The boy's dark eyes were not those

of an adolescent. The rest of him looked naive and young and innocent, but his eyes were those of a predator.

She slapped him. "Don't say that! Don't even think it this close to him." She laughed. "Not soon. After he succeeds. *If* he succeeds." Though not as loud her laughter was as wicked as that racketing around the globular cavity. "Who wants to inherit a disaster?"

The boy shivered. It was cold there, and gloomy, and something in the air reminded him of graveyards before dawn. "Why did he summon us?"

"Probably because he needs to proclaim his genius, and Lupo Provik doesn't feed his ego because Lupo refuses to be impressed." She palmed a bright plate on the corridor wall. "Father! We're here."

The show doubled in intensity. Lightning arrows thumped the wall near the corridor's end. Hologramatic monsters slithered the air, snapping and clawing, breathing fire and spitting venom. A black gondola manned by a skeletal gondolier approached unperturbed through the fury. Backlighting betrayed the hologram. The thing was a grav-sled and humanoid robot tricked up by the imagination of Simon Tregesser.

The sled nudged the wall. The woman stepped aboard. The youth hesitated, followed. The wing of fear cast one brief shadow upon his face.

His features hardened into naive inscrutability. He was learning.

One learned if one intended to survive amongst House Tregesser's ruling family.

The sled glided toward the heart of the cavity. A closed, transparent bell filled with dark smoke hung from the machinery there, which supported the thing inside and made of its will realities. The sled stopped ten meters away. Search probes tickled its passengers.

A grotesque face pressed against the inner surface of the bell. The smoke faded, revealed the wreckage of a body, one arm withered, the rest gnawed by fire, blind, all the handiwork of an assassin who had been almost lucky enough.

"Ah. My loving child Valerena. And her plaything."

"My son, Father."

A shrill cackle surrounded her. "I have eyes that see farther and deeper than these blind scars. But who or what you bed is your own affair." A moment. "Are you Valerena indeed? Or her Other?"

"I'm Valerena Prime."

"That's a comfort. Sometimes I think you send your Other when your conscience bothers you."

Guilty, Valerena tried to change the subject. "Why did you summon us?"

"The most pessimistic projections suggest that the beast is down on P. Jaksonica 3 and has been recognized. That entire Presidency will be crawling with Travelers carrying the alarm. We count the game begun. Soon they'll come sniffing up the trail. And we'll seize a Guardship for House Tregesser."

"You underestimate them." Valerena sounded tired. She had argued this before. "You risk the existence of House Tregesser against a quantity you know only from fragmentary reports that survived the *Enherrenraat*."

"I have shielding the equal of theirs. I have Lupo. The rest is firepower. When the Guardship arrives it will be cut off from the Web and under fire so intense its screens have to overload. It'll be surrender or die. The only choice they give the rest of the universe. Then House Tregesser will have its Guardship, Hellspinners, and the secret of lifting so vast a mass onto the Web."

"That's the strategy of the *Enherrenraat* revenant. *They* thought they'd win with firepower. They're extinct. The Guardships aren't. And they're five hundred years wiser now."

"Five hundred years more senile, child. Five hundred years more frozen into old ways."

Blessed stepped in. "Why did you call *me* here, Grandfather?"

"You're the heir of my heir. It's time you learned why your mother and I doppelled; so we can work on this unconcerned by the jealousies of lesser Houses and the spiteful interference of the Guardships. They can't suspect us of schemes and duplicities if their spies see our Others devoting themselves to the interests of House Tregesser."

The thing in the bell roared, "A thousand years has House Tregesser prepared! In our generations the hour has come at last!"

"Yes, Grandfather. Grandfather, where did you find a krekelen? They're supposed to be extinct."

"I have my resources, boy. Valerena! I need a woman. Send me one. And this time make her one with some juice left. That last one was a crone."

Valerena flared. "She was twenty years younger than I am!"

"Ah? Then maybe I should use you while there's a dollop of juice left in you." A pendulous, maggot-colored, impossibly huge organ slithered through a sudden opening in the floor of the bell. "Come here."

"No."

"Then send me a woman who will please me. Or take her place yourself. Go away. I have no more use for you."

The skeletal gondolier began poling toward the corridor mouth.

"Noah!"

A black, winged man dropped down between the gamboling lightnings. He lighted on a tongue of metal protruding from the great machine. "Lord?"

"How was I, Noah?"

"You were madness itself."

"Were they convinced?"

"I believe so."

"Ha! And will they try to kill me, then?"

"Someday."

"How soon?"

"Not soon. They will wait till after you capture the Guardship. They will want to steal a triumph."

"And they'll want to avoid the consequences if I fail, eh?"

"Yes, Lord."

"Does Valerena know she's not the first Valerena?"

"I think not. You indulge her too much, Lord."

"I have no other heir."

"It's your funeral."

"If I become so lax as to let her reach me here, then House Tregesser deserves more alert, more aggressive leadership anyway."

"Such is the custom."

"Watch them. See their every hair fall."

"And the woman they send you?"

"Yours, if you want her."

"Grace, Lord."


Simon Tregesser's bell clouded. Outside, the show ached up toward a shattering crescendo. Lightnings and coils of darkness slithered around the bell till no eye could have pieced it out of the chaos.

The bell rose into the belly of the machine. Chaos died. Silence took mastery of the cavity. A lone winged form glided the stillness.

Simon Tregesser's prosthetic eyes stared through the bell wall at his special secret. The thing had adopted an especially repugnant arrangement, almost demonic, perhaps in response to the show outside. Tregesser smiled as much as he could with ruined lips. Valerena did not know, but this *thing* from Outside would give House Tregesser its Guardship.

He hoped.

Down in the shadowed heart of him he nurtured the very doubts his daughter had flung in his face.

And he did not trust this emissary from Yon, this ally whose urgings had led him to push House Tregesser's plans beyond endless preparation to considered action. Simon Tregesser did not trust anyone or anything he did not own completely, excepting Lupo Provik. Lupo was his good arm and good body and, sometimes, his brain.

*An infantile display, Simon Tregesser. What do we gain by spawning machinations within machinations? There is but one goal. Let us devote ourselves with an appropriately holy fervor.*

Tregesser sensed its contempt. The disgusting monster. A shot of oxygen into that methane murk would set it dancing in the fires. Someday... the moment the Guardship surrendered. "You heard my daughter. Here, in private, between us, I second her doubts. You want me to dice with fate depending entirely upon your screens."

*They are the ultimate possible within the laws of this universe. They are identical with those deployed by Guardships.*

"So you say."

*Our observations during the* Enherrenraat *incident leave no doubt.*

"There's always room for doubt when you tempt the invincible. If you were that close to the action then, you were dead."

The thing did not respond.

"I suppose it's too late. I'm committed."

*You are committed, Simon Tregesser. Forever.*

Simon Tregesser's methane breathing ally set a thought

vibrating along the Web. Every development must be registered lest it be lost.

The Tregesser creature was right. To observe the Guardship screens under pressure, it had been necessary for observers to be too close to survive. They had left their data vibrating on the Web.

This creature, too, would leave such a legacy if the time came.

What mattered was that the Guardship should come. That it should be tested and, if conquered, be rescued from the false ambition of fools and unbelievers.

The Guardships threatened to doom the truths of the Shadowed Path.

Death did not matter. Death was but a destination. The Shadowed Path led away in ten thousand directions but always ended in the same place, the maw of the Destroyer.

Always better to be the knife than its victim.

## - 7 -

Third WatchMaster strode out the hatch. The stench and uproar and alien perspectives of the curving station dock hit him like blows, stunned him momentarily. Those creatures beyond the STASIS cordon... most were not even human!

His body kept moving till a portly, florid man said, "Commander Haget? I'm Schilligo Magnahs, Station Master. This is Gitto Otten, Director, Station Security and Investigation Section."

"Gentlemen." He clicked his heels. "The situation is?" He had no patience with ceremony. It wasted time.

"Static, Commander. The Traveler was brought to dock and locked in, per directive. STASIS seals were placed, quarantine was established. Not an electronic whisper has escaped. We awaited your arrival before proceeding."

"Satisfactory. WarAvocat will be pleased. Let's examine this Traveler that spits mythical aliens."

"Mythical, Commander?"

"Legendary and extinct, if you prefer. Probe showed the pod occupied by a krekelen shapechanger."

"But that's..."

"Exactly. Impossible. Yes. Soldiers are searching Cholot Varagona now. We'll have the thing soon. Then we'll see if it's genuine." Third WatchMaster continued to scan the dock, struggling with discomfort. He had not been off *VII Gemina* in too long. He had forgotten how mongrelized Canon space had become.

The Station Master sensed and misinterpreted his malaise. "Pardon the confusion and gawking, Commander. We see your people so seldom, curiosity tends to cause chaos dockside."

Third WatchMaster loosed a dry chuckle. "Diplomatically said, Station Master."

Station Traffic had brought *VII Gemina*'s courier gig in four bays from the Cholot Traveler. The walk was shorter than Third WatchMaster's daily trek to his station in Hall of the Watchers. It gave him no time to regain his equilibrium.

The quarantined dockhead was properly sealed and cordoned. Third WatchMaster overheard onlookers discussing his party.

"Bunch of bloody zombies."

"Think if one of them smiled, his face would break?"

Third WatchMaster looked at the man. He flushed, lost interest, hurried away.


The STASIS Director returned the comm to its cradle. "They're going to open up now."

Machinery grumbled. STASIS agents leveled weapons. Vehicle doors thumped on the concourse as drivers dismounted and prepared to take on detainees. The personnel lock of the

Cholot Traveler opened.

Third WatchMaster strode inside.

The Traveler's operating officers were shaky. One lean, red-faced passenger waited with them. The piping on his apparel pronounced him prominent in House Cholot.

A little man stepped forward, extended a hand that Third WatchMaster ignored. "Commander Haget? I'm Chief Operating Officer Timmerbach."

Third WatchMaster nodded. "How do you do?" He looked down the tight passageway beyond the crew, at the passengers. "Everyone turned out?"

"With the exception of two nonhumans requiring special environments."

"This farce must cease! I demand you end this absurd imprisonment immediately!"

Third WatchMaster did not glance at the civilian. He told the nearest I and I man, "That one fails the attitude test. Make certain he's the last processed out."

"Yes sir."

"You bloody... do you know who I am?"

"No. Who you are is a matter of supreme indifference."

"You bloody well better get interested. I'm Hanhl Cholot, of House Cholot Directorate."

Sweating, red, shaking, Chief Timmerbach tried to calm his owner's representative.

Turning away, Third WatchMaster said, "STASIS, after you process the Director, hold him as a material witness. If his attitude fails to improve, we'll transfer him to *VII Gemina*."

Cholot's attitude improved instantly, if not sincerely. Even a first trip downside functionary ignorant of the ways of the Web knew you did not get yourself dragged aboard a Guardship if you had hopes of feeling earth beneath your feet again.

*Glorious Spent* was exactly like every other Traveler. The

shipbuilders of House Majhellain constructed only three basic forms: the fat bulk cargo Hauler, the more common cargo/passenger Traveler, and the yachtlike Voyager for the rich. Every ship of a class was exactly like every other.

The horror Third WatchMaster found while inspecting passenger compartments was on the manifest. He had been warned by Timmerbach that *Glorious Spent* carried two aliens who had boarded on the Atlantean Rim. But...

One looked like a group-grope involving giant hydras and starfish atop a heap of exposed intestines. It was some sort of colonial, symbiotic intelligence. It was a methane breather, which explained why it had not turned out for the passenger muster.

It was revolting.

What the hell excuse was there for letting something that hideous run loose? What was Canon coming to?

By contrast the second alien, shimmering golden as it stared back from the corner of its cabin, seemed almost natural. Third WatchMaster did not recognize it. The manifest was vague. But its documentation was in order.

There was something calming about it. After a minute in its presence he felt relaxed and incurious. He moved on without asking a question.


I and I went over every millimeter of the Traveler. Every datum in every bank got sorted and tasted, then sifted and sniffed again. Nothing turned up. The Cholot Traveler was innocent of wrongdoing. There was only a feeble case for negligence. Any secrets there existed only in the minds of passengers or crew.

Those got sifted, too, excepting those of the aliens, for whom adequate probes were unavailable. Hanhl Cholot suffered examination three times, Third WatchMaster blandly excusing the harassment by wondering why the shapechanger had masqueraded as a child of House Cholot.

Hanhl Cholot was as stupid as the krekelen had been clever. He had believed its portrayal completely.

There was no guilty knowledge aboard. Third WatchMaster was not surprised. He had expected to learn nothing useful.

Maybe something would turn up once *Gemina* digested the data.

## - 8 -

Turtle looked at the soldiers, shuddered, sighed. Fear dragged the cold fingers of old ghosts across his flesh. He derided himself quietly. He had nothing to fear. His documentation was genuine. Fear was for when you had to risk the other kind.

But it had been so long since he had faced the disdain and suspicion of Canon troops, so long since he had put his nerve to the test. "Getting flabby," he muttered, and stirred himself before the indecision attracted attention.

Warned he would be coming, the sentries barely glanced at his passes at the UpTown escalator. They were more troublesome at the High City lift. The garrison did not much care if terrorists reached UpTown. But the holies of the High City must be shielded by every strength at hand.

The sentries in the lift could find no excuse to deny him. After all, he had orders from Lord Askenasry.

The soldiers took no chances. One rode up with him. Two more were waiting. They bustled him into an armored carrier more jail for those inside than protection from the world outside. He saw nothing of the High City's fairy spires, half energy construction skittered by rainbows. He saw nothing of the so-perfect people on their heavenly wind-washed streets. He saw nothing but metal bulkheads and the indifferent face of a Canon trooper whose conversation ranged from sniffs to grunts..

The machine whined to a stop. Turtle's companion did not move. Turtle remained seated till the back panel dropped and a vaguely familiar old woman beckoned him. He stepped out into a sun-washed courtyard. Surrounding walls masked the rest of the High City.

"Lona, is it?" It had been many years since he had been to the High City.

"I'm Carla. Lona was my mother."

It *had* been a long time. And he had forgotten that the Canon lords—those who stayed ahead of their enemies—rejuvenated themselves alone, not those who served them.

This woman might not have been born when last he had visited Merod Schene High City.

Lord Askenasry was a frail old stick figure, wrinkled, so black his skin had indigo highlights. A phalanx of machines kept him breathing. He had been past his prime when last Turtle had visited, but then had been healthy and virile and in command of himself and his environment.

One other man shared the sickroom. He stood out of the way, motionless, features concealed inside a cowled black robe, arms folded, hands hidden inside his sleeves. One of the physicians of House Troqwai, the unknowns, as much priests as healers, as much a harbinger of the inevitable as a hope. Turtle was uncomfortable under the creature's impassive gaze.

He thought of it as man, but it could as well have been woman or nonhuman. There was no evidence obvious to the eye.

The stench of decay permeated the room. Time, the great assassin, rested heavily there, its presence patient and implacable. The myriad sorceries of House Troqwai could hold the killer at bay for a time that seemed unimaginable to the harried children of DownTown, but still the murmurer gnawed and clawed and insinuated its dark tentacles through cracks in the walls. There was no escape for even the rich and the powerful.

Turtle recalled Askenasry as a merry youth, rambling the sinks of DownTown with rowdy contemporaries, accumulating the debt he would have an opportunity to discharge now. All those friends had fallen already. Now he was alone of his kind, like Turtle.

His eyes were open in slits. They tracked Turtle without emotion or apparent interest.

"I have come."

Askenasry's response came from a machine, a laryngeal whisper amplified. "You have taken your time." His words came in little rattle-tat bursts interspersed with soft coughing.

"I have come before."

"At my insistence. Refusing payment for a service."

The argument was ancient. Turtle refused the bait. Let the man fade into the darkness not understanding that he would have helped anyone that faraway night. The ancient did not need the strain of a clash of philosophical sabers. "I have come now."

"To collect? At last?"

"Yes."

"What is it? Passage? Credit? Documentation?"

"No. I want you to save some hotheaded young fools from the consequences of their foolishness. As I once saved other youngsters from their foolishness."

Askenasry stared the grey steel stare that had made him so intimidating in his prime.

"A krekelen came to Merod Schene. It carried the old whisper of rebellion. There were ears to hear it. And now there are hands to dabble at revolution."

"The krekelen were exterminated when I was a pup."

"A krekelen came. I saw it."

Askenasry did not argue. "Where is this fabulous monster now?"

"Aboard the Cholot Traveler *Glorious Spent* bound for P. Jaksonica 3. Cholot Varagona."

Disbelief faded to doubt in old grey eyes. "What do you want?"

"This time they call themselves the Concord. They have the usual plan for taking down the High City and making a punitive landing impossible by seizing the garrison arsenal. They are immune to reason. They do not believe in Guardships. I want you to whisper in the right ears. I want them forestalled till the Guardship comes."

"What Guardship?"

"The Guardship that will come after the krekelen tries landing on P. Jaksonica. Cholot Varagona lies under the Ban."

"This is all you require?"

"It is enough. Lives for lives."

"I have no power these days."

"People still listen when you speak, Lord."

"You would be surprised at their deafness."

"I doubt it. Your species' indifference to reason ceased to amaze me long before you were born. Let the garrison make a show of force. Let them round up known instigators. Let the boot rest heavily. Let it cause a howl. But stop the nonsense. So there will be a Merod Schene when the Guardship goes its way."

The old man did not respond. His eyes had closed. For a moment Turtle feared he had wasted his passion. He looked at the Troqwai, appealing....

The physician did not move. Turtle relaxed. The killer had not come. Otherwise the magician would have been plying his artifices. House Troqwai gave no quarter when it wrestled Death.

Lord Askenasry's eyes opened. He struggled after a smile.

"I'll do what I can. To repay you, not because I give a damn what happens DownTown."

"I understood that before I came. Your motive is not important so long as you do the deed." Turtle offered a slight bow, added that little propitiating gesture of crossed fingers expected by the Troqwai, backed from the room.

The physician moved toward his charge as though floating. He bent to look into the old man's eyes.

Carla took Turtle to the carrier. Soldiers hustled him aboard. He saw nothing of the High City going home, either.

## - 9 -

Tension chained knots of muscle across Third WatchMaster's shoulder and up the back of his neck. He lusted after another relaxant, dared not indulge. Another would turn him goofy.

It was the intimidating judicial formality of Hall of Decision. He hoped the inquestors would discover no reason to interrogate him.

Hall of Decision had been opened for the first time in decades. The Deified had come down from their screens and donned hologramatic guises.

Third WatchMaster shared the witness dock with the krekelen (wrung dry by I and I and passive as a potato), the soldier who had captured the beast, her battalion commander, several citizens of Cholot Varagona DownTown, Chief Timmerbach, Magnahs, and Director Otten. Facing them on a lone elevated throne was the avatar of the Deified Kole Marmigus, nominal master of *VII Gemina*. True power resided in the Dictats, enthroned at either side of Marmigus at a lower elevation. Marmigus's main function was to oversee the annual election of the pair who commanded the Guardship.

Significantly, one Dictat's throne was empty. Hanaver Strate had chosen to sit as WarAvocat, centering the rank of three thrones below those of the Dictats. He was unwilling to maintain a Dictat's objectivity.

Banks of thrones to the sides of the Hall were occupied by the Deified. This was the first Third WatchMaster had seen them all together.

So many! Hundreds upon hundreds.... But three millennia was time enough for countless deifications.

Third's gaze crossed that of the soldier who had captured the krekelen. She was tense and bewildered, out of her depth.

The ceremonials in honor of the tutelary ended. The Deified Kole Marmigus rose. "That's the folderol out of the way. Let's dispose of the cut and dried so we can get to the entertaining part."

Third WatchMaster was astonished. Marmigus alive had had a reputation for informality and irreverence, but in a formal inquiry dignity was mandatory.

"Up first, disposition of the krekelen. There is no ambiguity in the law. The damned things were judged useless. The only thing we can do is kill it. But WarAvocat has petitioned for a stay. He may be able to use it against those who loosed it. Anybody object? No? WarAvocat, you've got your pet."

Hanaver Strate was playing a strong hand these days, getting elected Dictat while he was still alive, getting this without demur from the contentious Deified.

"Next item. Disposition of the Cholot Traveler *Glorious Spent*. I and I and STASIS can't fabricate a case for detaining the vessel. Its Chief has asked that the quarantine be lifted."

Third WatchMaster snapped to attention, clicked his heels, shot a fist into the air.

"Commander Haget?" WarAvocat offered the recognition.

"Deified sirs. Stipulating that nothing concrete has been established, nevertheless I wish to insist that there is something very wrong aboard the Traveler."

Timmerbach cursed.

WarAvocat beamed down at Third WatchMaster.

Intuition had done him right.

Others looked at him like he was a treacherous shill for WarCrew.

Strate asked, "What disturbs you, Commander? The aliens?"

"Yes, sir."

"Isn't their documentation in order?"

"It's impeccable, what there is of it. But it's awfully thin."

"Exactly! Thank you, Commander." WarAvocat continued, but Third WatchMaster could not hear him. A pillow of silence had fallen upon the witness dock.

Timmerbach continued grumbling against fate in general and no one in particular.

WarAvocat appeared to be making an impassioned statement against resistance from the Deified. That made no sense. Arguments could be battled out in the electronic realm in picoseconds.

The truth struck him as a pair of shipboard security types entered the silence to fetter the krekelen. WarAvocat and Deified, krekelen and witnesses, all were part of a dramatization for slower biological minds. If any crew were watching.

"Sir?"

"Yes?" A sinking feeling. More security types had appeared.

"WarAvocat would like you to join him in his quarters. Will you accompany us, please?"

Third WatchMaster turned, marched, mind numb.

# - 10 -

Simon Tregesser kicked his closed personal grav-sled across Central Staff's vast Information Center, came to a hover behind Lupo Provik. He turned up the gain on his prosthetic eyes, still could not make out what interested his strategist.

"Fresh data, Lupo?"

A hint of exasperation faded from Provik's features as he turned. His plain face, shelled by ginger hair, assumed its habitual cool blandness. Only blue-grey eyes hard as diamond drillheads betrayed the man within. "The new gun platform just broke away. We've started siphoning the intelligence packet."

No honorific. Never an honorific from Lupo. Simon would tolerate that from no one else. But Lupo's loyalty did not need to be compelled or paid for in the coin of terror. Provik had been with him all his life. Provik had masterminded the gambit by which he had rid himself of a tyrannical and sadistic father. Provik found those subtle traps in Valerena's schemes his own genius overlooked. As bodyguard Provik had lapsed only once. And for that, unforgiving Simon Tregesser had forgiven him.

Simon did not understand Lupo Provik but willingly used and even liked the man, in his odd way. Lupo was as courageous, merciless, remorseless, and brilliant as Simon Tregesser imagined himself to be. And he was no threat. He had suffered one defensive lapse. Offensively he had been invincible.

Simon most appreciated the fact that Lupo was not intimidated by Guardships. Few were they of whom that could be said.

"Anything exciting?"

"Standard fare. Antiquated Guardship sightings. Nothing tagged for special attention." Provik was trying to create a model of Guardship movements. After years of work he could guess the whereabouts of six with a fifty-fifty chance of being right.

Easily disappointed, Tregesser drifted away. He spat curses at a pod of Chtrai'el-i computer technicians.

Aliens! Outsiders everywhere! Central Staff was infested. But it was impossible to recruit humans with balls enough to try it with the Guardships. Guts and determination! That was the recipe for accomplishing the impossible.

A vagrant curiosity ambled the surface of his mind. How many of these monsters were agents of what passed for Houses Outside? Most, probably. But it would not matter. Lupo would see to that.

Provik watched his employer drift away. He felt no irritation anymore. He had no feeling at all. Simon Tregesser was a device, a mask, a tool, the means whereby Lupo Provik worked his will upon a universe that must be manipulated with the tongues and fingers of the lords of great Houses. Simon Tregesser had his allegiance and protection so long as he shared a passion for empire building.

From the outside it appeared that Lupo Provik had no other passions. From the outside it seemed that Lupo Provik had no weaknesses or vulnerabilities. From the outside it appeared that Lupo had neither friends nor loves. From the outside it seemed he did not believe he was missing anything.

From the outside.

Central Staff was of a magnitude in keeping with its mission. In the slowest hours of third shift, five hundred beings were on duty in Info Center, controlling the forces outside. Financing had come from the same sources as most personnel. Outsiders desperately wanted to break the Guardships' deathgrip on the Canon Web.

Simon Tregesser managed one of his smiles. Valerena failed to appreciate a genius that got others to pay the freight and set them up to take the fall.

Tregesser stared from an observation blister, watching the new ship. It would come to Central to have Guardship-grade shielding installed—and its ability to get back on the Web removed.

When the Guardship came, no one would have the option

of retreat.

"Simon."

Tregesser withdrew his attention from the gunship. "Yes, Lupo?"

"One interesting datum did come in the intelligence packet."

Tregesser waited.

"*XII Fulminata* came off the Web at C. Payantica. It stayed only an hour, then climbed back on, presumably bound for Starbase Tulsa. This is the first sighting of *XII Fulminata* in sixteen years."

"It couldn't be the easy way." Tregesser glared at the gunship. *XII Fulminata!* "Starbase is only a dozen anchor points from P. Jaksonica, isn't it?"

"Yes."

"It would suit the drama of the thing, wouldn't it?"

"There's no cause to assume *XII Fulminata* will take the trail. But the possibility now exists."

"Does that change anything?"

"No. *XII Fulminata* carries no more firepower than any other Guardship."

"It would be one of the crazy ones," Tregesser mused. There was no response. He rotated his chair.

Lupo was headed back to work, satisfied that *XII Fulminata*'s reputation would not stall the project.

Tregesser snorted. He could not stop it if he wanted to.


Simon Tregesser suffered one nagging worry. The reliability of the thing secreted down below. Its great value was an ability to know what was happening countless stars away. As promised, it had known when the bait's Traveler had broken off the Web at P. Jaksonica....

It had delivered no news since.

Tregesser was... concerned. As was the monster, he knew. It responded strangely when pressed. Something was wrong.

He ought to get down and check. Lupo's news was not reassuring. *XII Fulminata*, indeed!

He keyed a signal to Noah to ready the bell.

Time to shed this damned toy, anyway. Nothing could make it comfortable.

Lupo glanced up as Tregesser drifted into the lift to his hideaway. He blinked as though trying to clear smoke from his eyes. "Be back in a few minutes," he told his staffers. He activated his beeper and headed for the shipping docks.

Valerena had asked to see him before she left.

## - 11 -

Five people were there with the serving robot: Third Watch-Master, the female soldier, Timmerbach, Magnahs, and Otten. Third WatchMaster stared at the deck and rummaged his mind for what he had done. Only Otten and Magnahs conversed.

Hanaver Strate walked in, flashed a grin. "Everyone comfortable? Had refreshments?"

Only the soldier had the nerve to respond. "Sir, what did we do?"

WarAvocat looked baffled. Then, "I see. You're wrong. It's not disciplinary. I intend deploying you against whoever sent the krekelen to catch a Guardship's attention."

"Sir? Someone sent it?"

"So the Deified say. The krekelen was a telepathically linked communal beast originally. The isolated individual became a low-grade moron that could be programmed like a robot. Our krekelen was programmed to give itself away."

"Isn't that a little unsubtle?"

"Only fools would expect us not to be suspicious. Someone wants us to react. Probably to backtrack.

"We have an advantage. Chance placed us here when the incident occurred. That puts us two and a half months ahead, that being optimum turnaround when a call goes out for a Guardship. Commander Haget, let's assess the I and I reports and see if we can't find a basis for your outburst."

Magnahs, Otten, and Timmerbach gave him dark looks.

"I'm sorry, sir," Haget said.

"The interruption was useful and timely. Saved me doing it myself."

"There wasn't anything solid, sir. Just my conviction that there was something wrong."

"Intuition?"

"It was more that I couldn't manage an interrogation. Whenever I tried the methane breather, I became so repelled I fled."

"But you went back."

"And ran again."

"And went back again. But I won't argue about standards you set yourself. What about the other one?"

"It bothers me more. The methane breather is a creepy-crawlie. The other seemed all right. It didn't bother me. But I never got around to getting anything from it."

WarAvocat asked Timmerbach, "Did your people have similar experiences?"

"Yes, sir. I even ended up moving all passengers off B Deck. They couldn't stand it near the methane breather."

"The other one?"

"No problem. It didn't socialize. It just wanted to look at the worlds we visited."

"Hunh. Commander Haget. Where did they come from? The methane breather has a commercially arranged temporary courier's credentials. The other has a Treaty World diplomatic pass."

"*Gemina* didn't know the methane breather, sir, and only that there's a Closed Treaty arrangement with the homeworld of the other, the one the Travelers know as Seeker of the Lost Children."

"Sounds like a job description."

Third WatchMaster shrugged. "The methane breather calls itself Messenger. Seeker's home is the Closed Treaty System M. Meddinia, which is in the Sixth Presidency, near the Atlantean Rim. It's a fixture on the commercial runs in the Sixth and Second Presidencies. It's been traveling without a destination for several hundred years. Like the Chief says, it's unsociable. But it pays well to be carried around and left alone."

WarAvocat nodded. "Thin. What about the other one?"

"A colonial intelligence previously unknown in Canon space. Even ships that trade Outside didn't know it. It boarded at A. Chancelorii 3B on open itinerary."

WarAvocat nodded. "Chief Timmerbach. Aren't the Manesa Systems, S.L. Manesica and B.L. Manesia, in the same Presidency as A. Chancelorii and M. Meddinia?"

"They're neighbors, sir. All part of the same cluster. The Web there is a tangle, there are so many interconnections between anchor points."

"And though it didn't cross paths with you till V. Rothica, the krekelen began its odyssey on the Cholot world S.L. Manesica 7. Interesting."

The Chief just shrugged.

WarAvocat leaned back, steepled his fingers. "The Deified say the chance of a connection between at least two of the aliens is close to unity."

Third WatchMaster had begun to relax. He had done a good job. No blame on him if he could not find data that did not exist. Might even be a good mark when advancement reviews came up.... The way WarAvocat looked at him aborted his confidence.

Strate was going to shaft him.

WarAvocat's thin lips stretched in what he thought was a comradely smile. "It won't be as bad as you think. You could end up elected to WarCrew without loss of grade."

What the hell? "Sir?"

"I thought you'd see it. The Deified want to go after this one. *VII Gemina* is headed for V. Rothica. While we're charging around looking for the krekelen's masters, I want you and a team with *Glorious Spent*."

"Me and a team? Sir?"

The soldier got it first. "Shee-it!" she muttered.

"I'm going to put you aboard the Cholot Traveler. The Sergeant will go along. You'll stay out of sight. Legwork will be handled by people we'll borrow from P. Jaksonica 3B STASIS on a TAD contract. Otten, I want three good ops, preferably volunteers."

Otten's thoughts left specters on his face.

WarAvocat continued, "The krekelen will be reprogrammed, set into Cholot shape, and put back aboard *Glorious Spent*."

Magnahs, Otten, and Timmerbach sputtered. Klass swore softly. Timmerbach found his voice first. "Sir! You can't do this!"

"We can and will, Chief. You'll be paid for your trouble. Might even be a lifting of the Ban on some Cholot systems. Can you cry about that?"

Timmerbach could but kept his mouth shut.

WarAvocat said, "Consider the circumstantial evidence. The krekelen started from a Cholot world and ended up on one, made the last leg from a Merod world disguised as a Cholot, carrying Cholot documentation, aboard a Cholot Traveler, accompanied by a member of the Cholot Directorate. Suppose you were dealing with *IX Furia*?"

Timmerbach blanched.

*IX Furia*'s style was to shoot first and forget about questions. Or, some said, to shoot first and then shoot the survivors.

WarAvocat said, "Thank you for coming. Commander Haget, you and the Sergeant get your kits together. You'll find sealed orders at departure bay. I'll talk to the Station Master, Director, and Chief while you're getting ready."

Those three did not look delighted.

Third WatchMaster shambled toward the exit, deflated. He wished he could extinguish himself in drink or drugs. The soldier said something he did not catch. He grunted, trudged toward his quarters. There were people who would kill for this opportunity. But they had to send him.

It felt more like punishment than reward.

## - 12 -

The wind licked and pranced through the ruins, muttering and chuckling. Superstitious DownTowners thought the ruins haunted. The wind carried voices that said something if you listened closely.

It carried dust and leaves, too. The dust kept getting behind Turtle's nictating membranes. "I'd forgotten what it was like out here," he told a squat Immune called Lonesome Mike. "Midnight can't come outside alone."

Lonesome Mike grunted. He was no conversationalist. He had not become Immune because of brainpower.

Turtle stared across the barrens at Merod Schene. "Looks like a dream city from here. Can't see DownTown at all."

It was the sort of view that ended up in tourist lures, Merod Schene glittering against the tapestry of a creeping orange sky, the High City wavering like seaweed amongst hurrying chubby clouds.

"How long we got to stay in that hole, Turtle?"

They had moved into the headquarters bunker of an archeological dig abandoned when an attitude shift among the House Merod Directors had cut off funds. It was comfortable but primitive. Lonesome Mike objected because he felt isolated from the action.

"Till we find out if Lord Askenasry can get out the garrison. Maybe only a few days. If he fails, we wait it out."

Turtle figured at least three months before the Guardship came. The Immunes had laid in supplies for six. No point worrying about the future beyond that. What would be would be decided by then.

The day began fading. UpTown grew sparkly. Then its lights were overwhelmed by the fairy fires of the High City. Turtle stared a while, motionless as the old block on which he sat. Then he went below for supper and the day's rancorous exchange with an emissary from the Concord.

Those fools flat refused to take no for an answer. As long as the Immunes rejected Concord, half the population of DownTown did. Turtle expected overt threats soon.

That was the night Amber Soul sent the messenger scurrying, heart ready to burst with terror.

Three nights in succession the Concord fools threw the darkest denizens of DownTown at the ruins. Three nights in succession Amber Soul sent them flying.

"As if murdering us will sell the justice of their cause," Turtle said. "Just it may be, but it's doomed. They never see that. They never think. And they never learn."

It was the fourth night. Shouts rolled down from the watchers. "Here we go again," Turtle grumped. "This time we send them home carrying their heads under their arms."

Amber Soul touched him. *It is not that. Lord Askenasry failed.*

"Damn!" Turtle raced to the surface.

The violence of the explosions was sufficient to send muted thunders tramping fifteen kilometers to the ruins. The elfin towers of the High City listed thirty degrees.

"They didn't have sense enough to sheer the mooring cables."

"Or couldn't."

"It's going to drop on UpTown."

The disaster was a long time coming, but come it did, the High City settling onto UpTown, UpTown's supports collapsing. Turtle imagined screams running with the thunder. "I'm going to pack."

"What for?"

"We have to go do what we can for the survivors."

"Not tonight." That was Lonesome Mike. "Tonight they're going to be even-ing scores."

True. Hell would be in session over there. It had to run its course.

All day a carrion bird of smoke perched on the bones of Merod Schene. With night's fall fires reddened the bird's belly. Turtle stared while the Immunes gathered for the long hike. Midnight complained softly, to no one but herself.

The grandfather of all fireworks shells burst over the dying city.

"Nuclear!" somebody yelled. "The blast wave..."

"No!" Turtle snapped. "There will be no blast wave. Nor any sound."

"But..."

"That was a Guardship breaking off the Web. They're here."

"How could they be?" Midnight demanded. "You said it would take months."

"It didn't. One must have been at P. Jaksonica. Or near enough to summon quickly. People, get back in the bunker.

And pray it isn't *I Primagenia*."

# - 13 -

WarAvocat stared at the wall. The data painted a grim picture. "Communications. Anything from V. Rothica station?"

"Affirmative, WarAvocat. A warning loop on a STASIS emergency band. General broadcast. Not a beam or pulse."

"Been a long time," WarAvocat said to First WatchMaster while awaiting data sufficient to determine the number of soldiers to waken.

Overhead, the Deified fussed and bickered, ignored.

"Move ship toward station," WarAvocat directed. The visual showed the big wheel naked of shipping.

"Planetary-based insurrections seldom intrude upon off-planet operations," Kole Marmigus observed from above.

"This one has. Probe?"

"There are people alive in there, sir. We're not yet close enough to distinguish their loyalties."

WarAvocat cast a sharp glance around.

"I'll handle that, sir," First WatchMaster said.

"Let it go."

"I can't let my people smart off to their superiors."

"Forget it." WarAvocat's gaze locked on the wall. It was bad down below. "Access. Hall of the Soldiers. Warm one regimental combat team for surface action."

A voice called, "WarAvocat, a small vessel just left station. Looks insystem. A miner or something."

"Very well."

Probe added, "There's nothing alive aboard it, sir."

"Headed this way, sir."

"Very well." A gnat. "We'll need people to clear the insurrectionists off station. Deified. Any advice? We've not boarded a station in my memory."

The Deified had access to everything *Gemina* knew. Also, it was politic to consult them occasionally.

"That miner is accelerating at nine gravs, sir," First Watch-Master noted.

"Very well."

Kole Marmigus said, "We suggest a battalion for the assault, WarAvocat."

"That many?"

"There are corridors and passages to be held behind the shock force." The Deified vanished. Station schematics replaced him, tactically significant points marked by red dots.

"More complex than I anticipated." Strate accessed Hall of the Soldiers and ordered appropriate forces warmed.

"Thirty seconds to impact, WarAvocat."

"Very well. Put the show on the wall. Split it with one view an approximation of what they'll see from station."

Two views appeared. One portrayed the wheel of the station, a slim sliver of distant moon, and the onrushing miner. In the other a huge, dingy white, slightly flattened lozenge crawled across the starscape, the miner dwindling toward its immensity.

"Ten seconds to impact."

"Battle screen maximum," WarAvocat ordered.

In the exterior view the Guardship vanished behind an oily shimmer.

"Five seconds to impact. Three. Two. One."

Both views died in a storm of light.

Then in the exterior view the Guardship ploughed through the nuclear fury. The great terror had not so much as shivered.

WarAvocat chuckled. "For a second, there, they were cheering over yonder." His humor vanished. "Let's take it before they purge the data banks."

"Are we taking prisoners?"

"I see no point, beyond SOP for interrogation. Deified?"

The Deified held their tongues. Thumbs down for the heroes of V. Rothica.

*VII Gemina* launched the assault battalion, then turned and followed other assault craft already headed for Merod Schene.

# - 14 -

Jo Klass composed herself before leaving her cabin for the social compartment dividing the suite. Commander Haget waited there, seated at attention. She supposed he was uncomfortable too, but she did not commiserate. The man was insufferable. He dealt with everything according to regulations.

Or tried. There were none to govern this. He was going crazy without precedents and rulings.

"Good morning, Commander."

"Good morning, Sergeant. The others will join us momentarily."

The STASIS people shared a similar suite on another deck. They were as enthused about the morning meeting as Jo was. Pointless. They could report if something happened.

Degas and AnyKaat, who practiced the quaint old custom of marriage, knocked and entered. AnyKaat was the more outgoing. She was a lumpy, overly wide-bottomed, stringy-haired dishwater blonde in her late twenties. She had washed-out blue eyes, a ready smile, and was too cheerful for her profession. Jo liked her. She was not sure about Degas.

Degas had wavy black hair, olive skin, dark eyes, and was two centimeters shorter than AnyKaat. He did not talk much. He was a technical sort, more at ease with things than people. He had a fawning manner that made Jo feel he was trying to excuse himself for being or trying to sneak up on something.

Jo suspected AnyKaat was grateful for this chance to travel. She seemed to be the only real volunteer. Degas had come to keep up with her. Era Vadja might have come under orders.

"Good morning," AnyKaat said, brightly.

Commander Haget responded with a calculated nod.

"Era?" Jo asked. She did most of the talking. Haget apparently considered even Era Vadja, a Canon reserve light Colonel and second assistant STASIS Director at P. Jaksonica 3B, beneath direct notice by one as exalted as himself.

Sometimes Jo wanted to bust him one.

AnyKaat shrugged. "Sticking his nose in somewhere. He'll turn up."

Haget frowned. Punctuality was one of his fetishes.

"Anything to tell?" Jo asked.

AnyKaat shook her head. But Degas growled, "There's a thing called Hanhl Cholot that's going to turn up with broken bones if he don't keep his hands to himself."

"Don't fuss yourself," AnyKaat said. "I'll handle him."

Jo had had her own encounter. She thought of asking for details but Era Vadja came in. Without knocking. Haget reddened.

"Sorry I'm late. Seeker was on the move. Thought I'd better stick."

Haget's mood shifted. "What happened?" Neither monster had moved before. The methane breather could not, of course.

"Not much. It went and stood in front of Messenger's door for twenty minutes. Then the krekelen's for ten. Then it went home."

Haget grunted. "Circumstantial confirmation of WarAvocat's hypothetical connection. How do we find the lie of it?"

Vadja said, "I got the feeling Seeker was not friendly toward Messenger. For what a feeling is worth."

"Worth as much as anything on this job."

Jo wondered if she had been chosen to balance Haget. She had gotten into it occasionally because she had a tendency to improvise.

Someone knocked. Commander Haget pointed the STASIS trio toward Jo's room. "Answer it." He retreated into his own cabin.

Jo gasped when she found herself face to face with Hanhl Cholot. "What are you doing here?"

He tried to grab her. His face darkened when she retreated.

Then he froze. The color left him. He stared. Jo noticed his pupils. He was on Jane.

Haget's eyes were steel. "Your manners still lack polish, Cholot. Maybe we should have concentrated on them more."

Degas came out, popping a fist into a palm. He wore his best STASIS scowl.

"You will forget you entered this suite. You will forget you saw anyone here," Haget said. "In fact, you will return to your quarters and stay there. Do you understand? Or do you require instruction more direct than what you got at P. Jaksonica?"

Jo had seen frightened people but none more frightened than Cholot. Even so, she did not trust his terror. He was too used to having his own way.

Era Vadja said, "That man could be trouble. He sits around brooding; he'll think up ways to cause us grief."

"Maybe," Haget admitted. "And maybe he'll find all he can handle. Klass. Keep an eye on him."

There was another knock. This one was diffident.

"Now what?" Haget pointed toward cover again.

Jo found Chief Timmerbach twitching in the passage. "I need to see the Commander."

She stepped aside. Timmerbach moved past like a man marching to his own execution. Haget came out. "What is it?"

"Problems with the Web. We may shift to an alternate strand

next anchor point. This one has begun to sag and mist. It shows feathering, too."

"Presence?"

"No feel of it yet. But we're running with the feathering."

"You've slowed ship?"

"To a crawl."

"Very well. I don't expect there's anything I can do."

"There never was anything anybody could do. I just wanted you to know we might fall behind schedule." He fled.

Haget observed, "A dozen ships a year disappear on the Web."

But never a Guardship, Jo reflected. Whatever it was, it did not trifle with the invincible.

## - 15 -

Valerena glimpsed motion down the corridor. "He decided to come."

Blessed said, "This is pointless. You can't suborn Lupo. You can't even make Grandfather think you suborned him. Lupo is the one man he trusts. And with good reason."

"What do you know? You're still a child."

"I know you can't reach Simon Tregesser without going through Lupo Provik. Lupo can't be bought. If you can't bribe Lupo, you have to kill him. And he won't let you."

Valerena sneered. She was sure every man had his weakness or price. "What course would you suggest, beloved child?"

"Patience."

"Patience? What kind of suggestion is that?"

"Simon Tregesser is old. He has physical problems. Let time do the dirty work."

"He speaks more wisely than I expected." Lupo Provik skewered Valerena with the ice of his devil eyes. "You wanted to see me?"

Valerena shivered. That look. It haunted her. It seemed she had faced it before. "What *is* your price, Lupo?"

"I'm priceless, Valerena."

Blessed giggled.

Valerena stifled her anger. "There's no hope you'd help me take control?"

"None."

"And you'd resist me if I tried?"

"Of course. But you have no need. Your father isn't immortal."

"What will *you* do when he dies?"

"Go on. My second loyalty is to the House."

"Would that be true if my father didn't die of natural causes?"

"When the man is dead, he's dead. I'll defend him but not his ghost. I'm no avenger. I'm a tactician and strategist." What might have been a smile tugged at his mouth.

"I see. Maybe you're right. Maybe I should curb my impatience. I do have all but the final power now, don't I?"

"Indeed. Your father has indulged your every whim. Occasionally he's regretted that."

"And will you support me as devoutly, Lupo?" Blessed asked.

Valerena shot him a venomous look.

"Of course."

"That will be all, Lupo," Valerena snapped. "I just wanted to make sure of what I already knew."

Provik responded with a slight bow. As he departed, he reiterated, "Be patient, Valerena. It's the safer course."

He was gone. She spun on Blessed. "You'd better watch that sarcastic mouth."

"Yes, Mother. What now? I can't picture you taking advice just because it's good."

Valerena glared. "Contrary to what you and they believe,

there *are* pathways to my father that don't lead through Lupo Provik."

Blessed smiled at her taut back as she stamped away.

# - 16 -

The first refugees reached the ruins soon after the uprising began. The Immunes accepted them though that meant a drain on resources. After the retreat to the bunker occasioned by that furious starburst, though, Turtle announced, "We accept no more fugitives."

Lady Midnight, who could find charity toward a viper, asked, "Why not?"

"Because we're going to get hit by a flood. And some will be Concordians. We don't want them around when the Guard-ship soldiers come. They assume guilt by association. They shoot if there's a doubt. The point of coming out here was to survive."

Midnight argued against turning anyone away. "These are the people who terrorized you! Amber Soul. Come with me."

The fugitives came. Amber Soul drove them away. But before they arrived, the sky opened and rained sparks on Merod Schene.

The brightest object in the nighttime sky, after the moon, had been the station, stationary above the equator south of Merod Schene. But now there was a brighter object. "The Guardship," Turtle said.

*It must be huge.*

"It's bigger than anything you can imagine humans build-ing."

A few hairs of fire reached for the rain of sparks. A pathetic few. Most of the garrison's arsenal had been destroyed in the city's collapse.

"Can you sense the city?" Turtle asked.

*Only as a great fester of fear and pain.*

Explosions limned the horizon and illuminated the bellies of scattered small clouds. "The last gasp of the Concord," Turtle guessed. "A booby trap no doubt sprung prematurely. This race never learns."

*The Guardships learn. Do they not?*

"The Guardships are immortal. They do not have to relearn lessons every generation."

*But they grow more nearly mad.*

"Some have gone strange," Turtle admitted. "Some have grown impatient and terrible, like vengeful old gods. But mostly they just do what they were created to do—with an efficiency that must keep the ghosts of their designers in a turmoil. Those old pirates didn't figure *they* would have to toe the mark, too."

"You know a lot about them, don't you?" Midnight had come out. Lonesome Mike anchored her against the wind.

"Knowing them is my life's work."

"You respect them. But you would put an end to them if you could. Wouldn't you?"

"They have kept the peace and expanded its frontiers for four thousand years, but at the expense of most of humanity and all of everyone else. The wellsprings of power have become frozen. End some things, yes, I would. But I would not alter the inability of the Houses, or anyone else, to rampage across the Web."

Lonesome Mike grunted. "I can think of ways to play conqueror without going head-on with the Guardships."

"If you can, someone else has and it's been done. Everything has been thought of and tried. What works without being crushed by the Guardships *or* Canon forces is too difficult and expensive for most Houses."

"And you would end the peace," Midnight accused.

"No. I would end the misery, the rigidity, the stasis."

"By bringing on the chaos?"

Amber Soul kept them invisible for a while. They sat in the rusty sunlight and watched scout flits run game through the barrens. They watched glimmering assault craft hasten off to secure the rest of the world.

"Concord didn't put up much of a fight," Lonesome Mike said.

"One regiment to conquer a world," Turtle muttered. "I wonder which Guardship it is? Guess we'll find out."

The soldiers, when they came, were as invisible to Turtle as he was to them. Amber Soul alerted him. *They are close. But I cannot fix them.*

Turtle studied the terrain toward the city. Soon he discerned the unnatural twitchings of brush and stirrings of dust that marked the advance.

"Careful buggers," Lonesome Mike grumped.

"It's not efficient to expose yourself to needless risk. Amber Soul. Tell everyone to sit still, hands in their laps. Then let the mask fall."

He had hoped the soldiers would not come but had not expected to be overlooked.

A massive battle suit flicked into existence a few meters away. Turtle stared into the mouth of a weapon for a moment, then looked for the soldier's tutelary emblem.

"What's funny?" Lonesome Mike demanded.

"It's *VII Gemina*."

"Is that good?" Midnight asked.

"It could be a lot worse. You'll be all right. They'll be fair."

But his heart sank on his own behalf.

# - 17 -

"Station is secure," the air told WarAvocat. Strate had moved to WarCentral, brain and heart of *VII Gemina* in combat. It made no difference where he was physically, but his presence there had symbolic value.

"Loyal personnel have been liberated. Little damage was done to the physical plant."

"The data banks?"

"Sound and secure, sir."

"Very good. Prisoners?"

"Five percent per SOP. Random sample."

"Very good." WarAvocat preened. "Prep station for return to service. Send the captives over. What's your casualty status?"

"Zero for Medical. They weren't set for a real fight."

"Excellent." WarAvocat turned his attention to the world below, where operations were going as smoothly. Rabble never put up a fight against professionals.

That could take care of itself. He needed rest. He went to the space reserved, said, "Access, WarCentral furnishings. Close the WarAvocat's night room." Fantasy walls snapped into existence. "Give me a bed."

The floor crept, coalesced, softened, rose. Hanaver Strate stretched himself out. He fell asleep in seconds.

A soft buzz wakened Strate. "Yes?"

"Noon reports from Peacekeeper One, WarAvocat."

"Very well." He rose, smoothed his apparel, ran thin, bony fingers through his hair. Two hours here was worth six in a normal bed. *Gemina* reached in and reworked the sleeping body, eased the tensions, hastened the outflow of fatigue poisons.

Noon reports. Merod Schene's day ran only a few hours ahead of *VII Gemina*'s. It would be early afternoon down there, just twelve hours after the first troops grounded.

An aide awaited Strate, walked with him. "No bad news?"

"No bad news, sir. Peacekeeper One is ahead of schedule with casualties nominal. The insurrectionists were unable to acquire significant portions of the garrison arsenal. Merod Schene is ninety percent secure. I and I have begun sifting survivors. Peacekeeper One has requested hospital and reconstruction units. He's dispatched his primary combat forces to satellite towns, mineheads and agricultural complexes where the insurrectionists routed the authorities. Our speed in recovering those facilities seems limited to the speed of personnel carriers in atmosphere at six hundred thirty millibars."

WarAvocat awarded the joke a chuckle. He seated himself at his command station. "Review noon reports," he told his desk.

The operation constituted an exercise. Most casualties had come accidentally, not by enemy action. He was into the I and I data before he found anything interesting. "Deified? Question."

His fellow Dictat, Ansehl Ronygos, materialized on a small screen. "Yes?"

"What's an Immune?"

"Immune is an honorary title from the lower social orders, usually indicating an unofficial magistrate. An Immune has no legal standing, but his word acts like law. Most Immunes are too strong, too tough, or too crazy to meddle with. Occasionally one is proclaimed for wisdom or artistic value. Immunity indicates a popular consensus that an individual be exempt from the hazards of lawlessness."

"Apparently the Immunes of Merod Schene opposed the insurrection."

"Yes."

"They tried to give warning that a blowup was coming."

"Yes."

"And the Deified are interested in these Immunes?"

"In one in particular. Possibly."

WarAvocat awaited clarification. None was forthcoming. Sometimes the Deified were that way.

He released the requested hospital and construction units, then reviewed the data from station. He gleaned seven prior visas issued to the krekelen. Two had not been known to *Glorious Spent*, nor recalled by the beast itself. The additions gave WarAvocat a solid picture of *VII Gemina*'s future course.

He hoped *VII Gemina* would not have to clean up every world along the way.

"Access, Peacekeeper One."

The commander of the landing force came back in seconds. "Yes, WarAvocat?"

"You have custody of locals called Immunes?"

"Yes, sir."

"The Deified are interested. Send them up."

"Will do, WarAvocat."

Hanaver Strate leaned back, closed his eyes, tried to imagine what those electronic spooks were up to now.

The night terminator had reached Merod Schene before the detainees arrived. WarAvocat inquired, "Deified, where do you want to interview the detainees?"

"Hall of Decision."

Startled, he examined the speaker. He did not know her. Her apparel proclaimed her one of the oldest Deified. First Millennium.

Strate reached Hall of Decision before the detainees. The old-time Deified were very interested. He spied several who had not appeared for the show with the krekelen and Commander Haget. Many lost interest in the outer reality after a few centuries in *Gemina*'s bosom.

What brought them out now?

One awed junior officer delivered the detainees to Strate as the only living being present. "What's wrong with that one?" WarAvocat asked, indicating a woman in apparent catatonia.

"I don't know, sir. About seventy klicks out she started screaming. Then that."

"I see."

"The others didn't know what was wrong."

"Uhm?" Strate ordered an envelope of silence and a security shield, then climbed to his Dictat's throne. He considered the detainees. With one exception they seemed overwhelmed.

"Deified? You wished to examine these... people?" It was hard to regard them that way.

Ansehl Ronygos suggested, "Relax the silence."

Strate reiterated the request as an order. The system would have responded to Ronygos directly, but the Deified liked to nag the living for having introduced unbreakable routines that prevented them from issuing edicts and making decisions without the consent of the living.

*VII Gemina* was trying to avoid troubles that had befallen other Guardships. *XII Fulminata*, without restraints upon its Deified, had gone cold and weird, ruthless, merciless, and almost suicidally fearless. *IV Trajana* was the spookiest of all Guardships, having subsumed its crew completely. Afterward, it had climbed onto the Web and been heard from again only briefly during the *Enherrenraat* incident.

Some thought *IV Trajana* was hunting the Presence that lived on the Web and appeared to be responsible for the disappearance of so many ships. Possibly. Ages ago *VI Adjutrix* had gone seeking the ends of the Web, which extended far beyond Canon space.

Ronygos said, "Let's have their names and origins."

The young officer hurried through the list. With one exception they were aliens or artifacts. How did the aliens get to V.

Rothica 4? Were phantom Travelers a problem again?

Several First Millennium Deified descended upon the detainees. They surrounded the one who seemed unimpressed. Then the old spooks just stood there staring.

WarAvocat checked the detainee's number. "Access, *Gemina*. Review the file on detainee number five."

A whisper in his ear: "Name, Turtle. Origin: Alien, species uncertain, probably Ku. May be an artifact. No other data available."

"Curious," WarAvocat mused aloud, watching the old Deified. Why was *Gemina* reticent about what was troubling them?

## - 18 -

Simon Tregesser was playing lord of thunders to distract himself. It was not working. For two weeks that thing in the tank had been useless. Half the time it was comatose, the other half it might as well have been. It said nothing that made any sense.

When a thing like that was terrified out of its mind...

He did not want to think about it. But when he put it out of mind, Noah slipped in.

Noah had been missing too long. Something must have happened. That bitch Valerena! Next time he killed her he would make it permanent. Lupo said Blessed showed promise.

He hurled thunders and lightnings with renewed fury. The whole damned universe was out to frustrate him. *XII Fulminata!* What the hell? Was some malign force ranged against him?

That was his most secret fear. That somehow someone or something was using him the way he used so many others.

A small red pin light came on. He was tempted to ignore it. But no one pestered him with trivia. Hardly anyone but Lupo and Noah bothered him at all. Neither of them wasted time.

"Who was that? What do you want?"

"Noah, Lord."

"Where the hell have you been? Get down here." He flung lightnings like spears for near misses as Noah swooped down the vast empty cavern. His laughter pounded the walls.

Unperturbed, Noah drifted to his perch.

Disappointed, Tregesser let the uproar die. The damned illusion caster was a waste. Nobody but Lupo and Noah saw his productions. You could not impress either with a black hole big enough to gobble galaxies.

"All right, Noah. What have we got?" Echoes chased themselves around the vast hollow.

"Valerena tried Lupo Provik before she left."

"Again? The woman shows no imagination."

"I'm not sure she's witless. And the boy is no moron. He knew the effort was pointless and understood why."

"Where have you been?"

"Tregesser Prime. There were implications to Valerena's behavior that intrigued me. She deserved a closer inspection."

Tregesser Prime. In the Canon catalog it was designated P. Benetonica 3. The Tregessers rejected that name, and as much else of Canon as they could.

"And?"

"As I said, this Valerena may be dangerous."

"Get to it, Noah."

"She has several Others in development. She has a Banat-Marath team installed in her castle. Her security is tighter than usual."

"Interesting. Why a crew of Others? Why not have Lupo produce them?"

"I also caught a hint that she may have obtained the control cues for the Simon Tregesser Other."

Tregesser might have been drilled by one of his own

lightning bolts. His speaker crackled for half a minute before he managed, "Indeed?"

"How she could have managed that escapes me, Lord. It seems unlikely. Yet my snooping—nobody pays attention to an artifact—convinced me something is going on. I've put together a scenario. It contradicts none of the known facts and ties the behavior of several individuals into a unified field."

Simon growled. Noah's manner could be frustrating. But neither threats nor rewards could change him. "Lay on, Noah. I don't think you can shock me more than you already have."

"Assume one of the earlier Valerenas enlisted one of the Directors. Plausible?"

"Probable. They're all vampires. They'd go for my throat in a second."

"Assume that Valerena made a mistake and you directed a changeover. Our hypothetical Director would not have to know about Provik's lab to realize he was dealing with a different Valerena. She wouldn't know things she should."

"Still plausible. This Director might tell her she was a replacement. That she was an Other. Hell. She must be terrified that we have a hold on her. We don't, do we?"

"No. You decided that was the lesser evil in the long run, where the welfare of the House was concerned. You directed Provik to produce replacements without controls. If he put them in, someone might learn about them."

"So there's a chance we've been dealing with the same Valerena through what we thought were several changeovers while she's been having Banat-Marath make Others she can sacrifice."

"Exactly, Lord."

"It hangs together, Noah. But what has she been doing with the replacements?"

"I wouldn't care to speculate."

"You wouldn't? Maybe I shouldn't, either. I might not want

to know." Tregesser pondered a moment: "This doesn't upset me as much as you might think, Noah. It tells me my offspring isn't as stupid as I'd feared. But it's still a step from explaining the central mystery."

"Mystery, Lord? What mystery?"

"The sense of what she's doing. Her motivation. What is it? I'm clinging to life with broken fingernails."

"If you'd send to House Troqwai..."

"I won't have it. They're jackals." Not true. He did not want to die. He would have been happy with a platoon of Troqwai's phantoms hovering. But not here. "A little patience and the whole thing will drop into her lap. So why risk everything, repeatedly, trying to rush it? That isn't rational."

"That's easy." From where Noah stood it *was* easy to see. "She hates you. She has only one way of expressing that hatred. Take everything you have: life, property, and power."

Again Tregesser might have been struck by his own lightning. "But she's my daughter!"

"Emotion played no part when you removed your father? That was unadulterated concern for the House?"

Tregesser snapped the lie. "Of course! I know what it is. She wants to steal my victory. She wants to be remembered for breaking the Guardships."

"You really think so, Lord?"

"I *know* so, Noah. Get out of here!"

"As you will. But why would she want to take that, too?"

Lightnings crisped the air around Noah. He banked, sideslipped, even looped. Those lightnings were thrown in earnest.

# - 19 -

Valerena lay on a couch in an open-air pavilion atop a small mountain on the Isle of Ise in Tregesser Prime's tropics. The structure was a replica of another of pre-Canon times, according to a memorial plaque. She did not care. For her history began with the conception of Valerena Tregesser.

Nobody cared about the Go Wars anymore, anyway. They would be forgotten if the Guardships were not still around.

Blessed settled into a canvas chair. "The artifact should have reached your father by now." He raised a tube to his eyes, turned a portion of the barrel.

"Must you play with that thing all the time?"

He pointed the tube at her, ran the tip of a finger across a heat-sensitive surface. A symbol appeared inside. This one was Valerena Prime. "They say the pattern is never the same twice. I'm checking."

"Have you found a duplication?"

"Not yet. Mathematically, I have to."

He had begun the project a year ago and had identified nine Valerena Tregessers so far.

"Put it away. You do it just to irritate me."

"Will your father do what you want?"

"Of course. He'll rage for a while. Then he'll brood. Then he'll rage again. Then he'll call Lupo Provik."

"You surprised me, Mother. Not in a thousand years would I have believed there was a way to reach him without going through Lupo. How did you find out?"

Valerena concealed a smirk behind a hand. "Each time he summons me he demands a woman. Always younger and more vulnerable. Just to show me how disgusting he can get. One of those women got through alive. She told me all he did was give her to the artifact. And the artifact, unlike Lupo, has wants and needs that Father doesn't fulfill. He had a pleasant stay on Tregesser Prime. All the women he could handle."

Blessed spied a speck moving swiftly above the burgundy sea. He fiddled with his kaleidoscope till his mother scolded him, put it down. "And you're sure Lupo will do what you want?"

"He'll try to steal a march. Set a trap. That's Lupo." A jewel on Valerena's bracelet flashed. "Who is that?" she demanded.

Blessed did not hear the reply. But he knew the meaning of the flash.

"You'll have to play on the beach, beloved son. I have company."

"Your friends from the Directorate?"

Valerena did not respond except to point.

Blessed held his breath till he was out of sight.

The screen was small and the image flat, but Blessed and his friends Cable, Nyo, and Tina had a good view of the visitors. One was no surprise. Myth Worgemuth was an old schemer who dated back to the days of Simon Tregesser's grandfather. But Linas Maserang had prospered during Simon's reign. What did he stand to gain?

Valerena, presumably. The fool.

His mother shed the slutty role she played for him. "Sit. Get comfortable," she said.

"Your message sounded portentous," Worgemuth replied.

"I've found a way to lure Simon out of his fortress, away from Provik." She gave the men an edited story, maybe eighty percent truth.

"Good," Blessed whispered, and slapped hands with his companions.

"Blessed!" Cable Shike hissed.

Worgemuth had noticed the kaleidoscope. "What's this?" The view wheeled.

"A kaleidoscope. My son's. He must have forgotten it when I chased him out."

Tina snickered.

A huge eye squinted at Blessed. "Haven't seen one of these since I was a kid."

Sound transmission ceased. When Worgemuth put the

toy down it sent a picture of the frescoes on the pavilion's ceiling.

Blessed was satisfied. He knew the identities of his mother's Directorate allies.

"I wonder what Lupo will really do?" he mused.

## - 20 -

Lupo stood beside Simon's enclosed chair, stared out at the end space. "Our course seems evident. What options have you considered?"

"Mostly I've been in a panic. I'm not handling the pressure here like I thought I could."

"You came right away. That's a point." Provik had not asked for Tregesser's source of information. He would not. But he had guessed.

Tregesser had fewer secrets than he supposed. Lupo was aware of everything going on around his employer. He knew about the artifact and the Outsider. He knew the artifact had been away. "Is it possible Valerena has gotten those codes?"

"I don't see how. But the impossible has happened before. Hasn't it?"

"Yes."

Lupo Provik had delivered House Banat-Marath to temporary Tregesser thrall after accidentally learning that Sandor Banat-Marath maintained a force-grown second self he put out front. The only difference between Sandor and his Other had been control codes built into the Other during the vatwork. Most artifacts came with controls.

Provik had invested years of prime espionage work. He had uncovered the Other's codes. Shortly afterward Sandor Prime vanished.

Nine years later an assassin got the Sandor Other and Fodor Banat-Marath succeeded. Provik lost that House but none of the secrets he had plundered. House Tregesser now created its own specialized artifacts. No one suspected. Artifacts were a Banat-Marath monopoly.

"You think I'm being set up, Lupo?"

So. The old boy had not been thrown completely. "There's always that possibility. To be sure, we'd have to wait to see if your Other behaved strangely."

"I don't follow you."

"Assume the Simon Other codes haven't been compromised since even I wasn't there when you programmed him. If your Other acts weird, we can consider the news about the codes disinformation."

"What? Your logic eludes me."

"Think Valerena. If she really had the codes, you'd never know. Right?"

"That's how you and I would handle it."

"Yes. That's worth remembering. We aren't dealing with people who think the way we do. Valerena can be brilliant, cunning, blind, and stupid all at the same time. That's why she's so damned dangerous."

"So what do you suggest?"

"Assume the worst. Do what your enemies want you to do, only as fast as you can move. Switch places with your Other."

"But..."

"Right now. As fast as you can. Make the change before they're alert. They'll expect you to move with your usual deliberation."

"So I'd play the Other. When the time came I'd trade, and they'd have the real Other across their sights."

"If we need the double switch."

"I like it, Lupo."

"*Nobody* can know. I mean *nobody* but you and me. Don't trust anybody."

Simon Tregesser grunted. "There could be nothing in the shadows."

"In my experience there's *always* something in the shadows."

"Have a Voyager readied."

Lupo watched Simon out of sight, then yielded to his chief of staff. He headed for the vast suite he maintained. He spoke a code word. His door opened. It was the only entrance and Lupo Provik was the only being the door would pass.

Lupo called, "One! We have a job to do. Get everyone together."

In moments six more Proviks joined him. No one, not even Simon Tregesser, knew there was more than one. Provik had done the vatwork himself. The even-numbered Lupos had been altered there to become female.

"Update time," Lupo Prime said. The universe saw most of him, but Lupos One, Three, and Five sustained his tireless, workaholic reputation.

The dread, mysterious mastermind behind the ascendant fortunes of House Tregesser was a sort of hive creature.

The ambiance became semi-telepathic. Little external boosting was necessary. The update took only a moment because it had not been long since the last. Provik insisted on two a day now the Guardship game was running.

When it was over he gave orders. "Two, Three, and Four go with me on the Voyager. One, take control here. Keep an eye on the artifact Noah."

Below, Simon Tregesser was leaving his Outsider ally. Once more he had been able to get no sense from it.

It just kept on about something called the Destroyer, blowing steam because the Destroyer was being thwarted. It acted like it was about ten percent there, with most of its minds trapped in a far abyss.

Weird. But without it there would be no ships, no guns, no screens, no ambush, no wealth to siphon off to House Tregesser. For all that he could stand a little weirdness.

## - 21 -

Turtle felt the sound shield go down. He glanced at Amber Soul. How long could she continue the total commitment needed to hide from VII Gemina? Not long enough, he feared. Even he could feel the probing edges of the great slow booming pulse of the somnolent thing that was the Gemina within and beneath the VII Gemina of ceramics, plastics, and metal.

It was the thing that was the sum of all that the Starbase builders had wrought, all the Guardship had learned, and all that had been input by Deification. It was the thing that made the Guardship so fearsome. It was the thing that, vaguely sensed, made all Canon shiver in dread and overrate a Guardship's terrible might.

Turtle knew the Guardships were not invincible. Not yet.

He noted movement among the silent, seated hundreds staring down at them, forgot Amber Soul.

So.

He did not recognize individuals, only uniform styles.

That was enough.

Here came people who knew that he knew about Guardships being vulnerable.

They surrounded him. And for a long time they just stood there, staring.

And for a long time he just stared back. Were these living creatures as old as he? Or were they *VII Gemina*'s dead somehow recalled to life? "They are great necromancers, humans," old Kote had warned him before he had donned the K'tiba and had taken up the sword of honor. "They master sorceries beyond our ken."

"The mightiest wizard falls at one blow of the sword."

Kote had clicked his tongue in amusement. "Become a wizard, warrior child. Become the greatest wizard of the Ku. For it is *their* wizards who wield the mightiest swords."

In short, learn to think like the enemy, then outthink the enemy—instead of going on trying to outgut him and outfight him.

And so he had done.

"Kez Maefele. Greetings."

He turned to the woman. Now he knew her. She had been WarAvocat *VII Gemina* when the Surrender was signed. When he and the Dire Radiant had defied lawful orders to yield their arms and had, instead, fled into the waste reaches of the Web to continue the struggle.

It had been she, and perhaps these others, who had stalked the killers of the Dire Radiant till no ship but his *Delicate Harmony*, tired and torn and limping on wounded legs, remained. Till he had given the order that he had despised.

He clicked his heels and bowed slightly, after the fashion of the conquerors. "Greetings, WarAvocat. It has taken you three thousand years."

"Close enough as makes no difference. What are a few centuries from this perspective?"

Turtle now knew the thing he faced was nothing of flesh. *They are great necromancers....*

"What mischief have you been up to, Kez Maefele?"

"Staying alive in a hostile universe."

"You've had more than your share of luck."

"Perhaps luck had nothing to do with it, WarAvocat. Till now."

"Luck has run out. The Ku Question has run its course. The symbol is about to receive its final blow."

"You do nurture a grudge beyond any rational limit, WarAvocat. I, who suffered the loss, do not recall your name, but you have fed a hatred so old and so strong you want to do murder after thirty centuries."

"Not murder. An overdue—"

A voice cut across the woman's. "There'll be no killing, whatever you call it."

The woman turned furious but betrayed herself as a being not of flesh. She did not look at her contradictor.

Turtle did, plundered ancient memories to get an estimate of the man. A Dictat. But he wore the insignia of a WarAvocat and was among the living still. The combination would make him the most powerful being aboard. And more dangerous than the ghost, whose motives were not shrouded.

The woman and her companions went transparent as their attention turned inward. The woman appeared determined to argue.

"This is a valuable resource," the living WarAvocat said. He descended from his throne. "I won't waste it to satisfy an ancient grudge."

A stir rippled those figures seated at either hand. Turtle realized they were all Deified. The man approaching was the only living being of stature present. Had it come to that here, too? That the dead ruled *VII Gemina* and the living obeyed in hopes of being elected to the company of immortals?

The woman spat at the living WarAvocat. Her spittle vanished instantly.

There were limits to their sorcery.

*They are ghosts,* he told himself. *But ghosts with a will to kill. Ghosts whose will could shape the universe.*

Amber Soul screamed.

The psychic wave staggered Turtle. WarAvocat halted. His mouth dropped open. His skin became more pallid. His eyes bugged and his hands fluttered. But he did not remain rattled. He came on.

Turtle glanced behind him. Midnight crouched over Amber Soul, wings spread. Good. Her mind was not empty all the time. The others followed her lead, masking Amber Soul.

WarAvocat paused beyond jumping distance. "You *are* the Kez Maefele of Dire Radiant legend?"

"I was a long time ago, WarAvocat. These days I'm Turtle, a nonhuman spacer stranded by the strictures of Canon law."

"The Ku are long-lived."

"Wizards and warriors, WarAvocat. Other *ghifus* have shorter lifespans."

"That's right. Your geneticists wanted those castes to live till somebody killed them."

Caste was no synonym for *ghifu*. But why correct the man? It was not worth the trouble. "It was a hope."

"And you came from a breed designed to combine both castes."

"An idea that bloomed too late."

"I'm a student of your tactics in the waste spaces. The Dire Radiant was effective far beyond its strength."

Turtle shrugged. "In the end it did no good."

"It never does. But they never stop trying."

"What do you want? None of us have done *VII Gemina* or Canon any violence."

"The Deified were interested. You made fools of them once. Now I'm interested. You refused to take part in the rebellion. You tried to warn the authorities. Why?"

"To prevent pointless slaughter. The Concord were idiots. They could not hear the cries of four millennia of idiots who preceded them and dragged countless innocents down with them. But the High City people were as stupid as all *their* predecessors. So they died. The Concord fools died. And the innocent are dying still. For nothing."

WarAvocat responded only by looking thoughtful.

Turtle wanted to check Amber Soul again. She continued

to radiate something that frayed his nerves. WarAvocat was not affected.

"What's wrong with her? Does she need medical attention?"

"She needs to be removed from *VII Gemina*. She is psionically sensitive. The gut of a Guardship festers with souls, all electromagnetically active, some marginally psionically active. She's straining to maintain her identity."

Turtle had no idea of the truth. That sounded good. "She'll lose unless she's moved out."

WarAvocat did not appear concerned. He started to ask a question.

"I've said enough. I owe you nothing. You've dragged these people here without right, unjustly, and illegally. I won't abet your crimes."

WarAvocat laughed. "You amuse me. *I* am the law. Justice and right are whatever I say they are." He started to ask a question.

Turtle turned away.

"Way of *kokadu*? That's a certain path to death, Kez Maefele."

"Death comes."

"Access." Turtle glanced back as a greenish shimmer slid over WarAvocat's shoulder. "WarAvocat for Peacekeeper One." The shimmer buzzed like insect wings. "Peacekeeper One, suspend all medical services and disaster relief till further notice." The insect buzzed. "It's being considered."

There was power at its rawest. "You would, wouldn't you?"

"It's all the same to me. Relief efforts cost us time better spent tracing the carrier of the rebel disease."

"Send the others home and I'll cooperate."

The shimmer buzzed at WarAvocat. He lifted an eyebrow. "Personal protection. Activate." A shimmer enveloped him. He moved forward, pushed the Immunes aside, lifted Midnight off Amber Soul. "That one stays. And the winged artifact. The rest go back to Merod Schene."

It was the best Turtle would get.

WarAvocat ordered the Immunes moved and the relief effort resumed. He settled into a seat. "Come here, Kez Maefele. Sit down."

Intensely aware of the scrutiny of several hundred Deified, Turtle sat.

"What is that creature?"

"Amber Soul? I don't know. Nobody does. I don't think she knows herself."

"How did she become an Immune?"

"Because she's so damned dangerous."

"Psionic?"

"Yes."

"There was a creature of her species aboard the Traveler that carried the krekelen to P. Jaksonica. It called itself Seeker of the Lost Children. That mean anything to you?"

"No." Turtle watched Guardship security lead the Immunes away. Midnight looked at him, lost, her wings drooping sadly, colorless. He tried to look apologetic.

Amber Soul screamed.

# - 22 -

Commander Haget paced. His clomping abraded Jo's nerves. She wanted to tell him to sit down and stop fidgeting.

"Sergeant."

"Sir?"

"Any suggestions about how to fill unstructured time? I've never had to do nothing before."

*Write your memoirs. That'll keep you busy for ten minutes.* She shrugged. "In WarCrew we freeze down for the long waits. Short waits we sleep, we drill, we play games. We screw a lot. Sir." She bit down on a grin. His reaction was what she expected. In WarCrew they would have a lot to say about an officer like him.

"Why were you selected for this mission?"

"I screwed up. I got noticed."

"You don't want to be noticed?"

"It's the same as volunteering." Where did this guy live? OpsCrew! Poor short-lifers. This guy wasn't old enough to remember Kole Marmigus alive. "We don't volunteer. How old are you, sir?"

He was surprised. As though that was too personal a question. Maybe it was. They did things differently in OpsCrew.

"Thirty-nine."

"You've done well, then. Made full Commander."

"I suppose I have. How old are you?"

"I was elected four thousand years ago." She grinned at his reaction. "Twenty-six, physical. But I got killed during the *Enherrenraat* business. I don't know how old that me was or how much experience I lost."

He got that funny look. Like he was talking to a ghost. They never really understood. But dealing with the Deified did not bother them, and the Deified were nothing but electronic spooks. Weird people.

Someone tapped on the door. Haget disappeared. Jo opened up. "Chief Timmerbach. Come in."

"I need to see the Commander."

Haget appeared. "Chief?"

"Could you come to the operating bridge, sir?"

"What is it?"

"The Presence, sir." The Chief's fear was palpable.

"You want me to stand witness to the fact that this isn't an inconvenience created for my benefit, Chief?"

"I guess that's one way of putting it, sir."

"Very well. Sergeant, will you accompany us?"

"Yes, sir." Jo felt more excitement than unease, and was surprised she felt no fear.

She'd never been into the command center of any ship. And the Presence was something she understood only intellectually. It was not something Guardships feared. It fled from them.

There was no hard proof it bothered smaller ships, either. Except that ships did disappear, and others had brushes with the Presence that left everyone aboard shaken.

Dead silence reigned on the bridge. They were not the only spectators. Hanhl Cholot was there, sober and grim. He crossed gazes with Haget. Haget nodded, accepting his presence. This was a Cholot Traveler at risk.

Haget joined Timmerbach before a screen four meters high and six wide. Jo stayed with them. Cholot followed.

A ribbon of yellow smoke curved away into apparent distance on screen. Jo got the impression the Traveler was moving through the outer fringes of the smoke.

Haget grunted. "We must be close."

"We're as near the edge as we dare go, moving dead slow for the Web. But we're gaining on it. The disturbances and the fogging are getting worse. Can you feel it, sir?"

Jo felt the directionless dread, the creeping spine chill. Something close was hungry and deadly and getting nearer.... But that made no sense. There was no concrete object for her dread.

"Yes. I don't suppose we'd have a turn node coming up?"

"No, sir." Timmerbach reached up to indicate a remote starburst. "This is J. Duosconica, anchor for eight strands. We'll be all right if we reach it."

The starburst moved closer slowly.

Jo had thought you were supposed to see stars from the Web same as in starspace. This space could not be vacant, could it?

There were points of light on the periphery of the screen.

Something ahead was masking everything but the brilliance of that anchor point.

The dread grew.

The foggy ribbon grew foggier.

That was not right. A healthy strand looked like a cable of fiber optics, brilliant with light, solid, gleaming when seen from afar. Like the strands coming off that anchor point.

Hager asked, "Can you break away at J. Duosconica? Lay over till it's safe?"

"The star is a white dwarf. Nexus is too close in. Too hot for us. We have to go on. And hope we get there behind the Presence."

The dread grew.

The shaking started. It began as vibrations Jo barely felt through her soles. In minutes the Traveler was bouncing like a light aircraft in heavy turbulence.

Timmerbach shouted at his bridge gang.

"We can't hold it any farther off the centerline, sir. We're risking premature breakaway now."

Jo grimaced. If they dropped off now, they would be almost a light year from the overly hot J. Duosconica. Climbing back on might be impossible. Misty as the strand was, instruments might not locate it.

Jo palmed her communicator. "Colonel Vadja. Klass."

After a moment, "Vadja here, Sergeant. What's happening?"

"Trouble with the Web. I'm on the bridge. I thought it might be interesting to see what our aliens are doing. Can you cover it?"

"Will do, Sergeant."

Commander Haget nodded. "Good thinking, Klass. Chief, time estimate to the anchor point?"

"Ten minutes. Roughly. We may have to move back into

the strand if..."

"Chief!" someone shouted. "We got something coming up behind us. Fast! Gods! It's a big mother... Saldy. What the hell is that? It's going to run us over!"

Timmerbach ran around, cursed, shook a fist at a secondary screen. "Take us in to the core! Maximum ahead. That's a Guardship! That's a goddamned Guardship, and it's going to smash us right off the Web!"

The Traveler rumbled and shuddered and surged. Jo staggered, grabbed for a handhold. The anchor point swelled. So did the darkness surrounding it. The strand grew more turbulent, the ride rougher. The Traveler creaked, groaned. There was a shriek of tormented metal somewhere aft.

The aft view showed a glowing egg ploughing through Web stuff, swelling. Timmerbach raged. "That bastard can see us! He don't care if he kills us! The goddamned arrogant asshole! Seligo. Pick a strand coming off the anchor. Now!"

"Sir, if I guess wrong..."

"Do it! Chances are five to one for us."

If they didn't catch the Presence first, Jo thought. If the Guardship didn't shove them off the Web headed toward J. Duosconica....

Timmerbach continued to rage, demanding more speed. The Guardship closed. Features became distinct. Jo blurted, "That's *IV Trajana!*"

Haget gulped air. For the first time he was rattled. "Can't be. Nobody's seen *IV Trajana* since the *Enherrenraat* incident."

"More speed!" Timmerbach fumed. "Damned Web, you can't go anywhere but in a straight line. Seligo! Calculate a cut course to the nearest away strand in case we get knocked off."

Jo guessed they were two light weeks from the anchor point. Seconds on the Web. Months in starspace.

Her communicator whispered. "Klass? Vadja. Messenger

was on a rampage when I went past. Seems catatonic now. The other one hasn't done anything."

"Right. Klass out."

"We may make it," Timmerbach said. He whirled toward the rear viewscreen. *IV Trajana* filled the field. "One extra minute, you bastard. Give us one extra minute."

*Glorious Spent* shook like it was coming apart. The dread had grown as thick as fog. Jo could almost smell it. She thought its smell was old death.

## - 23 -

The Tregesser Voyager *Elmore Tregesser* broke away from the Web well off Tregesser Prime's Optimal. Lupo Provik signed. Two went aft to inform the passenger. Lupo nodded to Three, poised to send false ID if challenged. They had to get in unnoticed by Canon agents and Valerena's partisans.

Provik eased the Voyager toward P. Benetonica 3F, a trivial station supporting insystem mining. If there was no challenge, the Voyager would pretend to be insystem itself.

It was the usual way Simon Tregesser slipped in and out of his home system.

There was no challenge. Traffic control was inept, haphazard. Simon Tregesser preferred it that way.

Lupo sent a code to his people on station. When the Voyager nosed in, its three-bay section had been closed. Only trusted people were on hand.

No sense taking chances.

When it was time to move Simon, none of the crew looked like Lupo Provik. They looked like rough asteroid miners who maybe belonged to the same family. The kind of people who would move a dangerous cargo without asking questions. The kind Lupo Provik would hire.

Soon a battered lighter headed toward a port north of

Tregesser Horata. Six hours later it touched down. An hour later still, the lighter's operators delivered Simon Tregesser to the basement of a building not far from the Tregesser Pylon, a six-kilometers-tall tower that rose from Tregesser Horata DownTown through UpTown, and up and up, through the sprawling torus of Tregesser Horata High City and up a kilometer more. The Simon Tregesser Other waited in a ball that tipped the Pylon's peak.

Lupo stood at a window, stared up the immense height of the Pylon. He did not like it. Too vulnerable. Big showoff thing. A monument to Simon's ego. He could take it down a dozen ways. Did Simon think nobody was crazy enough to kill thousands to get just one? He'd do it himself.

"This's the touchy part," he said. "This's where Valerena will move if her intelligence sources are what they should be."

"They aren't," Two said. "She doesn't have what it takes. She's lazy."

"She is. I hate Tregesser Horata."

"That's because you can't control it."

"Yes."

Sheer size made Tregesser Horata remarkable. Neither the High City nor UpTown could accommodate their appropriate populations. After the heart of DownTown had been cleared for the base of the Pylon, UpTown had dribbled down and taken the near ground. Now the social gradient ran downhill from the Pylon to the Black Ring, then rose again. Thirty klicks out there were hill-straddling palaces of a new superclass a step above the hoi polloi cluttering Tregesser Horata High City.

The biggest, a fairy fortress perched precariously on a precipice overlooking the natural absurdities of Fuerogomenga Gorge, belonged to Valerena Tregesser.

Lupo's House Security department occupied ten levels of the Pylon, even with the High City. He hated the structure but lived there when he was home.

Airboats drifted across the arc of sky between the bottom of UpTown and the polished ivory face of the Pylon. Insects, Lupo thought. Deadly insects. He watched every one, half expecting a suicide assault. It had been tried. There was a permanent dark stain a kilometer up.

Two said, "If you're that worried, call T.W. See what she's got."

"Can't reach her without telling somebody who I am. I'm not supposed to be on Prime."

Four said, "We're within time parameters. It's not like you to be impatient."

True. Usually he was patient as a spider. "It's that place. It's a deathtrap."

Two observed, "Valerena may pull it down if she takes over."

"*If* she takes over. When I talk to Simon about the succession, he gets shifty. He has notions. And I have mine." The others eyed him. "Blessed has the real stuff."

"Valerena isn't worried about him."

"She has all the Tregesser ego. Considering her horizontal lifestyle, it's doubtful she can imagine any male as dangerous."

"What would she put up in place of the Pylon?" Four wondered.

"Something as ridiculous as that castle, a hundred times bigger." Provik glared at the Pylon. If will could bring Simon down, he was breaking the sound barrier.

Three returned. "He's coming."

"Get him moved. I want the Voyager gone before Valerena even thinks about setting a watch."

The bell in the cellar was identical to the one that had departed. All identifying marks and serials had been duplicated. The creature inside had been mutilated to become an exact duplicate of Simon Tregesser.

Lupo studied the Other as they loaded the bell. He frowned. Simon liked to be clever. Would he outfox himself by pretending to be his Other going back, leaving his true Other in place?

He might. He damned well might.

Some test was in order. He mentioned it to Three and Four, made suggestions. They would take the Voyager back to the end space. He and Two were staying.

He had identities he and his family could assume. They belonged to people who arrived and departed mysteriously, with no apparent reason or rhyme.

He made a call after the lighter lifted. He and Two became a man and woman who were the scandal of Tregesser Horata. They pretended to be man and wife. Everybody knew they were brother and sister.

It gave people something to distract them from their own dark sins.

A tsunami of light hammered Tregesser Prime.

"Guardship!" Lupo cursed the fading starburst. "What the hell?"

What a time to have one break off the Web here.

# - 24 -

Lupo One met Lupo Three in the docking bay. Three said, "Simon didn't make the switch. He's pretending to be his Other."

One looked at Four. She nodded, gave him the rest. "A Guardship broke away while we were in transit from Prime to 3F."

"We seem doomed to nothing but glad tidings. Which one?"

"*VI Adjutrix*. It took station out of traffic and just sat there.

No signal of any kind."

Three asked, "Could it mean something? Could something have leaked?"

"Not likely. Nothing to be done about it, anyway. Let it sit. We'll know where one is. Let's move Simon. Keep an eye on him till we know his game."

The Simon whose bell appeared on deck boomed, "Lupo Provik, you old bastard! I haven't seen your ass since my big brother dragged it out here."

Not true, but One did not correct the Tregesser vision of reality. Simon was into his role. In private the Simon Other cultivated quirks in a grasp at identity, pretending it was more than a useful phantom.

"So this is the great end-space hideout. I want to see every nook and cranny."

"I'll arrange something. Right now we need to get you down where you can do a show. The staff are used to having you in their hair."

"Ha! If they have hair. I suppose. Did your people tell you a goddamned Guardship broke off the Web at Prime? Bastard like to ran us over."

When a ship broke away local space had to adjust. An energy storm raged till the shock damped out. With Travelers that energy ranged from long wave to visible light. With a Guardship the blast of white light was just the bottom end of the discharge.

One asked, "Were you inside the corona?"

Four nodded.

"Did you get any data?"

"Not much."

One grunted. That was the way luck went. They had not been a research ship sitting there waiting for it.

Simon Tregesser drifted across the great cavity, feeling

smug. He could come up with a twist of his own still. He got the bell integrated with the systems at the center, went inside to check his Outsider.

The damned thing was comatose. He could get no response. What the hell was with that thing?

Instrumentation indicated continued biological activity. It was not the body that had gone. It was the minds. If what it thought with were minds. If it thought.

The hell with it. He didn't need it to tell him what was happening. Every Traveler leaving P. Jaksonica was howling for a Guardship. It would not be long before one came sniffing up the backtrail.

Time to get on with it.

He lowered the bell and began playing with his thunders and lightnings and image makers. A little clumsily. He summoned Noah.

Noah came looping down between the lightnings, swooped to his perch. "Yes, Lord? Have you been unwell, Lord?"

Mad Simon Tregesser laughter hammered the cavity walls. But it was Tregesser laughter a calculated touch off key. "Let's just say I set aside the Great Mission momentarily. In order to confound my beloved offspring."

Simon's attention was fixed on Noah absolutely, seeking nuances of treachery.

Simon stood accused of countless crimes. But stupidity did not appear on the True Bill.

Noah gone a while. Acting a little odd when he returned. Lupo suggesting he trust nobody with news of the switch. Meaning Lupo knew about Noah. So what? Lupo knew about every damned thing. Lupo made knowing his business.

A few questions in the Pylon. Enough oddities about Noah's itinerary on Prime to convert suspicion into intuitive certainty. To give him an idea for double-dealing Valerena into a corner. Teach the little bitch that she was playing with the big boys.

Noah covered well but not well enough. His reaction damned him.

Tregesser understood instantly how he had been reached. Valerena had bought him with women. He had not given enough weight to the artifact's lusts.

He would not make that mistake again.

Noah would get no more chances. But he *would* make himself useful.

Carefully, carefully, Simon led Noah to the suspicion that he was dealing with his master's Other, swiftly switched the moment Provik had sniffed Valerena's move. Then he sent the artifact off on a trivial task.

Lupo One secured the communicator, yielded to his chief of staff, headed for the suite.

The family gathered. He said, "Simon just told me to ready a Voyager for a trip to Prime."

Six said, "And the artifact will go along? Under the impression the switch has been made already?"

Three said, "If we're going back, we'd better think about that Guardship. Be a bitch to sneak in without it noticing."

"I'll leave you to that," One said. "Consider, too, the chance Simon is being *too* clever."

Lupo One was studying a holochart of Canon space when Simon entered main sector Central Staff Info Center. It floated in midair, away from normal business. It had a beanish shape fifty meters long, thirty-three wide, twenty-four high. Three million plus stars and stellar objects were represented. At a touch he could add or delete or zoom.

One had the chart retreating into the past, one hundred thousand years to the minute. He had only a few select strands portrayed. Without looking away he asked, "What happens when natural stellar motion moves anchor points so the strands connecting them come into contact?"

"I wouldn't know, Lupo."

"We can find out a little over six years from now. The strand connecting B. Shellica and B. Philipia will cross the strand connecting N. Nuttica and B. Belnapii. It'll be the first such impact since humans reached the Web."

"B. Belnapii? Didn't we have an interest there?"

"We still have a strong interest. Shaga timber."

"Why are you playing with this?"

"Knowledge. Knowledge is power, Simon."

"Firepower is power. I had that put in so you could track Guardships, not so you could play games."

"Do you suppose they have something like it?"

"Better. They've been prowling the Web forever. And you know I'm not the Simon Tregesser Other, don't you?"

"I know."

"Which means you've figured out what I'm up to. You know about my pet artifact."

"Yes."

"Is there anything you don't know, Lupo?"

"I don't know what happens when two strands collide. I don't know what causes tag ends. I don't know how the Web came into being. There's a lot I don't know."

"Is the Voyager ready?"

"Yes."

"There'll be an extra passenger. But you knew that, too."

"I anticipated it."

"Damn! I ought to kick out and give the whole mess to you. The hell with Valerena and the Directorate. Let them chew dirt. Let somebody have it who can keep reins on the monster."

Lupo One switched back to the display he had been running. "I wouldn't take the Chair, Simon."

"You wouldn't, would you? You cold bastard. You don't want it. I guess that's why I trust you. I just wish to hell I knew what you *do* want."

"I want to know where the Web came from. I want to know how new strands appear and feathery old ones suddenly get mended. That's happened three times in my lifetime. Nobody knows anything but that it happened."

"Single-minded bastard. Get a crew together. I'll let you know when I'm ready."

One toyed with the holochart for half a minute, then glanced at the departing bell. Time for an update.

# - 25 -

A Saarica. J. M. Ledetica. C. Phritsia. In each system Canon garrison had isolated the infection, then had eradicated it. White corpuscles on the job. WarAvocat was surprised. He had little respect for Canon's troops or officers.

His own competence and motives were under fire. The Deified were at their meddlesome worst, carping and second-guessing.

It had been too long since *VII Gemina* had seen any excitement. They all wanted a piece. A bigger piece than anyone else got.

And there was the complication of his predecessor. The Deified Makarska Vis resented his having robbed her of old prey. If she could not rip out the Ku's heart she would have his instead. So far she had been only a spiteful nuisance. Even so, he was glad he was Dictat. The honor gave him powers with which to suppress her pettiness.

*VII Gemina* broke off the Web at the Goriot world M. Anstii 3.

A patch of air in WarAvocat's quarters buzzed, nagging him. "Damn it!"

"Shall I withdraw, Lord?" The artifact's voice was the whisper of silver bells.

"No." It was too late to stop. He could not let go till it was done.

It was too late for Lady Midnight, too. The first tremors of pleasure had begun to torment her. Even with a man she loathed there was an early point when there was no stopping till racking, violent spasms reduced her to a comatose state of satiation.

The gene engineers had made her a slave to her flesh.

How could anyone have discarded a creature so exquisitely useful? Was there some hidden flaw in her?

"WarAvocat," he told the shimmer. "I'm occupied. What is it?"

The artifact moaned, a little cry almost of despair.

The air murmured, "We're off the Web, WarAvocat. House Goriot has appealed for help putting down a rebellion. Situation data suggests it isn't as ugly as V. Rothica 4."

WarAvocat gasped. Didn't the artifact realize he had business? No. Of course not. There would be no thoughts in her head, only needs burning to be filled. "I'll be there as soon as I can."

His attempt to hurry Midnight was defeated by the skill of the engineers who had designed her. When held helpless, her body was more mercilessly demanding.


WarAvocat entered WarCentral dazed. He had trouble taking in the information displayed. Deified glowered down from their screens. Or, like the Deified Makarska Vis, they smirked. He had betrayed a weakness.

That damned artifact! She had the power to obsess a man with that body....

Awed realization. Never before had he considered an artifact as possessed of any power at all.

The M. Anstii uprising had followed the classic pattern. The rebels had broken Goriot Glume High City's moorings and had destabilized its grav suppressors so that it was adrift in the planet's upper airs.

Beyond the stupidities that plagued every insurrection, the local rebels had failed to take into account M. Anstii's special circumstances. House Goriot's principal business was natural gemstones. M. Anstii was blessed with a profusion, some existing nowhere else. Forever plagued by jewel thieves, House Goriot had developed an elaborate private security force. The rebels had overlooked it in the first blush of bloodletting. The force had had time to get organized.

Result: standoff.

The Deified began pummeling WarAvocat with questions.

He scanned the ranks of screens and allowed himself a smile bordering on contempt.

The Deified Ansehl Ronygos spoke for everyone. "What are you going to do about this, WarAvocat?"

"Nothing, Deified."

Babble of protest and criticism.

"Explain yourself, WarAvocat."

"I am bemused, Deified. With all the resources you command... But, then, those no longer among the living forget how the living think. Deified, the most effective thing *VII Gemina* could do was break off the Web. By now the rebels are scattering. The household troops are in pursuit. Access." The shimmer jumped his shoulder. "Communications, WarAvocat. Are you in contact with House Goriot?"

"Yes, sir."

"Any reports on current rebel activity?"

"The insurgents have begun to disperse, sir, in anticipation of the arrival of our troops."

WarAvocat surveyed the Deified, case made. Some vanished in a huff. Some returned his smile, approving. Some looked like they had gotten a taste of something bitter. The Deified Makarska Vis lingered for a moment, glaring at him with a displeasure almost too intense for an electronic entity. Had a cabal of bitter kindred led *XII Fulminata* to become what it had? *XII Fulminata*'s style would suit Vis well.

He thought of the artifact. Arousal was immediate. He tried to put her out of mind. He had not given the other two prisoners enough attention. The one continued her efforts at sorcerous dissimulation.

He laughed. To think of what the alien was doing in terms of witchcraft—he was letting the Ku's outlook intrude upon his own. Who could credit it? A spacefaring race so primitive in thought it still looked at the universe through lenses of mysticism and magic.

So the Ku were a species defeated and commercially enslaved, and when they died they stayed dead forever, unlike Guardship humanity, where immortality was assured. No one stayed dead long, though OpsCrew and ServCrew did not recall their former lives.

But *Gemina* remembered. *Gemina* forgot nothing and forgave everything.

He started thinking beyond the noncrisis of M. Anstii.

## - 26 -

The breeze off the sea carried the murmur of spirits and sprites and a coolness that kissed Blessed Tregesser's cheeks. He stared out at the waves, watched one after another roll in and smash itself on the foot of the cliff, a hundred meters below. Darkness slithered over the water. The sun was setting behind him. As it did the evening's party came to life.

He shifted his kaleidoscope and thought that his grandfather's scheme would be just one more wave crashing against the cliff of the Guardships. The waves might demolish the cliff in time, but not in one year or ten thousand. Maybe the smart thing was to accept reality and operate within its constraints.

Most of the Houses did, and prospered.

And in the genes of others, rebellion simmered on, a quiet inferno, consuming generation after generation. And nowhere was that more true than in House Tregesser. He could not shake his heritage. But he did not have to stoop to the stupidities of his forebears.

Behind him somewhere Valerena laughed. Blessed thought her laugh tight, contrived, premature for the progress of the evening. But she was the guest of Linas Maserang here, and was working hard to keep him entranced.

Maserang showed signs of becoming disenchanted.

"Blessed? Won't you come join us, son? You perching up here, staring out at Linas's bleak dark sea, is creepy."

Blessed faced the fraudulent smile and dead blue eyes of Myth Worgemuth. Behind him, Cable Shike shrugged as though to ask, "How could I stop him?" Beyond Cable servants began lighting paper lanterns. Blessed said, "Myth, I'm still young enough to be excused anything. You're too old to be forgiven anything."

A shadow moved behind those dead eyes. "What do you mean, son?"

"That you're old enough to know better. That there's no reason anyone should forgive you anything."

Worgemuth's smile remained fixed. "I think I've missed what you're trying to tell me."

"I doubt it, Myth. But I'll spell it out. A long time ago you helped my great-grandfather take the House. Then you turned on him and helped my grandfather take control. Now you're scheming with my mother to oust him."

Worgemuth's smile vanished.

"I'm not stupid, Myth. I can see what you're doing. I can even puzzle out the fact the poor senile old Commodo Hvar is being set up to take the blame if the plot unravels."

Worgemuth looked positively grim.

"And now, before you've even gotten my mother in place, you're around sucking up to me. Maybe figuring on getting a kid in there that you can control. You think my mother is too stupid or too silly to notice? Don't bet your life. She's a Tregesser."

Worgemuth's mouth tightened into a colorless prune.

"But why worry about it? There's a gala in progress. The interesting people are arriving, fashionably late." Blessed went down to greet Tina Bofoku and her brother Nyo. Worgemuth remained where he was, as though he had relieved a sentry post that kept watch on the sea.

"Trouble with the old-timer?" Tina asked. She was in a sparkling mood.

"Only for him. Your mother is over there. Later?"

"Absolutely." She made a face at Nyo.

Blessed entered the crowd without joining it. Even at the heart of the veranda he was an observer who watched from the outside. How many of these people belonged to Worgemuth? Not many. They would be innocents or, at most, potential recruits.

At first the guests seemed to be playing ocean, moving in little surges toward where his mother held court, rolling away. But soon Valerena retreated into Maserang's house. The population divided into equally spaced groups with cometary individuals between them.

Sometimes someone spoke to Blessed. Always he replied courteously but coolly, cultivating an image of distance that, tempered by warmth in private, might lead some to think they had wormed their ways into his confidence. Those would be the people he used.

As he spoke with an executive who seemed to think she could further his education and her career in private, he caught a snatch of conversation. He froze. The words did not register. They did not matter. Only the voice mattered. There was something frighteningly familiar about it. Something that raised the hair on the back of his neck. Yet he could not identify it.

He spotted the man. "Who is that?" he asked his companion.

"Nikla Ogdehvan. He and his wife do something mysterious for the House. Probably something sinister. They come and go and nobody knows where or when they'll turn up again."

Subtle stress on wife. Why? Marriage was uncommon and quaint but not socially unacceptable. "Thank you. Excuse me, please."

The woman's lips tightened but she did not protest.

It took minutes of drifting. Once he had his target fixed he listened intently, not to words but to tone and rhythm. The man spoke seldom, but when he did everyone listened. There was a hard edge beneath his gentleness. No one *knew* what he did. No one wanted to find out.

Half an hour later, when he received the summons from his mother, Blessed knew exactly what Nikla Ogdehvan did for the House.

Linas Maserang, Myth Worgemuth, and a third man waited with Valerena. Valerena said, "Myth tells me you've got everything figured out. With a mind like yours, you might be useful."

Was that sarcasm? "I presume something dramatic has happened to make you bunch up with so many witnesses around."

Valerena scowled. "Word just came. Father's Voyager arrived today." Exasperation. "Those morons up there didn't figure it out till a few minutes ago. They wouldn't have noticed if that damned Guardship hadn't challenged him."

"May I see the data, Mother?"

Maserang said, "Help yourself." *His* sarcasm was thick. He

indicated his personal Information Center.

"Just scroll the message from station."

Irked, Maserang did so.

Blessed read. "Four hours twenty-three minutes since break-away. Not enough time to dock and make the descent."

Valerena snapped, "Of course not! He's up there lying low. It says that right there."

"What we *see* Grandfather doing and what he's *really* doing aren't the same things, Mother. I submit that he *intended* to be noticed."

"Nonsense," Maserang said. "Why?"

"Because this is my grandfather's Other, who has been exchanged already, coming in to make the switch again."

"Don't let your imagination carry you away. It couldn't have been managed without our agents noticing."

"Neither you nor your agents have noticed that Lupo Provik is out on your veranda, among the invited guests, masquerading as Nikla Ogdehvan. And he's been on Prime for a week."

Dead silence. Stricken silence. Death might have drawn a talon through that room.

Maserang's Info Center buzzed. Irritated, he muttered, "I told them I didn't want to be disturbed."

The silence turned toward disbelief. Valerena said, "Amuse yourself at someone else's expense, Blessed. I no longer find your humor tolerable."

Maserang said, "You'd better take this, Val."

She went and snarled at the comm. She erected a privacy screen a moment after she started, though, so that Blessed did not know why she was growling.

She was deathly calm when she came back. "That was my father's pet artifact."

Blessed moved toward the door. "I'll go irritate someone else, Mother."

She screeched something obscene. He did not listen. He

went out to see how life was treating Lupo Provik.

## - 27 -

Timmerbach raged and wailed and scurried around, but not once did he lose control of *Glorious Spent*. He was a wonder. He railed against his deities, his employers, Canon, the Guardships, the Web itself, without prejudice—while occasionally pausing to give his techs advice in a calm voice. He sounded crazy most of the time but was just a man trying to save his ship and maybe his life.

Jo looked into the screen portraying the aft view. *IV Trajana* loomed ever larger.

One of the bridge crew beckoned Timmerbach. They muttered. Then the Chief jumped back and complained all the louder. "Commander, we're not going to make that anchor point. We'll come up several seconds short. We'll hang on till these bastards bump us off, though. May they get hung up and never find a way down."

Jo recalled stories of ships found caught on the Web, apparently unable to get back off.

*Glorious Spent* shuddered and jumped as though kicked. Warning lights went mad. Jo grabbed Haget and a stanchion. Alarms shrieked and hooted. Timmerbach yelled, "Kick it off! Kick it off now!"

And pray the systems had not been damaged.

Real Space. Starspace. The sense of having been relieved of a vast pressure. It took her several seconds to understand why.

The dread was gone.

She and Haget realized they were still in contact. She jerked away. "My apologies, sir."

"None needed, Sergeant. Chief. We're off the Web prematurely. Have you calculated the schedule delays?"

Timmerbach exhaled slowly, controlling his temper. "We

were close to the anchor when we broke away, Commander. Assuming our numbers are good, we'll be in starspace four days. We'll pick up another strand and be gone."

Jo did not listen closely. She was trying to keep an eye on Cholot and to watch for the monster star raging somewhere nearby, and for the school of stars in which it swam. Guard-ships' soldiers seldom got to see such sights.

Haget said, "Thank you, Chief. We'll get out of your way now."

Jo's communicator beeped. She raised a hand to stall Haget. "Klass?" the comm whispered. "Vadja. Seeker is on the move. Headed your way."

"Got you. Klass out. Commander, Colonel Vadja says Seeker is headed for the bridge."

Timmerbach heard. "That's all I need. A goddamned creepy-crawlie... Keep it away from me."

"Chief, I have no intention of allowing an alien near the controls of a Canon ship. Klass. Get everyone up here."

"Yes, sir." As she summoned Degas and AnyKaat, she checked the exterior screens. Amazing that something as terrible as the dread or as big as *IV Trajana* could pass unnoticed in starspace.

"Astounding, isn't it?" Haget said. "Chief, we'll wait for it in the passageway. Lock up behind us. Sergeant, check with Vadja. See if it's still coming."

She did. It was. "Why?" she wondered aloud.

Haget shrugged. He made sure the bridge hatch was secured, stood at an easy rest. "That business makes you appreciate the problems of operating a small ship, doesn't it?"

"Yes." Surprise. That was too human a remark for Haget. Jo assumed a stance aping his.

"Here it comes."

Seeker of the Lost Children looked taller and more regal. Jo battled an urge to kneel.

The impulse went as suddenly as it had come. It was replaced by a desire to step aside. "It's trying to manipulate me," she said.

"Stand fast."

The thing slowed, halted. Era Vadja appeared behind it, then Degas and AnyKaat. Those two had brought sidearms.

Haget said, "Passengers are not permitted in this part of the Traveler. Please return to passengers' country."

Seeker did not move. Jo tried to stand outside herself while emotions and urges not her own tugged at her. She did not yield.

Haget repeated his admonition. He added, "Canon law forbids your presence on the operating bridge of any carrier not operated by your own species."

*This vessel must turn back. I have erred. I have overlooked one of the children. She is in danger.*

Jo shuddered. That voice was *inside* her head....

"Sir, you must return to passengers' country. This is a lawful order. If you fail to obey, I will be compelled to enforce it by force."

Jo was amazed that he would be so patient and polite.

Seeker was not listening. *Move aside. I will have this vessel turned.*

Hammer blows, those thoughts of command. Excruciating, but not unbearable. Jo withstood them. Haget seemed to shed them without effort.

Seeker appeared surprised. And distressed.

Haget said, "We have us a situation, people. I can't be sure it understands my warnings. AnyKaat, set to light stun. Degas, you for heavy. I'll try talking one more time."

If Seeker understood, it did not respond. Nor did it react to Haget's repeated directive to return to its quarters. It tried its mind magic again. It failed again.

Jo said, "Careful, Commander. It's getting pissed."

It started forward.

"AnyKaat."

AnyKaat drew and fired with Guardship soldier's proficiency. The alien collapsed. Jo moved in carefully.

Haget snapped, "Vadja! Check the methane breather. Now! Degas. The krekelen. AnyKaat. Cover us while we lug this thing to its quarters."

Chief Timmerbach cracked the bridge hatch, peeked out, squeaked, and locked up again as Haget said, "Don't be shy about using stun."

Jo knelt beside the alien. It was not entirely unconscious. It no longer looked much like the thing they had faced, though flickers of that semblance ran over it like scampering flames on a cotton wad moistened with alcohol.

The aspect beneath was no more real. Spots of black appeared on it and vanished as rhythmically as a heartbeat. Jo sensed sorrow radiating from it.

"I don't think it's really belligerent, Commander. I think it just doesn't know how to make us understand."

He knelt opposite her. "Ready, AnyKaat?"

AnyKaat eased around so she would be behind them. "Ready." Very professional, Jo thought.

Her communicator squawked. "Vadja, Sergeant. We got us a snake circus back here. This methane sniffer has gone berserk."

Haget said, "Tell him to stand fast. We'll be there as soon as we stuff this thing into its den."

Jo relayed the message. Before she finished, Degas checked in. "Nobody home back here, Sergeant. Our protean friend has gone AWOL."

"Can it do that?" Jo asked. "I thought WarAvocat had it programmed."

"Evidently not well enough. It has. AnyKaat, help Degas find it after we put this thing away."

"Yes, sir." She sounded worried.

Jo felt some feather touch from Seeker. She could make no sense of it. "It's trying to tell me something, Commander."

"It can talk us blue in the face after we get the bees back in the hive. But first things first."

Bees? How did he know about bees? From a former life?

Seeker was light. Jo had guessed a hundred kilos beforehand but now she was thinking fifty. Fifty creepy kilos. She grew increasingly repelled....

"Vadja, Sergeant. You people better get here. The damned thing is trying to get out."

"Shee-it!"

"Out?" Haget asked. "But..."

"No shit. Bang!" Jo said. "Shoot it if you have to, Era."

"Where?"

"Good question. Hell, just smoke away." She looked at Haget. "That all right?"

He nodded.

They reached Seeker's quarters. "In you go, buddy," Haget said. They dumped it and closed the door. AnyKaat set her weapon to Kill and welded the door shut. Then she ran.

"We'd better collect our own arsenal, Sergeant."

That took only a moment. Then, hip to hip, they raced for the methane breather's deck. Startled passengers dodged them and stared. Vadja kept Jo's communicator squealing. "Shooting doesn't do much good. It's spread out all over in there and just getting madder. Damn it! It *is* trying to get out."

Haget grabbed the communicator. "If you can't stop it, get the hell away from it. Now!"

They burst into the passageway. Forty meters away Vadja started running toward them. Behind him a compartment door popped open.

"Down!" Jo yelled, and tripped Haget. They landed in a sprawl as oxygen and methane met.

Thunder, flame, and the indignant wail of alarms filled the passage for the few seconds that Jo retained consciousness. The last thing she saw was Era Vadja flying toward her, spread-eagled on the knuckles of the blast.

## - 28 -

Simon Tregesser's bell drifted out of shadow, onto the dock, as Noah secured the pay comm. The artifact left the booth, headed for a sanctuary whose location had been given him.

Valerena thought there was a chance he might be suspect, that he ought to run.

His pace slowed as the wrongness penetrated his self-involvement.

The silence screamed.

It had been a typical dock when he had gone into the booth. Dense. Loud. Hectic. Now it was as empty as if all life had been obliterated.

He froze.

In so short a time?

Short of cosmic intervention, there was only one power capable of clearing a dock so fast.

The crew of the Voyager appeared ahead and to either hand. Each carried a naked hairsplitter. They closed in.

Mad laughter rolled behind him. This time, he knew, he would not dodge the lightning.

But he tried, knowing he could not bluff his way through.

## - 29 -

The thing hidden at the heart of Simon Tregesser's end-space citadel sensed a quivering on the Web. The vibration beat upon it from every direction, like the subtle neutrino flux of the universe itself.

For a minute the message drove it totally sane.

By means provided it called, "Simon Tregesser!"

Simon Tregesser did not respond.

It called again. The news had to be related! A juggernaut of disaster was rolling down the Web, and only inspired improvisation would keep it from bursting into the end space long before it was due.

Fate had carved itself a big slice. Fate and the machinations of enemies the Outsider had not known it had.

Tregesser would not answer. The madman must be off amusing himself. If enough alarms sounded, he would have to respond.

The Outsider's period of sanity ended as it began stressing the limits of its habitat. It twitched, spasmed. Its components turned upon one another. A convulsion cracked a gap in a seal supposedly proof against violence. High-pressure methane squirted through.

There was no explosion. A three meter sword of flame stabbed a control panel. Heat interrupted circuits. Smoke boiled. Plastics began to burn. Alarms whooped. Fire-suppressant systems reacted too late or not at all. Temperatures went up and up and up. More systems failed.

Fire reached a storage compartment for chemicals used inside the closed environments of Tregesser and the Outsider.

The Lupo who first reached the cavity witnessed the blow, which sent shrapnel rocketing unpredictably off the walls. But the Outsider knew nothing of that. Its components were dead already, some of asphyxiation, some of oxygen poisoning, some of decompression, or, failing all of those, of being broiled medium well.

The Lupo watched the violence subside, shook his head, went back topside to see if instruments had recorded anything that would explain what had happened. He doubted he would learn anything.

He did not.

He did get to wondering.

# - 30 -

In a place no Canon human knew or would go by choice, in a murk of methane and ammonia, a dozen colonial intelligences harkened as another thrumming blast of agony echoed across the Web. Their components rearranged themselves in some expression of shared emotion. It may have been sorrow, or anger, or despair, or something no human could conceive. Certainly there was a period of inactivity that might have been memorial or mourning.

Then that council joined its multiple brains to consider new machinations.

# - 31 -

Turtle had been given quarters reserved for visiting dignitaries, the best living arrangements he had known since the Dire Radiant. A prison cell without bars. Only prisoners mad enough to attack their jailers would need restraint aboard *VII Gemina*. The Guardship was aware of every sentient corpuscle moving through its metal and plastic veins.

He had the freedom of the ship, with the exception of the Core. What harm could he do?

He was caught more surely than any fly in a spider's snare.

Amber Soul had been installed in the cabin next to his, where her pain was monitored remorselessly. Initially Turtle went nowhere else. He refused to pretend to be anything but a prisoner of the ancient enemy.

Midnight had quarters beyond Amber Soul's but seldom saw them. She spent her time with Hanaver Strate. Turtle felt no rancor. She had to be what she had been created to be.

He was sad, pitying Midnight her pain and Amber Soul her needless agony.

Maybe one of Amber Soul's own kind could penetrate her barriers. To Turtle it was as proof as a Guardship's screens.

Frustration at his helplessness translated into a restlessness he assuaged, eventually, by wandering. But he did so far from the habitats of living crew, out in remote reaches near the rider bays, the nests of pursuit and interceptor fighters, and the Hellspinner pits. There were places out there that offered direct views of naked starspace.

He suspected thousands of Guardship crew never saw space except as a telerelay. A screen had boundaries. A screen never portrayed more than a small, flat section of reality. These humans did not like to admit that they were of no consequence in the eye of the universe.

He found a dead Hellspinner pit. *Gemina* permitted him access. From the O Bubble on the Readying Room he had a view of as much universe as his mind could encompass. He could lie on the Twist Master's couch and subside into seductive, freckled darkness where there were no yesterdays, no tomorrows, no worries or fears.

He could get as morbidly philosophical as he liked.

WarAvocat found him the third time he visited the pit. Of course, *Gemina* would report. Amazing, though, that the man would come out and invest time visiting.

WarAvocat took the console seat, stared out at the void. *VII Gemina* was off the Web, doing Turtle knew not what. He could see a small moon, a station, the moving sparks of local traffic.

It looked as though he had nothing to say. When he did

speak, it was only a confirmation of what Turtle read from his stance. "It's restful out here. When I look back, I feel nostalgic only about my time as a Twist Master. Out here you're alone with yourself. Sometimes you end up facing yourself and what you might be."

He grinned, apparently without calculation. "Nothing like popping off a 'spinner and having a Lock Runner slide through and you have to twist a new one and get him before he gets you."

Turtle countered, "Nothing like banging through knowing you have to spot the pit and take it before the Twist Master gets you and your team. Are you really that old?"

"WarCrew sleep a lot. Did you pilot a Lock Runner?"

"I invented the tactic." Successful Lock Runners had deposited commandos on the skins of Guardships. Guardship soldiers had been no match for Ku warriors.

"It wouldn't work now."

"There are no more Ku. No other species has the reflexes. WarAvocat, where are the children?"

"The what?"

"Your children. Your little ones. I've been aboard three Guardships. When we took *XVI Cyreniaca*, briefly, before it blew. *XXII Scythica*, before WarCrew drove us out. And now *VII Gemina*. I have yet to see children."

WarAvocat puzzled it out. "We're our own replacements. Everyone aboard has been here since *VII Gemina* was commissioned."

"But... I know WarCrew age only on duty. But the others look like they live uninterrupted lives."

"They do—till they get elected or Deified. Most crew just die, then a recorded and edited version gets impressed on a young clone."

Turtle did not comprehend the rationale. "They live their lives over and over?"

"As the jokes goes, over and over till they get it right."

Turtle shook his head. It made no sense. He had studied these people all his life. They were predictable but incomprehensible.

"It works for *VII Gemina*, Kez Maefele. Other Guardships evolved other directions. They've gotten strange."

Strange. "They say nothing ever changes. They blame you. You are wonderful devils. But I have lived every minute of several thousand years. The entire universe has gone strange. You may not have noticed."

"Why wouldn't we notice?"

"You do not look outside as long as Outside does not fracture the rules you enforce. Canon has changed, WarAvocat. I mark the watershed when the rage for tier cities swept Canon. Before that there were few nonhumans in Canon space, except along the Rims and on the Closed Treaty and Reserved worlds. Artifacts were rare. Like me, they were created for noble purposes. Now they are everywhere, nonpareil toys, to be played with, abused, and discarded. Humans' worlds were choked with people. The Web was acrawl with ships. Trade was brisk Outside. Where have the trillions gone, WarAvocat? There are thousands more worlds now. But they should be filled. They are not. Few are more populous than that pesthole where you found me. Why? Your normals are not breeding.

"These days those held in deepest contempt are the glue binding what is left. Humans own Canon, but nonhumans and artifacts keep it going."

WarAvocat ruminated. "Is there a point?"

"Not if you don't see it already."

"Are you saying this long die-off is our fault?"

"I have no opinion. I am an observer. But others watch. Maybe they see with greater acuity. They are more free than I to roam."

"Food for thought, Kez Maefele."

"I will pass you hearsay, WarAvocat. There are races Outside with ambitions toward Canon space. They perceive a vacuum. But one force holds them at bay."

"Us?" WarAvocat smiled. "'What cannot be achieved by strength must be gained by stealth.'"

Turtle grunted. "You have studied me closely."

"You accomplished more with less than anyone before or since. Your tactics set the tone for every incursion and rebellion since." WarAvocat chuckled. "As long as they pursue tactics that almost worked instead of looking for what will work, I ought to be pleased."

"Is there a way?"

"There must be. There always is." WarAvocat mused, "I wonder if anybody considers what would happen if we got knocked off. Seems obvious that whoever did the job would be somebody nastier than us."

"I don't expect that aspect garners much thought." WarAvocat was right. Who defeated the Guardships would replace the Guardships, almost certainly with a grander tyranny.

He stared outside, unseeing, wondering if greed and cruelty and brutality were as much absolutes of life as entropy was an absolute of the physical universe. Did the climb out of the slime write programmes no mind could overcome?

# - 32 -

Two said, "The boy recognized you last night."

"He has a marvelous eye," Lupo replied. "And a mind to match. He capitalized on it instantly. He lessened Valerena in the eyes of her supporters, made them look incompetent to her, and pointed them out to us. House Tregesser will receive excellent leadership in his time."

"If he survives Simon and Valerena."

"He'll have to be nurtured. And weaned from traditional

Tregesser obsessions."

"You're very thoughtful this morning."

"Too much of what is happening is beyond my control. This, here, while our Guardship is moving toward the end space. You feel it, too. The need to be *there*."

"This will end today. You expect to fail out there, don't you?"

"If anyone can capture a Guardship, I can. What I doubt is that a Guardship can be captured. It hasn't been managed since the Ku Wars. It didn't take then. *XVI Cyreniaca* blew itself up."

"Overload won't suffice?"

"We'll find out the hard way. The Directors are gathering. I want to be there when Valerena arrives. Let's go."

Valerena was a Tregesser. She had had twelve hours to compose herself. She was a Tregesser. When the Tregesser rage reached the heat of molten lead, it transmuted into cold, hard gold. Tregessers were most dangerous when they achieved that elevated state.

It gripped her as she passed through the ground-level entrance to the Pylon, Blessed in tow and armed with the inevitable kaleidoscope. She had examined her position minutely, dispassionately, and the best she could call it was hopeless. Lupo Provik had penetrated the true nature of the gathering at Maserang's.

With no hope of profit and little of salvage, she had chosen a course she thought would surprise Lupo, an almost mystical acceptance, a decision not to defend, nor to argue, nor even to participate.

The ground level of the Pylon was vast and open, carpeted in yellow ochre living carpet that subsisted on spillage and droppage, though during off-peak hours keepers sprinkled it with water and fish food. Itinerant refreshment centers roamed the islands and archipelagos of furniture, their operators dispensing altered moods and states of consciousness.

The denizens of the Pylon were encouraged to mix there. Simon Tregesser wanted it known that he was a democratic guy. A waste management technician could relax with his head of section and defuse the age-old conflict between labor and management.

Valerena sneered.

It was crap. All crap, pure crap, and nothing but crap. Just a ploy to cozen the troops. It hadn't pulled anything over anybody's eyes.

Among the islands stood countless trophies of Tregesser triumphs. The refreshment barks were out tacking among them, business brisk even at this hour. But the refreshments were on the House. One of the little perks of working for Simon Tregesser.

Blessed said, "There's Lupo and his friend."

Valerena saw them. They would meet a few meters from the lifter banks, where that group were ogling some addition to the exhibits....

It was the artifact Noah, stuffed and mounted, looking like something out of mythology. She scowled at Lupo Provik.

"Very clever, Lupo," Blessed said. "Slick, even, getting Grandfather switched so quickly."

"There are times when you do what the adversary desires, but according to your own timetable."

"Who's your friend?"

Provik said, "You were quite clever yourself."

"I think Mother will finally take your advice about waiting." They entered a lift shaft as a group.

"Welcome news. If it lasts till we see what happens in the end space."

The surrounding walls presented ascending murals. But

Blessed stared at Provik's companion. "I'm Blessed Tregesser. Who are you?"

The woman just smiled.

Lupo said, "You're clever, Blessed, but don't let it go to your head. You lack experience and finesse."

The youth's hand jerked a millimeter toward his mother.

Valerena had been paying no attention, but now she let her gaze drift to the back of her son's head. She mulled that remark. Clever Blessed! Had he indeed, with a few words, demolished everything?

Lupo had given the boy a gentle caution against prying. He had missed it twice.

The unsubtlety of youth.

If the boy had... No. If he had done that, he was no child anymore.

Lupo looked at her over Blessed's shoulder, smiling. Then he stepped out of the lift. They had come as high as they could in this shaft. Now they came to the first security barrier. Lupo's companion followed him. Both palmed a reader and passed. Each barrier she did pass would be one more datum about her place in Provik's enterprise.

Valerena left the lift last. As Blessed palmed the reader, she plucked the kaleidoscope from beneath his arm, ran fingertips over its barrel.

"Clever, clever Blessed," she said, and dropped it into the waste receptacle beside the security officer's station. "Naughty, naughty Blessed. Mother has to remember that you're a big boy now, doesn't she?"

## - 33 -

Alarms wailed like newly orphaned children. A computer voice droned, "There has been an explosion on B Deck. Passengers please remain in your cabins. There is no danger.

Hull integrity has been maintained. Damage control parties are at work." Over and over.

Cold air stirred a wisp of hair lying on Jo's cheek. She cracked an eyelid, thought, *I'm still alive.* That seemed absurd.

What a mess! Metal and plastic torn, warped, melted, hammered into grotesque sculpture by blast and heat. But she saw no structural damage. House Majhellain built their spaceframes to endure the ages.

The air was shivering cold and fresh. That contaminated by the explosion had been evacuated. But she still smelled singed hair.

Her skin looked broiled. Felt like it, too. Flash burn.

"Oh!" she groaned, touching her scalp. What hair she had left was hair that had been shielded by her arms. She must look like hell.

"You all right, Jo?"

Haget had gotten himself into a lotus position, sort of. He looked ridiculous. She laughed weakly. "Yeah. Underdone."

She got her knees under her, started a painful crawl toward Vadja, three meters away, sprawled in a pool of blood. "Commander, we got a problem. Something cut the artery in his left arm. His color is bad. Pulse and breathing, too."

"Where the hell are those damned civilians? Where's that damage control party?"

"That's just to keep the passengers from panicking. Go get somebody. I'll get a tourniquet on him."

Haget crept down the passageway, grunting, cursing softly.

Jo could not resist. "Dignity, Third WatchMaster. Everything with proper dignity."

He by damned got up on his hind legs and tottered, one hand on the bulkhead.

For nothing. A pressure hatch opened. A man in a protective suit stepped through. Another followed. They expected a worse disaster than they found. They gawked at Haget. One ducked back. The ship's doctor popped in, a fussy little fat man who sized up the situation on the fly and went directly to Vadja. He looked at Jo's work, harrumphed, got busy. Vadja was on a stretcher, taking plasma, and headed for the Traveler's infirmary in the time it took Jo to get to her feet and gingerly approach the opening to Messenger's cabin.

Pieces of alien were splattered on bulkheads, deck, and overhead. That brought back memories of a bunker taken during the *Enherrenraat* mess. Stubborn bastards had ended up plastered all over the place.

Haget arrived as she backed away, trying to keep her lunch down. "I thought you were used to this."

"Stick your head in there. Take a whiff."

He did. His lunch did come up.

Jo said, "Whatever those suckers eat, it must have to be dead a month before they start. We'll need suits if we're going to poke around in there."

The atmosphere system was trying. Its best was not enough.

Timmerbach appeared, oh-mying, looking like he'd shove them through the nearest lock cheerfully if only he dared. Haget said, "We're building a real credit obligation here, aren't we? Though I don't think we had much to do with the thing going berserk."

Timmerbach grunted. His look said anybody who had to deal with Guardship people would go berserk. "Fifty-six hours till we get to the off strand, Commander. Then on to S. Marselica Freeheld, where House Majhellain has facilities. Hopefully we can part company friends."

Haget smiled thinly. "We won't be leaving you, Chief."

"I didn't think so. But I thought I'd suggest it."

Jo was trying to contact AnyKaat and having no luck. "This damned comm got bruised."

"Try Vadja's." The doctor had dispossessed Vadja of his gear before moving him. "S. Marselica wasn't on the itinerary, Chief."

"Neither was the Presence, a killer Guardship, a suicidal Outsider, or this gallivant across starspace. But here we are. With who knows what damage from the explosion and the beating on the Web. We have to get *Glorious Spent* in for a hundred percenter."

Jo tried Vadja's comm. It would not crackle. But that did not matter now. Degas and AnyKaat had arrived.

Haget said, "You're probably right, Chief."

AnyKaat asked Jo, "You all right?"

"Overdone around the edges. Otherwise, fine."

"You look awful."

"Thanks. You're one of nature's rare beauties yourself."

Haget asked Timmerbach for the loan of suits so they could invade the alien's quarters.

AnyKaat asked, "How's Era?"

Jo explained. "Unless that doc is a butcher, he'll be all right. Just shock and loss of blood."

Haget joined them. "Timmerbach will provide the suits, Sergeant. In the interim, I suggest we visit the infirmary. See about Vadja and if maybe the doctor hasn't got something that'll stop the stinging of these burns. What's Seeker doing?"

"Sleeping it off," Degas said. "Sir, what are we going to do now? I got the impression Seeker was tailing Messenger, maybe keeping it from doing whatever it was trying to do. Now it doesn't have a mission. And it wants to go back."

"I don't follow."

"We're supposed to stick and see what they do. But we haven't charged this one. It can do whatever it wants. Suppose next station it bails out and takes another ship?"

Jo grinned. "What he's saying is, how do you and me walk up to some other Traveler's Chief and bluff him into hauling us around? We'd be stuck. We don't have documentation. Him and AnyKaat have documentation but no credit. Timmerbach knows we're off *VII Gemina*, but if he gets pissed he could dump us and we wouldn't be able to prove a thing."

Haget scowled. "Don't give the little bastard any ideas. Hell. WarAvocat should have given us the necessaries. We'll work on the alien. It's out for sure? After the doctor we'll get cleaned up. Did you get any wind of the krekelen, Degas?"

Degas and AnyKaat shook their heads.

"Better work on that, too."

Jo came out of her quarters, found Haget ready before she was. She said, "That stuff does take the sting out. But it makes the red even redder. I look like some kind of artifact."

Haget grunted. He looked uncomfortable. He blurted, "Tell me something, Sergeant." But then he lost momentum.

"Sir?"

"Uh... what's wrong with me?"

"Wrong with you? Are you asking for an opinion of your personality?" She knew damned well he was, but if she pretended density maybe he would back off.

No such luck. He insisted. "Yes."

Shit. "You're probably a good officer. You wouldn't be a full Commander and a WatchMaster if you weren't. But you never go off duty. You probably sleep at attention."

He opened his mouth to snap, bit on his rejoinder. "I asked, didn't I? Qualities that are prosurvival in Hall of the Watchers but less important out here, eh?"

"You've adapted some, sir."

"I've tried." He did not know what else to say. So he fell back on the support system that had served him in the past: getting after the job. "Let's go visit Seeker and see if we can't communicate. Do you have a functional comm?"

"Yes, sir."

He strapped on a sidearm. "Tell Degas and AnyKaat we're coming."

Jo's eyes were vacant when she walked out of Seeker's cabin. Haget stepped into her path. She mumbled and tried to slide around him, headed for the bridge. He blocked her. "AnyKaat."

AnyKaat slapped her.

She shook her head, rubbed her cheek. "It got to me this time, didn't it?" It had been her fourth attempt and fourth failure. The alien was not interested in communicating, it was interested in getting *Glorious Spent* to carry it where it wanted to go.

"All right," Haget said. "We tried it one rational species to another. Now we do it my way." He drew his handgun, stepped inside, let the alien have it. "Two hours till it wakes up. Let's get the equipment installed."

His way amounted to crude operant conditioning. They would take turns trying to communicate. If Seeker tried to control instead of communicate, zap! Someone would sit monitor in Jo and Haget's suite, ready to administer the zap.

"There's no positive reinforcement in the cycle!" Jo protested.

Haget snapped, "The hell there isn't. The absence of pain. The opportunity to argue its case."

More than an hour passed before Jo realized that was what Haget considered a joke.

"You think we could try this on him, too?" AnyKaat whispered. "Zap him till he gets human?"

"He's basically all right. He just never learned how."

AnyKaat gave her a wonderstruck look.

"Shit," Degas said from outside. "Here comes the angel of gloom."

Jo leaned out. Sure enough, Timmerbach was headed their

way. He did not look like he had a social visit in mind.

"What you got, Chief?" Degas asked. "We falling into a black hole? Somebody undo the golden zipper of the universe? You find the krekelen holed up in the wardroom?"

Timmerbach was taken aback.

Jo said, "You never come around with good news. What's wrong now?"

"Where's the Commander?"

"Asleep," Jo lied. Haget had gone off to test the monitor. "And he said don't wake him up."

"You'll have to do. I don't have time to run after him. We're not going to be able to get onto the strand we wanted. It's the one the Presence and the Guardship used. It's too feeble to get hold of."

"I knew it," Degas said. "What did I tell you?"

"We're headed for another one?" Jo asked.

Timmerbach nodded. "It means another four days in starspace."

"Any problems with that? Stores shortages or anything?"

"No. I just don't like to be alone in starspace so far from help. Anything could happen. If we have a breakdown, we're dead."

Degas said, "Chief, the law of averages is due to catch up. Your luck is going to change."

Timmerbach's look said that while his Traveler was occupied territory, the only shift he expected was for the worse. That this was not worth whatever *VII Gemina* might do for House Cholot.

That things might have gone worse without them was irrelevant.

"I'll inform the Commander," Jo said. *I'll tell him you looked like a fat little boy with naughty thoughts who maybe ought to have his butt spanked just in case.*

She watched Timmerbach out of sight. "From now on we

watch Timmerbach and Cholot. No need to be discreet about it, either."

# - 34 -

Neuelica. J. Claeica. S. Reinica. The pageant of systems rolled. The roster of bloodsheds for naught lengthened. There was no pattern. No one House had suffered abnormally. None in harm's way had been spared.

WarAvocat had expected no less. The enemy's stupidity was not tactical, it was strategic.

In transit from K. M'Danlica to M. Colica, WarAvocat moved into seldom visited Hall of the Stars, down against *VII Gemina*'s Core, where everything the Guardship fleet knew about its territory was projected in a display. The detail was as exhaustive and accurate as four millennia of observation could make it.

WarAvocat spent a work shift adrift there, then half another, till he thought he sensed something. Then he sent for Kez Maefele.

Security brought the baffled alien. The Ku's bewilderment only increased when they just deposited him. "WarAvocat?"

"I want to solicit a professional opinion."

"Military? Isn't that absurd?"

"Some things change more than others. I've located a suit *Gemina* says will do you. The fit will be odd but you'll be able to do everything you need to in it."

"You want me to go EVA?"

"We're going into near vacuum, but right here. The place is its own best explanation. If you will?" He indicated the suit he wanted the Ku to wear.

"It's been a long time, WarAvocat."

"I'm watching you."

The Ku fumbled some with unfamiliar closures but he made

no mistakes. WarAvocat led him into Hall of the Stars.

"You've always had this? No wonder you defeated us. We made do with paper charts and our own memories."

"The same system was on line. There's more detail now." WarAvocat moved them to the quadrant of interest. "This is the corner where we're playing. The Sixth Presidency. Chart my first. The red line is the krekelen's track. The green represents the course *VII Gemina* has made. They don't match. We don't want it obvious what we're doing. And the earlier we get there the better our chance of catching them on the stool. Chart my second."

Blue set off a globe seventy light years in diameter. "I believe, and *Gemina* and the Deified concur, that the krekelen started out somewhere in here. That's where we'll find whatever we're supposed to find. I'm not taking the chase any closer. There'll be alarms. I'd rather not give our adversary warning."

"You appear to be maneuvering against what you would do were you running your enemy's game."

"I always go against myself. I'm the trickiest WarAvocat I've ever met."

"Why am I here?"

"If he plans an ambush, he needs a place to set it. Chart my third." The blue faded. "I used my own requirements for a site. Chart my fourth." Most of the stellar information vanished.

"Three tag ends. None with anything to recommend it as more likely than the others. None have been explored. I've eliminated everything else."

"So now we come to me."

"Yes. You operated in this starspace. The Dire Radiant explored at least two of those tag ends. Could you use one to ambush a Guardship?"

WarAvocat wondered if he had bet wrong. Makarska Vis would make big noises if he had.

"There's nothing off the ends of the farther two. The nearest is the only choice."

"Why?"

"There is a lot of cold matter there. Some large enough for major basing. And the basing exists. We used that end space a long time. And it was used by the Go and pirates before us. I'd bet it's been used by pirates since."

"Any other reason for choosing that tag end?"

"It has a back door."

"Explain, please."

"A month of hard running in starspace takes you to the G. Witica–S. Satyrfaelia strand."

"Chart. Show me the strand." WarAvocat studied it carefully. "I should have seen that." Would he have? Probably. In time. "Thank you for your help, Kez Maefele."

"I did not help you, WarAvocat."

"I know. You did it for the same reason you tried to warn them on V. Rothica 4. Access, OpsAvocat. This is WarAvocat. I have the information I need. Take us to Starbase."

As he helped the Ku shed his suit he said, "I think I just gained another month on the bad guys."

# - 35 -

Valerena pretended a calm she did not feel as she took her seat. The Diréctorate room was like many such in which the courts of power had convened through the ages. Quiet, large, comfortably furnished, overly warm. She, Blessed, Lupo, and his friend were last to arrive. Maserang and Worgemuth pretended she did not exist. Old Commodo Hvar looked confused.

Valerena was confused. Lupo had brought his friend into the room. They had assumed stations behind the refreshments bar. Never before had Lupo intruded here, let alone one of his people. Provik was not a Director.

Then, too, her father and his Other were both present. They occupied opposite ends of the room and were having a great time trying to out-Simon one another. There was no telling which was which.

Blessed slumped in his seat, the bored scion present only by compulsion.

Lupo made the Directors nervous. They knew who he was. His presence was not reassuring.

"All right! Let's have a little order here!" one of the Simons bellowed. As though anyone was being rowdy.

"A little order! Knock off the farting around. We got desperate business."

Only Blessed continued his show of indifference.

Everyone knew a conspiracy against Simon Tregesser had been discovered. Names had gotten around. Enemies of the accused were eager for the bloodletting. Friends viewed the future with trepidation. Maserang and Worgemuth faced it in stark terror.

Neither Simon mentioned the matter.

They went off on a zany duet about insurrections on worlds belonging to the House. According to them the Tregesser fortune was being bled white. The House was being gutted. All because of a few incompetent managers.

"We are being destroyed! Devoured! We have to act now, today! We have to get those fools out of there! We have to put in managers of proven skill and decisiveness. I call for—No! I demand!—a vote removing the following near-traitors, before they do us more harm." He named six names. Valerena knew none of them. They could not be much. Eager to get to the blood feast, the Directors approved the dismissals immediately.

"In this extremity our proconsuls must be the best and most reliable." He nominated Valerena, Blessed, Maserang, Worgemuth, and two old men he had loved to hate since childhood.

He demanded a vote confirming their appointments.

Blessed was not bored anymore. He sat rigidly upright. He stared at Lupo, who smiled at some private joke.

Her timing perfect, Provik's companion brought Valerena something aswirl with color in a tall, frosty glass. She said, "You owe Lupo a life."

Valerena looked at Provik. He nodded.

So. This was fetor from Lupo's brain. Clever. Cruel. Convince Simon that exile was a fate worse than death. She might have guessed.

And was it not more cruel? Was it not? To be marooned a thousand light years from home and the wellsprings of power and her own intricate systems of security? Lupo would make sure there was no way out.

Right around the table those smug, grinning bastards voted to throw her off Tregesser Prime.

What choice did they have?

Defeat had become a rout.

And the conqueror was not done exacting his revenge. "The times are desperate! There isn't a moment to waste! Voyagers await you, quivering to be on the Web and away! Hurry! Hurry now! The Voyagers await."

What a marvelous family and existence.

"I'm going," Valerena told Blessed. "But I won't let him harry me into a frazzled rush."

"Cover your home base, Mother. We won't be gone long. He won't last longer than it takes his Guardship to erase him."

The two Simons charged around, tried to drive everyone out of the room. "I thought this was supposed to be a Directorate meeting...."

"Mother! Even I know nothing gets settled here. Grandfather decides how the vote will go before he calls a meeting."

Valerena was thinking about her Others. In the tumult of a hasty move, some could get lost without being missed.

She smiled thinly. Then noted Blessed smiling his own smile.

What was that little wretch up to now?

"Will they be plotting against me again, Lupo?" Simon asked after the last Director left.

"Valerena and Worgemuth, certainly. Maserang is out of it. He was going along out of inertia."

"And Blessed?"

"Valerena dragged him along."

"I wish I could stick a knife in Worgemuth. But the old bastard has too many damned relatives."

"You going back to the end space now?"

"I don't want to miss this thing."

"It might be months."

"You're sure a Guardship will come?"

"Pure reflex. Of course."

"You have any doubts, Lupo?"

"Plenty. This's been tried a hundred times. All we've got new is those shields and a lot of crazy Outsiders to do the dying."

"We didn't send that krekelen out whimsically. You checked it right along with the eggheads. We have enough firepower. We have the Po-Ticra suicide pilots eager to die for their silly god."

"I know. It looks like a lock. But I've been thinking. We shouldn't have taken the Web-location modules out. We'll lose everything if it blows up on us. That's a lot of capital to burn."

"It's not Tregesser capital. If it goes bad, I want only two people getting out alive. You and me."

"You're the boss. But I still hate to waste ships."

# - 36 -

Lady Midnight joined Turtle in Amber Soul's quarters. "She isn't any better, is she?" There were tears in her eyes.

"Neither better nor worse. She must be trapped in her own sorcery. We Ku have dozens of stories about sorcerers who destroyed themselves with their own magic. I wish I knew how to help."

"Time will help."

"I hope so. Is he treating you well?"

Midnight blushed. "Yes. Better than most. But..."

"He's basically decent, within the mandates of his culture. He wouldn't willfully do you a hurt. Yet he can destroy a world or exterminate a race without a qualm. What is Canon's is Canon's. What isn't shall be." He muttered, "The dragon never sleeps." Then, "You said 'But.'"

"Someone has been harassing me. That woman who was there when they brought us here. She interrupts my sleep to call me names. And I don't even know who she is."

"She's a ghost gone rancid in her eternal life. It's not you she hates, it's me. I think we can circumvent her."

Did the Deified lose maturity with the millennia? Could an entire Guardship turn infantile?

Doubtful. This was a weakness of the ghost of Makarska Vis. "Excuse me? I was maundering."

"I asked if you know where we are. Not that it matters."

"No. But I know where we're going. Starbase Tulsa."

That name. It throbbed like the beat of primitive drums. Starbase Tulsa, the womb from which every Guardship sprang and to which every Guardship made its periodic hadj. If there was an object of greater dread than a Guardship it was that stellar citadel whence the invincible issued.

An entire mythology revolved around Starbase. It might be heaven or it might be hell. For the mass of humanity and those nonhumans adrift in Canon space, it was more of the latter. It was a place where devils spawned.

Midnight began to shiver. Her wings, which had lost so much of their luster and color already, drooped, faded. Her timidity could not withstand the onslaught of dread.

"We'll be no worse off than we are now, Midnight."

"I know. But I can't help it." Tears tracked her cheeks. She stared at Amber Soul.

Turtle did, too. "Stay with her. Try to get something down her. I think she senses our presence and concern, on some level, and that comforts her."

Midnight had a high empathy quotient and an inability to resist appeals. She would forget herself for a while, ministering to Amber Soul.

"I have a few chores to do. I'll be right back."

In his own suite Turtle examined the comm. Getting the Deified Makarska Vis was easy. In moments he had her on screen, looking vexed. "You!"

"Me. Greetings, Deified. Did I disturb you?"

"Yes."

"Good. You have been disturbing a friend of mine, presumably venting your spite on her because she is incapable of returning your vitriol."

The Deified Makarska Vis gushed filth.

"To me you are a ghost, a memory mummy impressed upon the motions of electrons. I am not awed. If you do not wish to be disturbed, you will stop harassing my friend."

Would it work? Was she possessed of sufficient determination to lock him out? He shrugged and returned to Midnight and Amber Soul.

## - 37 -

Among the satellites orbiting the ringed gas giant, there were a dozen moonlets that were natural only in appearance. They were created things half the size of a Guardship, sheathed in ice that concealed their true nature. The ice had been bombarded to give them an ancient, lunar appearance. Everything was camouflage here. This outpost was too near the frontier.

Blinding light ripped from one of the moonlets. Meteor impact? No. This came from within, sustained. Ice turned to water and water to gas. The light died, leaving a cone burned through the mask. The moonlet began moving.

A day later, far from its primary, it flicked out of existence. It had clambered onto the Web. Invisible, it hastened toward the Atlantean Rim of Canon space.

The intruder was invisible but not undetectable at close range. As the object breached the Rim, it very nearly ran over Guardship *XXVIII Fretensis*. Alarms sounded. The Guardship swept in pursuit.

## - 38 -

On impulse WarAvocat went to Kez Maefele's door. The Ku responded immediately. "WarAvocat?"

"We're due to break away soon. Approaching Starbase. I thought you might be interested."

"Am I that obvious?"

"I know your weakness now. Curiosity. I could use it to trap you."

"The Deified Makarska Vis took care of me when she was WarAvocat."

"By main strength and awkwardness. The woman's tactics had the subtlety and finesse of an ax murder."

"There is something to be said for overwhelming might."

"Speaking of Makarska Vis, word is you bluffed her into backing down."

"I am sure she did not stop harassing Midnight because I

told her to back off."

"No. Your suggestion got backing from *Gemina*. She'd begun showing divisive, political tendencies. I'm going to Hall of the Watchers. Their wall gives the best view. Are you coming?"

"Yes. You have a motive for doing this?"

Startled, WarAvocat said, "No."

"You did not mean to impress me with the power of the Guardship fleet?"

"No." He started walking. The Ku followed. "We are a less complex people than you think."

"Maybe. Few of you are subtle."

"We have no need."

"Remarkable. Especially considering the longevity and persistence of the players."

"It's gone funny on some Guardships. Here it hasn't because the soldiers nourish the roots of the culture. Soldiers tend to be direct and simple."

"And if something evades immediate comprehension, they blow it up or kill it. Ku warriors were the same."

It took an hour to reach Hall of the Watchers, by which time *VII Gemina* was off the Web and closing with some stellar concourse in the form of a triple wheel station, the rotational axis of which was a hollow cylinder large enough to pass a Guardship. Traffic was heavy.

WarAvocat observed, "Someone else has come in recently, for refitting. There's always activity but seldom this much."

"This is Starbase Tulsa?"

WarAvocat chuckled. "No. This is the Barbican, Starbase's only intersection with the universe outside. This is as far as outsiders come. They make deliveries here. Our own ships carry materials from here."

"Then the Guardship fleet is not self-sufficient?" Was that overdoing it? If not, it was on the boundary. WarAvocat looked like he was wondering if that ignorance was feigned. He had, after all, spent a long life studying the Guardships.

"You sound surprised."

"Not entirely. Logically, no system could be entirely closed. I know it was open long ago. But I have been out of touch. I assumed self-sufficiency had been attained."

"We work toward it. But it isn't an overriding concern. Someday."

"Then the system is vulnerable."

"Possibly. Not very. House Horigawa, who have the monopoly on supplying us, have remained faithful through the most trying tests."

"To their extreme benefit." That was no secret. House Horigawa had become one of the dozen richest by serving the Guardships.

"They did come out of the *Enherrenraat* incident very well." In part because they had betrayed the conspiracy before it had been ready to move.

Turtle watched quietly as *VII Gemina* entered the station's axial cylinder. "Masterful steersmanship," he said.

"You have to do it right," WarAvocat said. "We have secrets even from ourselves, I think. No one's ever told me why we run the Tube." *VII Gemina* left the Tube and began accelerating. "We go back onto the Web now."

"I fear I've missed the strategy here." Turtle did not have to feign ignorance now. "Why should everyone break off the Web here?" The answer, by remaining elusive, had kept him from bringing the Dire Radiant in here.

"No choice. This is the most unusual strand on the Web. There's a break in the strand here. The gap is only a few light seconds across, but it's enough. Any attacker has to come off. He has to cross the gap under fire. Messenger ships are always stationed at the tag end on the other side. You can take the Barbican by surprise, but anything beyond will be a deathtrap before you get there."

"Has it been tried?" He knew it had. What he did not know was why attacks against Starbase inevitably failed.

"Everything has been tried. That, half a dozen times."

"And there were no survivors to carry the news."

"None. The price of attacking Starbase is absolute and final."

*VII Gemina* climbed onto the Web with hydraulic ease. The wall, still carrying a forward view, flashed on a gleaming strand. The Guardship surged along it. In seconds the wall went nova.

The light storm cleared. The wall revealed the shine of a guttering red dwarf glimmering off the backs of two orbital fortresses and the complex they guarded. The primary around which the three scampered was a supergiant with a thousand moons, a planet a minim short of being fat enough to become a star itself. Turtle wondered how it had come to be paired with the red dwarf.

"By the right!" he murmured. "Starbase. I never imagined... no construct can be that big. Unless there is some trick of perspective...."

"No trick," WarAvocat assured him. "And it's not the biggest construct around. You'll see that, too."

The relative motions seemed odd. "We are moving past it."

"I told you this was the most unusual strand on the Web."

"Then this is not Starbase."

"No. We call it Gateway. It's a decoy."

"No one outside even suspects." He never had.

"No. It's totally automated. Its complement consists of dupes of Deified from the fleet. Starbase itself runs the same way."

The supergiant rolled beneath *VII Gemina*. Turtle asked, "What is in that atmosphere to give it those blue tones?"

"I don't know. I can access the information."

"Never mind. It isn't important."

WarAvocat watched the supergiant dwindle. He wondered why he'd never been curious about its coloration, nor been particularly cognizant of the planet's beauty, with those thousand pearls in its hair. Nor even much curious about a strand that had a double anchor, supergiant and red dwarf, with a gap between.

*VII Gemina* clambered back onto the interrupted strand.

The construct waiting off the nether tag end was much larger than Gateway. It was a vast rectilinear shape guarded by eight orbital fortresses poised on the points of a cube. The array orbited a feeble yellow star that had no planetary family.

One more curiosity on this particular strand. The star was there but the strand was loose. An end, period. There was no strand leading away in any other direction.

The Ku said, "A battery of adjectives suggest themselves. But none are adequate."

"I know. It still awes me. I used to see it as the ultimate construct, the product of a golden age, never to be equalled. Its builders probably thought that, too. But Starbase Dengaida will make it look like a pyramid raised by clever neolithics."

"Starbase Dengaida?"

"The inevitable consequence of being what we are."

The Ku looked puzzled.

"Invincible. Canon has grown so vast we have a problem with travel times. We have Guardships operating against pirates beyond the Roberquan Rim, which did not exist when you went into hiding on V. Rothica 4. Their patrols take them a thousand light years Outside. The Rim keeps advancing. It can take them six months to reach Starbase. A year in and back. The problem will worsen. Soon after the *Enherrenraat* incident, foreseeing the problem, Starbase recommended we build a new Starbase out there."

"Word never filtered down into Merod Schene."

"Wasn't meant to. I doubt anyone outside the fleet and House Horigawa has guessed yet. It isn't something we want broadcast. Construction works are vulnerable."

"And it will be bigger than this?"

"A lot. We couldn't find another site to compare with this one, though. So we had to make it tougher to crack."

The Ku's attention remained fixed on Starbase.

Cues on the wall said *Gemina* was in touch with the Guardship already docked. Data flowed both ways, and back and forth between *Gemina* and Starbase Core. He picked the ID code out. "Kez Maefele, the Guardship already docked is *XII Fulminata*."

The Ku eyed him. "You do not seem excited."

"They aren't a social bunch, *XII Fulminata* crew." He turned away. "Access, OpsAvocat. WarAvocat here. I'd consider it a great favor if you docked us on the same face as *XII Fulminata*. Out." He turned back to the Ku. "They want to cut themselves a slice of our action. I'm going to let them gobble till they choke. We owe them one."

Starbase was spotted like a domino, with eight black circles to a face, in rows of four. As *VII Gemina* approached the block it appeared to rotate, bringing another face uppermost. On that face one black circle had been obliterated. *XII Fulminata* docked.

WarAvocat did not look forward to his next few days.

## - 39 -

The Outsider broke off the Web in the Closed System M. Meddinia. It boiled off its mask as it drove toward the system's archaic, ramshackle station. It should have shed its disguise before invading Canon space.

It had not finished when its gaseous surround was back-lighted by the violence of *XXVIII Fretensis* breaking away.

The Guardship wasted no time asking questions. When the corona cleared, twelve riderships were running free and swarms of smaller craft were boiling off. *XXVIII Fretensis* seemed to be disintegrating.

A barrage preceded the riders. Boiling through space ahead of shells and missiles were a half dozen glimmering balls spit from Hellspinner pits. The best Twist Master ever had no hope of a hit at that range, though. The idea was to frighten the Outsider into raising its screen. Hellspinners terrified anyone who knew anything about them.

The Outsider stuck out its tongue. It did not raise screen. It took M. Meddinia 4A under fire.

The one Hellspinner that looked like the worst throw broke down and in and brushed the Outsider. Tonnes of matter erupted in a geyser of shattered nucleons.

The fastest attackers raced toward the hit, looking for a soft spot.

*XXVIII Fretensis* developed data on the Outsider's displacement. WarAvocat ordered a supplementary launch. A ship that large might carry secondaries of its own.

It did, but none were active. The Outsider had come expecting no resistance. In quickly, a message delivered, and out, silent and unseen....

The attackers closed in. The Outsider raised screen. Word went back: The screen was Guardship quality.

The Outsider could not have been in a poorer position. It could not deploy riders. A more powerful enemy lay between it and access to the Web. And it was deeper in the gravity well.

Attackers englobed the Outsider. They floated just meters off the screen. *XXVIII Fretensis* rotated to present its broadest face, closed to three hundred meters. At that range even the most inept Twist Master could not miss.

A hundred pulsating green eyes burned on the Guardship's face.

WarAvocat *XXVIII Fretensis* ordered his Hellspinners loosed. Those balls of mad energy drifted onto the Outsider's screen like the slow fall of a fine oil mist onto the surface of a summer-warmed pond. Rainbow points spread and faded slowly. Fighters darted to the impact points like fish to motes of food. They pounded those spots, probing for an opening or weakness.

The screen withstood the salvo. But the Twist Masters had permission to loose at will. No screen could absorb Hellspinners long.

The Outsider finally grasped the gravity of its situation. It began to move.

Its assailants moved with it.

Here, there, soft spots in the screen yielded. A one-meter gap opened and persisted for seven seconds. An interceptor put one hundred rounds of 40mm contraterrene shot through the hole. The Outsider's skin blossomed, a garden of small fires.

Other gaps opened. Some attack craft chose marksmanship, gunning for specific installations. Others just blazed away. None tried running the gaps. A screen shielded both ways. A fighter inside would become the target of every Outsider weapon otherwise unable to fire.

The gaps grew larger and lasted longer. The Twist Masters began pairing, hoping to get a second Hellspinner through a gap cut by a first.

The Outsider dropped inside the orbit of the station.

The riders armed their axial cannon, which hurled 250kg projectiles at 8,000 meters per second. The projectiles spun off slivers of contraterrene iron as they rattled through a target.

Orders went out to the attackers: Penetrate the screen and silence the Outsider's drives.

WarAvocat *XXVIII Fretensis* had guessed the reason for the

Outsider's move planetward. It meant to eliminate evidence by throwing itself into atmosphere.

Cluster shells began getting through. So did Hellspinners and massed barrages from the secondaries. The Outsider was ablaze within the envelope of its shield, surrounded by a shrapnel metalstorm. The attack ships that went in had to use their own lesser screens till they reached firing position.

The Outsider offered only token counterfire. And that soon fell silent.

One salvo stilled the drives. But too late. The Outsider was in a groove that would take it into atmosphere in thirty-eight hours.

WarAvocat *XXVIII Fretensis* ordered the attackers to concentrate on shield generators. When permanent gaps appeared, he began recovering his secondaries.

*XXVIII Fretensis* began laying in all the fire it could, including 100cm axial clusters at 12,000mps capable of penetrating to the Outsider's Core—if it had one.

On the Outsider's far side, which had suffered little damage, attackers began opening a path for boarding parties already on the move.

The invaders found nothing alive. In the few hours they had they learned very little. They collected biological and technical samples and got out in time for *XXVIII Fretensis* to pound the hulk into fragments unlikely to be large enough to do damage when they reached the planet's surface.

As the Guardship turned toward the Web, M. Meddinia station broke communications silence with a laconic, "Thank you, Guardship."

The only Guardship casualties were two bruised and embarrassed pilots whose interceptors had collided during a race to be first through a gap in the Outsider's screen.

# - 40 -

Jo slammed into the suite. She was in a grim mood. Vadja had the monitor. Degas and AnyKaat watched over his shoulders. Jo demanded, "Any sign of the krekelen?"

"Not a whiff," AnyKaat replied.

"What's going on?"

Vadja said, "We've maybe got a breakthrough, Sergeant. Course, I only hear the Commander's end. But it sounds like they're talking."

"Good. About damned time."

"Something eating you, Sergeant?"

"I just spent a watch poking around on the bridge. Making a pain of myself. It wasn't Timmerbach's turn to be on but he showed up ten minutes after I did. Looked like he dragged out of his rack in a panic. Worked his butt off trying to keep me from poking in the wrong places. But I still saw enough to know he stuck it to us when he skipped that strand. Him and Cholot are up to something. They think they're going to hand us the dirty end. Wish he'd hurry up."

"Want me to buzz him?"

"Don't bother. Time won't matter. I just want to break some bones."

Degas asked, "Did you get into the system deep enough to cull those biomass figures?" He was convinced that the krekelen had killed somebody and assumed his identity. Haget rejected the notion. Jo was drifting toward Degas's viewpoint.

Degas headed for the door. "I'm going to the galley. That thing has to eat."

Jo looked at AnyKaat, who said, "Instead of looking for the man, he looks for his footprints. Like checking with cooks and stewards on what meals went out when and where."

Vadja leaned back. "The Commander has had enough. He's working on his graceful exit."

Jo leaned past him. Haget was by-the-booking it out the door.

"Way to go, Commander!" Vadja enthused. "Look at there. He broke away clean."

Jo rested a hand on Vadja's shoulder. "How's your arm, Era?"

"Hurts bad enough. I don't think it's going to fall off."

Macho bastards were all alike, male or female. She had talked the same damned way. Was it just soldiers' territory? A defense mechanism that kicked in when you were vulnerable?

Haget shoved into the suite, flopped into a chair. "Jo. Can I impose on you?"

"That's what I'm here for."

"Ask a steward for an analgesic, some soda water, and whatever that liquor was you were swilling the other night."

"Headache?"

"Low grade. Nerves. It would have become a killer if I'd stayed down there."

"You got through?"

"Sort of. It's decided to cooperate. Sort of. Its thinking right into your head isn't as convenient as it sounds. It hurts."

AnyKaat called the stewards while Jo listened.

Haget said, "It's ground gained. Maybe we'll manage some back-and-forth now."

"Did you get anything?"

"Only that it's real anxious to get back to V. Rothica 4. It claims one of its own is marooned there, a child, that it overlooked when the Traveler was there."

"If it missed this kid when it was there, how come it knows now?"

"There's where communications break down. Maybe it couldn't explain. Maybe I just didn't understand. But it's positive and it can't figure out why we won't jigger the clockwork of the universe to help. Hell with it. I don't want to think about it. Answer the door."

The steward had come. He looked at them warily, the way Jo had come to expect. The STASIS people said law enforcement people faced that daily. Jo did not like it.

Haget asked, "Something bothering you?"

She told him about her visit to the bridge.

"Give me fifteen minutes. Then I'll choke Timmerbach till he tells us what's happening."

"Might do better with Cholot. Little sweater like the Chief, he isn't going to spit without orders."

"Uhm. Check the infocomm. See if you can access any Web data. See about this strand Timmerbach wants to pick up."

Jo did that. Timmerbach and Cholot, the twits, were slapstick comics at conspiracy. They had not locked inferential data out of the system.

"Commander, the second system down that strand is L. Caelovica 3, known locally as Karihn. Main city is Cholot Mogadore. Three stations. Only one handles Web traffic. Not much, but the only settled system on the strand. I'd guess only Cholot ships go there."

"That's enough. It ties the knot tight. We'll give them some slack and see how they hang themselves."

# - 41 -

There were few occasions when the crews of Guardships came in contact. WarAvocat had come face to face with *XII Fulminata* crew only twice. He had not been impressed. They suffered from an excess of arrogance and presumption of superiority.

Still, there was a trap in that end space and there was no reason to suspect that it had not been put together with care. This might be the time the villains had what it would take. Wouldn't hurt to go in with more than one Guardship.

"You think too much, Strate," he muttered. "Don't think, act."

The tramp of many feet echoed through the corridors of Starbase. *VII Gemina* was warming every body and turning everyone loose, to have most of their expectations disappointed.

This was not the Starbase of old. This Starbase was a ghost artifact, empty corridors echoing only to phantom memories of the bustle that had been.

Today it was all automation, machines pursuing ancient programmes, overseen by the ghosts of ghosts, carrying on without human clutter.

There were six completed replacement Guardships in the construction channel and a dozen more being completed at a leisurely pace. They amounted to a macro-exemplar of the process by which slain soldiers were replaced. If a Guardship was lost, a replacement would be impressed with data left during its last visit to Starbase.

*VII Gemina* began updating its file when it broke off the Web. That would continue throughout its stay. All crew would register a current personal file.

*VII Gemina* might be destroyed, but there would always be a *VII Gemina*.

Those who created the fleet had faced a problem as old as idealism: how to keep the fire burning. Children reject the dreams of their parents, and grandchildren hold them in contempt.

Their answer was to preserve the founding generation.

A whisper from behind told Strate his time was no longer his own.

He did not hurry. They could not start without him. And they would be irked with him anyway, having to deal with a Dictat-WarAvocat who was one of the living.

He was less than a minute late. The stir had hardly settled.

Was there any real point to this formalization? A face-to-face only highlighted the ways in which Guardships had evolved independently.

*VII Gemina* had turned out a parade: soldiers, gunners, Twist Masters, pilots, ridership crews, OpsCrew and ServCrew. *XII Fulminata* had sent a minimum of live crew, a few passionless senior officers to attend the six Immortals who ruled the Guardship.

The formalities were to be conducted over a circular table at the center of a parade hall. That table was surrounded by equipment that would allow *XII Fulminata*'s Immortals and *VII Gemina*'s Deified to participate. *XII Fulminata*'s delegation had not activated their images.

They waited till WarAvocat seated himself because in their universe the living snapped to attention in the presence of Immortals.

Hanaver Strate did not. "Ready? To remain in character you'll have a list of trivial complaints to demonstrate your superiority. Let's get them out of the way so we can get on with the job."

Thalygos Mundt winced. But Kole Marmigus looked at his opposite number and chuckled. WarAvocat *XII Fulminata* Delka Stareicha fixed Strate with his best cold stare. "You want us to break off into this end space first." He had turned up the chill on his voice box.

"You claimed the right by seniority. I happily yield the honors to so illustrious..."

"You think we'll go in there, take a beating, and look bad."

"Whoever goes in first stands a chance of hitting a firestorm. Whoever put out the bait believed he could take a Guardship. If you don't think *XII Fulminata* can handle it, you can run backup."

Stareicha was caught.

"You invited yourself, WarAvocat. If you want to play games

meant to validate *XII Fulminata*'s superiority, I'd as soon *VII Gemina* undertook the operation alone. Since neither first in nor second pleases you, why don't you return to routine patrol?"

Kole Marmigus chuckled again.

Prune-mouthed, Stareicha observed, "It must be getting near time to elect Dictats. Very well. *XII Fulminata* claims first honors."

History in the making. Formalities held for no better reason than so they could be recorded for posterity.

The shimmer behind Strate's shoulder murmured. Stareicha got a thoughtful look.

Another Guardship was coming in. *XXVIII Fretensis*. It brought news of an Outsider attack upon the Closed System M. Meddinia. The creatures responsible sounded like the methane breather aboard *Glorious Spent*. Curious.

Had *VII Gemina* stumbled into one grand skein of schemes, or two? There had been nothing to connect the krekelen to the aliens aboard that Traveler, but now there was a connection between those two.

Their races appeared to be at war.

That was not permitted in Canon space.

The brass of that attack outraged Hanaver Strate's sense of the natural order.

# - 42 -

Lupo could not shake a ballooning pessimism. He tried to study intelligence abstracts but his mind refused to focus.

Simon Tregesser cruised up. He was subdued, too. "I heard you had something." He had not recovered from finding his refuge destroyed by a berserk Outsider.

"We've had sightings of two more Guardships headed into Starbase. *VII Gemina* and *XXVIII Fretensis*."

"That's three pretty fast. Any statistical significance?"

"No."

"Why so glum, then?"

"The unpredictable variables aren't coming our way often enough to please me."

"You want to put the Web locaters back, don't you?"

"If it sours, we lose our investment."

"And I say that strategy, run to fight another day, is hopeless."

"But..."

"But you have some right to your argument, Lupo. Put the damned things back."

"They won't know they can run. I'll give them sealed orders to be opened only on receipt of an unlocking code."

"Good. Have you made plans to get us out, too? With your usual devotion to detail?"

"Yes."

"It's the waiting. Relax. Go play with a woman."

"Yes."

"Can you say anything else?"

"Yes. But it'd be on a subject you don't want to talk about. You have to consider bypassing Valerena."

"It isn't done, Lupo."

"The House will suffer."

Tregesser made burbling, grumbling, contrary noises.

"She is a Tregesser. But she comes up short on perspective, Simon. She has no sense of timing. She's lacking in the intangibles. She can't hang on to loyalties."

"If she's feeble, she won't last. That's the way it's done."

"Blessed will take it away from her. But at what cost? Suppose we catch a Guardship. You want to imagine Valerena having her own Guardship?"

"We grab a Guardship, Valerena won't get her hands on it. Get me one. You'll have no worries."

"You'll give it to Blessed?"

"The hell I will. I'll give it to me. I'll succeed myself. You can make me a new damned Other, a healthy one, and I'll move into it when you do the personality impression."

"That's an interesting idea. If you can get away with it."

"Why shouldn't I?" Tregesser did not notice Provik saying "you" instead of "we," though *he* replied with "I" instead of "we."

"No clone has ever been anything but an artifact, except Valerena. But officially only you and I know about Valerena."

"Be the same thing, Lupo."

"Hardly. How the hell would you hide Simon Tregesser suddenly turning up with a healthy body? The Directors would claim it wasn't you. They'd say it was some scheme of mine to take over the House. Hell, it's been tried before. Somebody works a deal with Banat-Marath and Troqwai and gives it a shot, and everybody cheers him for giving Death the slip, then they show him the door to the nearest DownTown. There's too much wealth and power at stake."

"Crap."

"Human nature, Simon. It don't work. It's the iron law. They'll let you cheat Death once if you're at the top but the price is you have to start over at the bottom. As an artifact."

"Bah! Crap, I say! Watch me! You're my man, aren't you? If we can flout the law and human nature and historical inertia to put together that mass of firepower out there, we can get around the Directors. Can't we?"

"No doubt." Lupo Provik maintained the neutrality of billet steel. He was Simon Tregesser's man, worthy of the trust he had been given, but his loyalty had been subscribed in the certainty that Simon Tregesser was not immortal.

"Hey! The more I think about it, the more I like it." Big mad peal of the old Simon Tregesser hilarity. "I'm going to get on it. Something to while away the hours. Ha-ha! Ha-ha! Immortality. Wouldn't that be a bitch!"

*A screaming bitch,* Lupo thought as Simon zipped away, roaring and treating his aides and allies with complete disregard. A bitch so big he would have to reexamine his commitments and undertakings if Simon pursued it.

Not that he objected to immortality per se. It was good enough for Lupo Provik.

## - 43 -

Midnight told Turtle, "You'd better come. She might be coming out of it."

Turtle secured the infocomm. "That's good news." *Gemina* had not been letting him at much. For instance, he could access nothing about Kez Maefele.

He followed Midnight to Amber Soul's stateroom. "You haven't been spending much time with WarAvocat."

"He's busy figuring out how to kill people." Her tone was peevish.

Turtle suspected some of those people needed killing. They had loosed the beast of blood when they had sent that krekelen on its mission.

Amber Soul did seem changed. The air around her had lost that charge of pain it had carried so long. She no longer looked human, only humanoid, in the shape she had worn most often in Merod Schene DownTown.

He began with a gentle examination, aware that *Gemina* monitored his every twitch and breath. He did not try misdirection.

"This might be a good time to get some nourishment down her."

The door snapped open. Four humorless ConCom security types tramped in. A junior officer looked around with the cold eye of the jackboot breed. Turtle accepted it with bland indifference.

They needed the fear, his type. They fed upon it. "You're to come with us."

"Fine."

"Get that onto the stretcher and let's move out."

Turtle glanced over his shoulder. Nobody there. "You talking to me?"

"Who the hell else would I be talking to?"

Turtle shrugged. "I'm not crew. I don't do crew's work. *Gemina* wants her moved, *Gemina* can move her." Something was wrong here.

"You'll do what I tell you."

"Or you'll put a bug down my shirt? I know you wouldn't be dumb enough to get physical with a Ku warrior."

The color left the officer's face. Odd response. Humans got red and puffy when they were angry.

One of the others whispered to the officer, who barked, "I know that, dammit! You and Blaylo get the thing on the stretcher."

The security men designated activated the stretcher's grav unit, moved Amber Soul aboard, set her floating into the corridor. They bothered guiding her only when the stretcher drifted near a bulkhead. Turtle remained close behind, keeping Midnight near. One security man ranged ahead, scouting. Another fell back to rearguard. The officer was nervous.

Midnight kept tossing Turtle questioning glances he ignored. But finally he asked, "Up to something sneaky, subaltern? Slipping through all these deserted passages. Who are you trying to put one over on?"

"Just keep moving."

"You can sneak but you can't hide. *Gemina* is watching."

The bearer's shoulder flinched. That had stung.

The officer snapped, "Close the mouth, Ku. Or we will give

the obsolete warrior a field test."

Turtle turned, took the man's cap before he could blink, shifted hands, put it back. "You're right. I'm slowing down."

The act was satisfying but not worth the scorn he got from Midnight.

They mostly went down, past the armored bulk of the Core, always through the kinds of passageways Turtle haunted when he wandered. The final passageway led to an exit lock.

They were leaving *VII Gemina?* For Starbase? That *was* a surprise.

The subaltern slipped outside and took the lead. He marched them down corridors that stretched for kilometers, into visual infinity. Occasionally he zigged out and down stairwells that had not felt the tread of feet in lifetimes. Finally, he ushered them into an empty room. The subaltern said, "Wait here." He went out with his troops.

An hour later Turtle said, "We've been ditched, courtesy of the Deified Makarska Vis."

Midnight looked like she might panic. "Do you recall the way back? I do."

"Yes. They didn't try to be confusing." Which was ominous.

Midnight jiggered the stretcher controls. It rose a meter. "There should be a comealong."

"They would have used it."

"Probably. Let's go. I have to do something or I'll lose control."

"You're doing well."

"I do better when hysterics are a luxury."

"We all do." He let her manage the stretcher. He did not press. He was sure it was too late.

He kept expecting to run into somebody who would want to know what they were doing. But they encountered no sign of the builders or their heirs. Starbase, Turtle feared, was a prison where they would serve life sentences for having offended the Deified Makarska Vis.

The entry hatch was locked. As he expected. He told Midnight, "Stay here. I'll find a way to get hold of WarAvocat."

She had her hysterics then.

## - 44 -

The spacers of House Horigawa saw something no one had seen since the days of the *Enherrenraat*, Guardships coming out of Starbase Tulsa, through the Barbican, in line astern, ready for war.

The news would go out. But no news traveled faster than a hungry Guardship.

## - 45 -

Jo staggered into the suite's common room, not quite knowing why she tried. She pointed herself toward the infocomm. As though that would do any good.

Vadja lay slumped over the board.

Forewarned was not necessarily adequately forearmed.

"Bastards," she mumbled as she fell. "You're dead meat now."

## - 46 -

Lupo was studying Web strands when the universe went white. In a voice almost sad he said, "Commence firing." The command was redundant. The outer gun platforms would have begun firing before the corona's light reached the asteroid. He touched his wrist comm. "Simon. Your Guardship is here."

He stalked the length of Control, stood before the vast

window facing the tag end. The rush and chatter, the wail of alarms and flash of lights behind him, did not impinge upon his consciousness. He touched his wrist again. "Our guest is here."

There was no response from his family. None was needed.

The night donned a mask of fire. The Guardship became the brightest object in the universe.

Simon slammed to a stop beside him. "What's it doing here already, Lupo? How did it find us so soon? Are we ready? Can we handle it? Which one is it?"

Lupo answered none of those questions. He couldn't. "Let's watch it on the main display. Lower the armor now," he told a technician. He headed back the direction he had come, noting that all activity was orderly, efficient, and without panic. The technicians had their confidence. They had been through this in drills so often everything was automatic.

Tregesser tagged along, keeping quiet only because he did not want to betray frailty to his troops.

The display had reset to local. Data from every ship, station, gun platform, and observation point fed into the new picture.

"Ha!" Tregesser roared. "Ha-ha! What did I tell you, Lupo? It's locked up inside its screen. Look at them pound that bastard."

"Uhm. Wouldn't you know. It's *XII Fulminata.*"

"Shit! Double shit! But look at it, man!"

"Its screens are holding, Simon."

"For how long? Eh? What're they doing?"

Slivers had begun sliding over the surface of the Guardship, behind its screen, roilsome as maggots in a carcass.

"Launching fighters. Holding them inside the screen."

"Why? They can't get them out."

A Tregesser ship, crawling the outer surface of the screen, laying down continuous fire, exploded.

"How did they do that?" Tregesser shrieked.

"He got too close, running with his own screen down. They fired a CT burst and opened a port just long enough for the shells to pass through. Our ship shaded the port."

While Provik spoke another ship blew up. They were too eager out there. He tapped his wrist. "Allkire Verkler! Get those ships off the face of that screen or I'll get me a new group commander."

Another blew before Commander Verkler made his adjustments.

"They aren't using Hellspinners, Lupo."

"They're not stupid. Hellspinners cause weak spots coming out." The course the Guardship had to run was a test to destruction, a tube of ships and gun platforms. The farther it advanced into the tube, the more fire it would take.

Tregesser said, "Those fighters are like bugs on the inside of a light globe." Then, "Hey! They're launching."

It was called a bubble-through launch though neither Provik nor Tregesser had heard of the tactic. It was used only by Guardships with little or no concern for living crew: *I Primagenia*, *III Victrix*, *IV Trajana*, *XII Fulminata*, others gone extremely strange. Losses in a bubble-through were heavy.

Fighters came out with their own screens maxed, osmotically. The gaps they exited never opened bigger than fighter and screen. The Guardship risked little. But fighter screens were of a lesser grade, and the ships they protected were easy targets for a moment. If they did not get through fast and start dodging, they were dead.

A lot got dead this launch.

But then the survivors were everywhere, making life miserable for the attackers, forcing them behind their own screens.

"They're as crazy as your damned suicide squadrons,"

Lupo said.

"It was a good move for them. It worked. Look. Magnum launch."

A cloud of fighters had begun boiling off the Guardship now. Heavier riders and gunships followed. *XII Fulminata* was deploying everything. Soon it looked like a wad of wire mesh.

"Magnum launch indeed," Lupo said. "You'd better send in the Po-Ticra before the heavy secondaries get maneuvering room."

There were Outsiders who would respond only to Simon Tregesser, apparently unable to understand that Provik spoke with his voice. Lupo thought that a bad way to do business. If Simon checked out, those personal alliances became void.

This battle meant more to Simon than he would admit. He did not have to capture a Guardship to profit. Destroying one should quicken a flood of Outsider support.

They wanted to shatter Canon Rim, of course. Simon, dancing on a tightwire, hoped it would not go that far. He just wanted a lot more for him.

Lupo wondered if the Outsiders would let House Tregesser gain a Guardship. Alien and stupid were not synonyms.

He issued orders, made adjustments, examined data. "Simon. The numbers say they can't win. They can't even turn around. Start your call for surrender."

"What's that? We did it? Did you say we did it?"

"I said we're going to do it. Unless something happens. These crazy Outsiders could screw it up."

"Eh? Ha-ha!" The mad laughter rolled. Then Tregesser began booming his brief ultimatum.

The Guardship did not reply.

*XII Fulminata*'s screen began to show signs of distress. Lupo noticed, too, that the Guardship had begun to accelerate. That made no sense. Unless they had decided to rip straight through the end space.

Cold chills.

Death's glance had passed your way, they said, when that creepy cold brushed your back.

Nova fire.

"What was that, Lupo? Lupo! What's happening?"

"You know damned well what it was, Simon. Another god-damned Guardship just broke off the Web." He looked around. They had a positive ID. "This is *VII Gemina* and they're into a magnum launch already."

More creepy chills. This time they lingered. He had caught Death's eye.

"What are we going to do, Lupo?"

"You're going to leave me the hell alone while I figure out what." First, pull the fighters off *XII Fulminata*. They were not contributing much. Launch the reserve. Shift the fire of the more remote gun platforms to the new target. Have Simon throw Po-Ticra suiciders at any gap in *XII Fulminata*'s screen. *XII Fulminata* could stop them only with massed Hellspinners. Most would miss and rip more holes in the Guardship's screen.

He executed as he thought, shifting from fighting for victory to fighting for survival.

The adjustments looked good. The numbers were iffy, but there was a chance....

Nova light.

"Are they sending the whole damned fleet?"

"Lupo!"

Provik tapped his wrist. "Family, we have to run for it. Get ready." He watched till the ID came up. *XXVIII Fretensis*.

Somewhere in the back of his mind he had been expecting a third Guardship.

# - 47 -

WarAvocat's anger dwindled only because he had no time to indulge it. The moment duty failed to distract him, the rage returned.

The Deified Makarska Vis would pay.

Their conflict was the talk of the Guardship. Sympathy ran heavily in his favor. It was certain he would be reelected Dictat if he stood, and almost as certain that the Deified Makarska Vis would bow before a motion of censure from the Deified.

"Ready on all launch stations, WarAvocat."

He surveyed WarCentral. *VII Gemina* was ready.

He had never felt so uncertain.

What did this crop of villains have? They always had something they thought gave them an edge. He dreaded the day when they were right.

"We have broken away."

"Commence launch. Riders recheck your launch sequence."

"Heavy fire ahead. No incoming."

Verbal redundancy informed OpsCrew and ServCrew what *VII Gemina* and WarCrew were doing.

Tens of thousands of ears listened. Even the least member of WarCrew was awake and on station somewhere.

"Holy shit," someone said. "Look at that."

"That" was the sort of firestorm about which WarAvocats had nightmares.

The trap was obvious. And good. It was a sock into which momentum would carry the Guardship deeper and deeper while enemy fire grew more intense. *XII Fulminata* could not be seen. That Guardship was the focus of enough violence to fuel a small sun.

"We're starting to take fire."

WarAvocat told the WarCentral duty WatchMaster, "Someone has been getting ready for a long time. There's no way out except through the other end. We can't even turn back because *XXVIII Fretensis* is coming in behind us."

"Can we handle it, sir?"

"We'll find out. Maybe I should have allowed *XXVIII Fretensis* second honors."

Data accumulated. The picture was not good. *XII Fulminata* had lost half its riders. The rest were damned unless recovered by *VII Gemina* or *XXVIII Fretensis*. *XII Fulminata*'s screen could take no more strain, yet it faced worse fire ahead.

"WarAvocat." WatchMaster pointed.

A swarm of fighters had broken away from *XII Fulminata*, headed for *VII Gemina*. Other viewscreens showed hordes of fresh fighters pouring out of remote chunks of rock. The enemy was committing reserves.

The nearest gun platforms, already under fire from *VII Gemina*, began shifting to the incoming target.

"They're quick," WarAvocat said. "Bet they've decided to forget capturing *XII Fulminata* and try for us. Comm. Anything from *XII Fulminata*?"

"No, sir."

"That stubborn bastard." WarAvocat examined the latest. *VII Gemina* would have all its secondaries away before it had to hide behind its shield. If it had to.

"Sir, their screens are as good as ours," WatchMaster said.

"Damn!" So they were. *XII Fulminata*'s secondaries had not been able to silence a single heavy weapon.

*VII Gemina* ploughed through wreckage left by *XII Fulminata*. "Must have done a bubble launch. The crazy bastards."

"Don't look like they had much choice."

"Probably didn't."

Screens threw up schematics of enemy vessels amongst the wreckage. Few were not of nonhuman manufacture. Probe delivered data on species spotted in the wreckage. Few were recognized by *Gemina*.

They overhauled an enemy cripple of ridership size. A dozen Hellspinners whipped out. Three made contact, devoured half the vessel. WarAvocat nudged course slightly to pass a gun platform closely enough to use Hellspinners.

Its screen *was* Guardship quality. But it did not withstand the barrage.

*VII Gemina*'s interceptors met the enemy attack ships. In seconds it was obvious the Guardship had the better pilots. But the enemy had the numbers advantage.

"They've been getting ready for a *long* time," WarAvocat muttered. Every weapon *VII Gemina* could target was in action. There was not yet enough incoming to mandate more than prophylactic screening.

*XXVIII Fretensis* broke away. WarAvocat *XXVIII Fretensis* assessed the situation and ordered his fighters forward to protect *VII Gemina* so *VII Gemina* could support *XII Fulminata*.

WarAvocat ordered, "Put out the mine cloud. If they come at us hard, we'll run behind screen till our support arrives."

The mine cloud consisted of explosive packets that would orbit the Guardship on attenuated grav strings.

*XXVIII Fretensis* began dumping velocity to deal with the enemy individually and to block access to the Web.

There would be no escapes.

The senior communications officer beckoned WarAvocat. "Just got a squirt from *XII Fulminata*, sir. Personal for you. The signal was a mess. We'll have it together in a minute."

So. WarAvocat *XII Fulminata* deigned to speak to his auxiliaries.

Another voice: "Fighters coming in."

WarAvocat faced a screen that segmented to portray multiple attacks. "None of those are of human manufacture. Hold screen till the last second. All weapons are free."

The fighters streaked in. Defensive fire reached out. Hellspinners rolled. One hapless pilot hit a mine. The screen snapped up at the last instant. It was too late for several eager pilots to avoid collision.

WarAvocat asked, "How many did we get?"

"Six on the screen, sir. Eight in the mine cloud. Thirteen with fire."

"Not bad." The enemy began sniping at the mines. They wanted room close to the shield. "Watch for Lock Runners," WarAvocat cautioned. There would be soft spots in the shield while the Hellspinners raged.

Most of the enemy fighters, though, went on to meet those from *XXVIII Fretensis*. *VII Gemina*'s contingent were overhauling *XII Fulminata*, laying fire on everything in sight, doing damage wherever the enemy had his attention too obsessively fixed on *XII Fulminata*.

"Message from *XII Fulminata* is ready to run, WarAvocat."

"Go ahead."

It began with a visual collage showing enemy tactics, a grim variation on the Lock Runner theme. The Lock Runner would pop through and spray small caliber CT slugs. The Lock Runner would race in firing and just crash and blow up.

WarAvocat *XII Fulminata* was terse. "Our shield is destabilizing. It won't hold. We're going shitstorm. Good luck, *VII Gemina*. *XII Fulminata* out."

WarAvocat muttered, "In character to the end."

# - 48 -

Lupo Provik cursed, exasperated. "Simon, I guarantee you I can't pull it off against three Guardships. They're eating us up. Will you get yourself into your damned Voyager and get out?"

Tregesser wanted to find hope where there was none.

"If it suddenly goes our way, you can turn back."

"What about you?"

"I'm covering you, dammit! I'll leave as soon as you're clear. Will you go? Do I have to drag you? You want to guess what it's going to be like here when these things realize they're all going to die?"

"All right. All right." Tregesser started moving. "At least we gave it a try."

"It'll help when we shop around Outside again. Go." Lupo scanned his data. Half his fighters gone. Half of everything suffering at least some damage. And that damned third Guardship just cruising in, doing execution duty, blocking the escape route. No point sending the signal that would free the troops to try for the tag end. He muttered, "But we weren't supposed to draw the whole damned fleet."

He watched the Guardships till he received word that Tregesser's Voyager was clear and running into the void, headed out the end space's back door.

"Mr. Provik!" The tone jarred. It was one of total disbelief.

"What?"

"The lead Guardship has dropped its screen."

"We broke through?"

"No sir. They shut it down. On purpose."

"That's insane." He scanned the incoming data, looked for the error. It was not there. The Guardship was spewing more fire than it was taking. Its output was not falling off as it should. He checked the visual display.

Pieces flew off *XII Fulminata* in all directions.... He caught something, adjusted scale. "I'll be damned."

*XII Fulminata* was peeling itself like an onion, sloughing layers a hundred meters thick in chunks and sections as they were destroyed. The layers beneath were as heavily armed as those blown away.

It was depressing. They always had something more to show you.

More and more, his gun platforms were forced to waste time shielding themselves. That made it more difficult to fend off the pinpoint attacks of enemy fighters.

"Damn them. They're as crazy as Simon's suiciders. They just keep coming. How do you whip somebody who doesn't care if he gets killed?"

Be interesting to find out why they valued their lives so lightly.

No time to worry about it now. He tapped his wrist. "Ready? It's time."

He drifted away when no one was watching. He joined his family on the operating bridge of his personal Voyager. As Lupo One backed it from its docking bay, he said, "*VII Fulminata* blew up a minute ago. Want to screen it?"

"Might as well."

Lupo felt tired beyond any weariness justified by exertion. It was the tiredness that comes after great stress, great failure. It was a weariness brought on by a certainty that half a life's work had gone for naught.

He had expected it, but that did not soften the impact of reality.

Behind the Voyager, fire and death clawed the face of the night and ripped the fabric of space.

# - 49 -

Absolute silence gripped *VII Gemina.* In every compartment boasting a viewscreen, men and women watched fire blossom on the field of stars, *XII Fulminata*'s self-chosen eulogy.

No Guardship had chosen self-destruction in two thousand years. Even in defeat that extremity had been unnecessary.

WarAvocat suspected it was a statement rather than a

necessity. *Fulminata* would not let anyone or anything external become the arbiter of its fate.

Characteristic.

WarAvocat surveyed the Deified. Makarska Vis refused to acknowledge his presence. He smiled. She was shaken. What support she retained, after her trick with the Ku, would dim.

He vandalized a holy silence. "Stand to, people. It's our turn."

The smell of fear tainted the air.

*VII Gemina* was deep into the deadly sock, approaching the point where *XII Fulminata* had dropped screen. Much of the enemy's resources had been destroyed. But a lot remained. Maybe enough.

A leaden weight dragged at WarAvocat. He did not want to follow *XII Fulminata* into oblivion. Could he have gone on without *XXVIII Fretensis* there to see?

The might of the enemy smashed in. In seconds *VII Gemina* was locked up inside its shield too tight to fire back.

He checked his secondaries.

*XII Fulminata*'s last few and some of *VII Gemina*'s were headed for *XXVIII Fretensis* to rearm. The *XII Fulminata* pilots would not be much use anymore, as exhausted and disheartened as they must be.

The enemy had begun recovery, too. Suddenly, he understood why Stareicha had seemed intent on racing to his doom. "Maximum acceleration ahead," he ordered, silently cursing the man or woman who had condemned him to follow this one straight course. "Connect me with all the squadron commanders. Off whichever Guardship. All secondaries to relay to anyone we can't reach directly."

Click! Every viewscreen reserved for the Deified became active.

"We have a net, WarAvocat."

"Access. All squadrons. This is WarAvocat *VII Gemina*.

All ships capable break off present action. The enemy is recovering for rearming. Pursue. If his bays are open, fire into them. Destroy ships moving in to rearm. Don't waste time on enemy batteries. When you need to rearm, do so on *XXVIII Fretensis*.

"*XXVIII Fretensis*, I'm going to run this gauntlet through, then work back outside it. Do you have reserve pilots sufficient to reman ships off *XII Fulminata* and *VII Gemina*?"

A simple "Yes," and that connection ended.

WarAvocat checked his shield. It was solid but under increasing pressure. That pressure would get worse. Maybe so bad he would have to follow Stareicha's example and hope *VII Gemina* cleared the sock before it was consumed.

Could he give the order to drop screen? He was not WarAvocat *XII Fulminata*, obsessed with an image of invincibility, ready to accept destruction if withdrawal was the alternative.

All those silent Deified, many of whom had been WarAvocat before him, stared, knowing the conflict within him, perhaps wondering if they could have given the order themselves.

"WarAvocat."

That voice was grim. He hurried to the woman's side. She tapped her monitor. It displayed a schematic of the sock ahead, aflicker with fields of fire. She cancelled that. A stark portrait and bleak prognosis remained.

"I should have figured." He had been thinking of it as a sock, not a tube. And the mastermind on the other side had shown no inclination to miss an opportunity.

The end of the killing tube was plugged with chunks of dead rock. "How many? Four?"

"Six. Two are small."

That was one decision made. It was too late to avoid a collision. He had to go into that with a shield. "We taking any fire from them?"

"No, sir. Probe shows only dead rock."

"Fields of fire again."

She brought them back. He studied them, ignoring protests from warning systems associated with the screen. He grunted. Only one thing to do, feeble as that was. He had to open a port forward and throw everything he could to reduce the masses of those rocks. Tube it like a gun barrel so it would channel Hellspinners. The Twist Masters could get off more if they were not aiming them.

He gave orders. *VII Gemina* hurled massed fire forward. He fixed his attention on the schematics, ignored the creaking screen. It would hold. Or it would not.

A lucky Hellspinner destroyed the smallest rock. A heavy CT shell blew the other small one into gravel. Hellspinners rolled, snapped chunks out of the four big rocks. "I want everyone strapped securely," WarAvocat directed. He set the example.

Twenty-eight seconds and the run would be over. *VII Gemina* would be clear of the killing zone and ready to get down to the business of massacre.

"WarAvocat! The screen is going!"

"Hold it forward! All weapons commence firing!" He was going shitstorm, want it or not. "Damn it, I said hold the screen forward! Get it up! Get it up!"

Two. One. Impact.

# - 50 -

Provik secured the stern view. "I was good enough to take out two Guardships."

"Only thirty to go," Four quipped.

"Good enough to take two, but they sent three. The same old story. You can't beat them if you play their game." He stared at nothing. "Our whole investment, smoke in a few hours."

Four said, "We knew the odds. We weren't doing anything

new. Just putting more firepower in one place. We had the Outside screen, but it didn't contribute much."

"Tactically, it had little significance," Lupo admitted.

"We need a *new* strategy," Four said.

"I'm open to suggestions."

Three said, "We need Hellspinners."

"Let's not fool around here," Lupo said. "As long as we're wishing, why don't we do what Simon did and wish for our own Guardship?"

That stifled conversation. Lupo reactivated the viewscreen, contemplated the receding battle zone. They were killing each other there still, but it was harder to see. The massed firing was over. The surviving Guardship would take its time and do the job right.

Had he covered House Tregesser well enough? That was his main concern now. That he might have left something that would point a finger. Not something important, like someone who knew something, but something trivial that would scream House Tregesser.

He had it all covered. Still, he would be watching over his shoulder for a long time.

"Do we have contact with Simon's Voyager?"

"Way out on the edge."

"Keep it there. Don't reply if he tries to communicate."

Everyone looked at him. One asked, "What are you thinking?"

"Not yet. It needs time to ripen. Or rot."

"He'll get irritated if we don't respond."

"He won't see us. Our system is better than his. He'll keep his mouth shut. He won't want the Guardship coming after him."

Lupo stared into that viewscreen and wondered if he had what it would take to do what he was contemplating.

# - 51 -

Jo broke a long silence to spit, "Chains! How absurd are these clowns going to get?"

Degas, AnyKaat, and Vadja—still groggy from drugs— burned with the same indignation. They wanted to bite somebody. Chains! In a pseudoprimitive cell, shackled with chains!

Only Haget was in a good humor.

Jo snapped, "What're you grinning about, you stiff-necked martinet? Are you getting off on this?"

His smile faded. It resurfaced quickly, though. "I can't help it. I keep thinking of the fun I'll have after the pendulum swings."

"The pendulum swings? You silly sack of shit, what do you mean, after the pendulum swings?"

Haget laid a finger to his lips. "Let them find out the hard way."

Jo muttered, "He's crazy. We're in the hands of savages and our fearless leader thinks it's a joke on *them*."

"It is, Jo. They played it on themselves."

Degas said, "Cholot was the krekelen."

Haget agreed. "Timmerbach wouldn't pull a stunt like this on his own. The real Cholot had the spite but not the balls."

"We've lost it. It'll get out of that Traveler and turn into somebody else."

"Maybe. But if you can figure it out, so can Timmerbach. We catch up with *Glorious Spent*, our krekelen will be there. Locked up. Bet?"

Degas mumbled, "You're right, Jo. He's got a wobble in his spin."

Haget said, "Two weeks at the outside, troops. Jo. Is that thing dead yet?"

Jo glanced at Seeker. It had not yet shown an inclination to recover. "It's still breathing."

"It'll come around. So let's lay back and enjoy the holiday."

"Listen to the man. Calls this a holiday."

"Fake it, then. It'll drive them crazy."

"Ha-ha. We've got a party now." Jo looked at Seeker. Had the damned thing gone into hibernation?

"Hi, guys," Haget told three humorless STASIS types outside the door. "Smile. It's good for you."

Jo pasted on a grin. "Eat, drink, and make merry. You don't have a lot of time."

They went away. Jo wished she felt as confident as she had sounded.

## - 52 -

Turtle established them in an empty office overlooking that cavernous birth canal where new Guardships came to life. For him the location was no better than any other. But it pleased Midnight. She could launch herself on fanciful aerobatic flights in the inconsequential gravity of the construction channel. Her wings had gained color and luster.

For six days Turtle worked himself to exhaustion. If Starbase had secrets it wanted kept, he could not detect the blocks locking him out. If there were living beings anywhere, he could not track them down. He could locate none of the Deified supposed to haunt the system. There seemed to be no omniscient observer as there was aboard *VII Gemina*.

He could find no evidence Starbase was anything but what it appeared, a half-forgotten fortress where no one had remembered to shut the gate, and the garrison were dozing at their posts. The neglect of absolute assurance.

No defenses were active.

Turtle could not focus on the monitor. He went to watch Midnight's ballet. "Castle Dreaming," he murmured, recalling a myth as Midnight looped. A fortress dire and invincible, defended by unkillable demons with claws of steel and fangs of diamond. But Tae Kyodo had entered unchallenged and had walked out with the Bowl of Truth because the demons were taking a siesta, confident their reputation would keep the bad guys away.

Up the cavern the automated factory went to work. Sparks flew. Midnight glided down. "That was beautiful," he said.

"It's easy where there's so little gravity. Did you find a way?"

"It's so easy it's pathetic. We just get on one of the shuttle ships. The Deified operating them aren't interested in what happens inside them. But once we reach the Barbican, we'll have problems. We'll have to change ships. And they will be alert for people who do not belong."

"I'm going to check on Amber Soul."

"All right." Turtle stared at nothing. Somewhere along his life path he had lost the fervor that had driven him in the days of the Dire Radiant.

All those years slinking through the shadows, peeking through the cracks, educating and arming himself against his next bout with the necromancers, and now his inclination was to lay his sword aside and declare peace on the Guardships. Revolutionary change would deliver Canon into the jaws of predators.

There was an evolutionary thing happening, and he'd just begun to recognize it—though he had listed symptoms for WarAvocat.

Canon grew as inexorably as a black hole. Growth would not stop while there were Guardships and Outsiders to offend them.

Give them that. The conquerors never struck first.

Within the ever-advancing Rims a vacuum was developing, consequent to human depopulation. The race was old and, maybe, beginning to fade from the stage of the Web.

The vacuum was pulling nonhumans off the worlds where they sulked, to fill empty shoes. Almost by capillary action, some were oozing upward into the hierarchies. This great empire, Canon, might be theirs to inherit. Ten thousand years hence, Canon law and the Guardships might be the only evidence of the human race's passing.

Circumstances argued that the greatest good for the greatest number sprang from the status quo.

How to get out? Just the one way. Stealth. Going without being seen, without leaving a spoor. But the Barbican stood athwart his path like a wall a thousand kilometers long and five hundred high.

"Turtle!" Midnight squealed. "Come here! She's waking up! For real this time."

He hurried into the office.

## - 53 -

Blessed Tregesser paused before leaving the cozy Voyager for the uncertainties dockside. M. Shrilica 3A. Not exactly the hub of the Tregesser empire. A financial loser. The insystem station, 3B, unaffected by Canon regulations, was almost completely shut down.

The world, too, was a source of negative profits. To recommend it, it had nothing but its value as a place to dump exiles.

Rash Norym, whose governorship he would usurp, looked like a woman who had received an unconditional pardon. She waited dockside with the Station Master and a platoon of functionaries who looked like they were doing life without parole.

"If we're going to do it, let's get it done." Blessed started walking. Nyo and Tina Bofoku and Cable Shike followed, willing companions in exile.

Shike was twenty-two. He came out of the darkest dark of the Black Ring. His eyes were the eyes of an old man who had seen all the evils that men do. Blessed hoped to make Shike his own Lupo Provik. Cable aspired to the role.

Blessed stopped in front of Norym, took her hand in his. "Don't question your good fortune. Make use of the opportunity. I'll do the same here." She seemed pained because her escape would be at the expense of another. "Nyo. The envelope."

Nyo handed it to Norym. "Transfer, travel authorization, whatnot."

She opened it. She read. "Tregesser Horata? The Pylon?"

"I pulled a string. It would be nice to have a friend inside. Somebody who would send the occasional letter telling me the latest gossip."

Her face closed down. She knew there would be more to it. A time would come when a major payback would be demanded. "I understand. Thank you."

"Good. The Voyager is waiting. Go when you like. I'll need to meet with your managers to see if we can't turn this operation around."

Rash Norym looked at him hard; a seventeen-year-old talking about turning around the worst loser in the Tregesser empire. "Lots of luck."

"We studied it coming out. Cable thinks he sees a way to cut our losses."

Norym glanced at Shike. "Like I said, good luck. I'll write when I'm settled." She was amused. But there was no humor in her companions. They had heard the deadly edge in Blessed's voice.

## - 54 -

Valerena stood staring through double armor glass into the high noon gloom of a mild and sunny day on C. Pwellia 2, a world in its toddler stage. It was so active tectonically nothing dared be built upon its surface. Everyone lived aboard the same airborne prison, a feeble giant of an imitation starship that could not rise above fifteen thousand meters with prayer boosting it.

"Tregesser Tzeged," she muttered. "Armpit of the universe."

C. Pwellia 2 boasted a crop of volcanos so vigorous the planet seemed to simmer. Its surface was a treacherous scum that could break up or turn over any moment. Sometimes the activity exposed concentrations of rare elements worth harvesting.

It was a low-budget operation, marginally profitable, kept in place by the Tregesser need to possess. If House Tregesser pulled out, some other House might move in.

Valerena wondered if the seeds of disaster might not lurk inside that attitude. If you were too stubborn about holding on you might not recognize when getting out was your only viable option.

She had brought a retinue of a hundred to this hellhole, where it rained only at stratospheric altitudes, and that a deadly corrosive rain. Her retainers were there behind her. She turned. "They sent us to Hell on a pretext. Let's shove it down their throats."

## - 55 -

Amber Soul ate ravenously for three days. Then they grabbed the first ship out to the Barbican. Turtle spent the time aboard explaining what had happened, where they were, and what they had to do to get away. Then he explained again. Then he zeroed in on the grey areas where she did not comprehend. Then he just hoped for the best.

And there was the thing she wanted to hear over and over again. "Your race inhabits a system called M. Meddinia, the fourth planet, a Closed Treaty world. Your people don't leave there often. Nobody could figure how you got to Merod Schene."

Then she would want to hear all about the member of her race who had been on the Cholot Traveler. He could tell her nothing but the name: Seeker of the Lost Children.

The passage to the Barbican was easy. The Deified managing the ship noticed nothing. The transfer to a Horigawa Hauler was more difficult, but Amber Soul covered them perfectly.

But they did register on several intruder sensors and got STASIS and a few technicians grumbling about ghosts and glitches.

The journey in the belly of the Hauler was as easy as the first leg. Running empty, the crew had no cause to check the holds.

Midnight became the problem. Her nerves were not up to this. Turtle had to keep calming her. "One more leg and we're safe. Two at the most. We go off the Horigawa onto some other Hauler. Get off that at a station down the Web and just disappear. Maybe find a phantom and make a move just to get thoroughly lost. They can't turn over the whole universe looking for us."

"But where are we going to *go?* What are we going to *do?* We don't have any documentation. We don't have any *credit.*"

For Turtle, with his timeless perspective, those were not problems. Given ten years he could develop either anywhere. He had done it often before going inert in Merod Schene.

They might not turn over the universe, but WarAvocat would alert STASIS and Canon garrisons everywhere. He represented a real threat now. He had to go to ground fast.

Where? That would be determined more by Midnight and Amber Soul than by his own desires. He thought of heading Yon. There were Ku Outside. But that was too far. He thought of Amber Soul's homeworld. But the Guardships would suffer no qualms seeking him there, treaty or no.

The Horigawa Hauler left the Web at the obscure, planet-less system N. Kellrica. It meant to collect transhipped luxury goods destined for the Barbican.

Midnight told Turtle, "Amber Soul doesn't want to leave."

"We have to get off here. This is a very minor nexus station. Perfect for losing our trail. Security will be feeble."

"There's something here that scares her."

"There is something about them all that will frighten us. We're fugitives, Midnight. They will hunt us. We do not have the option of choosing which fears we want to face. Tell her to come on."

Amber Soul came. In a state approaching petrification. Had security not been nonexistent, Turtle would not have gotten her off the Hauler, let alone all the way around station to the only other vessel docked, the Sveldrov Traveler *Gregor Forgotten.*

He had not counted on finding himself with no options but one. From what he overheard along the docks, though, it was a bad season for the old station. There might be no other ship in for months. He could not turn back. The Horigawa Hauler had departed.

A Hauler would have been preferable. A Traveler was more difficult to hide aboard.

Amber Soul did not want to board. Turtle could make no sense of her objections. Midnight shrugged. "She doesn't understand herself. She says she doesn't remember, but it's evil. She's been there before. Something like that."

"Damn! We have no choice. Unless we're ready to sit here

till *VII Gemina* comes. She doesn't want to go back there, does she?"

"No."

"Then we have to do this. And she has to hide us while we're aboard."

Amber Soul managed. But her mental state continued to deteriorate. Her thoughts, that leaked over at times, were flooded with terror and misty memories of something terrible long ago.

Something was very wrong. Amber Soul walked the edge of madness, continuously terrified. Still she could not explain. But it was that Traveler. That specific Traveler.

Midnight fell into a bleak mood of her own. She had begun to suffer because of her design specs. It had been too long since she had seen a man.

Turtle could lead neither out of shadow.

He began to suspect that there was indeed something sinister about the Traveler. Yet the passage began with promise. The crew remained unaware that they had been joined by unregistered companions. Till Amber Soul went into a sudden paranoid frenzy that ended with one of her psychic screams.

In her last moment of consciousness, she sent mind pictures of things writhing and people screaming for mercy where there was none while shadows murdered them brutally.

It made no sense, but it felt real, like something Amber Soul actually had seen.

Turtle understood only that because of the outburst he was not going to get away.

## - 56 -

Chief Timmerbach released the final coupling. Centripedal force eased *Glorious Spent* away from M. Carterii 4A. He had little to do. So he worried.

Had the Majhellain techs been thorough? Should he go ahead and incarcerate Hanhl Cholot? Should he backtrack and try to brownnose that prick Haget into letting him off?

Nova light.

"Guardship breaking off the Web," some genius said.

"Bet I could have figured that out for myself."

A less confident voice announced, "Chief, that's our old buddy *IV Trajana*."

Timmerbach's stomach went into freefall. He stepped to nav comp and brought up back course data. "Shit."

Hanhl Cholot—or whatever—said, "Take us back to dock, Chief."

"Like hell. I'm not dragging anybody else across their sights."

"That's an order, Chief. If you won't execute it, I'll replace you with someone who will."

"I doubt it." Timmerbach's bridge people continued turning the Traveler, laying it into the groove headed toward the Web.

Cholot started to bluster.

Timmerbach said, "Master-at-Arms."

A hard-looking woman approached Cholot. "To your stateroom, sir." She showed him a pacifier.

"Hey, Chief. Check this."

Timmerbach turned away as Cholot walked out ahead of the Master-at-Arms. "What?"

"Pair of fighters off the Guardship headed this way like they want to see if you can burn holes in vacuum."

Timmerbach sighed and slumped into his command chair. He had no reserves left. He was accursed, and he accepted it. He wanted to go to sleep and shut the universe out.

But he could not. He had an obligation to passengers and crew and House. He kept *Glorious Spent* in the groove, headed for the Web.

He understood why *IV Trajana* was here. Web geometry. The strands they had taken leaving that anchor point converged again here. That bastard Haget had seen that. He must have deadmanned the Traveler. "Should have known better. You can't beat them."

The fighters spread out. Timmerbach's last hope vanished as they began curving in. One took station ahead. The other came in on his quarter in firing attitude, snapped three sudden shots that scrubbed three Web tractor vanes. *Glorious Spent* could not run away.

"Guess that's a message, eh? All right. Guide on that lead fighter."

What the hell could he do? How was he going to deal with this? *IV Trajana* was not *VII Gemina*.

The fighter guided him straight to the Guardship, to an empty rider bay. The Guardship grabbed hold. It began accelerating, headed for the strand leading back the way the Traveler had come.

Warning lights flared. Main cargo hatch gave way. Timmerbach heard noises in the passageway. He faced the hatchway.

A pack of little machines scurried in, accompanied by a feeble ghost. The ghost surveyed the bridge, fixed on Timmerbach. It said, "Come."

## - 57 -

The wound in *VII Gemina*'s shoulder was three kilometers long and half a kilometer deep. It had been scarred over enough to ignore till the Guardship reached Starbase Tulsa. WarAvocat had no intention of heading there immediately.

A Voyager had been detected sneaking away just before *VII Gemina* hit the rock.

That mastermind was in for uncomfortable times.

The guns in the end space were silent. The task now was to root the survivors out and find out what other throats needed cutting. Thus far the sword of evidence only pointed Outside.

The one clue he found intriguing came out of the heart of the command asteroid, the wreckage of a monster artificial environment. A few squiggles of data suggested the system had been occupied by a monster like those aboard the Cholot Traveler and the invader destroyed by *XXVIII Fretensis*.

# - 58 -

The crew of the Sveldrov Traveler were unfriendly but surprisingly cautious. They isolated the hold and that was that, initially.

The Traveler broke off the Web at the first anchor point up, made station, then the crew surged in and tossed the stowaways out dockside. Then the Traveler scooted before Station Master or STASIS could act. It refused anything but responder communication.

Turtle was baffled. He could think of nothing that would explain such behavior.

"Remain calm," he told Midnight. STASIS personnel and dock workers eyed them warily. "Let me do the talking. Don't say anything if you can help it. If you can't, don't contradict me. I'm going to blow smoke in their faces." He looked at Amber Soul, no longer in a coma but certainly in a fugue of some sort, lying on the deckplates, panting, changing external appearances as though trying to find one that would protect her from what she feared.

What the hell had it been about that Traveler?

He told Midnight, "Just pretend you're too stupid to understand their questions." There were advantages to belonging to the underclasses. One was that you never disappointed the master race by being stupid.

Bureaucracy ground slowly where for ages it had had no need to handle the unusual. Turtle had plenty of time to rehearse an elaborate fable.

# - 59 -

Seated against the wall, Jo was first to sense the strange, short vibrations. They filled her with undirected dread. "Anybody else feel the station shaking?"

Everyone did. AnyKaat, Degas, and Colonel Vadja looked grimly uncomfortable. But Haget just sat there grinning. "I suggest you all get yourselves up to military specs."

Eleven days in close confinement had produced one plus. Seeker was communicating. Some.

*A killer ship has come,* Jo heard within her head. *It is attacking. It has not communicated with the station.*

Jo glared at Haget. "A Guardship is here. You knew it was coming. How did you do that?"

Haget grinned some more. "The routes *IV Trajana* and *Glorious Spent* took come back together at M. Carterii. When Timmerbach started acting strange, I rigged a deadman signal on a longwave transmitter and concealed it in the main hold. It carried a copy of our mission log. It had to be reset daily to keep it from broadcasting a mayday."

"Clever. And you kept it all to yourself."

"If I'd told you, I'd have been telling everyone else who happened to be listening. They might have moved us out of here. They're coming. Let's look like soldiers."

*I Am A Soldier.* Jo grunted, got up, joined Haget at the cell door. The others fell in behind them. Even Seeker prepared to move. Haget smiled pleasantly when Station Master, the STASIS chief, and a squad of retainers appeared. "Buck up, girls. We all screw up."

"Don't overdo it," Jo muttered.

The station people let them out and returned their possessions and equipment, loaded them aboard a bus. The bus took them to a docked ridership guarded by an unstable hologram of a youth clad in a style unseen for three thousand years.

"WatchMaster Commander Haget, take your party aboard. Station Master, I've surveyed your data reservoir. The following persons are to be delivered to me." Followed a list of forty-six, with job titles.

Station Master started to protest.

"I have loosed a Hellspinner. This station can survive no more than seven."

Station Master got the message.

"I am remanding to this station the crew and passengers of the confiscated Cholot Traveler *Glorious Spent*. All passengers will be delivered to their contracted destinations at the expense of House Cholot and will be reimbursed for their inconvenience and lost time."

There were no comforts aboard the ridership. Prisoners and rescuees alike were crowded into a compartment that soon stank of fear and excretions for which no facilities existed. Some prisoners babbled pleas to Haget.

"Be quiet. I'm no more in control here than you are."

The ridership settled into *IV Trajana*'s hull. The Guardship was in the groove and running for the Web.

The same uncertain hologram waited outside the exit hatch. It seemed blind to everyone but Haget. "Bring them out, Commander."

Haget nodded to Jo. She herded the prisoners out and formed them in a column of threes. They were beyond terror now, into that dulled, accepting, bovine antihysteria that grips the victims of great disasters and atrocities, glazed eyes becoming one-way glasses keeping reality at bay. Wake up some day and find it all a bad dream.

Ha.

Lights came on ahead and died behind. Physically the Guardship resembled *VII Gemina*. But it was empty. Haunted empty, leaving Jo feeling isolated and alone. Like she had been warmed from storage to find the entire Guardship abandoned but going on. Haulers and Travelers came off the Web that way sometimes. Without a soul aboard and nothing to show what had become of the crew.

It took half an hour to reach their destination. The same holo character awaited them. "Prisoners to the left, Commander. Your own facilities to the right."

"Jo?"

There was an electronic barrier. It parted. A light came on. Jo moved the prisoners.

Degas said, "Hey, look. It's our old buddy Chief Timmerbach. How's it going? Not so good?"

AnyKaat silenced him. "They left the lights on where we were, Degas."

The holograph told Haget, "I'm on the Web running for Starbase. *Gemina* will put in before and after the action against the pirates. I have little capacity for sustaining the living. I may dispose of the prisoners as I examine them."

"My WarAvocat would want the Chief off the Traveler. And possibly the krekelen."

In a moment of illumination, Jo realized Haget was talking directly to *Trajana*. Directly! No one ever spoke to *Gemina* direct, nor did *Gemina* speak directly to anyone. If that should happen, it would scare the crap out of the whole crew.

Bound for Starbase. For home. There was a lot of loneliness and uncertainty out here. She missed the familial closeness of the squad and platoon, the certainty of knowing who and what and where you were. She did not miss the rigidity, the lack of humor and humanity in the chain of command.

Things happened out here. Strange things, weird things, *interesting* things. Today's universe was alien to the one where she had been born.

Born? A woman she no longer remembered had carried her inside her body. Did they still do that, down on the worlds? She could not recall the last time she had seen a pregnant woman.

They did not have the several immortalities down there. That was not allowed. Somebody too strong might come along.

This place was the antechamber of Hell. Here the shadows of madness met and danced. She wanted out badly.

Once upon a time she had lived on a world, a child who could look up and see uncovered sky....What was the matter with her?

Shit. The place was creepy. And that damned spook *Trajana* was on a talking jag, going like it would not stop till it dumped them at Starbase. Yakking like some crazy old hermit who had not seen another human being in thirty years.

Spider momma, ate all her babies, cries because she's all alone.

## - 60 -

Blessed scanned the report again, pushed it away, shook his head, pulled it back, pushed it away again, looked at the others. "What do you think, Cable?"

"Improbable. But it fits the facts."

"A mutiny? A Canon legate and most of his staff murdered?"

"Killed accidentally, according to this. And the legate had not announced himself."

"They do that," Nyo said. "Especially when they're sneaking around."

Tina said, "Maybe that's what got them killed. Maybe they

found something out."

Cable said, "The Traveler behaved erratically from the moment it broke off the Web. It ID'd itself as the Hansa Traveler *True Ceremonial*."

"And Bligger says it isn't? Based on the pathetic data he has?"

Rolan Bligger was the Canon garrison in M. Shrilica system. An honorary, at that. But he took his appointment seriously.

"His ship records go way back. Only one Hansa *True Ceremonial* is noted. It vanished on the Web fifty-three years ago. He says this ship's markings were either Sveldrov, Pioyugov, or Volgodon."

"Stolen ship?" That meant pirates.

"That would explain their lack of interest in an investigation."

Blessed gnawed a hangnail. The business stank. And felt like it might fall on him. "So what do we have? An artifact and two aliens. Why would a legate drag them around?"

Tina laughed. "The artifact is obvious. For the same reason you drag me around."

Nyo simpered. "You really think she can cook, Tee?"

Shike smiled. He tapped one of three small holoportraits. "This one is mental. Psionic. Strong. Be handy if it was tame."

"What's the other one? It's ugly. And it looks mean."

"Bligger says it's a Ku warrior."

"What the hell is that?"

Blessed said, "Check history, Nyo."

Cable said, "I looked them up. They had it out with the Guardships a long time ago. Gene-engineered their whole species. Ku warriors were faster and meaner than anything human. If you were a Canon legate peeking in dangerous places, you might want a character like that covering you."

Blessed said, "It builds into an interesting picture. I don't believe them, but I'll give them a closer look. Bring them down."

"I took the liberty after I talked to Bligger. Smelled like something we might use."

As they awaited their interview, Turtle admitted, "I put it on too thick."

"Maybe that Traveler was extrasuspicious."

Of course. Amber Soul's seizure had not made those people produce false identifications. He had been asked about that repeatedly. All he knew was, he had boarded a vessel purporting to be *Gregor Forgotten*. Lord Strate had booked passage. Wasn't his business to know why. He was a bodyguard.

He had picked Strate because that was a name Midnight could remember and talk about endlessly—he hoped not too much.

If he kept them focused on him long enough, they would lose interest. Then it would be into DownTown and disappear and scheme how to get away before *VII Gemina* came.

A tall young man summoned them into an office. Turtle took his measure at a glance. A lifetaker. Doubly dangerous because he had a mind stacked atop the conscience of a spider. Carrying at least three weapons.

He rose and followed. Midnight knew he would do the talking unless she was questioned directly. Amber Soul could not stick her foot in her mouth if she wanted.

There were three more in the office, all younger than the thug. The leader would have stood out even had he not fortified himself behind an immense combination desk and info center. Turtle saw toughness and competence in spite of youth.

The one behind the desk asked, "Are you the one doing the talking?"

"Yeah." Turtle pitched his voice near the bottom of the

register of human hearing. Its undertones would make them uneasy.

"Name?"

"Sally Montengrin." An entertainer whose name was known throughout Canon space.

"What?" The boy was startled.

"You ask a stupid question you're gonna get a stupid answer, kid. You got it in front of you. You got the next answer, too. And the one after that. All the questions been asked five times each by fourteen different guys. They been cross-checked by three different computers. So cut the crap."

He had the boy rattled. Probably nobody ever talked back.

"Do you know who you're talking to?"

"Should I care? Some kid who thinks he matters because he's big in his House. But ain't nothing in Canon."

"I could make your life unpleasant."

"You can't make it worse than it is already, being here on the butt of the universe getting interrogated by a fifteen-year-old with delusions of importance."

Midnight touched his arm, cautioning him not to overplay it.

The girl laughed. "It *is* the butthole of the universe, Blessed."

The boy flashed her an irritated look. She sneered. The boy looked at Turtle. "You might be right. If your answers are a web of lies, I won't trip you up now. So what am I going to do with you?"

"Not being human, I don't get why you figure you got to do anything. But the human that's got the power always figures he's got to interfere. What would a Ku do? Ignore us because he'd figure we wasn't any of his business. Unless he got in a bureaucratic bind. Then he'd ship us off to Capitola Primagenia and let the Presidents sort us out."

"Most human administrators would agree."

"But you're not going to do that because you figure you might be able to use us somehow."

The boy's face went cold. One finger twitched.

Turtle seemed to do nothing but lean a little and take a small step backward. The thug flung past him in a surprised sprawl. He showed no animosity as he pulled himself into a sitting position. "That's enough, Blessed."

"An experiment," the boy told Turtle.

"If I'd thought you was serious, you'd all be dead."

Young eyes went hollow as young ears heard echoes of the whisper of the wings of Death.

The boy Blessed said, "You've made an impression, Ku. Seriously, do you know who I am?"

"Who you are, no. I've heard this is a Tregesser world."

"I'm Blessed Tregesser. My grandfather is Simon Tregesser."

Turtle looked at him blankly.

"Simon Tregesser! Simon Tregesser!" the girl chirped.

Her brother asked, "You've never heard of him?"

"No." He hadn't.

Blessed Tregesser stared for half a minute. "Tina, show them where they'll be staying."

The girl frowned but led them out of the office.

Turtle was satisfied with his performance. But now he had to get off this world. Before these people found him out. Before *VII Gemina* came.

Blessed waited till Tina returned. She came in and demanded, "What did you guys cook up while I was gone?"

Nyo said, "Nothing. We waited for you."

Blessed asked, "What did you think, Tina?"

"He was scary. And I think he played you like a magic flute."

"Uhm. Nyo?"

"He scared me, too."

"Cable?"

"He was telling the truth. He could have killed us."

"Tina's right. He played us like magic flutes. Am I the only one who noticed he wasn't alone? He focused everything on himself."

Tina said, "You had one without a mind and one that couldn't talk."

"I've got a habit of accepting nothing at face value. Cable. Can we use them?"

"Him certainly. If we find a handle. I've never seen anyone move like that. Not a millimeter of wasted motion. He could kill you so fast you wouldn't know you were dead. The psi-active alien might be valuable, too. If it can be controlled."

"That's the catch with all of them. That and the fact that they might be what they claim, and somebody might come looking for them. Research them. And cover any trace of them having come here."

"That'll take some doing. They made a racket coming in."

"Take Tina. If it can be gotten out of the system, she can do it. Nobody talks to people anymore. Unless they volunteer. Discourage that."

Shike smiled. "Consider it handled."

Blessed did. He always did when he suggested Cable handle something. Cable always got the job done.

## - 61 -

Simon Tregesser's Voyager had been running flat out, well into the red, for nineteen days. It was seven days ahead of the schedule Provik had posited for the run to the G. Witica–S. Satyrfaelia strand.

Tregesser's crew thought him mad. Nobody pushed a ship so hard so long. It was a miracle the Q had not gone.

Simon was no more confident than they, but he was riding a nightmare hunch that if he did not get to that strand *fast*, he was a dead man. He had no idea why. But he trusted his hunches. They had done him right before.

They would be coming up on the strand soon. He had them feeling for it now. He wondered how Lupo was doing. He had not seen Provik since the run began. He had stopped trying to communicate.

Maybe Lupo hadn't gotten out. That would be hell. How would he manage without him? Lupo had been his rock forever.

Simon was on the operating bridge, filling half with his bell, when the Guardship broke off the Web. Right there. In his lap. Six light years from anywhere.

"Aw, shit," he said without any force. "One more signal to Provik. Warn him off." He analyzed the Guardship's motion vectors and ordered a turn that offered a chance to reach the strand before the Voyager could be destroyed.

He would not be taken, that he determined.


Provik remained amazed. "Simon is going to complete the run a week fast. Or kill himself trying."

None of his family were comfortable running in the red, though his Voyager was more suited to it than was Tregesser's and there were enough of them to close-monitor the Q.

"He should be getting close." Simon's Voyager remained at the very edge of detection.

"Message coming in."

Guardship. Right in Simon's lap. Motion vectors thus and so. He was turning so. Fifty-fifty chance of outrunning death and getting onto the Web.

"Damn! Decision time."

Tension filled the bridge. Suddenly they were all there, all offering to share the pain, wondering if he could do what, for nineteen days, they had been deliberating.

Lupo stared at the comm board. The tight beam was locked onto Simon's *Voyager*. The code sequence was in. The circuit was armed. The machinery was ready. Was the man?

Could he kill Simon Tregesser?

He could. But could he live with Lupo Provik afterward?

"Damn it!" His hand stabbed. "Turn us into the Guardship's vectors and shut everything down."

He sat down and cried.

Shedding their own tears, his family began trying to make the *Voyager* invisible by reducing its emissions.

# - 62 -

WarAvocat feared he would have a minor mutiny on his hands if his move did not produce quick results. To hear OpsAvocat and ServAvocat fuss you would think *VII Gemina* would scatter into its component atoms shortly if it did not head for Starbase immediately. And that despite assurances from *Gemina* that the Guardship's wounds were neither deadly nor incapacitating.

There would be political consequences if the fugitive did not turn up. His reelection looked ever less certain. The cream of his support had been killed in that end space. The regrowth system would be a long time replacing them.

"Coming up on breakaway, WarAvocat."

"Very well." That bastard had better show.

"Breakaway."

Two seconds passed. "Holy shit. There he is."

What? Already? Impossible.

"Look at that bastard go!"

WarAvocat ran to where he could see it for himself, telling no one in particular, "He's got to have been running at the top of his red all the way. Why hasn't he blown his Q?"

"He's seen us, WarAvocat. He's turning."

WarAvocat scanned the motion vectors, range rates, relative velocities. The son of a bitch had a chance.

He gave orders quickly, moving *VII Gemina* not in pursuit but so as to cut off flight toward S. Satyrfaelia. Once the Voyager headed the other way it was dead. *VII Gemina* could overhaul it on the Web and run it till its master gave up.

Then the fireworks started.

The Voyager's Q went. The multimillion-degree fusion process erupted into the Voyager, obliterating everything inside before it reduced the more stubborn hull to stripped nuclei. Those inside the Voyager did not live long enough to realize what had happened.

Probe had time only to determine that there were five beings aboard, all apparently human.

Before the fire faded OpsAvocat asked, "Can we head for Starbase now?"

Lady Midnight fluttered into WarAvocat's mind. "It's your Guardship, Ops-Avocat. Condition Yellow One. WarAvocat out."

Nothing left now but the chore of hunting down the villains behind the ambush.

# - 63 -

Valerena watched figures scroll. She was pleased. The balance had shifted just enough to produce the first profitable week of the century. Better weeks would come. All you needed was the will....

"What?" she snapped. She loathed interruptions. And that was one lesson these people were too stupid to learn. She glared at the creature in the doorway.

"I was told to deliver a message." Sullen and without honorifics. "A Tregesser Voyager has broken off the Web. A man named Lupo Provik wants to talk to you. He's sending a shuttle."

Lupo? Here?

She was frightened. This should not be. He was supposed to be in that end space with Simon. Had something happened? Had they aborted?

She had a thousand questions and a hundred fears.

She was on the flying city's docking platform, suited, when the shuttle set down. The poison wind barked and whined around her.

She stepped onto the bridge of the Voyager. Lupo was there alone, waiting. There was something wrong with him. "Have you been sick?" she blurted.

He responded with a soft, sad, almost holy smile. "Only here." He tapped his chest.

She frowned, worried. Lupo Provik, of all people, going spooky and mystic?

The universe could not be that perverse.

"What's happened? Why aren't you in the end space?"

"Sit down."

There was an echo of the old whipcrack. She sat.

"It's over, Valerena. We blew it. They came earlier than we expected. *VII Gemina. XXVIII Fretensis. XII Fulminata.*"

"Three? But..."

"Three. We got *XII Fulminata* and *VII Gemina*. But *XXVIII Fretensis* finished us. Your father didn't get out."

Shock. She felt lightheaded, numb. Her brain closed up shop.

"Valerena? You hear me? Simon is dead. You're the Chair."

She nodded slowly. And for once told the complete and naked truth. "I'm scared, Lupo."

"That's what Simon said the day he took over."

"It's real, isn't it?" She knew it was. Lupo would not say it if it wasn't.

"As real as death, Valerena. I'm taking you to Prime. You have to be confirmed. You have to take charge fast. The Directors will panic when they find out we failed. They might get the idea they could profit by informing. They'll need supervision."

"Yes." Tendrils of self-possession insinuated themselves through her shock.

Simon Tregesser was dead. The Tregesser empire was hers. There were things to do.

Dead! "The bastard got me again. Dying in his own time and way."

Lupo smiled sickly. "He didn't die willingly or in a place of his own choosing."

"It *was* Simon who died? You're sure? It wasn't his Other?"

"It was Simon Prime."

"Will his Other give me trouble?"

"They always do. They don't want to die, either."

That was a snake's nest someone was sure to stir. The Simon Other had become a nonperson with Simon's death but some Directors might defy that, preferring the Other to her. Then, too, someone might try to make something of the fact that she was not the original Valerena. She was not popular with the Directors.

Did that matter? Simon hadn't been popular. He had been the boss. The king. The bloody damned emperor.

As she would be.

"Can we use it?"

Lupo paced. He milked his chin and stared at unseen infinities. "If you kept it out of sight, maybe. But we'd never dare forget it's Simon Tregesser in almost every sense." He faced her. "We can talk while we're on the Web. How soon can you leave?"

"Now. But how safe will I be?"

"Why would you... My loyalty is to the Chair. You're the Chair. I'm the one at risk."

"You are?"

"I've thwarted your ambitions so often."

Valerena examined her feelings. She entertained no resentment. He had been doing his job. "Will you do as good a job protecting me?"

"Probably better. Especially if I can convince Blessed to be patient."

"I could leave him where he is."

"You can't. He has to be on Prime, to learn. Just as you were, despite the frustration you caused your father."

"He bottled me up here."

"An emergency expedient. He was frayed. Too much pressure. You wouldn't have liked the solution he preferred himself."

"He wanted to kill me again?"

"All of you. I convinced him it would be more cruel to send you here. We're still saying things better said in transit."

"Then go, Lupo."

He nodded, touching something. "Two. Four. I need you."

Valerena watched the women enter. One had been Lupo's companion that day in the Pylon. The other had to be her sister.

Provik said, "We have a crash priority here, ladies. See if station will bump us to the head of the launch schedule."

Good heavens! The man had a sense of humor.

# - 64 -

Starbase! At last!

That damned spook *Trajana* had not shut up the whole time. How did you exorcise such a ghost? It had tried to keep its prisoners alive, a captive audience.

No one talked much except when humoring the ghost. *Trajana* was not just weird, it was psychotic. Two prisoners had spoken their thoughts. Their remains shared confinement with the survivors.

The ghost kept hinting that *Trajana* wanted to acquire new living crew. Each hour raised the tension level. Degas had the shakes half the time.

Haget handled it best. He could take *Trajana*'s ravings about the Presence without twitching a lip, feigning an interest in *Trajana*'s obsession. Or maybe he *was* interested. Maybe *Trajana* did have something to say behind all the shit about devil gods, death cults, and phantom Travelers.

Haget broke away from the spook. "Starbase, people. *XXVIII Fretensis* is in for post-combat refitting after a joint mission with *XII Fulminata* and *VII Gemina*."

Jo asked, "What's up? You look rattled."

"Unsettled. It was the trap WarAvocat expected. *XII Fulminata* was destroyed. *VII Gemina* suffered heavy damage and hasn't yet made it back."

AnyKaat blurted, "Somebody took on three at once?"

"Yes. They had the hair and almost enough firepower. And that's all I know. Except that *Trajana* wants to horn in on the follow-up."

Jo asked, "How bad was *VII Gemina* hurt?"

"*Trajana* has graciously offered us refuge if *VII Gemina* doesn't come in. We're docking now. We have health and dietary matters to attend outboard. Let's go."

Haget led them on a long hike. Jo brought up the rear, behind Seeker, who stumbled with weakness. They debouched onto a vast, empty, sterile dock. A lighted dock. A dock not foul with the stenches of wastes and decaying corpses.

To and around a corner. "Now," Haget said. He hugged Jo so hard he crushed the wind out of her. When she wriggled free, she hugged Vadja too. Degas and AnyKaat looked ready to couple on the spot.

Haget said, "One more day and I'd have started chewing the bulkheads. I'm going to scream the craziness out."

Jo whispered, "I know a better way."

He looked at her. "Yeah. Let's get Seeker to Medical before we have to carry him."

They reached hospital bay. Haget tried to get Seeker to tell him what he needed. Seeker did his best. Maybe Jo would have been a better receiver. They had developed a feeble rapport aboard *IV Trajana*. Jo ordered a feast while the others sought physicals.

Haget handed Jo a note. "See if you can come up with a broth with all that in it."

"All right."

AnyKaat stepped out of the physical scanner. "Am I alive?"

"Close enough," Degas said. "You'll do for what I've got in mind."

Vadja said, "There are indications of malnutrition, Any-Kaat."

"Surprise, surprise. Degas, get in there and see if you're man enough to live up to your brags."

The scanner pronounced Degas fit. An automated cart arrived with a consignment of Jo's feast. AnyKaat said, "What do I want to do most? Eat or get clean?"

"Eat," Degas said. "Getting clean is going to take a while."

"You talk a good game, anyway."

Haget said, "Give Seeker something with plenty of sugar."

"You notice something spooky?" Jo asked, handing Seeker a sweet roll. "There isn't anybody around. Last time I was here the place was crawling."

Haget grunted. "Long time ago?"

"Yeah. Come to think."

Haget began pounding a general info keyface. Seeker came

to the cart and studied the food. Vadja came out of the scanner judged healthy, arm included. He joined the assault on the foodstuffs.

Jo poured herself a cup of amber liquid, told Seeker, "Try this juice." She headed for the scanner.

Seeker drained the pitcher.

A second cart arrived. Seeker went to work on his broth.

The scanner declared Jo healthy. "Scanner's all yours, Commander."

"I got your answers, Jo. Most Starbase personnel were drafted into the crews of Guardships. A few are in storage."

Seeker made a hissing sound. Jo looked.

Several people had come to the doorway. Their uniforms were unfamiliar. "Commander. Company."

Haget rose.

A hard-faced, greying woman stepped forward. "Commander Haget? Commander Stella Cordet, Third WatchMaster, Hall of the Watchers, *XXVIII Fretensis*." She spoke with an accent. Haget accepted her hand in a numb parody of his usual crisp manners. "WarAvocat sent me to offer the hospitality of *XXVIII Fretensis* and ask if there's anything we can do. You must have had a harrowing experience."

"Harrowing?" Haget chuckled. "You might say that. WarAvocat is most gracious. I hope he'll understand when I plead a need to regain my wits and self-confidence before I visit an unfamiliar Guardship again."

The woman gave him a hard look. "He'll understand." Then the iron mask collapsed into a smile. "Frankly, I don't see how you didn't come out of there a raving lunatic."

Haget seemed faintly embarrassed. "You know what happened?"

"*IV Trajana* sent the data. I skimmed it and reviewed your original mission as described in the data *VII Gemina* left behind."

*Gah!* Jo thought. *Two of a kind. Efficient to the point of constipation.*

"If there's nothing you need immediately," Cordet said, "we'll just get out of your way."

"Uniforms, Commander," Jo suggested.

Haget looked at her. "Sergeant?"

"We need fresh, clean uniforms, sir."

"Yes. We do, Commander Cordet."

"Consider them on the way. I'll check back later, Commander Haget."

"Right. Thank you, Commander."

Cordet gave Seeker one brief look, marched off.

"Why didn't you ask about *VII Gemina?*" Jo demanded.

"I had other things on my mind." Shy smile. "I was thinking something might not work out."

Shit. She had to go through with it now, want to or not. Well, hell. It might be interesting.

## - 65 -

Blessed looked over his workscreen, with its ranks of strutting bugs, at Cable Shike. "I'm going to put a bell on you. How long have you been there?"

"Ten seconds. You got to stay alert."

"You sit here staring at production figures for six hours and see how sharp you stay. You're wearing your smug look. How come?"

Shike seated himself. "Had a lucky strike in the data mines. Station Master is a history freak. Worked up a fair history of the region. It was pretty active during the Ku Wars."

"And?"

"They got desperate toward the end. They engineered some special leaders. Only a few saw action. The most famous was a Kez Maefele who didn't stop fighting when the rest of the race surrendered."

"You going to tell me we have the original, one and only, live Kez Maefele in our hat?"

"Looks like."

"He don't act it."

"Would you?"

"No. You figure he might be more useful than we thought?"

"More useful than ten of me or a dozen Lupo Proviks. Look him up."

"I'm glad you have that strong self-image. How do we reach him? Where's our leverage?"

"He brought it with him. Here. Specs on the artifact. A production model with options. And some stuff on the alien. Mostly guesswork."

"What about covering their arrival?"

"I've got it scoped. I haven't scrubbed it. There's something weird about the in and out of that Traveler. I want to hold the data till I figure out what it is."

Blessed had confidence in Shike. "Keep my ass covered."

Shike rose, walked out.

Blessed thumbed through Cable's printout. "Nyo," he said to his comm, "bring me our guest artifact. Alone." He had been thinking about trying it. This made it business.

"You all right?" Turtle said into Midnight's tears.

"I did it again. I couldn't stop myself."

"I know. Why do you punish yourself?"

"He didn't have me up there for three days because he wanted a toy, Turtle. His bodyguard figured out who you are. He bragged about how he would have the famous Ku warrior Kez Maefele on his staff. In private he turns into a nasty, mean-spirited little boy."

Midnight was not as slow as she pretended. She assumed there were eavesdroppers.

"I've been around a long time, Midnight. This has happened before. It will happen again. Those who want power try to seize talismans of power. But such talismans are dangerous, like the magic sword that makes a warrior invincible but devours his soul."

Turtle was worried. What Midnight knew could set tides of adventurers rolling across the Web. Worse, she knew he knew more and knew how to capitalize on what he knew.

He was a Ku warrior. He had bragged in his interview with those children, but there were ways to force his cooperation. The plotters and schemers always found ways.

If he were one of *them*, he would be less vulnerable. He would have no conscience. He could show them a shrug when they threatened Midnight.

*They* ate their young and tortured their mothers.

He could take that attitude about Amber Soul. She could look out for herself.

Midnight forgot the listeners. "Can we get away from here? I don't like these people."

"I'm thinking about it."

"You sound unhappy."

"I'm suffering a bad case of cynicism."

"Can I do something?"

"Just go on being Midnight."

She hugged him. "Sometimes I wish you were human."

He understood. "Sometimes I wish I was, too." He extricated himself carefully. "My Swordsmaster had a motto. 'When in doubt, attack.' The moment seems appropriate. No. I don't mean physically."

She did not seem reassured, though.

He encountered the girl Tina before he had gone a dozen steps. She said, "Blessed wants you."

"I was just heading up to see him."

"You're amused?" Blessed demanded.

"Bored," Turtle said.

"Bored?"

"I've been around a long time, boy. You think I'm a virgin? Thieves have been trying to twist my arm for ages."

"Thieves?"

"You going to tell me you want me to join a holy alliance to make the universe a better place? Or admit you're out to grab whatever you can for yourself?"

Blessed grunted.

"Thieves."

"That's a harsh view of commerce."

"Commerce? We're talking predation. Except the true predator kills only to assure its own survival. You live better than all but a handful of beings. What *need* have you for more?"

The boy was off balance. He could come up with no rationalization quickly enough to counterattack.

Time would tend to that.

"You don't have a need. You have a want. Power. We Ku look at things differently. Our villains know they're villains and don't try to hide, especially from themselves. They don't understand what compels them but they recognize its impact upon external reality.

"You humans lie to yourselves."

"Is there a point to this?"

"Several. The least is that you and the Ku will both go ahead regardless. Your true purposes are not external. You are trying to placate a demon within. I want you to know that when your demon is whispering in one ear, I'm going to mutter into the other."

Blessed looked puzzled.

"You think Kcz Maefele might be useful. Perhaps. But I'll

always remind you what you're doing to others. I'll drench you in their heartbreak."

"Our research indicates that you were the most dangerous of your *ghifu*. That a literal translation of your name might be, 'Revenge of the Ku Race.' But you haven't been doing anything about revenge."

The boy's comm blinked as Turtle replied, "Of course I have."

Blessed listened to the comm with one ear. He snapped, "Bring in that antique maxiscreen we shoved in with those broken-down cleaning robots. I can look at it on that." Of Turtle he demanded, "How?"

"By constantly rubbing the villains' noses in the consequences of their villainies."

A staffer shoved in, pulling an old 220cm vision plate that crackled and popped.

"Over here. What's wrong with the picture?"

"It's all right when the plate isn't moving."

"That's good. Right there. All right, Ku. One of the real villains of our time has just broken off the Web."

"A Guardship?"

"*VII Gemina.* Probably headed for Starbase. Our strand is one route in. But they don't stop here."

Turtle looked. "It's been in a fight. Must have run into somebody tough."

Blessed glanced at him. "I wonder who won."

"Self-evident. The Guardship wouldn't be here if it had lost."

"Yes."

The Guardship had found the mouth of hell somewhere. It had not recovered its secondaries. Its exterior had been slagged.

"There's the ancient enemy, Ku. Suppose you could command a battle fleet again. Would you?"

Turtle stared at the wounded Guardship. "I might." The genes. He could not be one of the villains, could he?

"Could you give them a better run?"

"I could. I could have before, given the tools. But those tools are rare and dear. I don't believe they could be gathered." By the Prime! He was being tempted.

"Not in Canon space. But there's a lot of Outside."

Turtle concentrated on the Guardship, willing his wizard side out of hibernation. He had to be very careful.

The boy had grown tense. His games had ended. Because of that Guardship.

"It might be arranged, Kez Maefele."

"I might be interested. If I knew what you were talking about."

The boy studied the Guardship, too. Then, "We're at a point of no return, aren't we?"

"Are we?"

Blessed left his desk. He paced. Turtle reached into the past for tools with which to calm hormonal storms. The Prime was determined to drag him past the mouths of the guns of fate.

Blessed stopped. "I learned most of what the artifact knows."

"She can't help herself."

"What you see is my grandfather's handiwork. He may be dead now, along with a man named Lupo Provik, who might have been your match. They had the help of aliens from beyond the Rim." Blessed looked at him hard. "Two people in this system know what I've told you."

A child had put a knife to his throat.

"Grandfather must have made a showing."

A hell of a showing. It spoke well for the alliances he had forged.

"That, and your name, would make great arguments when we go back to those creatures. There they go. They weren't looking for you."

The Guardship had climbed back onto the Web.

It was walking-through-the-fire time, staying-alive time, and being the fastest and deadliest thug around was not going to be enough. Was he ready to take up the lance and enter the lists for one more tilt with the dragon?

The boy hurled his comm unit at the vision plate. The plate crackled and popped. He said, "That was Cable Shike. The Guardship helped itself to station's data while it was here."

"That's routine."

"There was stuff about your arrival still in the system. Think about that. Then think about the fact that we're stuck here till I get a parole from Tregesser Prime."

Turtle stared at the now blank plate.

## - 66 -

WarAvocat wakened relaxed. He swelled a little with the thought that he would see Midnight soon.

It had been tense there, off the Web, getting that runaway drive well damped, more because of the carping of Makarska Vis's coterie and Ops and Service people than because *VII Gemina* was in any danger.

But the crisis was over. The bad feelings had bottomed out. The technicians should have the well relined, new casements set, and the tractors recalibrated before *VII Gemina* reached Starbase.

No. The bottom line was political. The Dictat election had delivered some disappointments. OpsAvocat, hoping to become the second living Dictat of the century, had drawn only cool support while Hanaver Strate, whose campaign had consisted of an admission that he would stand, had drawn approval from sixty-eight percent of the electorate.

WarAvocat's new fellow Dictat was the Deified Aleas

Notable, a little known former WarAvocat taking office for the first time. Her genius was a cipher. She had been one of the longest reigning WarAvocats ever, but her term had run smack in the middle of the longest period of peace in *VII Gemina*'s history.

WarCentral was quiet. The boards and wall had nothing interesting to say. Quiet time was useful, though. This he could use to establish a working relationship with Aleas Notable. They had to get along for a year.

A staffer said, "Sir, there're rumors Tawn has been seen."

"Really? Where? It's been a couple hundred years."

"The usual places. Empty corridors and whatnot. One man supposedly touched her. She paralyzed him with the fire in her eyes."

"I might look into it. I'd like to meet her myself."

"Nobody who goes looking for her finds her, WarAvocat."

"You're right." Not even the Deified could find the Guardship's tutelary spirit. *Gemina* claimed she did not exist. Even so, Tawn turned up after every spate of combat. A savant once suggested Tawn was a dream. *Gemina* had enough spare capacity to create a platoon of phantoms real enough to touch.

A spare, youngish woman said, "WarAvocat, would you look at this?"

He accepted a data pad. "What is it?"

"An abstract of data taken during routine scan while we were off the Web. *Gemina* tagged it."

WarAvocat skimmed it. "A phantom?"

"The info came off the abandoned 3B station, which was in a conjunctional mode during the incident. There was no comparable data from the 3A source. *Gemina* thinks someone was purging and weaving in so there wouldn't be a noticeable hole."

WarAvocat scrutinized the ID data. *Gemina* said the phantom could not be either of the ships it had claimed to be. *Gregor*

*Forgotten* was on a regular trapezoidal run between L. Maronia, K. Foulorii, M. Bemica, and D. Sutonica-B. Always had been and always would be. The Hansa Traveler *True Ceremonial* had been lost, but it had been found by *XVII Macedonica* twenty years ago. Pirates. No known survivors.

"A phantom phantom? That's a new one."

Phantom operators did borrow the identities of ships which could be counted on to remain safely far away. But to underlay one falsehood with another hinted at something more sinister than smuggling.

*Gemina* had caught no whiff of a true identity.

"Curious."

Insofar as *Gemina* could determine, no one had boarded or departed the Traveler during its inexplicable approach to M. Shrilica 3A.

"Run it through the Starbase pool when we get there."

Starbase.

He was an old fart. He should not be moved by anything. But he could not suppress his excitement when he thought of the artifact. *VII Gemina* would be in repair dock a long time. His duties would be light.

"WarAvocat. Word from *XXVIII Fretensis*. *IV Trajana* is in."

"*IV Trajana?*"

"It brought in those people you put aboard that Traveler at P. Jaksonica. It rescued them from a Cholot prison."

They had *dared*?... He would get the story. That Haget would be sorry if he had screwed up....

He ordered the artifact and two aliens brought as soon as *VII Gemina* entered repair dock.

What artifact and two aliens?

WarAvocat brooded. Then, "Access, *Gemina*. Priority input.

I want a council of Deified WarAvocats. Mandatory. No excuses accepted. Input immediately." In seconds all the former WarAvocats were present.

"During our previous visit to Starbase, the Deified Makarska Vis put three guests of mine off the Guardship. They aren't there now. Think about that."

They saw the peril before he finished.

Someone offered a motion to recall the Deification of Makarska Vis. It failed. Barely.

# - 67 -

"Why is that damned Guardship still out there?" Valerena demanded.

"Why not go ask?" Provik snapped.

"Hell. I might." She knew he was tired of hearing about it. He feared she had fixed it as an object for all her frustrations.

The transition was going well because of the failure in the end space, because the stakes were high, because there was a Guardship in the sky. Somebody had to be in charge. And Valerena was the designated heir.

Beyond that general agreement, though, the Directorate fell into factions trying to get the advantage of one another.

The Simon Tregesser Other, acting in an advisory capacity, was cautious and cooperative. It did not want to be shut down.

Provik said, "You have to recall Blessed. No matter how insecure he makes you."

"I know. Soon."

"Real soon. The Directors won't tolerate having the heir apparent kept isolated and ignorant. They'll make it an issue."

"Screw them."

"They're scared, Valerena. They're going to be scared for the rest of their lives. I can tell them ten thousand times there wasn't anything in that end space to connect House Tregesser and they're not going to believe me down in their guts. They're going to wake up every morning wondering if this is the day the hammer falls."

Valerena grunted. She understood. She felt it herself. She told the nearest window she wanted to look outside. Sometimes staring down at Tregesser Horata had a calming effect.

"*Can* they find us?"

"I don't think so."

"But they never give up. They never forget."

"They can be distracted. Simon made a lot of friends Outside. They'll consider the ambush a great success. They'll be primed for anything. The Simon Other would be priceless as a go-between."

"All right. See who's outside."

Somebody wanted in. Lupo asked who it was.

"Simon."

"Speak of the devil. Come ahead."

Valerena watched Provik move to the best vantage point. She had seen him dispose himself like that for her father a thousand times. She was tempted to move, just to mess with him.

Lupo said, "We were just discussing you. I told Valerena we shouldn't dispense with you because you could be valuable as an ambassador Outside."

Valerena controlled a lip twitch. The bastard could say a lot without saying anything directly. She asked, "What brings you here?"

"That sonofabitch sitting up in the L5 is using our mining drones for target practice."

"What?"

"It just blew away an empty headed for the Pyrimedes moons."

Valerena could not think. Why did she freeze like this sometimes?

Lupo asked, "Why?"

"Who the hell knows? Maybe they're bored. Maybe they didn't know the gun was loaded."

"No provocation? The drone didn't buzz them?"

"Hell, the bastard was five million K away and headed out. They showed off a trick shot with a CT slug."

"Have they been asked for an explanation?"

"They aren't talking."

Provik said, "Valerena, the Directors will be in a panic. Someone will have to hold their hands."

"You do that better than me. You scare them more than a Guardship does."

"I'm usually more immediate."

"Calm them down. I'll try to find out what's going on."


Provik stepped into the down shaft behind the Simon Other's bell. As they descended, the Other asked, "What was that about me being an ambassador Outside?"

"They're used to dealing with Simon Tregesser."

"Why drag it under her nose?"

"Trying to give her reasons to keep you alive."

"I'd think you'd want rid of me."

"Why?"

"You got out of that end space by dancing around a Guardship you expected. If you'd wanted Simon to get out, you would've seen to it. He didn't get out. That makes me a living reproach."

"He overstepped."

"His immortality thing. I warned him. He thought he could bring you around by offering to share. He couldn't survive without you, anyway."

Lupo said nothing.

"I owe you, Lupo. Had he done it his way, he would've gotten rid of me." The Other drifted out of the shaft. "I won't mention my suspicions."

"No. You won't."

The Other would have to be monitored. No way it would not try to use what it knew.


"They're settled," Provik told Valerena. "What's the story upstairs?"

"No story. It won't talk. But it keeps taking potshots. Nothing that can't be dodged, though somebody could break off the Web and get blasted before we could warn them."

"This is screwy, Valerena. Guardships don't play games. They kick ass and say goodbye. Send a Voyager to Starbase for help."

"What? Us ask them for help?"

"It's their job. Coming back, the Voyager could collect Blessed."

"That's a joke? It's a lousy one, Lupo. Where did Simon find you, anyway?"

"Down in the Black Ring. Before there was a Black Ring. The same way Blessed met his jocko boy Cable Shike."

"That's at least the tenth story you've told." Who the hell was Cable Shike?

"I never tell the same one twice. It's nobody's business. But one of the stories might be true."

"Sure. I'll send for Blessed. But no Guardship. I'll go handle this personally."

"Manage that and you'll shut up the Directorate permanently." He left.

"Why did I say that?" Valerena asked her reflection in the window. "I'd better start thinking before I talk."

She made a call to her castle, then sat down to think. *Would* she stifle the Directors if she dealt with the Guardship?

Lupo was right. There was something bad wrong with it.

# - 68 -

Haget had reverted. He was relaxing at attention. Degas and AnyKaat seemed numb. Vadja was in some sort of relaxing trance.

Unable to sit while WarAvocat thumbed through a mountain of hard copy, Jo approached Seeker. "Are you all right? Still feeling well?" His health had improved radically.

*I am well, thank you. This is the man to convince?*

"This is the man?"

WarAvocat flipped back and forth, comparing. He looked up. "Pardon my manners. I've just gotten a glimpse of a mystery that makes me uncomfortable. During your travels, did you hear anything unusual about the phantom trade, missing ships, or ships found empty on the Web? Other than apocrypha?"

"We heard a lot about the subject on *IV Trajana*," Jo said.

"I have *Trajana*'s remarks here. Twenty-six hundred forty-one single-spaced pages, eighty-eight lines to the page, one hundred twenty characters to the line. A preliminary report, yet." Thin smile. "I wouldn't believe it even from a Guardship—from that one, anyway—if it weren't for incidents involving *XXVIII Fretensis* and *VII Gemina* returning from that end space."

WarAvocat checked a particular page again, shook his head.

"Sir?"

"We had to leave the Web to stabilize a drive well. Routine scan on local stations found an anomaly, a Traveler that had shown two identities, neither genuine. Just a nervous phantom, I thought. Till I spoke with WarAvocat *XXVIII Fretensis*.

"A few anchor points away, by chance, they stumbled on a Traveler caught on the Web. They maneuvered it into a rider bay, broke through a cargo hatch. Crew and passengers had been tortured and murdered and mutilated. Ritually, *Fretensis* suspects. Six passengers listed on the manifest were missing. So was much of the cargo."

"That doesn't make sense, sir. Pirates would put people aboard a Traveler, sure, but they wouldn't just kill everybody and leave the ship. A Traveler is worth more than any cargo."

"You're right. Ships are mostly what piracy is about. But *Trajana* really talks ritual. And when you slide into the supernatural, you do leave all rationality behind. But I'm getting away from the subject. I want to hear what happened out there. Commander Haget?"

"Have you seen my report, sir?"

"I have."

"Then you're aware that I gave new meaning to the word incompetent."

"I didn't see that. Sergeant. Do you consider the mission a failure?"

"A grim time, sir, but not a failure, considering we had no fixed brief. And a success in that we established communication with Seeker. He still won't tell us anything substantive, but we might get it with a little work."

WarAvocat cut her off. Damn. She wished she were somewhere else.

"I have to explain why you've been isolated. There has been a catastrophic polarization among the Deified during your absence. *Gemina* fears you might worsen that."

Shit. That was all she needed, to get caught in the power games of the Deified. Screw them.

WarAvocat looked at Degas, AnyKaat, and Vadja. "I've screwed your lives around too much already, but I'm in a bind where all I can do is jack you around some more. We can't take you home till we're spaceworthy. *IV Trajana* is willing. Interested?"

He got no takers.

"I thought not. I'll express regrets."

Jo indicated Seeker. "There were things we didn't put on the record, sir."

"And things you weren't told. For example, *XXVIII Fretensis* came into the picture by aborting an Outsider attack on your friend's homeworld. Handled quickly and efficiently," he assured Seeker. "Without damage or casualties."

Jo asked, "Did you really have one of his people here, sir?"

"Yes. She and two companions. A Ku and an artifact." He explained. "They're walking bombs. They could blow up on us any time."

The sly bastard was sneaking up on something, Jo thought. She had a cold feeling. She would not like it when it came.

She wanted to rejoin her squad. She wanted to sleep off the rest of this nightmare.

I Am A Soldier.

Yeah.

"I'd like to question Seeker," WarAvocat said. "I had no chance with the other one. She was in a coma the whole time she was here."

Haget said, "Sir, it would be best to handle that through the Sergeant. He trusts her more than the rest of us."

Jo shot him a killing look. He did not shrivel. Maybe he thought he was doing her a favor.

"Makes sense. Commander, I'm sure you have friends you want to see. Indulge me and put that off till I've reviewed the data."

"Yes, sir."

"Colonel Vadja, I'll explore the possibility of alternative transportation. Meantime, be patient and enjoy our hospitality. Commander, if you'll show everyone to VIP, I'll get on with Seeker and the Sergeant."

Bloody hell. She felt like an animal caught in a trap.

WarAvocat studied the soldier. She was scared. He glanced at the alien. It wore a human guise but not well. As though to ease the discomfort of those around it but not to deceive.

"Is there some way I can help you relax, Sergeant?"

She started. "I don't think so, sir."

"What about your friend? Would he be more comfortable sitting?"

"Not in a human chair, sir." She looked at the alien. Something passed between them. "He's anxious to hear about the one you had aboard."

"I have some tape made during her visit. If he can move to that viewscreen?"

The soldier explained through speech and gesture. WarAvocat set the tape running. "How good is this rapport, Sergeant?"

"Feeble. You have a fifty-fifty chance of getting through. If it's simple and concrete. What I get from him turns into garble easy. I can't catch the odors they use like we use gestures and expressions. They don't hear quite like we do, so they lose some of our verbal stuff. And our odors confuse them."

"I sensed hollow spots in your report."

"Not intentional, sir. I'd never done one before. I spent most of my time learning how to write one."

"He's agitated. Why?"

"I don't know, sir. Don't interrupt him. He gets real single-minded. You have to take things in series."

"Who and what is he?"

"That's hard. Seeker is more a job title than a name. A long time ago his people sent eighteen children to Capitola Primagenia. They wanted to understand humans better. They sent children because their minds are more flexible. They were supposed to stay ten years. But they never came home. When the first Seeker went out he found out they'd never gotten to Capitola Primagenia. But then, later, they got signals that some of the children were alive."

"Then what?"

"That's where we run into a wall, sir. I can't figure it. They *knew.* So they sent another Seeker. Him. He's been out ever since. And he's found several Lost Children. Near as I can figure, the Traveler they were on got hit by pirates. Methane-breathing Outsiders had something to do with it."

"Curioser and curioser."

"There was a methane breather on their Traveler. Some of the human passengers grabbed the bridge and stopped the ship on the Web. Another ship came. It brought more methane breathers and a crew of humans and aliens. They boarded..."

"On the Web?"

"Yes. They boarded but didn't do anything till the Presence arrived. Then they started killing people. When they started on the children, though, they made them stop. I don't know how. Seeker isn't a storyteller. He stated facts. If he doesn't, I can't follow him."

WarAvocat glanced at the alien, engrossed in watching one of its own do nothing. "How did our Lost Child get to Merod Schene?"

"I gather the children cooperated as long as the pirates didn't hurt them. So the pirates abandoned them one by one, on outbacks like V. Rothica 4. They couldn't talk, didn't know how to survive in a DownTown, and were kids. Solution to a problem."

"How long ago did this happen?"

"From context, shortly after the *Enherrenraat* crisis."

"That long ago?"

"They're functionally immortal. They don't die from natural causes. The tape is done. He's upset."

"Find out what you can."

He gave up trying to follow the exchange, reflected on fate's penchant for hatching villains. This phantom phantom pirate bunch might be the most bizarre yet. And ambitious, if they were behind the ambush.

He punched up data delivered in response to an old query.

No known, suspected, or rumored connection between any House and pirates. On the other hand, most Houses indulged in smuggling.

"Sergeant. Was it chance he was on the Cholot Traveler the same time as that methane breather?"

"No. He heard the thing had entered Canon space. He made arrangements to get onto the same Traveler."

He heard the methane breather had entered Canon space? How? And after missing the Lost Child on V. Rothica 4, later, suddenly, six hundred light years away, he *knew* she was in trouble? How mental could you get?

The soldier said, "He's very agitated, WarAvocat."

"I noticed."

"This particular child is about to go through a transition from adolescence to young adulthood. That's sudden and traumatic and could kill her, or worse, if there isn't an adult there to guide her."

"Or worse?"

"That's what he said. He says he's *got* to hunt her down before the crisis comes."

"Uhm?"

"They go through life stages. Like insects. Only more stages. The early stages they can handle alone. He says they can delay the final transition consciously as long as they stay in control of themselves. But if she was under stress and retreated inside herself—which she did—she might not be able to hold the change off."

"He wants to look for her?"

"With our help?"

"Want to go along?"

"Shit! I knew it would be a fucking when it came."

"Sergeant?"

"Sorry, sir. I am a Soldier."

"The idea doesn't appeal?"

"No, sir. I've been away as much as I want. The trip was interesting but I didn't enjoy it."

"I thought it might be a way to track the others I mentioned. One is the Ku warrior Kez Maefele. You might examine his war record."

"Yes, sir."

"For now, learn from Seeker. He'll cooperate because that's his best chance for finding his Lost Child."

"Yes, sir."

"That will be all. Don't talk to anyone. I'll get back to you."

"Yes, sir." She started trying to make the alien understand that they were supposed to leave. It did not want to go.

"Complete information on the Other's stay with us is available in his quarters, Sergeant."

That did it.

WarAvocat arranged that, then leaned back. The thing to do next was obvious, if unpleasant. He had to visit *IV Trajana* personally.

## - 69 -

Valerena surveyed six identical versions of herself. A little unnerving, looking at all those Valerenas. Only they were not exactly Valerena anymore, were they?

To work up a proper Other, you had to put time into the details, especially motivation and indoctrination. But she was always so damned busy.... Face it. She did everything half-assed. These were her six best Others, but she had no idea how they would jump if a shitstorm hit.

She fixed her attention on viewscreen and controls. The shuttle's inertial system was up to max. The escape and evasion programme was poised to zag out on the first shot. On screen, the Guardship filled the entire field. Its surface seemed worn, abraded, even scruffy. It made her think of old, old stone, barren except for patches of lichen.

She thought the thing looked unhealthy.

The comm kept squirting a semi-hysterical "We come as friends" message. There was no response, but there was no shooting, either, and the shuttle was well inside the traditional killing radius.

The color of fear is brown. Those old farts on the Directorate were dribbling it down their legs. After this none of them would dare say anything about her courage.

Only a few kilometers now.

She was soaked inside her EVA suit. Her hands trembled. What was it Simon had said about the day he and Lupo had taken the House? "Going in with assholes so tight you couldn't drive a nail up them with a sledge." She knew what he'd meant.

She was having trouble breathing, gobbling air in gulps. Her suit cautioned her against hyperventilation.

She exploded in one of those goofy laughs that had become her father's trademark. She understood that now, too. It bled the tension.

She glanced at her Others. Buttoned up the way they were, she could read nothing.

Eyes to the screen. Still nothing from the Guardship. It was not showing lights. Wait. To the left there, just above her line of approach. A bay door had opened.

That was message enough.

She laughed again before forcing trembling hands to make course adjustments and switch on forward lights. A fighter nest. She made out a dozen pursuit ships. Like the Guardship, they looked neglected.

Nothing but ominous shadows moved in there.

She eased the shuttle in, rotated it to face outward. Like she really expected she could make a quick getaway. The bay door closed. Fifteen centimeters of armor, proof against any weapon the shuttle carried.

No Tregesser had come this close. In this she had outshone Simon already. "Just the beginning," she promised herself. "Grab it by the horns and ride it."

Shuttle said no atmosphere was being released into the bay. She swallowed a big dry egg.

No turning back.

One of the Others cycled the personnel hatch.

"Better take hand torches," someone suggested. Not only was there no air, there was no light.

"Right." Take charge. Do something. "Full kit. In case the whole dammed thing is this way."

She had asked Lupo to brief her. He had given her a big nothing.

He divided Guardships into four kinds: Normal (thirteen units), Strange (four units, including *I Primagenia* and *XII Fulminata*), Weird and Deadly (three units, *II Victrix*, *IX Furia*, *IV Trajana*), and Insufficient Data (all the rest, including *VI Adjutrix*). Based on its current behavior, he suspected *VI Adjutrix* was Weird and Deadly.

And she had jumped right down the dragon's gullet. Like some silly sacrificial virgin.

Personnel egress from the bay was sealed but not locked. The corridor beyond was empty of air and light too. Surface paint was cracked, chipped, peeling. There was dust everywhere.

"Is it deserted?"

"Somebody shot at our drones."

"Somebody opened that bay."

And closed it again, too.

Valerena took the lead.

Hours passed. Nothing changed. Was it all for show? A test to nervous destruction?

Maybe. She was riding the edge of getting spooked. They came to a huge hall. It was dark but there was a trace of atmosphere. "We'll break here. Feed ourselves."

Valerena swallowed a mouthful of liquified slop. Four hours already.

"Hey!"

"What?"

"I saw something. Over by that display."

Six lights beamed that way. Valerena examined the instrument pack she carried.

"There!"

"I didn't see anything."

"I saw it, but I don't believe it. He was naked."

"Put the weapons away," Valerena cautioned. "Sit tight. See what happens." The pack said there was somebody out there.

The watcher hung around the edge of the light, shy as a fairy. Valerena glimpsed him once. A young him. He wore no protection against cold and vacuum.

Fed, rested, less rattled despite the improbable observer, Valerena said, "Let's catch him."

Ten minutes later, she knew they were being watched more closely than was possible for one pair of eyes. She could not surround him. She was being led. That imp stayed right there at the edge of the light.... She let the chase continue because he was the only contact she had made. Impossible as he was.

He left bare footprints in the dust.

Valerena saw the boy slip through a hatchway a hundred meters ahead. "I'm ready for another break."

Someone said, "I feel like I'm caught in a fairy tale."

The adventure became more unreal by the minute.

Valerena stepped through the hatchway—into intense light, acceptable warmth, decent atmosphere. The place appeared to be a battle command center. "Spread out and squat. This is the place." A minute later, "This is getting too weird. Did I have some damn fool reason for coming here?"

Time passed. Some of the Others cracked their suits. The boy flitted, watching. He grew more bold. But not much.

"The hell with this shit. I'm crapping out. Long as we're all right don't wake me up."

## - 70 -

Turtle glanced up as Midnight bustled in. "What is it?"

"We're going to Tregesser Prime. A Voyager just came for Blessed. He's taking us with him."

He just looked at her.

"Aren't you excited?"

"No."

"Oh."

He had explained his moral quandary. She understood but was not worried. He was Turtle, and Turtle did not hurt people.

He wished he had faith in himself. Temptation and rationalization had him back-against-the-wall. "Have you seen Amber Soul?"

"Yes. She wasn't excited, either."

"I'd better pack if I'm going traveling."

It worked. Midnight said, "Oh! Me too!" and fluttered out.

Turtle did no packing. He had none to do. He settled back to ponder an odd question Blessed had asked recently. Had he ever heard of a stardrive, overdrive, hyperdrive, whatever, that ignored the Web?

He had. But in no context suggesting such a thing was possible. It was the intellectual toy of fantasists who carped against the restraints imposed by the Web.

Turtle had asked why.

"Curiosity. My hobby is trying to figure out where the human race came from. It didn't evolve on any of the worlds it occupies today. It didn't migrate into Canon space on the Web. Its first contact with the Web came a thousand years before Canon's founding, when the Go visited M. Vilbrantia in the Octahedron. All eight systems there had been occupied for several thousand years before that."

"Pity about the Go," Blessed had said.

In its first millennium on the Web, humanity fought eighteen wars with its benefactors. There was no need for a nineteenth. The Guardships came onto the stage of the Web in triumph complete and absolute.

Blessed scowled at Nyo. "Let the bastards grumble. I don't move till everything is set. I want nothing left for Provik's scavengers or the Guardships. Cable."

"Yes?"

"What's the data situation? They haven't come back, but that doesn't mean they didn't get something. Did they?"

"I don't think so. I can't find a hole that would've caught their attention."

"What're you doing now?"

"Trying to figure out how to get our guests into Tregesser Horata."

"Anybody going to get suspicious if I turn up with an artifact for a playmate?"

"No."

"There's one covered."

"Artifacts come and go. Ku warriors don't."

"It's your competence. Where's Tina, Nyo?"

"Fussing around trying to get everything on the lighter."

"And I've got everything loaded but live baggage," a voice said from Nyo's wrist. "Will you come on?"

Blessed glanced around. "I always feel like I'm forgetting something."

Nyo grunted. Cable did not say anything till they were on the launch platform. And that was something Blessed did not want to hear. "We'll have to bring Provik in on this eventually. There's no way around it."

"That means handing the whole damned thing over."

"He'll have somebody on the Voyager. He'll have somebody around us every minute. There won't be any way to hide the Ku."

The first person Blessed saw aboard the Voyager was that woman who had been Provik's companion that last day in the Pylon.

She smiled her enigmatic smile.

# - 71 -

N Etoartsia 3. Tregesser Hyxalag High City. Myth Worge-muth sneered. He had seen DownTowns that pleased him more.

The High City was bedecked with special effects. It was some damned holiday he did not understand and had no intention of understanding, though he was hosting a gala for Tregesser Hyxalag's cream.

Be barely better than scum in Tregesser Horata, he told himself, and kept smiling.

He looked out at the High City, sneered again, glanced at his guests. The locals ignored him. He could slide out for a dip without anyone noticing.

He slipped.

He was dipping from a jar of Jane—the finest True Blue —when he realized he was not alone. A figure in black moved toward him. "Who the hell are you?" The figure unnerved him. He backed toward the doorway.

"Go ahead and snort, Myth."

"Valerena? What're you doing here?"

"Take it, Myth."

He looked down the half-meter barrel of a hairsplitter. Its compressed sodium bullet could cook his brain beyond hope of reclamation.

He snorted a dip. The euphoria started immediately.

"Do one on the other side."

Voice frightened but growing languorous, he protested, "That would put me out of it."

"Do it, Myth."

He did it. He had no choice, did he?

Two minutes later he needed help standing. The woman in black helped. She led him to the rail of the balcony, where he could support himself. She dropped his jar of Jane. A fortune spilled across the balcony. He did not notice.

"Goodbye, Myth." She squatted, lifted his ankles, flipped him over the rail.

He giggled for a while, having fun flying. Then he stopped doing anything at all forever.

## - 72 -

The *Trajana* ghost bustled around WarAvocat, babbling, straining his patience. But he was learning more than he wanted to know about phantom phantoms.

The ghost never did catch on.

He found no breach in the closure of *IV Trajana*'s Core. *Trajana*, having subsumed its crew into a single character, had become neurotic and lonely but not diseased. The Core tissue remained safely sterile.

# - 73 -

Valerena wakened certain something was wrong. She rolled over. The boy jumped up and tore away.

The Others were sleeping. Some had shed their suits. The boy had been squatting over one with an impressive erection.

Valerena laughed through a dry throat. She had a handle on him.

She needed a drink.

As she took a long draught off her canteen tube, she noticed the time.

Two days gone? A night in Elf Hill for sure. No wonder she felt awful.

But they had not been harmed. She supposed they had been studied, but how and why was not evident.

She ate. She drank. She did not waken the Others. She watched the boy, who had gotten a console between them but had not continued his retreat. "You have a name?"

No reply.

"Are you alone?" A bored kid with a battle center as a toy would explain the sniping incidents. She closed her mind to the larger questions that made the whole surreal.

Concentrate on the narrowest possible focus. Get her hands on the boy and work from there.

She rose slowly. He was poised for flight but did not go. He watched, fascinated, as she shed her suit.

It was a matter of time till the moth dipped a wing in the flame.

There was something weirdly exciting, even erotic, going on here. That surprised her. Her couplings had become little more than desperation transactions, brief and usually unsuccessful attempts to escape.

Four Others were awake when Valerena brought the boy to the group. He was hers. Or any woman's who wanted to manipulate him.

She settled on the deck, pulled him down beside her. "This is Tawn. He's amazing." She trailed her fingers up his inner thigh. He responded instantly. "He'll do whatever we want as long as we do what he wants."

"Artifact?" one asked.

"Sort of. He's an organic hologram projected by the Guardship's subconscious. We've got a very horny Guardship here."

"You say if you screw the kid you're screwing the whole damned machine?"

"Near as I can tell."

It looked like House Tregesser could take possession of a Guardship through simple sexual manipulation.

Maybe.

There was a lot she did not yet know. Where were the crew? Why was the Guardship sitting here like a derelict? Why was it in such bad shape?

She let her hand drift into the boy's lap. He would tell her.

It was outrageous. Absurd. Unbelievable. It was a surreal and spooky universe.

## - 74 -

It was the first time the Barbican and House Horigawa had seen Guardship soldiers. Everyone dockside stopped to stare. One of the soldiers feigned a charge.

Jo snapped, "Hoke!"

"Aw, Lieutenant, I was just—"

"Working on getting the shit details. As usual." She spotted AnyKaat up the curve, with a small, brownish man who should be the purser of the chartered Horigawa Traveler. AnyKaat waved.

The purser spoke first. "Is this the lot, Lieutenant?"

Trying to be cool. Like having his Traveler rebuilt and taken over was nothing new. "All the personnel. There's still cargo in the system. Where are the others?"

"The two Colonels are on the bridge, putting in black boxes. The other one is snooping."

AnyKaat smiled. "Degas being Degas."

"Where is the alien?"

"In his quarters."

AnyKaat asked, "Want me to show your people where to go?"

"That's my job," the purser snapped. "Come along, you people."

Jo dismissed the soldiers, asked AnyKaat, "Are they all like that?"

"All of them. Working real hard to show us they aren't impressed. Wait till you meet the Chief. You'll wax nostalgic for Timmerbach. Though Colonel Haget has his number."

"That's TDA brevet-Colonel Haget." Jo grinned.

"Be like him to insist we use all that luggage, too. Wouldn't it?"

"What the hell. You can't have everything. He's good in bed."

"Wouldn't he love to hear you tell me that."

"He'd shrivel up and die. How's Seeker?"

"Settled in and eager to go. Except he don't know where. I gather his Lost Child has to have a seizure before he can sense her."

AnyKaat guided Jo to her cabin. This time there would be separate quarters for whoever wanted them.

"He's awfully evasive."

"Wouldn't you be?"

"Damned right. I don't say I don't understand, only that I don't like it." She began removing her combat suit. "I'll drag this back to the armory later. This cabin is huge."

"Want a ball of string?"

"Wise ass." She had room but the appointments were not plush. The Horigawas were a spartan crowd. "Guess I better report."

As they approached the bridge, Jo asked, "Why did you guys volunteer?"

AnyKaat grinned. "Great pay. Short hours. Nothing else to do but wait around till WarAvocat sent us home."

"Really?"

"No. We weren't ready to go home."

"Uhm?"

"We were all born on P. Jaksonica 3B. Era is the only one who's been off. A year for Staff College. My mother was STASIS, too, till she moved to Admin. She always wanted to travel. Fixing it so I could was the next best thing. Degas's mother is a dock worker. She'd throttle him if he didn't work this for all he could."

Jo stopped. This was all news. After months in AnyKaat's company. She'd never wondered about the woman's background. Soldiers did not think about anyone having antecedents.

"What's the matter?" AnyKaat asked.

"Just being awestruck. You probably see your mother sometimes."

"Every day. Another good reason for going away."

"Mine died while *VII Gemina* was being built. I was in storage." She resumed walking, shaken. "What about children?"

"We have a son. Tobias. Be turning four soon. He's staying

with Degas's mother. I miss him." Just like that. And that was all. "What about you?"

Jo shivered. "We're all sterile." Without knowing why, she was sorry she had opened the subject. She increased her pace, arrived on the bridge briskly. "Combat team is aboard, Colonel."

"Ah. Lieutenant." Haget smiled. "I rehearsed. I'll probably call you Sergeant the next ten times. We're almost set. What about cargo?"

"Last of it should be loading now."

"Vadja's in Operations running test routines. When he's ready, tap station data and see if you can get a line on our aliens."

"You're pretty calm. Considering."

"Of course. The Deified will be along in an advisory capacity only."

"And if you don't follow his advice, there goes your career."

"Only if he's right and I'm not."

"Are they ever wrong?" Jo did not want the Deified along. There were a lot of angles to this mission she did not like.

"Your soldiers good for anything besides kicking ass?"

"Tell them what you need, they'll try to do it. I'll see what Vadja's got."

Haget pretended to notice AnyKaat for the first time. He beckoned her over and asked how he might best utilize her and Degas. Another angle Jo did not like. The thing was being thrown together, without formal manning for the systems being jammed into the Traveler. She left the bridge, stepping between stonefaced Horigawas pretending they did not mind having their ship rebuilt around them.

What had been crew's quarters and mess decks had had the partitions removed so the space could be made an operations center. The entrance lay only a few steps from the bridge hatch.

Once the cargo bays were filled and passageways were cluttered with cables and everything was connected and integrated with the Traveler's systems, the ship would have many of the espionage and data-processing capabilities of a Guardship. There would be nothing like it on the Web.

"Can I get into the system yet, Era?"

"Jo. Hi. Sure. Funny. You don't look any different."

"What?"

"I thought you might have a mystic glow now that you're an officer."

"Shit. You're all going to get cute, aren't you?"

"Sure. Want to watch something you'll never see again?"

"What?"

"*XXVIII Fretensis* heading out."

She joined Vadja at a viewscreen. *XXVIII Fretensis* was just leaving the Barbican. It was impressive.

"Good hunting, guys," Vadja said. He had worked up a definite dislike for Messenger's species.

"There you are." Jo dropped a sheet of hard copy in front of Haget. "You said the ten most likely departures so I got you ten, but if they didn't go out on one of the first three you can have my comet."

"Why so sure?"

"All three were docked in the same section. The ship from Starbase docked in the next section. They all left within ten hours. And the Barbican had false alarms on its intruder watch there at the right time. STASIS decided there was a self-correcting glitch or a rodent off one of the Horigawas."

"All Haulers. What do you think, Smokey?" The Traveler's Chief's name was Hide Yoreyoshi but he insisted on Smokey.

"Ore carriers, Colonel. They bring in metal billets."

"Why the intermediate stops?"

"Picking up special order stuff."

"If you were the fugitives, which Hauler would you have taken?"

"They were flying blind, Colonel. Probably whichever had the sloppiest dockside security."

Haget grunted, stared at the sheet. "Anybody think of a reason the Ku wouldn't get off the Hauler first chance he got?"

Nobody offered one.

Haget circled each of the first three stops. "There's our itinerary, Smokey. If we don't find anything, I'll spank the Lieutenant and we'll think of something else."

Jo snorted. She knew she had this step of the search in a lock.

## - 75 -

Lupo Provik gazed out his office window, at a level with Tregesser Horata High City. He saw nothing that pleased him. "What is she *doing* up there?"

Four said, "Still no word."

"Doesn't she realize how much mischief the Directors can do? Especially now?"

Blessed's Voyager had broken off the Web two hours ago. Lupo and the family had gathered to await Two's report.

Three said, "What's Two waiting for?"

Four asked, "Blessed wouldn't have neutralized her, would he?"

"No," Lupo said. "We won't catch him in that kind of mistake."

One had been on station since yesterday, waiting to escort the crown prince.

Five and Six had comm duty. Six said, "Stop fussing. Two is on."

They clustered as Two took shape. Lupo felt mildly foolish.

He should have suspected she was waiting to get close enough to send holosignals. She asked, "Am I coming through?"

"Perfectly," Lupo replied. "Got anything interesting?"

"Blessed is making a show of model behavior. For now. Main point is that though he took only three people out to M. Shrilica, he's bringing eight back."

Two vanished. Holoportraits replaced her. "Cable Shike. Nyo Bofoku. Tina Bofoku. They went out with him. Kharsen Bhentus. Oral Stang. Specialists in financial forecasting exiled by Simon Tregesser."

"I recall the incident. Not one of Simon's better days."

"Bhentus is human. Stang looks like an artifact trying to pass. The M. Shrilica records are inconclusive."

Lupo glanced at Three and Four. They were researching the names already.

"There are no records on these next three. Lady Midnight. Artifact. Function self-evident. Amber Soul. Artifact with a question mark. Of alien manufacture? Whatever, it gives me the creeps. Turtle. Alien. Actual name unknown. Race probably Ku. Supposedly Shike's assistant."

Lupo sensed what was on Two's mind. "You think it's a ringer?"

"This one, yes. Maybe more than one."

"We're on them. One will meet you on station. Brief him. Stick to Blessed. We've got us a situation."

"The Guardship?"

"Part of it."

Two said, "We saw a Guardship, too. *VII Gemina.*" She secured comm.

It was very quiet there till Lupo managed a chuckle. "Seems I was a little optimistic about our success in the end space."

Nobody said anything. No point going into it till Two arrived with the whole story.

"Let's bring those last three images back and see what we

can get out of the bank."

The one artifact was in the Banat-Marath catalog, a standard item. The alien was a Ku warrior, possibly useful to Blessed, noteworthy only for its rarity.

That left Amber Soul.

Strange name. Not in the Banat-Marath catalog. Not in any damned file. Human? If so, she was the ugliest woman Lupo ever saw. Alien? Alien artifact? Wouldn't do any good to run that.

"Lupo."

"Uhm?"

"Call from Goshe. Just had somebody come at him with the right codes, wants a face to face. Name is Kim Chingamora. I ran him. A class three, reliable, second purser on the Medvihn Traveler *Federal Lotus*. There hasn't been a Medvihn in here in eight years. He took an emergency leave and came here on his own credit."

"He's got something hot."

"Something he thinks will set him for life."

"Clear out. Four, you stay."

Goshe arrived with the guest, did introductions, faded. Four bustled around offering refreshments. The agent, not on the regular payroll, had yielded enough good material to rate the grade three. He said. "This is my first visit to Tregesser Horata. Impressive." He was nervous. He had mortgaged his future to get here.

"Relax. If what you have isn't what you thought, we'll still cover your expenses and lost salary. You've done good work before. You're the kind of operative we want to keep happy."

Chingamora laughed nervously. "Better get to it, hadn't I? If I've got fool's gold, I'll have to hustle back to my Traveler while they're holding my berth."

Lupo nodded

"All right. I brought a holocassette and a regular video cassette. It's like this: We picked up a passenger at C. Colignonica who wanted to charter a stopover at N. Etoartsia 3. Nobody thought anything about it. The rich do weird things. And a charter is the only way you can get some places. We were supposed to wait at station for her. She was only going to be down a while."

He offered the video cassette. It was a one-minute excerpt from local news reporting the death of planetary governor Myth Worgemuth. Authorities wanted to question an unidentified woman with whom he had been seen talking before his fall.

"The holo ties this up?"

"You be the judge." Chingamora gave Four the other cassette. A shape formed in the projection cube. "Hold this frame. This is the woman we saw publicly, when she left her stateroom. But the day before she was due to leave us, she called the purser's office for help setting up an itinerary that would get her to N. Compeuia. I popped this while I was going over schedules with her. Next frame."

It was not a good holo but it was good enough. Lupo said, "You have an excellent memory."

"I done good?"

Lupo laughed. "You done great. Count on a bonus."

"That's a load off."

"Wait in the outer office while I talk to my technical people."

Chingamora nodded, stepped out. His nervousness had not abated.

"One of Valerena's ⌐ ˙ ˙." Four said.

"Yes. Which explains why he's nervous. He didn't know she'd taken over till he got here."

"Going to be some excitement when the news comes."

"Some, yes."

"And Linas Maserang is next."

"Apparently. And it's too late to stop it."

"You think she wanted to be spotted?"

"I don't know. We'll find out. Six!" Six came in. "You catch all that?"

"Yes."

"Assume the Other will head for Tregesser Prime when she's done with Maserang. Find a choke point and go wait for her. Go back in the other room while I talk to Chingamora again."

"One thing first. Valerena called. Almost hysterical, she was so excited. She's off the Guardship. Wants to see you as soon as she gets down."

"All right." He opened the door. "Mr. Chingamora. Staff wants to know if you'd be interested in full-time work." Chingamora looked surprised. "First assignment would be to accompany my assistant to identify and grab the woman who chartered your Traveler. She's been impersonating Valerena Tregesser. We want to know why."

Kim Chingamora looked immensely relieved.

# - 76 -

There was enough randomly accumulated data in the Starbase pool to pinpoint the source of the meddlesome methane breathers with a sixty percent chance of being right.

*XXVIII Fretensis* broke off the Web in a magnum launch. Forty minutes later there was no doubt it had come to the right system.

The Outsiders were completely surprised. But they were not unprepared. Moon after moon came to life and joined the contest. Twenty hours after his arrival, WarAvocat consulted his Deified about the advisability of withdrawal.

*IV Trajana* broke off the Web as the debate raged. It attacked with a ferocity and self-disregard that left WarAvocat *XXVIII*

*Fretensis* agape.

Eighty-two hours later, the last orbital fortress succumbed. *XXVIII Fretensis* assumed a polar orbit around the gas giant. *IV Trajana* moved into equatorial orbit. Both began probing for targets below.

Such sieges lasted for however long they took. The Guardships had the time.

There would be a small difference this time. This gas giant was but one of a hundred dewdrops on the Web.

Canon did not know. The Guardships had not guessed. Simon Tregesser had not known, either. His Outsider allies had not been frank with him.

## - 77 -

Turtle watched Tregesser Prime grow. He was impressed. The system was the most vigorous he had seen in a thousand years. Did it matter that its masters represented everything he loathed in the human species?

It mattered. A lot. But temptation was a siren.

He tried concentrating on getting a feel for Lupo Provik, met on station. Blessed had said a lot about Provik.

Provik did not look dangerous. He was a plain man with no sinister aura. But some were that way. They did not wear their character like a Ku.

Provik seemed interested only in Amber Soul. Why her, particularly?

Another shuttle grounded within moments of theirs. As they debarked, Blessed whispered, "That's my mother. The Chair. What's she up to?"

Turtle saw four of the woman. And she did wear her character where it could be seen.

"Oh, Turtle!" Midnight enthused. "Look! Have you ever seen anything like that? Isn't it magnificent?"

Turtle eyed the white fang of the Pylon, rising through the tiers of Tregesser Horata. It was an impressive sight. And *it* had a sinister feel. Almost an aura of menace. "Yes. It certainly is."

Valerena felt like hugging Blessed when she saw him. She confined herself to a wave. He returned it uncertainly.

It was a sin they had to eye each other like fighting dogs. Especially now.

Who were all those people with him? One she knew. He was that accountant that had pissed off Simon so bad he'd exiled him.

She spied Lupo and his girlfriend, for a moment felt a cold something slide down her spine. But, of course, he would have met Blessed. He had promised to stick to Blessed like a second skin.

Provik left the other party, took charge of her own security. "Lupo, you'll never believe what I've done."

"I doubt if anything you did would astonish me."

"This will get you."

"Save it till we're inside the Pylon. Four days ago we caught a spy here with a camera and sound gun."

"What? Working for who?"

"No telling. She destroyed herself. An artifact created for the trade. We get them all the time. Not much you can do but hope what they get isn't all going to the same place."

"I'll bust keeping it in, but all right. What about Blessed?"

"He's going to behave."

She glared at the Pylon. "Its days are numbered, Lupo."

Lupo took Valerena to his office rather than hers. He claimed he had things to do that could not wait. She told him he should have gone before he left the shuttle. That earned one of his tired smiles.

He rejoined her changed, refreshed, relaxed, looking like a new man. She supposed he had taken a stimulant.

"Tell me now," he said.

"House Tregesser has a Guardship. Actually, Valerena Tregesser has *her* Guardship."

He just looked at her.

"I'll change its name. *VI Adjutrix.* That sounds so... I don't know. Dull. How about *Horido Segada?* That sounds dramatic and menacing."

It meant "Black Storm Rising." She had heard that somewhere.

"It's sure to catch the imagination. That's what the Go called their Main Battle Fleet."

"So I'll think of something else. What matters is, I've got a Guardship."

"How?" Cool Lupo. Over his shock already. Probably the biggest shock of his life.

"I seduced it."

His eyes narrowed.

"And now it will do anything I tell it to keep me liking it. It'll get a steady diet of Valerena Others."

"How many of those are there, Valerena? How reliable are they?"

"Why?" She did not like his tone.

"Others can be troublesome if you haven't kept them on a short leash."

"There were some things my father kept to himself. I'll follow his example."

Lupo shrugged. "We have a Guardship to discuss. I suggest you don't reserve anything there."

He was right. He was the Guardship expert. He could tell her if she had made a fool of herself. So she told it all, from first impulse till she set foot on Prime again.

He gave her his absolute attention. He had that knack, of

shutting out everything but you. She'd never held anyone's complete attention so long. He listened gravely, the way, as a child, she had thought a father ought when his little girl brought him tales of her adventures.

"Did I do good?"

"You did marvelous. I may revise my opinion of what kind of Chair you'll make."

While the spell held, she asked, "What should I do now?"

"Move it. We'll have to refit and recrew it. We do that where it sits and every ship through here will run off to tell the universe."

"It can't get back onto the Web. That's why it stayed here. It barely remembers that it was headed for Starbase. If it wasn't a machine, I'd think it was sick."

"We'll head it out past the mines. Maybe to Wodash. I'll find an orbital path that won't get any attention. On record we can open a new mining facility to account for the traffic. It can move in starspace, can't it?"

"Yes."

"This will be harder than managing that ambush was. We didn't have to do that under the noses of everybody on a busy strand."

"I really did something that's never been done."

"You made history. If we handle this right, you'll be the most famous Tregesser ever. But if we screw it up, there won't be any House Tregesser."

"Yes." She was tired, suddenly. "Don't you get bored, being right all the time? Figure out what you want to do, then set it up."

"First we need cover stories...."

Valerena left her seat. "Don't waste time. I want that Guardship for my headquarters. You like the Pylon, you can have it. Blessed can have the place on the Gorge. He needs something better than that old relic in the High City."

Lupo nodded. She thought she detected a hint of strained patience. Every time he talked to her... It hurt. He was worrying about the future of the House again. When he did that, she worried too, wondering if she was incompetent and a peril.

It made her want to scream, "You bastard, I'm trying! I'm doing the best I can! Stop listening to what I say when I'm running my mouth and pay attention to what I'm doing! *Help* me!"

Provik rose too. "We'll talk again after you've rested. I have a thousand questions about the Guardship."

"When I get the chance."

As he opened the door, Lupo added, "I really would like more information about your Others, Valerena. It could be important."

She went without answering, wondering why the sudden interest.

Lupo stood looking at the door. The family joined him. One said, "I refuse to be amazed by anything ever again."

Lupo said, "I think it's time to grow us some brothers and sisters. Otherwise the workload is going to bury us."

One suggested, "You might consider doubling T.W. a few times, too." T.W. Trice was the second name on the chart of the House Tregesser security apparat. She was the one person Provik trusted completely. She was the perfect manager, taking most of the routine load off his shoulders.

"I've tried. She won't do it."

Two observed, "Valerena was sensitive about her Others. She's worried. Does that mean some of them are out of control?"

"Probably. She had to go churn them out to confuse us, then just turned them loose. We'll have to find them all, tag them somehow, and keep them under surveillance. The workload keeps growing."

"And you love it," Two said. "You're practically running House Tregesser now."

"Just this side. They can keep the business end."

# - 78 -

Haget was in a mood where he thought everything he said was funny. Everyone else thought he was being nasty. Jo was tired of making allowances.

They had visited the first two stations. They had come up with zeroes. All right. So it was not going to be a stroll. They had known that. Why get irritable and sarcastic?

The Traveler was coming up on the third station now. Everyone, including Seeker, had a job. This was no time for emotional distractions.

Jo and her squad were convinced. This was the jackpot. They were ready.

Breakaway. Haget went to the bridge to oversee communications with the station. AnyKaat offered Jo a compassionate glance.

"Kark! Look at that thing!" Degas said. "Straight out of the Stone Age." He and Vadja were in charge of plundering station data.

AnyKaat said, "I make it three ships docked. One Hauler and two Travelers."

"Curious." Jo looked over her shoulder. The schematic had Travelers docked side by side around the wheel from the Hauler. "Suggestive?"

"Maybe. But an old station might have a wobble it damps with its porting arrangements."

Jo looked around. Too early to have gotten anything else.

Haget stepped in. "They aren't pleased to see us. You'd think a tramp station would be eager to suck anybody in."

"Wouldn't you?"

"Watch them, Jo."

What did he think she was doing? "Yes, sir. Have they assigned us a berth?"

"Eight. Beside a Hauler."

"Why am I not surprised?"

AnyKaat said, "Lieutenant, I'm starting to get heat readings from both Travelers."

Jo looked. She was only a touch more familiar with the equipment than AnyKaat. "Colonel, can you look at this?" He had been a WatchMaster.

"They're warming up to pull out," he said. "We've made somebody nervous. Yell if they undock." He returned to the bridge.

They would have seen nothing had they been a normal Traveler. Civilians did not need gear that could see such things.

The Probe team began to get results. "Lieutenant, there's a lot of running around going on."

Why? Guilty consciences? Making with coverups they did not feel were needed for a Hauler?

There was a *ping*. Degas said, "Jackpot."

They had penetrated the station's system, starting with the obvious, records of arrivals and departures. The entry following the departure of the suspect Horigawa Hauler was:

DPT SVELDROV TRAV GREGOR FORGOTTEN.

The Traveler that had behaved so oddly at M. Shrilica. Interesting.

"That Hauler is Horigawa," Haget tossed in the hatchway.

Jo felt a touch, found Seeker beside her. *There are some of Them there.* Mind picture of a Messenger thing. *Three. Possibly four. They may sense my presence.*

"Would that explain the activity?"

*Perhaps.*

"Activate the weapons systems. Warm screen generators."

"All *right!*"

"Hoke!"

"Yes, ma'am," sheepishly. Hoke was on a CT cannon he wanted to try.

"Probe. Do we have anything nonhuman?"

"Three possibles, Lieutenant. Not enough resolution to confirm yet."

Good enough. She went to the bridge hatchway. "Colonel, we have at least three Messenger types on station. One or more in the hub and two headed for the Travelers."

Haget smiled. "That's interesting. We can take off the mask, Smokey."

Jo returned to her post. Degas and Vadja had pinned the identities of both docked Travelers as false. "What do they have for defenses on that dump?"

"Nothing. Not even shield generators."

"Then all they can do is run."

AnyKaat interjected, "Those Travelers are heating up fast."

Probe said, "The alien in the hub is headed for the Travelers, Lieutenant. It's a big one."

Haget stuck his head in. "What're they doing?"

"The Travelers are getting ready to run."

"Shoot their asses off so they can't do anything if they undock. Then suit a team to go take control."

He was having fun now.

So were all the Weapons team. She gave the signal. Twenty-five seconds passed. Time. Twin-fire lilies blossomed. "Hey! All right!"

"Get those targets assessed, Hoke. See if you need to pop them again. The rest of you get suited. Full armor and weapons." The squad hurried out, leaving their stations live. AnyKaat, Degas, Vadja, Haget, and Seeker some, could cover the critical functions.

"Got them both, Lieutenant," Hoke said, rising. "Those

suckers want to go anywhere they'll have to put out oars and row."

"Stay. The Colonel may need a trained hand on weapons. Colonel Vadja, it's all yours."

Jo ran to the after-refrigerated hold, which they had converted into an armory. The squad was climbing into their suits. She stripped. "Let's be careful. We don't know what we'll run into. Those Outsiders are fucking crazy."

They got suited, through the activation checklists, armed, and forward in plenty of time. Jo checked her command channels. AnyKaat told her one of the Travelers was adrift. Degas, covering Probe, said station personnel had stopped running around. She had them send schematics.

Haget told her, "We'll offload you and back away. That loose Traveler has a couple popguns. Don't want it butt-shooting us."

"I understand."

"Jo... Do you have to go yourself?"

"I *am* a Soldier, Colonel. It's my command." Her tone was cool, but she was pleased.

"Of course. What support do you need?"

She put the schematics up on her faceplate. "Tell that Hauler to get its people aboard and button up."

"Already done."

"Good. We'll move out against the spin, pushing them ahead of us. Once we clear the section, knock a hole in it and let the air out so they can't sneak up behind us. We'll breach the radials as we go."

"Right. Don't take chances, Jo."

*Chunk! Clack-clack-click-clack.* The Traveler was in, held by drive. Some station genius had secured the docking mechanisms. A demo charge opened the station side lock. Jo checked the schematic. Probe saw nothing that looked like resistance.

But there were people out there, apparently carrying on with business. "Go!"

The first two out covered the rest. They drew no fire. When Jo hit the dock she saw a lot of nothing. In the distance several civilians ran like hell up the curve. "Let's move."

Four soldiers went left, to seal the accesses from the next section. Two went to breach the radial to the hub. There would be few EVA suits on station, none designed for combat.

She assigned two soldiers to seal the lock behind them. She did not want the section decompressing before they left it.

Station shivered as charges holed the radial. Jo started up the curve. Her people spread out. Those with assignments would catch up. She came even with the Hauler. It was closed up tight.

So quiet.

She did not have outside sound. She switched on and got all she could handle: breach alarms, riot alarms, computer voices repeating calm warnings.

She found a dozen frightened civilians caught at the section boundary, unable to pass the decompression doors. She checked them over while she waited for the welders.

Degas came on. "Looks like an ambush shaping up ahead of you, Jo."

"I see it. Colonel Vadja. Can you get into the station system deep enough to override the commands to this decompression door?"

"Can do, Lieutenant."

"Open on my mark, then."

She moved the civilians out of the line of fire, disposed her troops, relayed her schematics on squad tac, assigned someone to each of ten targets.

The ambush had been laid in the expectation she would use demos to come through one of the personnel hatches.

"Now, Colonel."

The big door shot up.

The shooting started.

The shooting stopped.

Five ambushers were dead. Three were wounded. Two were in flight.

Another fusillade.

Nine dead now. One escaped. For the moment.

"Move those civilians over here. Colonel, shut the door after we're through. Hoke, blow that section as soon as he does."

Degas came on. "Jo, you've got them all stirred up around the other side. The big alien is headed back for the hub."

"Feed that to Fire Control. Hoke, when that thing gets halfway along the radial put one right through it."

"I can't hit the spoke from here, Sarge."

"Then move the damned ship. You're Weapons." She grinned at her faceplate. Hell. She was WarAvocat here. Even Haget had to take her orders as long as the team was engaged.

The station staggered as Hoke put two CTs into the section just cleared.

The alarms went berserk.

"Let's move up."

Station shivered again as Hoke took out the Outsider.

They received sporadic rifle fire, mostly inaccurate. None was effective. The other side had no weapons capable of dealing with Guardship soldiers in full combat armor.

There was a brisk, one-sided fight at the next sector boundary. They took several prisoners.

Hoke came on net. "Lieutenant, you want that section breached after you're out?"

"No. Let's not do any damage that isn't tactically necessary. We got to leave something for the honest folks. Degas. That next section shaping up as hairy as it looks to me?"

"Yes."

"How many of those people you figure for civilians?"

"No telling."

"I'm not getting my ass shot off for their sake. Colonel Vadja. This time open all the accesses so they don't know where we're coming from. Shut them as soon as we're through. Hoke. When the doors close behind us put a round through the section. They can't fight if they can't breathe."

"I might hit you...."

"Put it through the far end." She disposed her troops, sent the civilians and prisoners back up the curve so they would not be hit. "Open up, Colonel."

The doors opened. Massed small-arms fire poured through. It died as gunners realized they had no targets. She let them sweat for six minutes before she ordered, "Go!"

They flung through behind grenades, got down, got behind things. The doors slammed shut. Seconds later the far end of the section flared with the blinding light of matter annihilation.

Jo waited till the pressure had fallen below a level that would sustain life. "Let's see what we've got."

"What we got is a lot of dead people," somebody said.

She let it slide. He was not a false prophet.

She was surprised there were so many. And few were civilians because they were all armed.

"Sarge!"

One of the methane breathers, inside some kind of pressurized, motorized tank, was headed toward her. She shifted to microwave output and gave it a whole charge pack in one blast. Its tank exploded.

"I think it wanted to talk, Lieutenant."

"Tough shit."

That was the last shot fired on station.

The picking through the ruins began.

# - 79 -

Lupo scanned the report again. "What business could she have in the Black Ring?"

For three days a Valerena Other had been seen going into the Black Ring. The past two Provik ground people had tried following her and had failed. This Other seemed to have no existence outside its jaunts. Where it came from was as mysterious as where it went.

"Smells to me," Three said.

"You and Four go see if you can pick her up today. Be careful. Have the regular team back you up."

Three and Four left before he changed his mind, fleeing routine.

Lupo returned to work but twenty minutes later yielded to a hunch. "One. Call Operations. Tell T.W. to scatter stationary watchers around where she turns up."

Four trailed Three by twenty-five meters, self-conscious there in the fringes of the Black Ring, though nobody paid her any attention.

Three gave the Other more room. The two men of the regular ground team kept pads across the street.

Four became uneasy as they approached the area where the Other had vanished twice before. She loosened her weapon.

It was a wide open aisle between ranks of warehouses where surface transports could maneuver into loading docks. But there were no transports there. There were no workers. The warehouses had been sealed up and broken open again by thieves and vandals. The walls were enscribed with folk literature that was short, pithy, anything but ambiguous.

Three hesitated, stepped out after the Other. Four exchanged looks with the ground men, shrugged, followed.

She saw it coming before it started. She was amazed that

Three did not.

She shot the Other before it finished giving the signal to the assassination team. Shooting with mechanical precision, she blew three of those out of their hiding places before the ground men reacted.

One had icewater for blood. But the weapon he chose was a camera. He stood there taping while the shit flew. The other shot back, with no more luck than the rattled ambushers.

Four shot three more before the rest ran for it. She shot two of those. Two got away while she slapped a new charge pack into her weapon.

No matter. She knew where to find one of them.

She went to Three, knowing there was nothing she could do. He'd been hit at least twenty times.

The Other groaned.

Four stepped over. The Other looked up, eyes appealing.

"Goodbye."

"No!"

Four shot her once through the forehead. The burn looked like a small caste mark.

She shot each of the attackers the same way, alive or dead. Then she set for a wide beam and worked her way back, collecting weapons and charring the right hand of each corpse.

It was a message from Lupo Provik nobody in the Black Ring would misinterpret.

She crisped the Other's face, too, so nobody would connect it with Valerena Tregesser.

"What about him?" the man with the camera asked.

Without exception the captured weapons were House issue. Their charge packs could be used as grenades. Each had a timer that could be set for a delay up to twenty seconds.

She told the ground men what to do.

They did it, then ran.

There was enough energy in the captured charge packs to

consume Three and turn the eight weapons to slag.

Four shouted, "But they even had House weapons!"

Lupo looked at her. She had kept cool till she had gotten back. She'd even retained the presence of mind to isolate the ground men. But now she had broken.

"I tell you it's too pat. Come. Let's do an update." To spread some of that emotion around, to dilute it, before it poisoned her.

"Don't you even care?"

"Come and find out."

After the meld Lupo asked, "Were we supposed to notice where the Other came from or only meant to follow her into a trap where I could be burned?"

Two said, "The Worgemuth kill."

"Right. Valerena didn't order that. Blessed couldn't have. We need to see him." He fiddled. A street map appeared on one wall. "Four. Here's where the stationary observers picked up the Other. Coming this way. Suggest anything?"

Four's hysterics had vanished but her emotional state remained ragged. The meld could not adjust hormonal balances. "That's a hundred meters from the place we used to slide Simon in and out of the Pylon."

"Right."

"Have you been in there yet?"

"No. You and Five go watch it. Don't disturb anyone. Two and I will see Blessed. One. Hang on here."

# - 80 -

Valerena grumbled. Everything wanted attention at once. She could not keep up even with her Others helping. She summoned the most trustworthy from the adjoining office.

"I just had a call from my father's Other. He wants to talk to me about Lupo. Right now. I don't have time. Go down and listen to his latest paranoid fantasy. Nod in the right places. Don't mention the Guardship."

The Valerena Other entered the new office assigned the Simon Other. He greeted her with crazy laughter. She asked, "What about Lupo now? I'm pressed for time."

"The load will lighten soon, Valerena."

"What about Provik?"

"What about Provik?" More laughter. "This about Provik. He's dead."

"Since when?"

"Since an hour and a half ago down in the Black Ring." The Simon Other's bell drifted to one side. Another Valerena Other stepped from behind it. She carried a hairsplitter.

"What the hell?"

"The Others are running amuck, Valerena. They're taking over the world." More mad laughter.

The hairsplitter rose.

"Wait a minute…!"

Sodium shrapnel cooked her brain.

The Valerena Other dropped the hairsplitter, started stripping the still twitching body. "Damn! She shit herself."

"Just put on her outer clothes. Rinse them out if you have to. Hurry. Before Blessed or T.W. hear about Provik. If you don't get control of the security forces, we're dead." He started grumbling about the massacre in the Black Ring. It had claimed a quarter of his hired hands.

The Valerena Other left smiling. As far as anyone would ever know she *was* Valerena Tregesser.

Valerena glanced up as the door opened. "What did the silly sack want this time?"

The Other gaped. Her jaw moved but no words came out.

A chill struck Valerena. This was not the one she had sent.... It was trying to pull a gun....

Valerena dived into the knee space beneath her work center. "Blazon!" she shouted. "Enemy!"

A roaring whir, like the beating wings of ten thousand small birds. The desk thrummed. Glass broke. Things fell. The Other mouthed one gurgling scream.

"Code Sane! Code Sane!" The whir ceased.

She crawled out shaking, dragged herself upright. The needle storm had demolished the office, had shredded the Other.

She lost her lunch.

"What happened?" One of the Others from the outer office stood in the doorway.

"Get out! Get out! Get out!" Valerena flung herself at the door, slammed it, locked it, leaned against it while the heaves doubled her over. Then she stumbled to her desk to call Lupo.

The comm system had been destroyed along with everything else.

She was trapped. With a corpse. With no way to summon help.

# - 81 -

Turtle returned the comm to its cradle.

"What was it?" Midnight asked.

"I'm about to get a close-up look at Lupo Provik. He's here to see Blessed. Blessed wants both Cable and me there."

"Don't show off."

"I won't."

Shike and the Bofokus arrived before he did. Blessed asked, "You didn't come armed? Never mind. It's too late."

They were in a vast room in the rear of the second level of

the High City home Blessed had taken over from his mother. Valerena had used it for large parties. Blessed settled in a chair against a wall. Tina sat at his left, Nyo at his right. Shike stood farther to his right. Turtle took his place at Tina's left.

A man and a woman stepped through a doorway fifty meters away.

They moved with polish, disposing themselves without a word or signal, the woman falling back and drifting out so Provik was exactly in Shike's line of fire when they halted.

They had read him as unarmed and Shike otherwise. The woman could shoot him and Shike both before he could reach her.

Blessed asked, "What brings you slumming, Lupo?"

"Some gunplay in the Black Ring."

Blessed frowned. "There're gunfights down there every day."

Turtle relaxed. He read Provik as having no violent intent. He tried to get a feeling for the man. It was difficult. There was nothing obviously remarkable about him. He would not stand out in a group unless he chose to.

Turtle eyed the woman. He saw the same qualities there.

Provik replied, "I was lucky enough to get this on tape. I want you to see it."

Blessed frowned again, off balance. "Tee? Would you take that? There's a player over there." He rose, started walking. He said something to Provik's companion. She just smiled.

The tape was brief. It began in the middle of the action, with a man collapsing while Provik's friend gunned down everyone in sight. There was no need but Provik let it roll through the coup de grâce.

Turtle looked at the woman. There was that little smile, just for him.

Very, very dangerous.

"One of Mumsie's Others," Blessed said. "Leading your

people into an ambush? Why come to me?"

"One of your mother's Others, yes, but she wasn't what brought us here."

Provik's companion was watching Shike now. Turtle stepped forward. "Excuse me, Tina." He rolled the tape back, zeroed in on the moment he wanted, froze the action. Two men in flight, one looking back. "Can we blow this up, Tina?"

She did it. Blessed said, "I see what you mean, Lupo. But Cable hasn't been out today."

"So who is that man?"

"Cable?"

"I have a half-brother."

"Is that him? Would he get into something like this?"

"It might be. He would if he was paid. If he didn't know it was House politics."

"I'd like to talk to him. Could you arrange it?"

"If it was a chance to get him out from under whatever's hanging over him."

Blessed glared. That was not the answer he wanted from his number one boy.

Provik's companion snapped into motion with the suddenness of an unexpected explosion. As she turned she produced a hairsplitter with her right hand, a House issue energy gun with her left. She never looked at Turtle but the energy gun flew straight to his hand.

Provik moved half a heartbeat behind her, drawing identical weapons, throwing his energy gun toward Tina.

Turtle snapped the weapon out of the air. The hairsplitters made *thwock thwock thwock!* noises at people charging into the room. He shot twice himself and moved forward, on the woman's left, while the people over there were dumbfounded by the failure of their surprise.

He glanced at the woman, saw a hunting animal totally intent on its prey.

She was not as fast as a Ku. Neither was Provik. But she had begun moving *before* anyone had come into the room. She and Provik had begun shooting as targets materialized. Despite the range, the woman dropped four and Provik two before he took his own first shot.

Turtle glanced back.

Shike had Blessed and the Bofokus down behind a couch, was estimating the best way to get them out.

A man with a four-tube rocket launcher leapt through the doorway. Hairsplitters pellets hit him before Turtle could shoot.

They *were* anticipating.

That was worth remembering.

The dead man launched his missiles by reflex. Into the floor. Two warheads exploded immediately. The other rockets ricocheted. One proved a dud. The other blew a hole in the ceiling.

Turtle stood. He shot pieces of furniture, to blow them apart or set them afire. Provik and his woman picked off the people they sheltered when they tried for new cover.

His charge pack went dead. He got down.

He glanced back, saw Shike push Blessed through a doorway, jump through after him.

Blessed was angry. "Who the hell do you think you're shoving, Cable?"

"The guy I'm going to keep alive. Even if I have to knock him in the head and drag him away."

"He's right, Blessed," Tina said. She was calm. Nyo was the rattled Bofoku.

Shike said, "Let's keep moving. There were at least twenty of them. The Ku and Provik won't beat those odds. Tina. Rearguard. Nyo, stay in front of him. I'll lead."

Blessed demanded, "How did they get past the alarm?"

"Your mother used to live here."

"She's trying to kill me?"

"Maybe. But Provik was getting at her Others. Be quiet. Analyze it after we're safe."

"I can't just be a lump while you take the chances."

"You'd better. The way I hear, your grandfather ended up in a bottle because he had that attitude."

Two men appeared ahead. They looked like household staff. Shike shot them both. He approached warily, toed a dropped hand communicator blinking for attention. "Nyo. Get their weapons."

"Where are we headed?" Blessed asked.

"Out. To Tina and Nyo's place."

The hall turned twice and ended on a balcony hanging seven meters above the lobbylike entry foyer. Shike looked down at an empty floor. He heard a voice.

"Keep after them. If even one gets out, we're dead." That voice belonged to Valerena Tregesser. It came from beneath the balcony. There was a cloakroom down there. Someone hidden there could cover the entrance, both stairs, and the freight and passenger elevators beside the stairs.

A second Valerena voice said, "I can't get Chocki. They must have gotten past him."

"Then be quiet. They'll be here soon."

Shike backed away. "Tina, go around the balcony as far as you can. When I wave, shoot at the cloakroom. Take an extra charge pack. Nyo, cover the hallway." He took a captured charge pack himself, along with his own hairsplitter and extra magazine. He ran along the crescent balcony in the direction opposite Tina, to its end, where it met a black marble wall. He waved.

Tina was no sharpshooter. She hit the cloakroom only four times.

Good enough. A cursing Valerena showed enough of herself

to shoot back.

Shike hit her shoulder with his hairsplitter. She screamed and kept on screaming. She stumbled out.

Blessed cut her down.

Shike emptied an entire magazine into the cloakroom hoping to start a fire or get a hit with a ricochet. He failed.

A bolt missed Tina by a handspan.

They could not get past.

A second hallway, which led to the room where the shooting had started, opened on the balcony near the passenger elevator. Four men and a woman stumbled out, the men in pairs supporting injured comrades, the woman firing back along the hallway.

They never had a chance.


Lupo moved onto the balcony carefully, stepping over bodies. Tina Bofoku and Cable Shike relaxed as they recognized him. He moved toward Blessed, who was slicing cloth away from a burn on Nyo's leg. "That should be all of them."

Shike said, "There's another one in the cloakroom. I couldn't figure how to get her."

Lupo looked over the rail. "There were two?"

"It was their command post."

"We don't have to use the front way."

Blessed turned Nyo over to Tina, joined them. "Valerena. You're the last one left. You want to die in a closet?" He looked at the Ku, who had followed Lupo. "She doesn't come out, go get her."

"You're too ambitious for me, boy. You want her, *you* go dance through the gunfire."

Lupo observed with interest. The Ku did not act like a hired hand.

The Valerena walked to the center of the serpentine floor. She saw Lupo. "You're not dead."

"Not yet."

Blessed shot her five times.

Two stepped off the stair and stood beside the passenger elevator, hairsplitter held loosely at her side. Lupo said, "That's all for now, Blessed. Though I'd like to see Shike's brother sometime."

Turtle watched Provik descend the stairs and move to the front door, where he stood relaxed while the woman made the last leg of her withdrawal. "That's a dangerous man, Blessed."

"I know."

"I mean more dangerous than you think. I don't think he can be killed."

Blessed was in a foul mood. He wanted to argue. Turtle refused. "He left that tape in the machine. I want to see it again."

But there was no tape there when he checked.

The woman must have gone back while he and Provik were chasing the survivors.

Maybe they were right when they said Provik made no mistakes.

## - 82 -

There was a caution waiting at the lower watchpoint with Goshe. Lupo called One. He listened briefly. In the privacy of a lifter, he told Two, "A couple of Valerena's Others, from her office, turned up asking for protection. One's been putting them off hoping we'd get back and handle it ourselves."

"Sarcastic, are we?"

"He could have handled it."

"Then got bitched at because things were happening and you weren't being kept informed."

"Probably. I reserve the right to be unreasonable, inconsistent, and arbitrary in an unreasonable, inconsistent, and arbitrary universe. What did you think of Blessed's new bodyguard?"

"Deadly. And smart, maybe. He never stopped studying us."

"We'll keep him in mind. Now let's worry about our Valerena trouble. I can't help recalling that she left three of them on that Guardship. What mischief are they up to out there?"

A minute later, still smelling of fight, they stepped into the office where the Valerenas waited. Lupo questioned them only long enough to get a glimmer of what had happened. He signalled One. "Call Blessed. We need him here. Use your imagination if you have to. Then get T.W. up here. I'm going to check on Valerena."

He hammered on the door. "Valerena! It's Provik."

Muffled, "It's unlocked."

He eased the door open, spied the shredded corpse, the demolished furniture. He went in slowly.

He found himself facing a cutter.

"It is you."

"I think so."

"You took long enough."

"I was in the High City keeping Blessed from getting killed by your Others."

"Blessed too?"

"All of us. They tried me this morning."

"A clean sweep."

"Except for T.W. Come down to my office. They don't know they didn't get you, either."

"Of course they do. Two got away when I did that." She indicated the corpse.

"Those two are all right. They came straight down to let

me know you were in trouble. If they'd been on the other side there would have been another try."

"Unless I'm not Valerena Prime."

"I'll know about that after I get you to my office."

T.W. got through so quick her call had to have been expected. "T.W. Trice!" the Simon Other boomed. "How the hell are you? I haven't seen your ugly puss since—"

"Can it. I'm not in the mood. Lupo got himself killed this morning." She had been Provik's lover once and was well known as his designated heir.

"Killed? Lupo Provik?"

"Lupo. I know. It sounds unlikely. Since Valerena took over, I've had orders to get with you if anything happens to him. Can you come down?"

"Why don't you come up? More private here."

"I can't. Somebody tried to burn Blessed and got the bad side of his bodyguards. I'm riding monitor on the cleanup."

Pause. "I'll be right down."

"Use the freight lift. I'm back in the big office." She secured. "That good enough, Lupo?"

"Perfect. He'll be foaming at the mouth, worrying."

Two came in. "Blessed is on his way. He brought the Ku instead of Shike."

"He knows we wouldn't let him in armed."

Blessed arrived moments before the guest of honor. There was no time to brief him. The Simon Other came out of the freight lift booming, "T.W! Where the hell are you, woman?"

"In here."

The bell came sailing in. "What's this shit about somebody trying to... Hell."

T.W. said, "I'll leave now, Lupo."

"You don't have to."

"I want to."

"Go ahead." Provik faced the bell. "You and Simon wondered how it would come out if we went head to head. Now you know. You were clumsy, hasty, sloppy, overconfident, and your communications and reserves were inadequate. You defeated yourself. I didn't see it coming."

"I had one throw of the dice. I took it. And you know damned well victory don't always go to him with the most resources. I don't have any regrets. Do what you have to do."

Lupo allowed time for Valerena or Blessed to comment. Neither spoke. He wished he could read the Ku. The alien seemed amused.

"You've overlooked your value to the House. Or maybe you didn't. Maybe you were counting on it."

The Simon Other did not respond.

"You're the Chair, Valerena. What do we do with him?"

"What do you think we should do?"

"You're the Chair. It's your job to decide. Mine is to carry out your decisions. I never let Simon duck responsibility for the unpleasant things we did, and I won't let you, either."

"You're a bastard."

"I know." He watched Blessed obliquely. The boy remained a cypher. "But this does have to be resolved."

"Can we deal with the Outsiders without him?"

"Probably. It may take longer."

"I don't need the aggravation of always having to watch for a next time."

Lupo smiled thinly. How often had she tried to get to her father? "Blessed. You have an opinion?"

"No."

Just here. Just watching. Just learning what it meant to be a Tregesser. "Go home, then. My people will come clean up. Don't relax. There could be a few severed limbs of this thing flopping around still."

Blessed left without a word, his alien drifting behind him.

"What was that thing?" Valerena asked.

"A Ku warrior. His bodyguard. Ready to talk about your Others?"

"Yes. But I have a problem with it."

"What?"

"After what happened in my office I realized there're several of them I can't account for."

"That'll be my next project. After we dispose of this body and equipment."

Two had shut the Simon Other down while Blessed was leaving, before it could leave a legacy of distrust by mentioning its suspicions about the circumstances of Simon Tregesser's death.

# - 83 -

It took four days to clean up the station. Haget put together a long-winded report and entrusted it to the Horigawa Hauler. Then he ordered the Traveler on to M. Shrilica.

"He didn't even mention how well you handled the station, Jo," AnyKaat said.

"He's busy."

"Stop making excuses. You know what he's busy doing? Using that station as a median point to develop a descriptive probability from which to predict which other stations might have been infiltrated."

"It has to be done."

"At Starbase. We got a job. Catch the runaways."

Jo did not want to argue. Especially since AnyKaat was saying what she was thinking.

Haget was having trouble handling an ongoing relationship. He was evading by burying himself in work.

They visited M. Shrilica station. They made the locals

nervous for two days. But the more sure Jo, Degas, and Vadja became that there was something worth finding there, the more perfunctory became Haget's attitude. Fifty-three hours in he decided to go after the phantom phantom.

Five strands anchored on M. Shrilica. One led toward Starbase, one back to the station already policed. Haget presented a search program moving outward from the next anchors of the remaining strands.

"He's screwed up royal," Degas said. "Why doesn't the Deified jump him?"

Jo could not defend Haget.

Vadja said, "Not to worry, Jo. We scavenged every bit of information except what's locked up inside human minds. He'll come back. When he does, we'll know what questions to ask."

Vadja launched a record pod that would lie dormant till a Guardship broke off the Web.

Jo worried for Haget. Everybody thought his decision stupid. The Deified probably did, too. But he exercised no opinion. He never spoke. He just watched. It was easy to forget he was there.

Eight months. The Horigawa Traveler visited a hundred systems, finding no sign of a Lost Child or phantom, catching only an occasional whiff of a methane breather long gone.

The venture was not a waste. It established with certainty a sinister rot spreading throughout that end of Canon space. Which scared Jo.

They had stumbled onto something big.

Haget assembled Jo, Vadja, and the Chief. "This search was a mistake. You've rubbed it in, never saying a word, making me wallow in it, good little soldiers carrying out every order. Waiting for me to run out of ways to save face. All right. I'm out. I fucked up. I made a dumb decision and compounded it by not backing down." He gutted himself.

"Let's get back in stride. Any suggestions?"

Vadja said, "Back to M. Shrilica, sir. Between the phantom's visit and ours, only two ships stopped there. One was *VII Gemina*. Data from the abandoned insystem station suggests the phantom did approach station close enough to have docked briefly."

"So?"

"Six days later Canon's only agent there, tolerated because he was an honorary, was killed in a freak accident. Following his death there was a twenty percent rise in shuttle traffic between Tregesser Xylag and station. That increase was noted by the old station but not by the new. No personnel transfers are noted officially, but new names begin appearing in official reports and old ones are not seen again."

Haget maintained his composure. He dared not ask how long Vadja had possessed that information. Vadja would tell him. It would go on record.

"Lieutenant. Is that the place to start?"

"Yes, sir."

"Smokey. Head for M. Shrilica."


The Traveler broke off the Web.

Seeker's thought was a bellow. *The methane breathers are here!*

The Traveler lurched. Its screen activated without a murmur of command. The ship rotated violently, facing back the way it had come. Its weapons belched CT projectiles. A long black needle of a ship, a type like none Jo had ever seen, became a garden of flame.

Though that ship had been in ambush, it never got off a shot.

Bruised, abraded, bleeding from mouth and nose, Jo picked herself up and blessed WarAvocat for having stuck them with that miserable damned spying Deified.

AnyKaat said, "There are five more ships near station."

Haget snarled, "Let's go get them."

# - 84 -

The siege of the gas giant was frustrating. Outsiders kept arriving and making themselves obnoxious.

The situation grew less irksome after the sixth month.

*XII Fulminata* arrived and assumed picket duty, eating reinforcements as fast as they appeared.

# - 85 -

Hanaver Strate burned with frustration. He was going to spend his entire second term as Dictat in repair dock. It had taken Starbasė only five months to re-create *XII Fulminata*. Meantime, *VII Gemina* languished, always facing an endless series of repairs.

Guardships came and went, mostly to learn what was happening. *V Gallica. VIII Furia. X Gemina.* Most recently, *XII Victrix. III Parthica* and *XXVI Ulpia* had come in in tandem after a twelve-year campaign beyond the Mauvain Rim. Both were on the Web now, carrying news and warnings to Starbase Dengaida.

And *VII Gemina* languished. And the only amusement for an otherwise unemployed WarAvocat was running a minuscule fleet of chartered, armed Horigawas.

The data supplied by Haget's team had been electrifying. The Deified had authorized commissioning five Horigawa privateers. The Horigawas had been seduced by the prospect of claiming prize ships.

Where the hell had Haget gotten to since?

A three-ship section of the Barbican had been converted to support the privateers—and only days after WarAvocat loosed them, their prey had vanished from the Web. Everywhere. Though they left ample evidence that they had been around.

Amazing. All this had been going on for centuries. But even a Guardship could overlook something it was not seeking.

Nor had the mess gone unnoticed. *IV Trajana* had gotten onto it—but no one would listen.

A grim picture. A big one.

He was confident that he had seen but a shadow of a shadow so far.

What the hell had become of Haget?

## - 86 -

"Let's get the bastards!" Haget said. And the Deified spoke for the first time.

"Negative, Colonel. There are five of them. Get onto the Web. You know the destination of the Voyager that visited the system. Follow it up."

Jo let loose a breath she had not known she was holding. An ambush. Maybe special for them. Why? That ship they'd just killed... that had not been built for anything but fighting. No Traveler was designed for combat. In Canon battle was the province of Guardships.

The Traveler clambered onto the Web. Seeker was pleased. They were back on the trail of his Lost Child.

Jo was sure they were off to scare up another dead end.

## - 87 -

Lupo left the update feeling melancholy. Times were quiet. Tregesser Prime, Tregesser Horata, and the Pylon had been tamed. Likewise the Valerena Others and the Directorate, despite the Worgemuth and Maserang murders. The killer's testimony had exonerated Valerena.

Five Valerena Others survived. The most reliable was ensconced atop the Pylon. Valerena herself spent all her time aboard "her" Guardship.

Blessed had taken over his mother's castle and seemed content to bide his time. He amused himself with absurd theme parties and expanding the alien zoo he had begun collecting. He was scraping them out of every DownTown in the Presidency. He had gathered another four Ku, to Lupo's certain knowledge.

Putting together his team. Maybe riding the wave of the future. There were few competent, imaginative, innovative, uncommitted humans around.

The renovation of *VI Adjutrix* was going well. Valerena had the damned thing eating out of her hand.

Week after week, month after month. Routine.

Which left time for the old game of Guardship watching.

Something big was taking shape. Starbase traffic was heavy. To his dismay, *XII Fulminata* had been seen coming out. *VII Gemina*'s survival he could accept. But *XII Fulminata* had been destroyed. He had tapes.

At least three Guardships were operating beyond the Atlantean Rim, for the first time in millennia, in the direction whence Simon had drawn support. Unsettling.

There were reports of armed Travelers roaming the Web in *VII Gemina*'s name. An unprecedented tactic. That word had killed the shadow side of commerce. It spoke of ships destroyed and stations savaged by Guardship soldiers.

What were they after?

Two stepped in. "An armed Traveler broke off the Web a while ago. It's ordered us to turn over the cumulative ship's logs for the Voyager *Marion Tregesser*. It invoked the name of *VII Gemina* as its right. It also wants Blessed, Cable Shike, and Nyo Bofoku."

Lupo let the shock subside. "Why?"

"Call Blessed and ask him."

Turtle shared a barrackslike room with five Ku who had survived the Dire Radiant and the ages since. Such a pathetic few. But there were more out there, and word was spreading.

He did not know if he would become the thing Blessed wanted. He told himself he was going through the motions to protect Midnight and Amber Soul. But, oh, the aching temptation.

As if Amber Soul needed protection from anyone but herself.

It was one incident after another, never her fault because she initiated nothing, always her fault because misunderstanding could be avoided if she would unbend and adapt.

Something dramatic and grim had happened within her. Even he could not reach her anymore.

Turtle led his Ku in ritualized exercises as old as the warrior *ghifu*. An ensign of the Dire Radiant graced one wall. Someone had drawn it in colored chalks. Turtle had not bothered to have the wall cleaned.

Midnight scurried in. "Turtle! You've got to come! It's Amber Soul!"

"What has she done now?"

"She's gone into a trance. She just stands there sending, 'He's here. The Old One is here.' The walls and ceiling have gotten all creepy. I think she's going to have an attack."

"I'll be right back," Turtle told his companions.

Tina looked troubled. "What's the matter?" Blessed asked.

"There's a call. Lupo Provik. I don't like the way he looks. If it was anybody else, I'd say he was scared shitless."

"What does he want?"

"You."

"I can take a hint." He punched the baroque comm that had belonged to his mother. "Lupo. What can I do for you?"

"Tell me what you've been up to. We've got an armed Traveler in, acting for *VII Gemina*. It wants the logs for *Marion Tregesser*. And it wants you, Shike, and Nyo Bofoku. All couched in the usual lyrical 'Do it or your ass is dead' Guardship style."

Blessed said, "Shit!" He looked at Tina, then at Cable, whom she had summoned. They had gone colorless. "Lupo, not on comm. Stall. You want to come out here or you want me to come there?"

"Here. That'll put you closer to the shuttle. Don't forget Bofoku and Shike."

Blessed said, "Shit!" again.

Cable said, "I couldn't have missed anything."

"It couldn't have been much. It took them eight months. Tina, get Nyo. Guys, I want to *hear* brains at work."

"We can throw ourselves on our swords," Cable said.

"It may come to that."

"I wasn't joking."


Sixteen kilometers off station Jo said, "This's the busiest we've hit."

Vadja said, "Home station for House Tregesser. One of the big ten Houses. One of the contrariest. They've never accepted a Canon presence."

Seeker stepped into Jo's head. *The Lost Child. She is here. I sense her pain.*

Vadja exploded, "There's a Guardship here! There's something wrong with it."

"Where?" Haget asked.

Jo told Haget what she had heard from Seeker.

The Deified, reviewing pirated data faster than Vadja, located the Guardship. "*VI Adjutrix*. Has been exploring the Web beyond the Rims for several centuries. Behavior here suggests regression to preadolescence. In past instances, this has resulted from failure in the Core closures, inviting infection. Take me to *VI Adjutrix*. I will enter the system and assume control."

Haget looked bewildered.

Jo said, "We have a mission here, Colonel."

"Where is this Guardship?"

The Deified said, "Having realized it was irresponsible and a hazard, it inserted itself into a slow cometary orbit. It is above the orbit of the innermost gas giant at an elevation of ten degrees, bearing three one three relative. At optimum acceleration it will take—"

Jo closed the Deified out. He had decided to rewrite the mission orders. "Colonel, we have the Lost Child confirmed as on-planet. The Ku and artifact are likely to be there. We don't want to give anyone time to disappear."

Haget fidgeted. The Deified said, "Drop the Lieutenant off."

"By myself?"

Haget calculated. "Take Seeker and three soldiers. And AnyKaat."

"Thanks." Haget missed her sarcasm. She beckoned Seeker and AnyKaat, selected the three reluctant volunteers. In the passageway, she said, "You're right, AnyKaat. He's a total dipshit."

Jo and the soldiers left the Traveler in full battle dress with complete combat kit. She figured the intimidation factor would be all she had going.

Two told Lupo, "They're sending a team of six to make arrests. I assigned them a House shuttle. They've added those creatures of Blessed's to their list."

"Only six? Confident, aren't they. Blessed better have a hell of a story."

"It gets better. The Traveler is headed for *VI Adjutrix*."

Valerena went into a state of nerves the moment she heard about the Traveler. Now it was headed her way. She was near panic.

Tawn was no better. He was sure he would lose her, was sure this meant his end as a corporeal being.

Valerena told him, "We can go hide Outside. They'll never find us there."

A minute later *VI Adjutrix* began moving inward, accelerating as only a Guardship could.

Lupo was aghast.

Blessed was maybe three-quarters through his story and already Provik was ready to shriek in exasperation. Blessed held in his hands the secrets of Starbase and had kept them to himself. Valerena had a Guardship that, with the Ku's knowledge, could have penetrated Starbase.

Imagine that. The invincible fortress in Tregesser hands.

The opportunity of four millennia squandered. Unless he could snatch it back from these *VII Gemina* predators.

Two came in looking grimmer than ever. "Hot news from beyond the sky, Lupo. Valerena blew the Traveler away and headed for the Web."

The news nets got it before it could be squelched. Jo heard it aboard the shuttle. She ignored the material about the Guardship's past misdeeds. One thought rang in her mind: *Rogue!*

She told the others, "When we hit ground, we form a square. AnyKaat, you and Seeker stay in the middle."

"Degas is gone," AnyKaat breathed. "And Era. Like that. It doesn't seem real. Is it real, Jo?"

Jo comforted her the best she could. "Only for a while. You're all on record at Starbase."

"It wouldn't be the same. It would be like having his ghost."

Jo knew that. She had been through it. "There's a way around that, too. If you want it bad enough."

"Here's an idea," Blessed said. "We open a window and see how far we can walk on air."

Lupo muttered, "That might be appropriate. But we have our obligations to the House."

## - 88 -

Once on the Web Valerena began to gain confidence. It was not as bad as it looked. Lupo would see that. He would have everything into an information pattern that would put the House in the clear. Guardships had gone rogue before. And the fleet would not come looking where she was headed. If it did, well, *her* Guardship knew the Outside Web better than they did.

She would find her father's allies, flaunt her prize, get moving on the next phase of the struggle.

First she must score a diplomatic coup to please and placate Lupo. Then she would dig her Voyager out of its rider bay and head for home, to mend fences. Yes. And tell Tawn not to let any creepy-crawlies close while she was away. If they stole his secrets, they might cut House Tregesser out.

She must not lose sight of the fact that they were not human. And that they had their own agenda.

As breakaway neared, Valerena's excitement grew almost

sexually intense. Would she be remembered not only as first to take a Guardship but also as the one who had caused their downfall?

She, Tawn, and all her Others but the one in the Pylon gathered. The most trustworthy of the workers caught aboard were allowed to join them, to witness something never before seen by people not of the Guardship fleet.

The viewscreens went white.

Before they cleared Tawn said, "They're here, Valerena."

A viewscreen cleared, revealed a monstrous shape of gleaming metal. Characters scrambled across the screen, proclaimed XII FULMINATA.

Lupo had destroyed *XII Fulminata!*

They would come within meters of colliding.

Another screen showed a gas giant with schematic orbits labeled XXVIII FRETENSIS and IV TRAJANA. In seconds *VI Adjutrix* would pass *XII Fulminata* and be caught in a pocket from which there could be no escape.

"Hellspinners," she muttered.

As *VI Adjutrix* swept down the flank of *XII Fulminata*, too close for the latter to raise screen, the Hellspinners went mad, devouring that side of *XII Fulminata* two-thirds of the way to its Core, doing it so suddenly and unexpectedly *XII Fulminata* could do no damage in reply.

There was no way to avoid diving into the pocket. Momentum could not be defeated. "We have to turn and get out of here," Valerena cried.

*XII Fulminata* did not like that idea. Already that Guardship was launching secondaries and rotating its good face toward *VI Adjutrix*'s fire.

*VI Adjutrix* launched, too.

Another first. The chance to see a battle to the death between Guardships.

To hell with that noise!

The displays had gone crazy. She could not take in a hundredth of the information. But the tactical situation became obvious quickly. *XII Fulminata* meant to hold *VI Adjutrix* till the other Guardships arrived. *VI Adjutrix* would keep probing the hurt already dealt *XII Fulminata* in hopes of a quick kill or at least of forcing *XII Fulminata* out of position long enough to dash to the Web.

Time flowed glacially, yet swiftly, according to where Valerena concentrated her attention. Came the moment when she knew *XII Fulminata*'s cries had been heard by *XXVIII Fretensis* and *IV Trajana*. Came the moment when their indignant replies returned and it was certain they were accelerating toward the action as violently as their frames could stand. And *XII Fulminata* would not give a millimeter, though its destruction was assured if it did not.

Tawn came out of his fugue momentarily. "I've done the hard part. I've beaten *XII Fulminata*. The other two have nothing left. I can take them, too."

They were all insane. Tawn wanted to fight. Tawn wanted whatever laurels there were from a triumph over three Guardships.

Damn!

"Why are they coming if they can't win?"

"They have to. And what they *know* isn't what they *believe*. My love, I must leave you for a while. I must preside over the execution of *Fulminata*." He smiled. "I never liked *Fulminata*."

Valerena watched briefly. She saw no evidence that *XII Fulminata* was beaten, awaiting a coup de grâce.

She summoned her Others. "This isn't shaping up good. He wants to fight even if he gets the chance to run. Ready the Voyager. I'll join you in a few minutes. We'll pretend to be a rider moving out to attack *XII Fulminata*'s wounded side. When we're over there, we'll run for it. Get going. Casual."

She watched *XXVIII Fretensis* and *IV Trajana* on a split screen. Half showed what actually could be seen, which lagged reality by the time it took light to bridge the intervening gap. The other half presented *Adjutrix*'s estimate of what the Guardships were doing in realtime.

They were coming up on turnover, where they would begin deceleration and launch secondaries.

They began decelerating.

Moments later, observation proved estimation incorrect.

Both had begun deceleration, but *XXVIII Fretensis* was pulling ahead of *IV Trajana*, as though planning a high velocity firing pass.

Something was wrong. Bad wrong.

Valerena began walking, betraying no emotion. But she did not sustain that false calm long. She ran.

Her run ended within sight of the Voyager lock.

Tawn stepped into her path. "Why are you trying to leave me, my love?"

"I don't want to die."

"They are the ones who will be destroyed. Come." He grabbed her wrist. She could not break his hold. "You were going to your homeworld? Yes. I see. We will go there when I finish this. I will need refitting again."

She tried to hang back. He dragged her. "For you I turned upon my own. Though it takes them a thousand centuries, they will hunt me down. They will hate me more than any mortal foe." More gently, "I have abandoned immortality for you, Valerena Tregesser. You will spend the rest of your life with me, be that ten minutes or ten thousand years."

Insane. Raving insane.

He began laughing as they approached the big hall. She had not heard him laugh before. It recalled Simon's crazy laughter. He said, "*Fulminata* is dead. Shells reached the Core."

He dragged her into the hall.

*XII Fulminata* did not look dead on screen. Erratic, yes, but still very much in action.

Did Guardships have reflexes, like killed animals?

*XXVIII Fretensis* and *IV Trajana* were sufficiently close that the split screen went to one view. *XXVIII Fretensis* was not leading the charge now. *IV Trajana* had pulled ahead. Neither should be able to slow enough to engage.

There was something bad wrong.

*IV Trajana* began accelerating.

Valerena saw it coming but did not believe it. Not till Tawn came, eyes moist, sorrowful. "I was wrong, my love. You were right. I'm sorry. Hold me. Please?" And a moment later, "We had so little time."

*IV Trajana* rammed *VI Adjutrix* at sixteen kilometers per second, flinging *VI Adjutrix* back into the remains of *XII Fulminata*. Three Guardships perished in a nova of violence.

So much did they hate and fear one of their own gone rogue.

*XXVIII Fretensis* slid by and clambered onto the Web, headed for Starbase with all the information *VI Adjutrix* had transmitted during its final seconds. *VI Adjutrix* had not turned on the fleet out of hatred and did not leave that final duty unfulfilled, though the fleet was casting it into oblivion.

Not a word about its lover did it betray, though.

Seconds before impact, the Valerena Others gave up waiting and flung their Voyager out of its rider bay. Gas and debris buffeted the vessel, tossed it about. They regained control and limped away, climbed onto the Web only minutes behind *XXVIII Fretensis*.

A debate began. They did not want to die. But their Prime was gone. Their lives might be forfeit. Yet they were Valerena Tregesser genetically and by conditioning. They had her sense of obligation to the House. And the House could not be kept ignorant of this disaster.

# - 89 -

The survivors among those who decided on the gas giant did not understand what had happened. They did see that the siege had lapsed and that three Guardships had perished. There might be fragments that would yield Guardship secrets.

Their world had been devastated. They could not investigate themselves.

They took hold of the Web and sent word vibrating across the strands of that otherspace.

# - 90 -

Lupo glanced from the woman to Two and back. "Lieutenant, you're the most single-minded woman I've encountered since last I saw my mother."

"You've stalled me five days. I'm out of patience. Deliver those people."

It would be amusing if she was not so serious. "And if I can't?"

"I'll take them into custody myself. Using whatever force is necessary."

"Just four of you. I admire your confidence."

"Are you a moron, Provik?"

"I try not to be. Why?"

"There are four of us *here*. There are thirty-two Guardships out there."

"And you wonder why we love you." Lupo glanced at Two. She nodded. She, too, thought the woman serious.

"Lieutenant, I don't have those people. I doubt they exist. You won't believe me, so you're welcome to look to your little stone heart's content. As for Blessed Tregesser, Cable Shike, and Nyo Bofoku, the Chair says go screw yourself. Bring in thirty-two thousand Guardships."

That startled her. Then she shrugged. "They're of no consequence. You have till sixteen hundred hours to produce the aliens and the artifact." She walked out even though she needed a guide to get out of his office alive.

Lupo said, "That woman has balls that drag on the floor."

"She raised the stakes as high as they get."

"If we don't give in, we get wiped out. If we do, we get it anyway."

"So?"

"We've got nothing to lose. They've made their plan?"

"Yes. Shoot out the gravs on the north and east side of the High City so it'll crash into the Pylon. A diversion to cover them heading out. Where they'll go I don't know, and neither do they. The only one of them who gives a damn about staying alive is their alien."

"They're not putting that on? They don't suspect we see and hear everything?"

"They debug. But they don't have the technical sophistication to suspect beat-up, standard bureaucratic wall paint."

"I'll bet they aren't gaming us. Get the family in here. And all the tapes. We've got six hours to fix this."

Jo started awake when AnyKaat touched her shoulder. "What?"

"Your Haget act worked. That Provik's assistant called. They've found our creatures. They'll deliver as ordered, except Amber Soul. They claim she can't be moved. Medical reasons. They're willing to prove it."

"You buy it?"

"Seeker does. He says she's been over the edge for three days. The only way these people would be able to cope would be to confine her. He wants to go."

"All right. Will you take him?"

"I figured it would be me."


"It's in your hands, Kez Maefele," Blessed said. "Make a commitment, one way or another. No more pretense."

He had not been fooling anyone. He glanced at the plain, impassive Mr. Provik, whose plain snare off that tag end had dealt the Guardships their worst hurt of the millennium. A master of improvisation.

Turtle saw the shadowed, twisted shape the thing would have to take. "Innocents will perish."

"Either way. For House Tregesser there's no choice. Who dies and where are all we can influence. We won't accept destruction stoically."

"I understand that. I realize you won't turn Lady Midnight over, especially since these people don't know her. I realize that if I don't agree, you will isolate me and allow one of my more fanatic brethren to assume my identity."

"I'd rather do that anyway. I don't want to risk you."

"I also see that this would not be possible were it not for Amber Soul's crisis."

"We still need to know where you stand."

"Blessed offered me supreme command. That is my price."

Provik exchanged glances with Blessed.

"A genuine commission, Mr. Provik. Not 'Let's tell the alien what he wants to hear.' The alien is a dangerous beast."

"Give him what he wants," Blessed said. "The campaign—if there ever is one—will have to be carried out by Outsiders. They'd respond to a Ku better than they would to us."

Provik nodded. "But I can only speak for me, not for the Chair."

"You can't make Mother do whatever you want? Hell. If she

gets stubborn, tell her I'll guarantee her freedom from worry about keeping the Chair."

Provik frowned.

"I'm eighteen. I'm not ready. I don't even want it right now. So what do I lose?"

"Not much. Kez Maefelc. Where do you stand?"

"Committed till you cause the sword to turn in your hand. You must leave soon. I would like to ride with you and suggest some less bloody way of terminating your risk."

Provik nodded.


Jo did not like it. They were too cooperative. Either they were up to something or they had no idea of the Ku's value. In which case they were wondering why she was so determined to get him.

Damn it all! She was a Soldier. She was not cut out for intrigue.

And that damned Seeker! He had to go complicate it by flat refusing to move his Lost Child for four months. She could not hang around here. WarAvocat needed to know what she had learned.


AnyKaat came in looking exhausted.

Jo said, "They'll be here soon. Anything I ought to know?"

"The Lost Child looked as bad as Seeker said. He said to tell you his people will remain friends of the Guardship fleet."

"What about the other two?"

"They got into a flitter with Provik. They left before I did. The story around the place—you got to see it to believe it, Jo—is that Blessed Tregesser is foaming at the mouth. He's so obsessed with the artifact he would've shot it out with Provik's security people if his mother hadn't intervened."

"What about the Ku?"

"What about him?"

"How did they act about him going?"

"Indifferent. He worked as a bodyguard. Staffers I talked to said the only reason the aliens were around was because they came with the artifact."

It fit. WarAvocat had talked about the danger of the Ku, but it was the artifact he wanted back.

Hoke stuck his head inside. "They're here."

Provik and his assistant were waiting with the Ku and artifact when Jo stepped outside. Provik looked irked. Always before he had been the soul of neutrality, if somewhat sarcastic. "Delivery as ordered," he said. "Two free citizens of Canon. And may I express the Chair's wish that you not grace Tregesser Prime with the honor of your presence any longer?" He climbed into his vehicle.

Jo glared, exasperated.

Provik's companion said, "Lupo had orders to say that. I have mine to extend his apologies, insincere as they are."

Don't let them bait you. "Apologies accepted."

"One thing. I know you people don't inconvenience yourselves with the forms and practices of the law, but to threaten mayhem in order to compel us to permit the abduction of a halfwit pleasure artifact and a senile alien makes no sense. What the hell are you doing?"

Jo glared. The woman was not intimidated. She smiled a thin smile. Jo said, "I am a Soldier." If she did not understand that, tough. "You two. Come with me." She beckoned the artifact and Ku.

Inside, AnyKaat said, "They don't like us much, do they?"

Jo shrugged.

"What now?"

"Now we find out if they're going to let us go." And if WarAvocat's emergency credit package was any good. She went to the comm and tried to make shuttle reservations. After several frustrating minutes she said, "AnyKaat, you try this. I'm either being jacked around or I don't know what I'm doing."'

"Passage for seven, first available?"

"Yes."

AnyKaat came up with the same thing she had.

"They're jacking us around."

A woman came on. "Are you having difficulty with your booking, ma'am?"

"Yes," AnyKaat said. She explained what she wanted. "The system keeps pushing us back to one A.M. tomorrow."

The young woman fiddled. "That's correct. Nothing available sooner. Is it imperative you lift earlier?"

"Yes!" Jo snapped.

The woman fiddled, saying parties on a tight schedule should make return arrangements before leaving station. "I can get everyone off the ground by nine tonight if I distribute you..."

"We go together," Jo said.

"Shall I transfer you to our charter department?"

"I want you—"

"Jo!" AnyKaat turned from the screen. "Some problems can't be solved your way."

The woman asked, "Which Traveler are you booked out on? It might delay departure."

She became distinctly cool when she learned there was no such booking. AnyKaat covered the sound pickup. "We wouldn't be safer on station than here, Jo."

"Are they messing with us?"

"You're not used to commercial travel."

"You deal with it."

"Do you want the charter?"

"If there's this much trouble getting off the ground, you'd better figure out what we have to do to get off station before anything else. Next month might be soon enough to go up."

AnyKaat thanked the woman, went to work trying to find passage to the Barbican. "Jo, here's five possibles the next five days. No direct passage. Not unusual. We'll have to change ships at least twice. Three times by the fastest combination."

Jo looked it over. The fastest way was the most convenient in relation to shuttle availability. "Book it."

"You realize there's no guarantee we'll get anything but lounge space on those next three ships? They can't know we're coming till we get there."

"I learned that much on the Cholot Traveler." She checked her prizes. The Ku watched her impassively. The artifact huddled behind him. The Ku was a mean-looking bastard. "Next time you run off, WarAvocat can find you himself."

The Ku seemed amused. "He will, I'm sure."

## - 91 -

Lupo grinned as the information came in. "We've got them. And all the investigators in the universe won't find a thing because we haven't done a thing. Lupo, sometimes you're so clever you scare yourself."

"Don't crow yet," Two cautioned. "That woman may not understand the real universe, and she may not be a genius, but she's stubborn. Don't underestimate her."

"I won't. Four. What were you so anxious to say a minute ago?"

"Valerena's Voyager broke off the Web. She wants to see you up there. She wouldn't say why. She sounded scared. Station says she hasn't asked for docking."

"Odd. Tell her I'll be up soon. We have to go, anyway. See if Blessed has his people ready."

"They're headed for the port. Ours are, too. We can lift whenever *you* get there."

One of the Valerena Others met Lupo at the lock. She led him to the operating bridge. Three more Valerenas there, exhausted from working ship. But no Valerena Prime. "What's going on?"

"Valerena is dead. We've brought back information on the circumstances. Our duty to the House. But we won't dock without assurances for our safety."

"I couldn't get rid of you if I wanted. The situation here requires a Valerena in charge. Blessed says he won't take over before his thirty-eighth birthday. Guarantee me you won't try something like the Simon Other did and you've got twenty years sure. Your natural lives if you behave."

Lupo Provik's word was good.

"Let me see what you've got."

What Valerena had obtained impetuously she had squandered. That was a shot to the heart. That Guardship had become the core of his vision of the future.

"Come see me when you get down. We'll work out details. Right now I'm running an operation and can't take time. Don't tell *anyone* about this."

Lupo contacted One during the crossing to station, prepared him for the Valerenas and their bad news.

Why go on? Nothing ever worked out.

## - 92 -

The gates of the repair bay unfolded. "At last," WarAvocat murmured. On the track of the villains at last.

He thought of the artifact. She haunted him even now. First stop, M. Shrilica. Should have been something more from Haget. Long since.

A Guardship broke off the Web. "WarAvocat. Signals from *XXVIII Fretensis*."

"Here it comes," he murmured. The end of a quiet passage. Before it began.

The air behind his shoulder whispered. Rogue. *VI Adjutrix.* *IV Trajana* and *XII Fulminata*—again!—accepting destruction in order to take out the rogue and ensure *XXVIII Fretensis*'s escape into Canon space. *VI Adjutrix*'s final contrite act.

OpsAvocat asked if there would be a change in plans.

Of course. "After M. Shrilica, we're headed Outside. There were riders that couldn't be recovered." He began reviewing the data in detail.


M. Shrilica's outworks had been destroyed. Only gutted shells of stations remained, and an old capsule from Haget's Traveler that was useless. And, near breakaway point, there was the hulk of a ship unlike anything seen before.

It took four days to extract a coherent story from survivors in Tregesser Xylag.

Five ships had come. They had lain in wait for months. Someone had come, finally, had blown one of them away, and had fled before the others could close in. The survivors had destroyed the stations and gone in pursuit.

"Haget," WarAvocat told the Deified. "Who else would they be gunning for? He left no message capsule. Or it was destroyed. I have no idea why he didn't run to the Barbican."

The Deified Thalygos Mundt suggested, "Maybe they didn't let him."

"Perhaps. His first capsule is useless, too."

"And the hulk?"

They knew. But they wanted to make him tell it. "The type hasn't been seen before. The design is strictly combat. It contained no technical surprises except a geometric inertial system the equal of ours."

"And the creatures who operated it?"

They did want him to state the impossible before the crew.

"They appear to be of human stock. With differences science staff say can be explained by isolation from the main gene pool for fourteen to twenty thousand years."

They wanted crew to know, but they did not make him remind them that known history predated Canon's founding only a few thousand years.

The Deified Ansehl Ronygos asked, "Explain your plan of campaign."

"First, D. Zimplica to inform Presidency General Secretariat. Then Outside."

WarAvocat ran the Web hard, twice forcing commercial carriers off into starspace. The pause at the Presidency capital system, D. Zimplica, lasted ten minutes. Then on to the Outside system where three Guardships had died.

He broke away in a magnum launch, into a swarm of ships trying to mine the wreckage. There were no surviving riderships.

It took eighteen hours to cleanse the system. Nothing escaped. He gave the Twist Masters ten hours to obliterate the remains of three Guardships. Then he proceeded to the next system in the empire of the methane breathers.

WarAvocat foresaw a six-year campaign softening defenses for Guardships to follow.

Tawn was seen twice after the fighting. He went but she was not there when he arrived.

# - 93 -

Lupo felt good going into D. Zimplica aboard the Raintree Hauler *Indefatigable*. He had shifted operatives like game pieces. He had collected on favors done and had assumed a few debts. The operation was set so it could be carried out without any anomaly an investigator could hook onto.

There would be no ship in or out that was not regularly scheduled. None would have any known connection with House Tregesser. If it worked, nothing would happen to hint that the Lieutenant's party had done anything but change ships.

He would arrive two days before they did. He would have time to scout. And the two days of their layover to do the job.

He asked Two, "What can go wrong?" She had just walked in looking like something had.

"A Guardship just broke off the Web. *VII Gemina*. Mr. Stefens ought to make an appearance on the bridge."

G. Stefens was the Hauler's passenger of record. Stefens was a high official of House Raintree.

The Chief said, "Ah, Mr. Stefens. We'll dock shortly. Have you visited Belladonna before?"

"Yes." D. Zimplica 3, Belladonna, was a Freeheld World, owing allegiance to no House, as well as the seat of Sixth Presidency General Secretariat. "It's probably the most attractive world in the sector. It's a shame it's already claimed."

"Yes. I suppose you're interested in the Guardship."

"Yes."

"It's gone. Stayed only ten minutes. Squirted something at the Secretariat, then left."

"Thank you." That was nice. That was beautiful. But it did not drain the water out of his legs. What message had it sent?

Lupo knew within the hour. The Secretariat had posted it to every ship. A Guardship fleet directive. An instant law.

Every ship docking at every station was to have its documentation examined. Any vessel making a nonscheduled arrival was to be searched and all persons aboard required to furnish documentation. Any creature of the description... (methane breathing colonial intelligence that Lupo recognized)... was to be destroyed upon discovery, without exception. Non-Canon ships barred from Canon space. Vessels without license to be destroyed if they refused internment. Severe restrictions on trade beyond the Atlantean Rim. *Severe* penalties for noncompliance.

"A fun bunch, our protectors," Lupo observed. Then he scanned the unusual justificatory appendix. Piracy. Smuggling. Espionage. Mass murder. Attacks upon Guardships. Attacks upon Canon star systems....

Lupo was not given to anger. He was so angry now he could do nothing but mutter "M. Shrilica" and nurture fantasies of revenge.

There was nothing he could do, of course. When he calmed down, he observed, "We're in trouble, Two. We have no leverage on those Outside things. But they know who we are. They can use that against us. We've lost the initiative."

"We still have the Ku."

Jo looked up at AnyKaat. "What did they say?"

"No."

"Damn!"

"They aren't picking on us, Jo. It's the way things are done. You don't let people hang around after you've gotten them where they're going. You have to get ready for the next bunch. And the way things are, you make a fuss and we're liable to spend a month in STASIS detention explaining."

"What?"

"This." Jo accepted something official. "*VII Gemina* was here day before yesterday. Just long enough to send that."

Jo read while her heart sank. " Missed them that close?" And, "They wouldn't tell it all here. Things must be bad."

"That's what I thought. That's what people on station think. So let's try to do things like everybody else and not get burned."

"You're right." She felt empty. Missed *VII Gemina* by a hair.

"I've reserved space in a hostel near our departure dock-head."

"What about our connection?"

"In dock, plenty of room, and it'll leave on schedule."

"I don't suppose they'd let us board early?"

"Jo, a station needs what travelers spend at the concessions to survive."

Jo tapped the directive. "Know what this means? WarAvocat wrote us off. Presumed dead."

The Lieutenant said, "Don't think about making a break, Ku. You wouldn't last even if I didn't kill you."

Turtle paid no attention. That was nervous talk. She was more an alien here than he was. He watched the crowd for a sign the operation was on. Provik could have overestimated his ability to pull it together.

He caught a passing smile, a man of Blessed's.

Two said, "They've taken a quad and a triple on separate levels. The women, the Ku, and the artifact are in the quad. The soldiers are in the triple."

"Let's work on the soldiers first. The Ku can handle the women if he has to."

Hoke slipped out early, to try his luck in the social whirl of the station. It was his lucky day. He ran into a woman who started panting the moment she saw him. But after the preliminaries he had no place to take her. So he followed her back to the Hauler where she crewed.

Hoke's comrades gutted it out for six hours before deciding

they had to do something.

They got lucky. Asking around, they ran into two crewmen off a Hauler who recalled Hoke on account of he had gone off with a woman from their ship. They were amused. One said, "She's probably eaten him alive by now."

The other snickered. "Pauli uses them up."

"She do keep them long off watches from getting boring."

"Speaking of which, old buddy, it's about time."

"Yeah. We got to head out. You guys want to walk down and see if that's where she took your pal?"

The soldiers went. Small talk kept them unsuspicious. At the docking bay one asked the purser, "Fredo, Pauli bring a guy home with her?"

"Yeah. Must be something. She's had him in there four hours and he ain't yelled for help yet."

"He's a pal of these guys and he's going to miss movement if they don't latch onto him. All right if they go drag him out?"

"Don't let the Chief see you."

"We got him cornered now. Come on, guys."

One of the soldiers was reluctant. The other muttered about the time. They went aboard.

Three men resembling the soldiers left the Hauler. They called one another by name. Two looked sour. The happy one smiled vaguely but talked enthusiastically about Pauli.

There really was a Pauli. And she was a minor legend.

Use reality, Provik said. Don't abuse it.

Jo fidgeted. When she could not hold it anymore, she said, "Hoke's late. Call them, AnyKaat."

"Ten minutes, Jo."

"Guardship soldiers aren't late. They're especially not late when they're supposed to relieve their commanding officer."

"No answer, Jo."

"I'll have his balls."

"What?"

"Want to know what happened? Hoke snuck out looking for some action. Jug and Shaigon got worried and went after him. Damnfools probably got lost." Jo flipped her passcard for their room. "Take a look. I don't want to be wrong. If they're not there, check around. But don't be gone too long."

"You be all right?"

"They're asleep. And I'll keep a gun in my hand."

Twelve minutes later there was a tentative tap at the door. "What?" Jo snapped.

Muffled, nervous, "Hoke, ma'am."

Jo headed for the door. "The famous eunuch to be."

Lupo hugged Two when they brought the Lieutenant aboard. "We did it!"

Jo sat on a rough Hauler bunk, back against the bulkhead, trying to understand. The Ku had been sound asleep. But when the door opened, he had plucked the weapon out of her hand.

The door there opened. A man stepped inside.

Lupo Provik!

"Good evening, Lieutenant."

"You can't get away with this."

"I already have. I'm tempted to let the people who replaced you go on to Starbase."

"Replaced?"

"Tomorrow the Merod Traveler *Fanta Palonz* takes on passengers. Seven answering the descriptions of your party, with proper documentation, will board. They will disappear at D. Chuchainica 3B."

Jo was scared like she had not been scared for a long time. "Why tell me?" The fear stemmed less from her circumstances than from recognition of the ruthless efficiency with which they had been engineered. In that moment she knew who had engineered the ambush in the end space.

"I want you to understand the full compass of your predicament, Lieutenant."

"I'm dead."

"No. This has been a bloodless operation. My associate Kez Maefele has scruples. He'd like it kept bloodless. His solution appeals to the poet and gambler in me."

She refused to ask.

"He wants to take your arms, credit, and documentation and dump you in a DownTown on a world pacified by *VII Gemina*. He thinks someone from a Guardship ought to experience that life. He says that's more just than spacing you."

"It's murder all the same."

"No. Real murder would be to eject you with the trash while we're running the Web. Which is your other option."

"You're a real smooth talker, aren't you?"

"I try. The point is, you and your people can get out alive. If you don't try to be heroes. I try to keep the Ku happy. No. Don't consider it. I'm a killer."

Jo relaxed. If he read her that easily, he might be as good as he thought. "You do what you want to do. But if you turn me loose, I'll find you again."

"That's the spirit. Keep it up. You might pull it off." He left Jo wondering what kind of man he was.

# - 94 -

It took Turtle four months to weave the cautious itinerary that let him deliver the Guardship soldiers. The fleet directive was no trouble. The soldiers themselves were. Provik's preferred solution looked much better toward the end.

Getting them through station was easier than he anticipated. Almost two years had passed since the Concord nonsense, but disorganization persisted for lack of qualified survivors.

Nothing had been done to clear the wreckage of Merod Schene. The surface survivors still lived in camps set up by *VII Gemina*. House Merod had evacuated their favorites and then downscaled their interest. The left behind could do as they pleased.

Seeds of a new society, scattered on soil fertilized by blood. Turtle almost wished he could stay to watch its evolution.

The worst of the survivors, the weird and deadly and crazy, lived in the ruins still and favored the night.

Turtle explained that to the Lieutenant. "You find the Immunes. Mention me. Line up with them. Show the world how mean you are. Don't tell anybody you were Guardship soldiers. Ever. Stick together. You and the other woman are reasonably attractive. That will cause problems. Different rules obtain here."

"Why are you doing this?"

"Repaying a debt you would have to be Ku to understand." He offered her a plastic box. "The interest on that debt. Two handguns. Two rechargeable charge packs. Treasures greater than serviceable women. Use them sparingly and guard them well. Goodbye, Lieutenant."

"Not goodbye, Ku. Till we meet again."

"Don't, Lieutenant. I will kill you the next time." Turtle left them. He felt sad. They were all on the skids to Hell.

It took him two months to reach Tregesser Prime because of the dislocations caused by "the War."

The most feared woman on V. Rothica 4 joined the two most

feared men. "It was them."

Cable Shike snapped, "About damned time. I'm sick of this hole." He had not wanted to come. Blessed had insisted.

Four and Five were sick of Merod Schene, too.

Shike said, "Let's whack them while they're dizzy and get out."

The letter of Lupo Provik's word was good. Provik had given the Ku what he asked. But there had been no promise not to tie up loose ends after the five reached Merod Schene.

Five said, "Guess I'd better get Crash."

"He won't play it straight," Shike said. "He'll give you that frog grin and say he'll go with the job, but he'll only go till he scrubs the three men. No way is he going to spiff those women."

Crash Gutsyke was a second-rate gang boss. He had ambitions.

Five said, "I know the type. Thinks he'll claim his pay, drill you and me, then expand his harem by one more." Five laughed.

Even Four was amused.

Just by moving in a careful formation, they drew attention. The bold came to look. The timid moved away. Jo tried to swallow her contempt and could not. Never had she seen such scum. Like the dregs of Canon had been dumped here.

Their search for shelter took them ever nearer the ruins.

At first she was unsure they were being stalked. But the camp became less crowded toward the city. It became obvious. There were ten of them, at least. She passed the word. Everyone had noticed.

She had given her weapon to Hoke though the Ku had meant them for her and AnyKaat. Hoke was an irresponsible dickhead, but he had been regimental small-arms champ and under fire was liquid helium.

Three very large men stepped out to block the lane ahead. Others began closing in, hauling out knives and swords.

"Kill," Jo said.

Jug had point. He kicked the middle blocker in the nose, driving the bone back into whatever the man used for brains. Hoke shot another and turned, began shooting to the left. AnyKaat was a beat late but started shooting to the right.

Jug broke the neck of the last blocker and looked around for another victim. He lurched. Fire and gore erupted from his back.

Hoke had killed another six men when it happened to him.

Jo dived for his weapon. She came up with it, looked around, saw the survivors in flight, shot two, saw Shaigon's head explode.

AnyKaat, using both hands to steady her aim, squeezed off a shot at three people on a rusty knee of the ruined city. One pitched backward. "Shit. I hit the wrong one."

Jo got behind Hoke's body. "Get down!"

AnyKaat zigzagged toward the ruins.

Jo tried to give covering fire. Twice Hoke's body jerked and belched fire and blood.

Jo got three more shots before her charge pack went. Only the last did any good. Like AnyKaat, she missed the gunner and hit someone else.

She jumped up and zigzagged after AnyKaat, making sudden pauses to snatch weapons from the dead. The air blistered around her, too close to believe anyone could shoot that straight and guess her next move that well. Then the gunner decided to worry about AnyKaat.

Jo found AnyKaat in the shade of a slab of rusty iron. She was seated on rubble. Her right calf was bloody.

"Bad?"

"Shrapnel. Just a little chunk taken out. Direct hit would

have taken it off. I won't be dancing for a while. One of those people was Cable Shike. Blessed Tregesser's bodyguard."

"We know where we stand, then." She popped the charge pack out of her weapon, placed it in sunlight. "That might pick up enough power for one or two shots before dark. Give me yours."

AnyKaat's weapon had power enough for three more shots. Just enough. "Somebody comes along, you don't act like that won't work. Point it at them and make them get down on their belly. Then stick them with this." She gave AnyKaat the longest blade she had collected. "Don't hesitate. We got no friends around here."

"What about the guys, Jo?"

"They're dead."

"Where you going?"

"In there. I'll be back."


The shadows were taking control of the ruins when Crash Gutsyke lumped his froggish shape into sight.

Shike and Five had dressed their wounds but moved slowly. Cable said, "Here comes Fuckup Charlie."

Five said, "That was some class you showed us out there, Crash."

Gutsyke's third of a meter of tongue lashed the air. "You never told me they had guns."

"We didn't know. I *did* tell you they were pros and they wouldn't be easy. From what I saw they could have taken you apart without the guns."

Gutsyke's tongue hit the air again. "About them guns you was going to pay us off with..."

"You didn't do the job. We took the three that are gone. There are two more out there."

"Give me them guns and we'll finish it."

"No. Finish it, you'll get the guns."

Gutsyke's tongue came out again. He was scared. "I had sixteen men this morning. Now I got three counting me. Word gets around, I'm a dead man. I got enemies."

"We all have enemies. You want the equalizer, take out those women."

Gutsyke tongued the air steadily.

Four moved slowly in the darkness, concentrating on the men Crash had brought to back his play. The rearguard had moved up a little but was not close enough to be a factor. The other two...

Gutsyke said, "You don't hand them over now, I'll take them."

Five chuckled. "You were right, Crash. You're a dead man."

Four took the backing pair with a burst, then put one into Gutsyke's spine...

... as two bolts ripped out of the darkness, striking Shike and Five.

Shit! That damned Lieutenant.

The third bolt hit her as she brought her weapon around. It was maybe half power. It hurt like hell but it did not put her down. She let the fucker have all thirty-eight rounds left in the hairsplitter.

# - 95 -

Five months after Lieutenant Klass left, Seeker was satisfied that his charge could travel. He approached Blessed Tregesser uncertainly, fearing he could not make his need understood, fearing it would be denied.

The humans surprised him. They spared one of their ships to take him to another system, where they chartered a Volgodon Navigation Traveler for a direct passage to M.

Meddinia. They even sent along people to ease friction with the authorities.

The Volgodon Traveler reached M. Meddinia without incident. The old station was almost completely automated, which made for slow handling of what little traffic there was. Sixteen hours passed before Seeker and Amber Soul began their descent to the homeworld she did not remember. Their station's one shuttle was ancient and quirky and slow, but utterly dependable.

The companions sent by House Tregesser were not themselves strictly human. They were products of Lupo Provik's secret lab, expendable artifact operatives. A condition of the Traveler's charter required it to stay at station till it verified the arrival on-planet of its passengers.

As the shuttle entered atmosphere the station's fusion plant went berserk. Its Q blew. The electromagnetic pulse triggered a device that set off a similar disaster in the Traveler's power plant.

That double blast vaporized the Traveler and seventy percent of the station.

Lupo Provik had kept his word—while making sure an alien who knew too much would not get back into circulation.

## - 96 -

Six months after *VII Gemina*'s fleet directive, twelve Guard-ships were involved, six beyond the Rim. At Starbase Tulsa new construction proceeded at capacity, concentrating on fighters and riders.

The methane breathers had not anticipated the utter ferocity of the onslaught, nor the suddenness with which it would come. In the seventh month they regained their balance enough to launch a limited counterstrike.

Six battle groups penetrated Canon space. Four thousand years of Outsider incursions made them predictable. The fleet was ready.

A group headed for Starbase found a Guardship waiting off the Barbican, supported by a quadruple complement of secondaries.

A group for D. Zimplica broke off the Web into a tunnel of death maintained by secondaries ferried in earlier.

Of the six groups only one succeeded. Only a few ships survived to scurry home.

# - 97 -

Jo crawled out of the ruins the next morning, squandering her reserves in order to reach AnyKaat before she passed out again.

She made it.

"What the hell happened, Jo? You're all torn to shit."

"Ricochets. She never hit me solid."

"Could have fooled me. She? Who?"

"Provik's girlfriend. They were the other two. I got them all. We're safe."

AnyKaat laughed sickly. "Right. Two women shot to hell in a place where women are bitches and bitches are commercial property."

Jo did not argue. "Can you walk? They had a lot of good stuff. If we don't grab it, somebody else will. And maybe use it on us."

"I'll manage."

She did. The stuff was there. But what had become of the bodies?

# - 98 -

When they brought Four in, she still had not recovered physically or mentally. The family, now including Seven, Eight, Nine, and Ten, and a new Three, took her information in an update and tried to remove her pain.

Afterward, Two told Lupo, "Blessed will be upset about Shike getting shot up."

"That was the risk he took, sending him out. But he'll patch up. I've seen Troqwai fix worse."

"You want to send someone to see if that AnyKaat woman survived?"

"No. If she did, she won't last. What we need to worry about is Four's trauma."

Two winced. No one would say it, or even wanted to think it, but the family had to decide if Four had been too badly damaged to be taken back. The meld had been agony. Four was convinced her ineptitude had killed Three and Five.

Two said, "It would have to be unanimous."

However much it might hurt, Lupo could not imagine his family being less than unanimous about anything.

# - 99 -

WarAvocat felt old and tired. Was it time to step down?

*VII Gemina* had fortress-busting down to a mechanical routine. But each new system threw up a more hysterical defense. Nowadays he needed another two Guardships backing him.

He stared at a viewscreen showing a fortress he meant to kill. It was the biggest yet. And only one of five. The system was a sector capital.

*VII Gemina* came to rest with respect to its target. "Project the tube," War-Avocat directed.

Screen generators strained to produce a shaped field. Twelve modified riders moved into the expanding bubble, feeding it with their own shaped-shield generators till it expanded into a tunnel with its small end firmly against the fortress's screen.

"Loose the Hellspinners."

Hellspinners preferred the path of least resistance.

The Twist Masters cut loose. Hellspinners tumbled down the funnel and collided with the enemy screen. They gnawed through. After the Hellspinners splattered the fortress for several minutes WarAvocat introduced a pulse into their flow. Axial cannon CT shells flew. After those opened a pathway, thermonuclears followed, killing the fortress's shield.

WarAvocat moved to the next fortress. The other Guardships finished the first with their Hellspinners.

Systematic. Routine. Too much time left to think about the chain of chance that had brought *VII Gemina* here, point ship in a war no one understood but that looked likely to persist for years. *VI Adjutrix*'s data had been incomplete.

There were a hundred gas giants, as reported, but *VI Adjutrix* had failed to mention the other species the colonial creatures dominated.

The Guardships focused on the methane breathers, but the other side's dying was done by subject species. WarAvocat hoped that with continued fleet successes the subject races would shift allegiances.

All this because *VII Gemina* had stumbled over a krekelen shapechanger.

WarAvocat smiled gently. Some House had set that up hoping to grab a Guardship. They had enlisted Outside help without realizing what they were getting. They would have lost *VII Gemina* instantly had they taken it.

The artifact crossed his thoughts. What had become of her? Had Haget caught the Ku? The Ku haunted him.

The new Haget was a staff officer with one of the ridership squadrons. Klass was in the pits, an apprentice Twist Master. The civilians were in storage.

Space behind *VII Gemina* turned purplish. The barrage pounding the fortress had sparked a self-sustaining Hellspinner reaction.

So damned tired. He really should consider stepping down.

## - 100 -

Lupo asked, "Are you stupid, Szydlow?"

The Canon legate dropped the hand he had begun to extend.

"Five months ago we told you you would be given dockage only if you invoked Article Ninety-One. You did. But Ninety-One wasn't written to support the ambitions of itinerant bureaucrats. We've soaked you the limit for dockage and service fees, and we've refused you exit from your Traveler. No one will take your calls."

Szydlow sputtered.

"Don't sit down. I didn't invite you. We haven't been subtle. We don't want what you're selling. Go away. Stop taking up dock space. Your credentials have been rejected. You have no immunity. If I offed you, the Chair would pardon me." Lupo produced a hairsplitter. "Whump. The asshole quotient of the universe drops a point. Goodbye, Szydlow."

"I shouldn't have threatened him. I don't let people provoke me."

The Valerena said, "You don't scare his kind with threats. You frame them for child molesting. Bad press deflects career trajectories and destroys retirement points."

"Hoo! Should have thought of that. Frame him, try him,

give him twenty years on a labor gang. I'll do it if he makes a pest of himself."

A year fled. Canon legate Szydlow returned to Capitola Primagenia. An expected tide of commerce raiders came and receded. The War had no impact on the lives of most people and little upon commerce. House Tregesser noticed it because Provik spent fortunes keeping track.

He suspected the Guardship fleet had gotten bogged down. The Ku agreed. Big doings near Starbase suggested the deadlock would be broken soon.

Then three Outsider humans walked into Lupo's office.

He had expected that since *VII Gemina* issued its fleet directive.

He gathered the usual group. Blessed brought a recovered Cable Shike and had his new Other listen in.

Two of the Outsiders were lean, slight, with narrow skulls. Their features were sharp. They were dusky. Their hair was a glossy black. They wore it identically. Their eyes were a startling blue. They wore black. They seemed emotionless. Lupo guessed them to be in their thirties.

The third man, twenty years older, shared their height, hair color, and eyes, but weighed more. His clothing was stark but would have drawn second glances nowhere in Canon.

Two announced him as "Gif the Hand, Voice Appointive to the Godspeakers of the Shadowed Way, Master of a Hundred Torches." When Lupo lifted an eyebrow, she added, "Don't ask me. The clown said to introduce him that way."

Gif the Et Cetera snapped, "You're an arrogant and obstreperous breed." His speech had an odd cadence. "The Godspeakers directed that you be disabused of false notions of who is master."

Those two men were fast.

Two shot one through the arm. The Ku caught the other by

the back of the neck, lifted him overhead. Cable Shike placed the snout of a hairsplitter under Gif's chin. Two's man looked more astonished than hurt. She gestured for him to get down on his face. He refused.

She blew his brains out.

Lupo said, "Mind telling me what other lessons you have, Gif?"

Gif looked at the corpse. "That's impossible."

"If you say so. So. The Guardships are kicking butt and they're getting desperate out Yon. They sneaked you in to twist our arms."

"Grace of the Godspeakers, the Guardships have been stopped. The counterattack will begin soon."

"The Godspeakers those things that look like a puddle of raw guts?"

"Soon you will speak of them in pure terror."

"I doubt it. Your bosses smell the fleet getting ready for the killing push, which is why you're here. But House Tregesser won't go down with you."

"You have no choice. There's your role in the ambush of three Guardships."

"Right. And if we help we'll harvest wonderful rewards."

"Yes."

"Liar. Gif, your side won't win. Unless I let it."

Gif gave him a bug-eyed look.

"The Guardships are going to squish those gut piles till there aren't any left. Then they'll stomp whoever worked for them. You ought to be trying to cut a deal with the fleet."

"You are an enemy of the Guardships."

"Sure. And before that I'm an agent of House Tregesser. You're only offering a chance to trade an unpleasant status for something worse. Why do you think we'd be willing? Two, take friend Gif to Research. Send somebody to clean up."

Two left. The Valerena said, "You're sure about this?"

"It was a high-risk mission for them. So on the record they didn't get through. Right? It'll be months before they're sure the mission failed."

Events Outside prevented the appearance of another mission for a year and a month. The second followed the routine of the first. Tregesser security invaded the Hauler that brought the envoys. A methane breather was found in what should have been a refrigerated hold. They killed it. There were witnesses. The incident had to be reported.

The raids started a month later. Every Tregesser system suffered at least one. A new level of pressure. None of the raids did serious damage. The Ku had had two years to prepare.

# - 101 -

VII   *Gemina* took no part in the operation that broke the deadlock. That was the greatest strike ever launched. Ten Guardships assailed the world where the methane breathers had evolved.

They thought highly of it. They shielded it with an unimaginable array of war machines. It took the Guardships six months to clear those and sterilize the planet.

Till then no Guardship had been lost. In that struggle seven perished.

In the end, Guardship soldiers stormed and captured a huge orbital fortress. They degraded its orbit. Four Guardships hammered it with Hellspinners till a self-sustaining reaction started. They let it go down to start a world afire.

There were no offers of surrender, no pleas for an armistice. Plainly, the struggle would go on for years.

## - 102 -

Jo and AnyKaat made themselves Immunes, of sorts, by virtue of their weapons and willingness to use them. But even after two years they dared not let one another out of sight.

Jo felt tired, beaten down. In the beginning they had wanted to acquire wealth enough to get off and buy passage to P. Jaksonica, where AnyKaat could lever them back into the real universe. That had cracked up on the realities of Merod Schene. They had lowered their aim again and again. Now when the rare shuttle landed, they went out to see if they could get a message to AnyKaat's mother.

Jo's spirits were at low ebb. And for months she had been having nightmares about Seeker—or something alien—invading her mind whenever she slept.

She was afraid she was cracking.

## - 103 -

It took Seeker a long time with Amber Soul to grasp the meaning of his experiences among the humans. And even she, who had been so long among them that she could not now fit among her own, did not comprehend them well.

They rewrote the faces of worlds.

They were an abomination in the eye of the universe, yet they had brought to this sand grain something unknown before their advent, the unyielding rule of law.

Their law did not always make sense. It was skewed to the advantage of the few. But it was as inflexible and predictable as any natural law and could no more be bent or twisted.

In their way, the humans were into the afternoon of their time, waiting for the twilight, but they had created this one great thing, this bubble of order and peace that hung like a jewel upon the tumultuous Web. With Chaos's own sword they chastised it, striking off its heads one by one, each time wresting from Chaos another shadow-thin slice of its dreadful empire.

There was a darkness upon the Web. It was a shadow of horror that left the strands thrumming with pain. It was an evil risen from the heart of Chaos to challenge the march of law. There was grave concern among the elders. They petitioned Seeker to burden himself with separation again.

Strange, strange Amber Soul begged to share his quest.

Lieutenant Klass had become like one of the Lost Children, abandoned somewhere on the vastness of the Web, without lightmarks to sign the way to her. Could he find her while it mattered? The thread they had spun between them had been slender.

His people activated the signal that would alert a visitor to the system that there were passengers to collect.

## - 104 -

Turtle came and went as he pleased. He was a trusted agent of the House creating a planetary defense.

Like it or not, he was a public figure and object of debate. He headed a band of aliens and artifacts numbering a hundred. Their presence in positions of trust caused grumbling.

The Directors had a grudge. The Chair no longer consulted them in any but the most mundane business. They knew nothing of its secret agendas. But they did know snakes were stirring. The Ku's gang and Provik's security forces were everywhere. Provik's monetary demands gnawed the belly out of the House's profitability.

Turtle was more content than he had been since leading the Dire Radiant. His moral cavils bent easily in the wind of a need to do what he had been fashioned to do.

The legacies of Valerena Tregesser included the Isle of Ise, for which Blessed had no time or love. That had become Turtle's place. There he heard a thousand echoes of childhood. He went there with Midnight, his frequent companion lately. Blessed was trying to fulfill an obligation by providing himself with an heir.

"I spent my first dozen years in a place like this," Turtle told Midnight. They had climbed to the pinnacle of a basaltic eminence hanging a hundred meters above a lapis lazuli sea. Below, a band of ivory sand sketched the limits of the sea. The sand had been imported for Valerena.

Midnight was in a bleak mood. Talking about his past usually distracted her. This time it did not.

This was not the Lady Midnight, righteous and frightened, who had come to Tregesser Prime. This was a Midnight without reservations, a Midnight who had been with one man too long. Blessed could do no wrong. Separation became wrenching agony.

Most men found such devotion suffocating. Midnight carried the scars to prove it. But Blessed came close to reciprocating. Flighty and flutter-brained as she was, she was his rock.

"She's going to take him away, Turtle. I know it."

The ultimate fester, never to be healed: She could not compete with a true woman anywhere but in bed. So long as that was true, she could not be secure.

"Tina? No. They're just friends doing something that will benefit them both. Blessed will make his heir and gain the backing of a strong faction in the Directorate. Tina gains an alliance with the Chair and becomes the mother of the Chair. Her heart isn't set on Blessed. She wants Cable Shike."

"Being mother to the heir could get her killed."

"The succession will be more orderly with Lupo to supervise."

"Lupo could get killed."

"There is more to him than meets the eye. He would be hard to kill."

Midnight stared out to sea, perhaps tempted to dive into the salt breeze and spread her wings against that turquoise plain. But she dared not. The gravity of Prime was too great. When she must fly, Blessed sent her to 3G, a resort station. When he especially wanted to please her, he joined her.

"I'm doing it again. Bothering you with trivia when you have an empire on your mind."

"Pain is not trivial, Midnight. It has the power to define us. Your fear of losing Blessed is as potent as mine that I have pledged myself to the wrong standard."

The wizard could not unravel the schemes of Lupo Provik. Maybe because Provik was weaving something whose ends he could not see. His one certain goal was to slide the House out of the closing jaws of Guardships and Outside.

"Is something happening?"

"Soon. Provik has heard of a big battle."

"The Guardships won?"

"They always win. The Outsiders will be desperate. We won't be able to evade much longer."

"What will you do?"

"That depends on Provik."

"Why is it always Lupo, never Blessed or his mother?" She did not understand Others. When she saw more than one Valerena or Blessed, she became bewildered. She could not get it through her head that the Valerena who mattered had died.

"Blessed defers to Provik's experience and talent. Provik is the only one who can pull the House out of this crack."

"*Could* you capture Starbase? If that's the price?" Her voice trembled.

"Maybe. It would have been easier with *VI Adjutrix*. I'm not anxious to try."

"I don't want you to. Any of you. There's a boat coming." An arrow of white wake reached toward the island.

"Yes." He had known for some time. His vision was more acute.

"Maybe Blessed got a chance to get away." She unfolded her wings. They were brilliant. She was happy.

"Maybe." But he doubted it.

## - 105 -

WarAvocat was reluctant to give the order. It meant he would surrender his role as force commander.

The worst was past, though. The methane breathers had their backs against the wall. Now it was a matter of wearing them down.

*VII Gemina* was no longer combat effective. After three years even the Deified were tired.

It was time to go home.

He gave the order.

Starbase had changed. Construction channels were storms of sound and fire. A millennium's hoard of materials had been consumed. A few more years and the fleet would begin to feel the drain.

He tried catching up on what had happened inside Canon space. Incursions and provocations everywhere, answered ruthlessly as diminished forces tried to hold the Rims.

Canon would double in volume before the plague of violence ran its course.

The fleet had to be expanded. It was able to cope now only by employing its nameless reserves and because Starbase Dengaida could provide some repairs and replacement secondaries.

Starbase agreed. Expansion was necessary. Canon had grown

but the fleet had not.

Starbase proposed expansion to one hundred units and construction of five more Starbases. Twelve Guardships to be assigned each Starbase with twenty-eight palatine units at Starbase Tulsa able to reinforce in any direction.

Starbase had other suggestions. Enrollment of five million new volunteers. Continuous recruiting afterward. Renovation of Canon's administration. The enfranchisement of nonhumans, who made up the majority of the population in Canon space. And a long list more.

WarAvocat wondered if Kez Maefele had found some way to tamper with the system.

But Starbase had been ruminating upon Canon's next two thousand years for some time.

WarAvocat was intrigued by one report originating outside usual sources. Its having reached Starbase at all was enough to make one consider reevaluating the certainty that there was no Divine Providence.

It came out of House Tregesser, unloved by Canon officialdom. As witness the wilderness of coda, addenda, and subscripts the report had accumulated, meant to vilify House Tregesser, whose main crime was that it refused to be gobbled by the bureaucratic machine.

House Tregesser claimed to be the object of an Outsider effort to take advantage of its maverick status. The House had defended itself and had captured several Outsider humans.

They had no idea of their origin. Their memory was one memory. Their history was one history. Alliance in worship of the Destroyer. They had been prowling the Web, with the methane breathers, committing holy atrocities, for ages. Their allies had no idea whence they sprang either.

The Godspeakers were so called because they could summon the Presence to grisly rites carried out by their human cohorts. They could communicate over any distance through the medium of the Web.

Though the Godspeakers set down colonies wherever they found suitable worlds, they were not empire builders. Nor were they true proselytizers. Those sprang from their human companions.

WarAvocat paced, bewildered. His experience with superstition was limited to an uncertain belief in Tawn, *VII Gemina*'s tutelary. He was repelled and revolted by those creatures. He felt no impulse toward mercy.

He was tired and slow. Maybe he *was* too old. He considered potential successors. None could cope any better.

"Access, the Deified Aleas Notable, if she's willing." They had become friends during their year as Dictats. He had not stood for reelection. She had been reelected the twice she had stood.

"Hanaver? Are you brooding again?"

"Me?"

"You."

He asked if she had reviewed the data just received.

"I have now."

Disconcerting. "And the commentaries filed in response?"

"Ah. I see what you mean. This struggle will have no end short of extermination of the methane breathers and their creed. It's the most evil thing we've ever encountered."

"Have you reviewed Starbase's recommendations?"

"No subject has ever exercised the Deified as much. But I doubt any have reviewed the Outsider info—and I suspect its implications are the predicates upon which Starbase's recommendations are based. You wanted me to see that? I've passed it on."

"I want an opinion. Should I retire?"

The face on the screen went vacant. Then, "You want a

vote of confidence? You got it. Nine to one against your retirement."

"My confidence doesn't need buoying. I'm burned out, Aleas."

"And thinking about the artifact still?"

He had told her. "Yes. Damn it. I'm lonely."

"*Gemina* has her specs. We could run a copy."

"Politically unacceptable."

"We'll think of something."

"I'm sorry for disturbing you."

"Hanaver Strate! You... Forget it. I have things to do."

WarAvocat grunted. If he got to work, he would not have these lapses. He would not have the time.

He put the Tregesser report aside, reviewed what other Guardships had learned about the enemy empire. The information would not take shape as a whole. Maybe if he went to Hall of the Stars....

Something had begun to nag. Something to do with star charts. Spots of blue.

"Access, *Gemina*. I need the visual data gathered by the soldiers who stormed the orbital fortress used to neutralize Objective Thirty-Eight." He had reviewed the material once and found it uninteresting. "Specifically, what was taped at the fortress's heart."

One company had gone all the way. The heart had proved to be a hollow sphere containing several thousand points of blue light. Twenty-some methane breathers had lain heaped in bowls on the surface of that hollow.

Could those blue points be some kind of chart?

He ordered them examined on that assumption. *Gemina* justified everything into the human sensory range, presented it three-dimensionally. "It is a chart, then?"

AFFIRMATIVE.

"Of what?"

INSUFFICIENT DATA.

"Find correspondences with our own charts."

Blink-blink-blink, a wave of about eighty flashes, SYSTEMS SUSPECTED TO BE OCCUPIED BY METHANE BREATHERS. THERE ARE NO REPRESENTATIONS FOR SYSTEMS NEUTRALIZED. A lot of blinks, SYSTEMS INHABITED BY SUBJECT SPECIES.

"What's our viewpoint? Show me the Rim."

A red gauze curtain sliced off part of the egg. Blue points floated on the Canon side. "Damn. Match those with known systems. Then eliminate everything associated with a known system."

As blue sparks vanished, he noted the presence of a brown sparkle similar to those representing subject systems not associated with blue sparks. "Knock out the brown spots not associated with a known system."

All those went. Several hundred blue sparks remained. He toyed with them, concluded they represented methane breathers on the Web.

They could track one another on the Web!

ACTION INCUMBENT?

"Advise Starbase. Suggest directives to all systems noted our side of the Rim. Also suggest penetration of additional orbital fortresses to obtain longer tape exposures."

He sat down, leaned back, closed his eyes, pleased with himself.

"That quick interplay of analysis and intuition is why the Deified won't accept your retirement."

"Aleas?"

"In the flesh."

He opened his eyes. "What the hell?"

"I had myself reanimated. *Gemina* approved. That's some response, Hanaver. When I was this age, I was considered reasonably attractive. By the standards of the time."

"Or any other." This was an act of friendship that prostrated him. And one he did not know how to accept.

"It'll take me a while to learn how to handle a body again. I'd forgotten so much. Especially how limited you are."

"Aleas..."

"Never mind, Hanaver. I know you better than you think. It's worth a try."

## - 106 -

Again there were three men in the embassy. These three were accustomed to Canon ways. Their spokesman was a florid, heavy man who smiled a lot even when he was alone with his own kind.

"Their top gun," Two told Provik.

"Yes. Anything more from station?"

"It's done."

"Set the stage, then."

Two brought in a Valerena Other, Blessed, the Ku, and Cable Shike. Lupo said, "Sorry we ruined your holiday, Kez Maefele. You deserved it. Have you heard the word from J. Belaria?"

"Yes. I expect it explains why they are conciliatory."

"I didn't think it would work. Nobody ought to be so dumb they run from decoys into an ambush."

"You knew they were decoys. They could not tell what was real and what wasn't. They should now think House Tregesser much stronger than it is."

"Let's find out. Let them in, Two."

Blessed asked, "Why the hell do you call her Two?"

"It's her name."

"It's weird."

Even the Valerena smiled at that from someone named Blessed.

Blessed blustered. "Can't she talk? She never says anything."

"Of course she can. When she has something to say."

Two winked at Blessed before she opened the door.

Lupo got up from behind his desk, met the florid man. "Welcome to Tregesser Horata, Mr. Korint. It's been a while."

Startled reaction. "You know me?"

"You were often there when Simon was arms shopping. You preferred the name Rejins." Lupo resumed his seat. "We appreciate your coming in civilized instead of like pirates. Though the presence of that Godspeaker thing was a provocation. We disposed of it. Let's get down to business."

"You messed with the Godspeaker?"

"No. We killed it. Those things aren't welcome in Tregesser space."

Korint was aghast. Likewise, his companions.

"I want you to understand that I find your religion loathsome. It deserves everything the Guardships are doing. But I don't let prejudice get in the way of business. What do you have to offer?"

The encounter had Korint turned around. "A chance to survive, Provik."

"Are we in some danger? We've had nuisance level problems with pirates but haven't had any trouble handling it. Heard about J. Belaria? Twenty-four pirate ships destroyed?"

"I've heard."

"Good. You're against the wall. You want help. We might be willing. If there's something in it for us."

Korint opened his mouth.

"Don't tell me you'll betray us to the Guardships. We rewrote that chapter starting when the shooting stopped in that end space. You've helped our image, trying to leverage us."

Korint forced a smile. "I was told you could run a bluff with a straight face."

Lupo set a cosmetic jar on his desk. "There's Jane in this. You know Jane?"

Korint knew the lady well. His companions would not

approve. Who had who?

"Come, Mr. Korint. What do you have to offer?"

Blessed said, "We're as sure of ourselves as the Guardships are. We have something to sell." He leaned against a wall instead of sitting.

Lupo said, "We can't give you victory. But we might sell you a stalemate."

Blessed said, "Your Mr. Marin, of the second mission, had an intimate knowledge of your assets inside Canon space."

The Valerena Other said, "We had to neutralize those in a position to trouble House Tregesser. We left the rest undisturbed. They'll help us more where they are. For now."

One of Korint's companions muttered, "You're a murderous bunch."

Cable Shike giggled. Lupo glanced at him, startled. "Sorry. It was him getting righteous."

Korint snapped, "Let's cut the shit, Provik. You claim our only leverage is financial."

"We can be bought."

"You no longer cling to the idealism that obtained in that end space?"

"Hell no! The Guardships arc awake now."

The Ku said, "The dragon never sleeps, Mr. Provik."

Korint said, "I can't see that we have a basis for discussion."

"Then what the hell are you doing here?"

"The Godspeakers are used to taking what they want. But you're right. We should hear you out. What do you have?"

"The key to Starbase. Two of my people have been in there." That put the fire in their eyes. "We also have talent to rent. Kez Maefele, formerly of the Dire Radiant, whose strategies have made your attempts to harass us so costly." They recognized the name.

They looked at the living legend. He looked back. Lupo

hoped the Ku would not have one of his moral seizures before the game was snared. If he sold this, they might be home free.

"I'll relay this," Korint said. "How would you price knowledge and talent?"

"Megatonnages of platinum, palladium, iridium, rhodium, transuranics, other rare elements. Information. Like everything you ever collected about the Guardships but haven't shared. What you know about the Web that we don't. Put a package together that will blind us, triple it, remember your alternative to going broke is getting wiped out, triple it again, and come back. Because you planned to screw us in the end space, we'll want payment in advance. We'll pick the time and place. Outside."

"And we'd have to trust you?"

"House Tregesser keeps its word. It's House policy. Consider. We *do* have a commercial interest in keeping you in business."

Three pairs of eyes drilled him with javelins of contempt. Korint said, "We have no authority to negotiate."

"I said, go see what it's worth. We'll wait. When you come back, don't bring any monsters. That would upset us. Two, turn these people over to T.W. Tell her to see to all their needs."

Turtle refused to react to the face of what he had seen. Provik was up to something. No point assuming a stance till he knew what that was.

Provik stared at the door after the Outsiders left. "Our problem is, they *can* take us down."

Blessed asked, "You going to tell us what you're thinking?"

"It's only starting to shape up. Till now I wasn't sure we could work anything. Now I know it won't be anything mutually beneficial. Now I know they were going to screw us in the end space. If they pull off the miracle of the ages and dump the Guardships, we're cooked just as done as if the fleet finds us out."

"You just offered them Starbase."

"We have to look like we're helping. In a way that will convince them while showing the Guardships nothing. That's why I offered. It's what they'd expect of a commercial enterprise, where the only god is profit. The rest I threw in because they wouldn't believe it if I said we were rooting for them. They know what we think of them. The ideal strategy would be to help but in some way that would take a long time. They'd keep quiet while the Guardships ate them up."

Turtle agreed.

"Kez Maefele. Can you fit your moral and ethical sets to that framework?"

"Yes."

"We couldn't sell them any of your contingency studies. They depend on Starbase not being alert."

"I have an idea that should appeal. If the Godspeakers have any vanity. An operation predicated on their ability to communicate across the Web."

Provik said, "You've been holding back."

"Of course. We're comrades in arms but we're not fighting for the same things."

"I see. And there's a little something you want from us."

"More or less."

"What?"

"There's no rush, Mr. Provik. Does House Tregesser undertake censuses of its empire? Particularly on worlds other than Tregesser Prime?"

"Periodically. Their accuracy is suspect."

"You might review those, perhaps running back a thousand years."

"That's all you have to say?" Provik was vexed.

"For now. There will be time later. When you have a contract with those devils."

## - 107 -

VII *Gemina* eased away from Starbase. Routine patrol inside Canon. Outsiders likely to be encountered only as commerce raiders. A vacation.

WarAvocat did not intend to let it become dead time. He ordered the Guardship to P. Benetonica.

"I'm not surprised," Aleas said. "What do you expect to find?"

"Who knows? People like this Provik who filed the report reserve anything they can exploit. Also, tenuous a thread as it is, M. Shrilica is a Tregesser system."

"Tenuous for sure. This war is a watershed, isn't it? Canon won't be the same."

"No. This will catalyze changes that have been taking shape for centuries. This may send the Houses into eclipse."

"I'd think massive new territories would mean a boom. People have to be transported. Stations have to be built. Onplanet infrastructures have to be assembled."

"It also creates a more mobile, more politically interested population. Especially once the edicts take effect. It'll be an interesting universe, Aleas."

"We won't change."

"Guardships are Guardships are Guardships. The dragon never sleeps."

## - 108 -

Turtle watched Provik greet Blessed with the respect due a Chair, then Shike with a nod. His own military genius got a spoken greeting that placed him on the spectrum between the two.

Provik said, "I took your suggestion, Kez Maefele. I was unaware that so dramatic a shift in population character had taken place. Though I should have known. Simon opened the technical and supervisory ranks to nonhumans because we couldn't recruit competent humans. It's been a battle with the Directors. Some would rather have an illiterate from the Black Ring manage a division."

Turtle settled into the chair Provik had had built for him. "That's human nature. And not exclusive to your species."

"I suppose not. But we ought to restrain our prejudices in the face of necessity. Have you seen the forecast Blessed's financial wizards turned in?"

"No."

"It's on the machine. Give it a skim."

Turtle went and scrolled the report. It was not an easy read. Blessed and Provik chatted about Placidia, the heir Tina had produced. Blessed was taken with the child, who was toddling now. They moved on to Midnight, then to the whirlwind of socializing that had befallen Tregesser Horata, gossiping in immemorial fashion.

Turtle finished. "Grim. If your future is tied to one of the Houses."

"I didn't see it black," Blessed said. "We won't lose wealth or property. We'll even keep growing. We just won't control as much of the whole. Cable, you take a look too. It shows us our place in a Canon expanded by a sudden one-point-five to one."

Turtle made way for Shike. Cable went after the report like he understood every word. Amazing. But Cable might have surprises for everyone. Especially Blessed.

Blessed asked, "What's up, Lupo?"

"We need to think about this future." He steepled his fingers. "Kez Maefele suggested I study census reports. I did. Our unskilled and semiskilled employees are mostly nonhuman or artifact. With no reason to stay loyal. Our skilled workers and supervisors run half and half."

"And?"

"Your report ignores the composition of the work force. It could desert us. Particularly given this." He passed out three-sheet handouts.

Blessed glanced at his. "When did this come in?"

Turtle missed the reply. He was engrossed. It was a fleet edict and, therefore, as immutable as natural law.

They wanted five million volunteers. Any Canon citizen who felt capable of surviving the screening.

That alone was enough to alter the shape of the future. But it was just the beginning.

The shocker was a paragraph that extended full citizenship to any resident of Canon space who, never having stood in arms against Canon, claimed it formally.

Nonhumans aboard the Guardships? Could it happen?

Provik asked him, "What do you think?"

"I think this is the most dangerous document you're ever likely to see. It stuns you with the call for volunteers. While you're numb, it codifies what are de facto practices already. It takes a few nibbles at House prerogatives but balances them with hammer blows to the power of Canon's bureaucrats. There isn't one thing there that will offend any significant portion of the population, yet it is a revolution, a legal recognition that Canon is a multi-species entity."

Perplexed, Blessed said, "I don't like this, but it doesn't look that dangerous."

"The next one will be just as gentle. And so will the one after that. Those people see things millennially."

Provik's woman stepped in. "Lupo, *VII Gemina* just broke off the Web." She looked numb.

Turtle reflected that the Prime certainly enjoyed the

occasional ironic twist. *VII Gemina!*

Provik asked, "Blessed, Cable, is there anything in the system—*any* system—to give us away?"

"We're clean. Unless they use brainprobes."

"You're sure?"

"There are no oversights," Shike said. "We learned from M. Shrilica."

Two agreed. "I've tested it. They've rewritten reality completely."

"Not quite," Turtle interjected. "You better hope they're as focused on information systems as you. Suppose one of them tunes in a commercial news broadcast? I or my soldiers or our developing defense works get mentioned every day." He had complained before that they had allowed him to become a public figure. No one had taken him seriously.

"A point," Provik said. "I want a news blackout, Two. With sanctions that will make it stick."

Two raised a finger: wait. She had the fingers of her other hand pressed to her ear, listening. Then she said, "They're here about your reports on the Outsiders. They're sending their own experts down."

Provik shrugged. "Give them so much of what they want they can't see anything else."

Turtle told Blessed, "Don't let Midnight know *VII Gemina* is here. She has friends aboard. She might try to contact them. She does not understand security."

# - 109 -

WarAvocat glanced at the screen to his left. P. Benetonica 3. A very old world orbiting an old star. He tried to recall when last he had set foot on a planet. Ages ago. He had been a combat soldier. How would he take it? Often soldiers on-planet experienced a sort of nostalgic melancholy.

He shifted attention to a tentative list of members of his landing party. About the experts there was no doubt. *Gemina* had picked them. But he was uncertain about the rest. Especially the Guardship soldiers from the chartered Horigawa. Would they be useful?

He had a hunch they might.

What could it hurt? They would expect him to bring an escort.

Aleas joined him. "Want to hear something?" She sounded amused.

"What now?" She had an irreverent sense of humor.

"Our people haven't had any luck getting into the local data pool. They just got an access-unauthorized response, whatever they tried. Till they pissed the system and it told them they'd be arrested and given five years to life at hard labor if they tried to get in again."

That *was* amusing. "Somebody screwed up?"

"Not really. The probe during our first visit to M. Shrilica warned them they needed better safeguards. You think they'll arrest the whole Guardship if we try again?"

He chuckled. "It is useful to know when you've been found out. We'll keep digging. Though it's unlikely we'll find anything now."

"*Gemina* says it's not Guardship-specific. The Tregessers don't like anybody nosing into their business."

WarAvocat grunted. "You coming down?"

"Try and stop me."

Lupo and the Ku watched the visitors debark deep in the roots of the Pylon. He had gotten a panic signal from Six, who had met them at the port…. "It's that damned Lieutenant! What the hell is she doing back?"

The Ku bent nearer the screen, shocked. Then he relaxed. "No. That's not the same one. That's a copy."

"Good." Lupo hated to think that more than one had gotten away on V. Rothica 4.

"This is the one to watch," the Ku said. "WarAvocat Hanaver Strate. I'm surprised."

Strate fit Provik's stereotype of a Guardship officer perfectly. "Recognize anyone else?"

"The woman. The apparent companion. As a face in a crowd. I don't know who she is."

Lupo tapped his wrist. "Two. Have they broken into that data system yet?"

"Yes."

"Good." He slipped a receiver button into his left ear, told the Ku, "Monitor the show. Give me any hints you can. Does this Strate have weaknesses?"

"He's lonely. Loneliness is epidemic aboard *VII Gemina*. Anyone off that Guardship might be vulnerable to a manipulation of that. He's also vain of his personal accomplishments. He's fond of women. As a general rule, don't underestimate him."

"He's the man who beat me in the end space. I plan to be careful."

WarAvocat could not hide his awe of the Pylon. In its frame of reference it was as impressive as Starbase.

He refused to bow to the paranoia that was the consequence of leaving *VII Gemina*. He let the Tregesser woman put his people into the lift however she would.

Why had they made so little fuss? They had sent only one woman to meet them. She had driven them herself. There were no obvious security arrangements. As far as he could see, there was no effort to keep anything out of sight.

A series of lifts took them to a reception area that suggested the level was a headwater of power in the Tregesser empire.

The woman palmed a wall plate. A door opened on a vast,

mostly brown, and mostly empty room. A woman stood looking out a window. A man sat in a chair, reading. He looked up, put his papers aside, considered them coolly. A second man sat at a work station against the wall to the left, dealing with callers.

"Shoot the bastard," he told one. "The rest will forget the idea." He cut off, switched, said, "Sorry. Family crisis. Look, the injunction will come through. Tell Deccan to concentrate on the lawsuits. For what we pay him he ought to castrate every fatass bureaucrat on Capitola Primagenia. I have visitors, Rash." He cut off, looked them over, lifted an eyebrow, came forward. "I see you've kept well, Lieutenant. Welcome back to Tregesser Prime."

"Who the hell are you?" Klass snapped.

"Same winning personality, too."

WarAvocat scowled. He should have warned Klass.

The man said, "I'm Lupo Provik. Head of House security, doer of odd jobs. Today I'm mouthpiece for the Chair. The gentleman there is Cable Shike. He represents Blessed Tregesser, heir to the Chair. The lady is Tina Bofoku, representing Blessed's daughter and her own, Placidia Tregesser. Whom have we the honor of addressing?"

WarAvocat frowned. This was not what he expected. "Hanaver Strate, WarAvocat *VII Gemina*, twice Dictat. The Deified Aleas Notable, formerly WarAvocat *VII Gemina*, thrice Dictat." This Provik set off alarms.

"I presume that means you're important. I'm not familiar with the fleet. My one encounter was when the Lieutenant threatened to destroy Prime unless Blessed let her abduct several houseguests. He doesn't think well of you. He was infatuated with the artifact."

WarAvocat allowed himself no visible reaction. "We'll talk about that. If the Lieutenant exceeded her instructions…"

Provik betrayed a ghost of a sneer.

Klass handled it. Most soldiers, walking into a former incarnation cold, would have shown cracks.

Provik said, "I'm told you want to follow up on our research on Outsiders of human stock. Why tie up a Guardship on that?"

"A man in your position seldom tells a lie but never tells the truth. I want to know what you didn't report."

Provik denied nothing. "Might I suggest an information swap? To maintain the dignity of the laws of thermodynamics?"

He was a bold rogue. "I'm open to suggestions."

"It's trivial, really. But I'm curious by nature. The question: Why were the artifact and alien so important the Lieutenant threatened general mayhem to get them?"

Why did he keep after Klass? "The artifact and two alien companions had been guests aboard *VII Gemina*, Mr. Provik. One was the Ku warrior Kez Maefele, who commanded the Dire Radiant during the Ku wars. Some years ago, in our haste to engage an enemy, we pulled out of Starbase without them. During our absence the three fled Starbase with information that might have been deleterious to fleet security. Somehow they reached the Tregesser system M. Shrilica."

Provik looked at him. He gulped air. His expression grew black. He turned slowly toward Shike, who had appeared astounded, skeptical, and grimly defensive in succession.

"You had that in your hands? And all Blessed could think about was wetting his one-eyed snake? Do you have any idea what we could have done with that?" He skirted his work station. "We could have traded it for a couple of star systems. Hell, for Capitola Primagenia! Blessed don't think with anything but his balls, but you're supposed to have good sense. Didn't you bother to find out what you had?"

"They were DownTown stuff, Lupo. We wouldn't have bothered with them if the artifact would've let Blessed break the set."

Provik shouted at him. The Bofoku woman tried to intervene, ended up getting drawn into the shouting match on Shike's side.

They did not care who knew they were villains, did they?

Two determined women burst in, pushed Provik and Shike apart. One forced Shike into his chair. Provik retreated to his work station. His voice quavered, promised murder. "Cable, you drag that cretin out of whatever bed he's in and take him to his mother. T.W., get ahold of Valerena. Tell her he's coming. Tell her why. And don't anybody say anything about this. If the Directorate finds out what we blew they'll hand us our heads."

Well done if staged, WarAvocat thought. You could smell the anger and hatred.

Staged or genuine did not matter. The central fact was inescapable. If these people had known what they had, they would have exploited it.

"Get him out, T.W."

Provik closed his eyes, took deep breaths. He slapped his desk, muttered, "We had it all."

He was shaking still when he opened his eyes and looked at his guests somewhat vaguely. Was he unstable? A man would have to be a little insane to attain Provik's position in one of the great Houses. "Two. Tell Research to put together whatever we've got on the Outsiders."

He looked at them. For an instant raw hatred peeped through. He pressed his hands down onto his desk to still their trembling. "Tit for tat, sir. The thing I reserved was the fact that the Outsiders revealed details and identities of the agencies inside Canon space. I neutralized those in a position to harm Tregesser interests and left the others to their mischief."

Aleas asked, "Don't you have any loyalty to Canon?"

He looked at her like she'd just offered to show him a

grotesque physical deformity. "To the extent that the Outsider alternative looks worse. Your kind doesn't make a rite of torture and mutilation—that I've heard. I presume some of these people are research and technical staff?"

"Yes."

"Six. When we're done, take them down and let them get started. Tell Linver to give them whatever they want. Clearance is from me."

"It's plain you have no love for us," WarAvocat said. "Why are you cooperating?"

"Pragmatism. Having a Guardship insystem is murder on business. Guardships get what they want. Yours will, too, whatever I like. When T.W. comes back, I'll have her fix you up with documentation. Do be careful wandering around. Security staff won't be told who you are. They get bonuses for shooting people who turn up where they don't belong. You want to go somewhere, clear it with T.W.'s office. We have our own politics to survive. Anything else?"

Aleas whispered, "You're not a demigod here, Hanaver. Just a nuisance." Which amused her.

Provik awaited some response. WarAvocat declined. He had made a mistake, challenging these people on their home ground. Here all the intimidations belonged to them.

"A rest, a meal, a chance to freshen up would do us the most good, Mr. Provik."

"As you will. Six. Forget the labs. Take them to Residential." Provik turned to his screens. He was done with them.

WarAvocat noted that the man's hands still trembled.

One, Three, and Four entered as the outer door closed. One raised four fingers. Lupo nodded, watched them place the bugs in isolation boxes. "That's all?"

"We saw every twitch."

"Give them to Research."

"You put on a hell of a show."

"I almost believed it myself. Shike did better than I expected."

"You pointed them straight at us."

"If we're vulnerable we might as well find out."

"I wish we all were as confident of our ability to walk the edge without falling."

"You are." And that was the truth. He only hoped circumstances would let them step back from the brink someday.

WarAvocat said, "Stay with us, Lieutenant," as Provik's woman led them around, assigning quarters. He owed her an explanation.

The techs started sweeping the moment the woman departed. They found an ample scatter of listening devices. They would have been troubled if they had not.

"That Provik bothers me," WarAvocat said once it was safe. "I don't know why. Maybe it's potential. Sit down, Lieutenant. I'll tell you the story."

Turtle studied Provik, trying to fathom his game. "You have grown too subtle for me."

"Just baffling them with bullshit."

Turtle wondered, though.

# - 110 -

WarAvocat gave the order to pull out reluctantly. He stared at the image of P. Benetonica 3, dissatisfied. "I can't shake the suspicion that I've been suckered."

"*Gemina* is satisfied," Aleas said.

"*Gemina* hasn't met Lupo Provik. That man... I don't want him loose in the universe."

"You're going to try to trace the Ku, aren't you?"

"I don't want him running loose, either."

"He has a long head start. He hasn't done anything with what he learned. If he did learn anything."

He caught her gentle warning. The Deified had their eyes on him.

"The war will be waiting when we get there." He glared at that world. Six days down there and he had not found a chink. And did not know much more about it as a world. He'd even missed the famous Fuerogomenga Gorge.

"There's something rotten down there, Aleas. Too much has happened for it to be unrelated, coincidental. The Ku. The rogue. The Outsiders."

"The Ku didn't reach M. Shrilica by choice. The rogue had been Outside for centuries. You can't connect them, Hanaver."

"Not logically. But they connect. I'm sure."

Aleas gave him a troubled look.

*VII Gemina* ran the Lieutenant's trail out. WarAvocat was not surprised when it turned to smoke. He did not dig deep. He was aware of the unfriendly scrutiny of the Deified.

"That damned Ku is out there scheming, Aleas. If those Outsiders get him...."

"Speaking of Outsiders?"

"I know. We're supposed to be showing them the light. My esteemed predecessors think I'm obsessed. They think I'm using the Ku as an excuse to look for the artifact." He ordered Ops to take the Guardship to M. Meddinia. He was WarAvocat. He could not be overruled. "We'll see some truths pretty soon. And the grumblers will be silenced again."

"I hope so. For your sake."

So. Even she had doubts.

M. Meddinia presented no surprises but plenty of frustrations.

Even *Gemina* could make only limited sense of exchanges with the ground. But it did seem that Seeker of the Lost Children and Amber Soul had come home before the destruction of the station, presumably by Outsiders. But neither was down there now, near as *Gemina* could figure. It was possible the locals meant they were dead.

WarAvocat gave up, ordered *VII Gemina* back to D. Zimplica in the face of protests from the Deified. He paused there only long enough to issue a Fleet Directive offering a reward for the Ku. He did not include Amber Soul because he saw no reason to fear it. He did fear Lady Midnight but ignored her for political reasons.

He had maneuvered himself into a precarious position without quite knowing how.

And he caught his sole friend watching him worriedly when she thought he would not notice.

## - 111 -

Turtle looked at Provik. Provik looked back. "This is it, isn't it, Kez Maefele? Your hour."

"Yes." He did not just have to go into that next room and sell those dour Outsiders a strategy for killing Starbase, he had to go in having sold himself. And he had not yet conquered Doubt, the devil that gave him no peace.

He had been too long among humans, or not long enough. He understood them too well. Their thinking had infected his own. But he did not yet understand them well enough to become one of them. Those grim old torturers beyond that door had more in common with Lupo Provik than Kez Maefele ever could.

"I can do it," Turtle said. "I will do it. But I could do it more easily if I believed I was doing the right thing for the right reasons. The motive is as important as the deed. Have you never done the right thing for the wrong reason?"

Some shadow of memory darkened Provik's eyes. "Sure. And the wrong thing for the right reason. But that was then and this is now. Why lose sleep over it? You want more motivation, remember they put a price on your head."

Was that a threat?

"No. Wrong choice of words. We weren't smart when we started. People on Prime know your name. Some are the type who would try to collect the reward. Be hard to avoid them all. Unless you spend your life locked up in the Pylon the way the Chairs do."

"Or I can go out there with the Outsiders and fight back?"

"You know their conditions. We go through that door and we're committed till they turn us down or turn us loose. The Valerena and Blessed can dodge it. You and I can't."

"Can't you?" Turtle eyed Provik narrowly.

Provik was startled. And understood. "How long have you known?"

"Since they tried to kill you, Blessed, and Valerena. They *did* kill you. It was on that tape. But it was you who brought the tape, and a female with impossible reaction times."

"And you never used that."

"I'm not human," Turtle said, which he suspected Provik would take to mean that he had not yet found a reason to draw the bolt from his quiver.

"I owe you one."

"Not necessarily."

One of the female Proviks appeared, escorting the chosen Valerena. She raised an eyebrow. "Another moral crossroads," Lupo said. "We're going to survive it, I think. Where's Blessed's Other?"

"On his way. Says he'll be a few minutes late. I think he wants to be the last to arrive."

Provik grumbled something. "Well, Kez Maefele, there's the

final curtain. Can you bring yourself to save this House?"

"You go to save your House, Mr. Provik. I'll go to raze the dragon's lair."

There were few Ku left. A few thousand were scattered across Canon. A few tens of thousands lived on the old homeworld, their backs resolutely to the stars and yesterday. And beyond the Rims there were tiny, scattered guest colonies and a few nomadic ships surviving by carrying whatever cargoes they could acquire. In all, surely, fewer than a hundred thousand Ku, fading from the stage faster than their conquerors, lacking any real will to survive.

Provik had let him spend a fortune to find out how hopeless his people were.

There was not a one of those Ku who did not know the name Kez Maefele. Maybe if they heard that the legend lived and had stormed the fortress unvanquishable, the spark of will might be breathed back to life.

Most especially if he got himself killed. Most especially then. All the best heroes did.

The Ku loved their martyrs.

He wore a replica of the uniform he had been compelled to give up the day of the Surrender, a gift from those scruffy volunteers hiding out at Blessed's castle. "Come follow me through the final curtain."

There were twenty-eight of the bastards in the room and none were like any Outsider who had come before. Those had been soldiers, necessarily flawed. These were masters. These were perfect. One wished he had let one of his brothers come instead.

Four felt the chill, too. She moved a step closer. The Valerena did the same. The Ku did not seem affected. One wondered if anything intimidated him.

These were the real bosses of the Outsider empire. These

were the men who talked to the things that talked to the Destroyer. These were the men who decided what words the Destroyer had put into the Godspeakers' minds.

One had no doubt that, however much and whatever they might believe, these men had their high priests saying whatever they thought it was best for them to say. These were the true creators and rulers of the Outside empire, however servile they might be in the presence of the Godspeakers.

He stepped to a rostrum. His companions seated themselves. He looked around. Everything had been set up right. The Ku's gear, sideboard with food and refreshments enough to sustain a siege, toilet facilities which allowed privacy but no egress.

"Good day, gentlemen. I'm told you've provided yourselves with an adequate translation system. If not, we have a good programme...."

"Proceed," said a grey box occupying a front row seat. "We note the absence of one ordered to appear here."

"Maybe I'd better bring in our system. I see a problem with yours already. You don't 'order' us. Mistranslation could cause misunderstandings. But we'll keep your system's flaws in mind. For the record, Blessed was detained but should arrive momentarily."

"Get on with it."

Their speaker was the man he expected, a skinny, leathery, wispy-haired old character who looked like a mummy wrested from its tomb and reanimated for the event. His ornate title boiled down to First Speaker. He came without a personal name. He was a generation older than his companions and dead set against any alliance of convenience. He was so old and so near death, the last of his contemporaries, that he could afford doctrinal intransigence.

One said, "Life extensions approaching a thousand years are not impractical in Canon space." Sowing a seed of temptation just for the hell of it.

"Our agents visited yours in the Hemebuk Neutrality. They found the payments offered generous and sufficient. Five, Six, Seven, and Eight had taken Kez Maefele's commandos and a dozen armed Tregesser ships. They had seized the treasure convoy to forestall the treachery planned by these wicked old men, who did not yet know that. The treasure had been awesome in magnitude.

"We've decided to accept your commission. We'll take Starbase. Providing you approve. Kez Maefele will outline how he expects to accomplish the impossible."

Blessed made his entrance.

Damn!

He had brought Midnight. Which made one thing absolutely, incontestably clear. This was not the Blessed Tregesser Other, this was Blessed himself.

The damned fool!

No wonder he had arranged to be late. There would be no arguing with him now, in front of the Outsiders, who believed they were getting the real things as hostages.

The damned fool! For the sake of an artifact!

Two darted into Lupo's office. "Cue up the meeting. Blessed pulled a fast one."

Provik did it, saw the artifact, cursed, called Cable Shike, Nyo Bofoku, and Tina. They were scattered everywhere, the former two sent out on business by Blessed. All three claimed ignorance. The Blessed Other, from the Fuerogomenga Gorge castle, said, "He wanted to get away. He wanted to spend more time with Midnight."

Lupo disconnected angrily. "That damned artifact. I knew she'd be trouble."

"What're you going to do?"

"What *can* I do? Live with it. Hope for the best. Too late to change it. The sneaky bastard."

Turtle glared at Midnight. She seated herself primly, undaunted. She was too happy. This madness brought her closer to what she wanted, Blessed all to herself. She did not comprehend what it meant to the House. And did not care.

And maybe the universe would be a better place if more people shared her priorities.

Turtle activated his star chart and presented a fifteen-minute outline of his strategy.

It was incredibly complex, would require every ship the Outsiders possessed, and battalions of Godspeakers, without whom it could not be coordinated. It would span the Sixth and Second Presidencies and nothing would be done the way it usually was. The first strike against Starbase would be made not by warships but by a flight of constructed projectiles with the mass of moderate asteroids. The battle fleet would approach from a direction the Guardships could not anticipate, after making a prolonged starspace crossing. The operation, once launched, would take ninety-six days to complete.

"Mr. Provik will distribute copies of the detailed proposal. It examines the operation at several levels of ambition. It proposes four result scenarios, including worst case, best case, median, and most probable. These were generated using data available through House Tregesser's intelligence services. You will find them promising."

It was a seductive report. Not that these men would need much seducing. They were desperate.

Provik distributed documents, insisting each visitor sign for his copy. Turtle explained that only thirty existed, one belonging to Provik, another to himself. Each was numbered. Its whereabouts had to be known at all times.

One found the silence unnerving. The Outsiders showed no

more animation than robots. They accepted their documents, signed in a strange but perfect cursive, began reading.

Did the Ku suspect that Lupo possessed a thirty-first, un-numbered copy, to be used or not as he thought would best serve the House? He might. The bastard was too damned smart.

One settled beside Four, waited while the Outsiders read. She touched his hand. If they survived, it would be years before they would be with their family again.

For a while there was no sound but the rustle of pages or the soft clink of dinnerware at the sideboard. The Outsiders stayed away till their mummylike captain finished reading and helped himself to a spare lunch. He selected portions only from those dishes his hosts had sampled.

Suspicious old jerk! Wouldn't do him any good. Everything was spiked with just enough Jane to put everyone in a better mood.

When everyone had eaten, the old man said, "There are critical data missing from this report."

One responded, "Operational details only. We can't give the thing away."

The mummy scowled at the Ku. "I note that some phases would be directed by yourself and your lieutenants."

"We have no doctrinal or political axes to grind. We have no personal ambitions or enemies to cause us to take false steps in order to make someone look bad. We have one enemy and one goal.

"You have no trained, competent commanders. You have men who carry out their orders. Your book on strategy contains two pages. Attack till the objective is achieved, no matter the cost. Defend to the last man. The Guardships love you. You get in line to be killed. Given the resources you commanded, I could have conquered Canon by now."

That got them.

That got One, too. The Ku was not given to exaggeration.

The mummy man glowered. "We will confer." He switched off the translator.

Lot of good that would do him.

Two told Lupo, "They're going to buy it. The Ku got them with a crack about how he could have conquered Canon with what they had."

"I wonder how."

"He did say Canon, not the Guardships."

"Any guess why they're being easy?"

"Desperation. And the notion that if the Ku comes through, they can get him to win their war."

Provik nodded. Kez Maefele had become a mythic character. "He won't win for them. He's decided the Guardships serve a useful purpose."

"And Blessed's little game?"

"We lay back and let T.W. front. And take a strong interest in guarding and educating Placidia. It's not likely we'll ever see Blessed again."

## - 112 -

Cable Shike brought his aircar to ground beside Nyo's flitter. He had made good time but Nyo had done better. He hoped Nyo had himself under control.

It was coming together....

He forced himself to stroll through the castle. It was anyone's guess how many agents Provik had there. You couldn't find them all.

It was coming together perfectly.

Shike paid no attention to the opulence, handed down by Blessed's mother. He took it for granted. But ten years ago the setting would have paralyzed him.

He made the long climb to the viewing veranda where the walls met in a peak on the tip of a promontory overhanging the wildest section of Fuerogomenga Gorge.

Nyo was there already, attacking a platter of sandwiches. Shike settled opposite him, back to the vertiginous view. "Trying to put on weight?" He grabbed a sandwich.

"I was too nervous to eat before."

"You need anything else, Cable?" Blessed asked.

"No."

Blessed dismissed a servant, one of the Ku's aliens. A hundred would be left behind.

"How are you?" Shike asked once the alien was out of earshot.

"Going through withdrawal."

Nyo said, "I plain don't understand what you're doing. You're legally the Chair. Why the rigamarole, sending Midnight off with your Other to fake everybody into thinking you ran away with your lover? I'm with you all the way. I always am. I'll do my part. But it helps when I understand. And this time I don't see the point."

Shike said, "Your reasoning eludes me, too." Though he had nudged Blessed along the path.

A thunderclap overrode Blessed's reply. The table danced. The castle shuddered and creaked. "Close," Bofoku said, glancing toward the parapet.

"It's active today," Blessed said. "Sunspots or something."

Shike forced himself to go to the edge, will in mortal combat with phobia. One such bolt often presaged a cannonade.

Fuerogomenga Gorge was four and a half kilometers deep here, and thirty wide. The bottom could not be seen. Cold air from the north flowed down into the moist air above a thousand hot springs and kept the canyon deeps veiled in mist. The region below the mist was known only through radar and infrared scan and unreliable remote telemetry.

Men had tried going down there. Most had turned back. Those who had kept going had not returned.

Sudden scatters of lightning shot between the ten thousand spires and buttes and islands which rose from the mist. Shike gripped the protective rail so tightly his knuckles popped. Six billion years of geologic history lay exposed down there, in those variegated layers. An eon and a quarter down, nearly two kilometers, there were what appeared to be artifacts left by an unimaginably ancient civilization. No one had yet recovered any of them, exciting as they were, though Blessed suggested that was because of House policy rather than any lack of ingenuity in providing safety for scientists and explorers.

From the beginning the Tregessers had had an almost superstitious dread of a world history so deep it had produced three evolutionarily independent sentiences. Maybe four, if that down in the chasm was of native origin.

"I'm going down there someday," Cable told Blessed. Determined. Nyo came up on his other side, facing his own lesser phobia.

The Gorge was so vast only the foreground seemed real. The distance gave no sense of depth of field. It seemed like a background matte painting.

The spider dance of the lightning played out. The reverberations faded. Nyo said, "You ever really go, I want to go with you." He leaned out, looked across at Blessed. "You were going to say something."

"There are things involved here. Including my ego. The way it works best is for me to *take* the Chair."

"How do you take what you've already got?"

"Who knows that? Us. The Valerenas. Lupo. His girlfriend. Not the Directors. They don't know what year it is. Lupo won't tell them."

Nyo grunted. He got that part. Provik was going away. The Valerenas could make a move since the Directors didn't know about Valerena Prime.

"Who runs this House, Nyo?"

Nyo shrugged.

Shike concentrated on the Gorge.

"Lupo Provik does. The Valerenas keep the Directors off his back. He decides everything. And he hasn't done an awful job, except he's really only interested in his shadow games.

"I may be Chair but he doesn't let me in on anything. And I don't think he'll ever turn loose. If we both live two thousand years he'll still be regent because I'll be learning."

A lightning firelight broke out up the Gorge. It sent light and shadow chases scampering their way.

After a while, Cable said what Nyo was probably thinking. "Head to head with Lupo Provik isn't smart, Blessed. People get prematurely dead that way."

"I thought one Cable was worth several Lupos."

"Maybe in a footrace. Not in a fight. I changed my mind after him and his girl took those people when the Others tried to get us."

Blessed chuckled. "That woman intrigues me. I wish he hadn't taken her with him."

Cable was uncomfortable. He thought Provik had accepted the Outsiders' conditions too readily. Did he have himself covered? Or was he just that sure of T.W. Trice? "Blessed. You recall Rash Norym?"

Glazed look. Computer mind running a file search. "Governor at M. Shrilica when we took over."

"You set her up in the Pylon. In case we needed a friend inside. She's got a mid-level job in security now. You'd better call that one in."

Nyo agreed. "We don't have to hurry. Provik will be gone a long time."

Cable said, "If we do this let's do it right. Not like your mother always did."

"We'll do it right."

The lightning began to play down the Gorge. The display was not as impressive as the one below the castle. Valerena had built where she had because the promontory overlooked the wildest discharges.

Shike pushed away from the rail, closed his eyes. That was the one way he could convince his hands it was safe to let go. "Call that one in, Blessed."

Nyo asked, "What about Tina?"

"From now on she stays out in the dark," Blessed said. "She's not with us anymore. We don't have to stop being friends, but we can't forget she has a different loyalty now."

"Yeah. That's sad, you know? Hey! Cable! Wait up."

Shike was headed inside to calm down. He paused but did not turn around. He resumed walking when Nyo caught up.

"I still don't get it," Nyo said.

"I don't think that matters. It's what he wants. It makes sense to him."

Nyo snorted. "How can he all of a sudden do without Midnight?"

"Symbolic gesture. Telling the world he's all grown up now. He's throwing away his last toy. And I think he was scared of the hold she had. He figured this would be the smaller pain."

"Not to mention her being out there will keep his Other headed the right direction."

"There's that. Can it. We don't know who belongs to who here."

Cable went to his quarters, to his desk, slipped a tape in to view, leaned back, chewed a hangnail. The tape was an oddity, nothing but Tina doing mother things with Placidia.

# - 113 -

Turtle prowled restlessly, wishing he was over on *Anton Tregesser* with his brethren. But the Outsiders were not that trusting. His followers had a pair of Outsider pilots who could not be coerced. He and the hostages were here on a Traveler wearing false ID, babysat by a hundred commandos. The councillors were safe on a Traveler also masquerading, excepting a handful who had gone out on a fourth ship to talk it over with the Godspeakers.

His people would be alert for the courier, ready to start shooting if the answer was "No." They would cripple this Traveler and try to board before the Outsiders could dispose of their hostages. They would take out the Outsider delegation, for whatever pain that would cause.

The Outsider soldiers stayed out of his way but kept him in sight. They did not trouble him. He had lived most of his life surrounded by enemies.

Midnight, though, did trouble him.

His pacing brought them face to face. "You've been avoiding me, Turtle."

"Yes. I don't know how to make you understand."

"Why are you doing this?" Ignoring what he had said. And not appealing for information but accusing him by asking a question for which there would be no acceptable answer.

"Because I am what I was made to be. Like you, I have no choice." That should make sense to her. "I was created to battle the dragon."

Midnight would not be able to grasp a long-range plan. She lived in a perpetual now, with only the vaguest feel for any future more than a few days distant, and had no more grasp on the past. Did she even recall WarAvocat or Merod Schene? She never spoke of them. She no longer asked what had become of Amber Soul.

"Do you have to, even when it serves a greater evil?"

She might not illuminate the universe with her brilliance, but she could arrow in on the hard questions. He did the one thing she always understood. He hugged her.

He stepped back and really looked at her. And was troubled by what he saw.

She had Blessed to herself now, without competition from Tina Bofoku or the House. She should be radiant. But she seemed a little frayed, her wings a little off-color, wilted, like a leaf just begun to fade. He felt a touch of sorrow.

The breath of time had fallen upon Lady Midnight.

An artifact of her sort stayed looking young longer than women of woman born, but not forever, and when age did come it came quickly. Soon she would be capable only of a crude imitation of her dance in flight, and then only in free fall. Her wings would fade, then wither and stiffen, then would fall off. And if she did not take her own life in despair, she would have only a few months more.

She would not know what was coming. She would be puzzled and hurt but innocent. By that much was her inability to focus beyond the moment a boon.

She had, at the most, ten years. Likely closer to five.

Such were the sorrows of being a Ku warrior trapped inside this time-linear human culture. The friends all fell while the enemy went forever on, persistent as the stars themselves.

He hugged her again. There would be little time left in which to know and appreciate her.

Alarms hooted. He felt the electric crackle as inertial systems cranked up. "The courier has broken away. Go to your cabin. Stay there till we know what happened." He used that tone he knew she would not question. She went, hurrying.

He went to his own quarters to await the decision of fate.

Lupo Provik looked in half an hour later. "They went for it."

Turtle knew. He would have been dead or rescued by now

had the decision gone the other way.

## - 114 -

Jo and AnyKaat put three meters between them, approached the shuttle cautiously. An unscheduled shuttle was unprecedented. One that asked for them specifically, claiming it had orders to lift them topside, seemed impossible. Had one of their letters gotten through? That had become too much to hope.

Far easier to believe that House Tregesser had sent someone to finish what Provik had begun.

One nervous spacer stood at the base of the boarding ladder, watching. Above, a scab-on weapons turret turned slowly. They were inside its angle of depression. Promising, but not entirely reassuring. The killers might want to make sure they hit the right targets.

The spacer sweated the weapons centered upon him. He gulped air before he croaked, "Lieutenant Jo Klass? Is one of you her?"

Jo asked, "What about it?"

"There's a Traveler at station looking for you. If you're her. They chartered us to get you."

"Who?"

"I don't know."

AnyKaat said, "I don't like it, Jo."

"If it's our friends from… the ship, they might not want anybody to guess who they are."

"Neither would our enemies."

"Still the best chance we're going to get. We'll be off the ground."

AnyKaat could not argue with that.

"You want to go in first? Or should I?"

AnyKaat darted forward.

"Wait a minute!" The spacer grabbed and missed. The muzzle of Jo's hairsplitter came to rest beside his left eye. "She can't go in there."

"Why not?"

"Klass is the one we're supposed to get."

"It's your lucky day. You get two for the price of one."

"But..."

"She goes. Or we all stay." She drew the weapon given her by the Ku. "One pop from this and that skin isn't fit for vacuum. Right?"

The turret whined. The air barked a baby thunderclap. Somebody watching had gotten too excited or too close. That would be the only warning shot.

"You got a way with words, Lieutenant."

"You want to get out of here? Let's move."

The spacer climbed a few rungs, stopped. Jo prodded him. He climbed.

AnyKaat waited inside the hatchway. She had another one sprawled on the deck plates. She guessed, "One more in the turret and one in Control. Four is all they have on one of these."

"Control, then."

AnyKaat led. The spacers followed sullenly. The shuttle, despite the turret, was not set up for rough trade. Control's hatch could not be locked and was not closed when they reached it.

The man at the controls was overweight and balding. He eyed women and weapons, shook his head, clucked his tongue. "STASIS can sort this one out." He punched a button. "Come one down, Mag. We're gonna lift."

AnyKaat took one of two empty seats. The older man rolled his eyes. "Plant yourself, Mark. Rest of you get back to the cabin so we can get this circus off the ground."

Jo eyed him, then nudged the man who had lost his seat.

"Let's go. Watch comm, AnyKaat."

"I'm on it."

The turret operator was down when they reached the passenger cabin. She was a match for the older man. Was this a mom and pop operation? These days? But this was V. Rothica 4, almost wholly abandoned by House Merod.

Liftoff came so smoothly Jo barely noticed. She divided her attention only two ways, between the people she watched and the people she might encounter soon. The latter had become the greater worry. These seemed content to let station deal with two hardcases.

The shuttle clunked into its dock. Systems wound down. Jo popped her harness and backed to the Control hatchway. "How does it look, AnyKaat?"

"They behaved."

"What have we got? You get a visual outside?"

"There are two Haulers in, one Merod and one Majhellain Specialized. The Merod has been here five months with a down tractor vane. The Majhellain came in last week and is replacing the Merod's vane. I got a visual confirm. The only other ship in is a Pioyugov Traveler, *Dawn Watch*."

Which meant nothing. Pioyugov Navigation were mercenaries of the pure blood. They worked for anyone who met their price and would play all ends against the middle to squeeze the maximum profit.

"We'll go out with these four. How far around from the Traveler are we?"

"A kilometer."

"Great. What's the visual on dockside?"

"Dead except for a standard docking crew for a shuttle, a crabby looking bitch in Admins, and a kid wearing Spacers with Pioyugov patches. Looks like he might hit puberty any minute."

The shuttle's master shoved a gigantic smoke stick into his mouth. He did not fire it. "What kind of desperados are you broads, anyway? Besides crazy? This is V. Rothica 4 station, not some pirate hangaround."

"We're live desperados," Jo told him. "Going to stay that way, too. Get it shut down and let's go."

He went to work, shaking his head. "The people you got to deal with in this business."

Ten minutes later it was time to leave. Jo put the shuttle crew in front, which they accepted with more amusement than resentment. The older man went straight to the woman waiting dockside. "Made it one more time, Cyn." He gave her a cassette. "Twenty-six tonnes dry atmosphere. Credit us."

"Two passengers? I've only got paperwork for one. What's going on?"

"They're real convincing."

"Which one is Klass?"

"The mean-looking one. Have fun." He started walking. His bunch followed. Jo saw no reason to stop them.

The Admin woman glared at something in her hand. "Klass, Lieutenant Jo."

"Yeah?"

"ID and documentation."

Jo showed her the business end of a hairsplitter. AnyKaat watched the dock workers. They did not seem interested. "This is all the ID you're going to get. Let's take a hike over to that Pioyugov Traveler."

The woman looked at the weapon, maybe not recognizing the type but certainly the threat. "Regs say I have to..."

"Are regs to die for?" AnyKaat asked. She caught the Pioyugov boy's arm. "Where you going? Stick around. We need you both. Something happens, we want you right in the middle of it."

The woman said, "You people are crazy."

"And still alive after all these years." Crazy could be

situational, sometimes. "Start walking."

No one paid them any heed the whole kilometer, except for normal curiosity.

The boy got restless as they approached the docked Traveler. AnyKaat told him, "Don't even think about running. You look like a nice kid. Be a shame to blow a hole through your head."

Same song, third verse with the Pioyugov purser. He didn't have any Karwin AnyKaat on his list. He relented when they showed him heavy-caliber boarding passes.

"Operating bridge," Jo snapped the instant they were inside. "You two go ahead of us," she told the purser and boy. She had let the Admin woman go. "Hurry." They would be hearing from STASIS soon.

"Let's don't get trigger-happy now, Jo."

"I've got it under control."

A normal watch was on bridge for a Traveler in dock. They were startled when the human wave rolled in. Hands flew into the air, jaws dropped, one spacer cursed softly, thinking they'd been boarded by pirates. Jo thought they probably looked it. She wasn't wearing her dress blacks. "I'll cover. You hit the boards and see what's going on."

"Right." AnyKaat dragged a Pioyugov out of her seat.

The watch officer demanded, "What the hell...?" His question evaporated as Jo pointed the hairsplitter.

AnyKaat fiddled for several minutes. It had been a long time and she was not sure what to look for.

Jo heard something in the passage outside. She did not have her back to the hatchway. "Company, AnyKaat. Cover."

"Right."

Jo spun to cover the passageway.

*Lieutenant Jo. I have found you at last.*

"Seeker? You old sonofabitch! AnyKaat. It's Seeker. I think. What the hell is this? Was that really you in my nightmares?"

*It was a thin thread and a weak one, Jo Klass. It has been a long, hard search.*

"You found us. I could kiss you. Couldn't you kiss him, AnyKaat?"

"Yeah. Station's on with a bitch, Jo."

"Screw station." She had a thousand questions.

*Now we must find your commander.*

"Haget? He's dead. Long gone. You know that. You were there."

*The one called WarAvocat Hanaver Strate Dictat. There is much to tell him.*

"You bet your ass we're going to find him. We're going to let him know what the hell has been going on, then we're going to kick some ass."

"Jo."

She looked at AnyKaat. She saw a lot of pain that would not have awakened had they never broken free of Merod Schene. AnyKaat had a kid she hadn't seen in more years than they had figured out. Just one anchor point away. A lot closer than this station had seemed from Merod Schene till a few years, hours ago. "Yeah. Right. Seeker, we got to go on down the strand to P. Jaksonica. *Got* to."

*There, AnyKaat. That do it?*

She fought the panic that boiled up from the pit of her stomach. All those days of peril, all those nights of fear, all those years, with nothing constant, nothing trustworthy, but AnyKaat. Gone on so long it was programmed into her cells, it seemed. And now maybe about to be lost.

Jo suffered an almost paralyzing dread of being alone. It had been bad down below, but now it was worse. Now it was not something she could hold back by being the fastest and deadliest gun around.

"Station is all excited," AnyKaat said. "Somebody is going to have to deal with them before STASIS gets righteous."

Seeker faced the senior Pioyugov. The man's half of their exchange made it sound like Seeker's people had all but bought the Traveler. The Traveler's operators seemed inclined to do anything he asked. If they could understand what he wanted done.

The crew went to work. AnyKaat drifted out of their way. Jo told the purser, "Guess you'd better show us where to bed down."

He glanced at her hairsplitter, said, "Yes, ma'am."

## - 115 -

The convoy left the Web twice before crossing the Rim, each time so its commanders could pass information, each time far from any anchor point. Turtle was impressed. The Outsiders were more daring than Canon operators, who dreaded leaving the Web away from carefully calculated optimum insystem points. Few Canon-based ships were prepared for extended stays in starspace.

A Godspeaker ship waited at the second pausing place. It relayed the news that Tregesser commandos had uncrossed the planned double-cross in the Hemebuk Neutrality.

They could not make an issue of it. But Turtle was sure they would try to even scores later. He would have to keep them thinking they had not reached his useful limit.

The convoy made a long passage to the nether reaches of the Outsider empire, broke away into the wildest waste space Turtle had ever seen.

Interstellar gas and dust were so dense the galaxy outside could not be seen. Parts of the cloud were in such rapid motion that its electromagnetic voices formed an endless chorus of screams. Gasses and dust and clouds of cold matter ranging from sand to planetoids were torn this way and that by mad gravitational tides. At the waste's heart was a binary consisting of a black hole, a neutron star, and a living giant star that was being gutted by each in turn as the three whirled in a rapid orbital dance that distorted the very fabric of space. The cloud was no more than five light years across, yet Turtle could discern another dozen stars or protostars with his naked eye. Their fires lighted the dust, making sprawls of angel hair that braided into a firestorm spanning the entire sky.

Fourteen strands led into the maelstrom. Not a one was anchored.

Provik was intrigued. He thought a study of local conditions would reveal something about the Web, the study of which, for him, was something more than a hobby yet not quite an obsession.

"I tell you, Kez Maefele, if we survive this, I may just retire. The older I get, the less it seems worth the trouble. Shike would love to take over. I could give it to him. Take me a Voyager and go kiting off, trying to figure out what the Web is, why, where it came from, all that." There was real excitement in his eyes.

"An honorable pursuit," Turtle said. And not an original one. The Web intrigued everyone who came to it, of whatever species.

So far as anyone knew, the Web had always been. Yet it could not be explained by any physics or cosmology, scientific or religious. The Web had no physical right to exist. It should not do what it did. Yet it was there.

One of the mysteries of the Web was that no one ever found it independently. Every species that gained access learned how from a race already using the Web to beat the iron tyranny of the photon.

Dammit, that was like the universe itself. No matter how deep you dug, you could not come up with a First Cause.

"An honorable pursuit," Turtle said again. "But I've never heard of anyone making real progress on it. Even Valerena's Guardship, which spent centuries at it, did not do much but chart reaches not yet known."

Provik grunted. He did not want to hear that his dreams were impractical.

The convoy moved into the waste space slowly, following beacons, traveling with screens up. The clutter was so dense and unpredictable no chart remained reliable. Two days after leaving the tag end, it reached a spinning canister of a station in a pocket kept swept of dangerous cold matter.

Soon after breakaway Turtle knew the Outsiders believed they had him in complete control. They began feeding him data of a sort a WarAvocat would kill for. Its delivery guaranteed his best chance for success. And that the Outsiders had no intention of releasing him, ever.

At one point Provik observed, "Now we know how they came up with such outrageous quantities of rare metals. Must be stars blowing up here all the time."

Several score ships budded the station. They betrayed the varied concepts of shipbuilding of at least ten races. The lean, swift killer ships of Outsider humans predominated. Standing off, too massive to snuggle up, were three of the vessels operated by the Godspeakers themselves.

Industrial-type construction was under way nearby. "They are preparing their last redoubt," Turtle guessed. "They do not have a falsely optimistic view of their military chances. A pity we Ku could not have had access to a region like this."

"Why?" Midnight asked, awed by the fury of the waste space.

"We would be fighting still. The Guardships could not have rooted us out. They could have done nothing but contain us, and that would have required the efforts of half the fleet forever."

The Outsiders knew they could not win. They had acquired him to buy time to develop the waste space as a hiding place of the mysteries of a dark faith.

The Godspeakers would not be too concerned about the loss of an empire. The pain of that would torment their human pets-slaves-allies.

The waste would be no boon to those. Those who retreated here would have to hide far deeper than this station lay. They would have to stay on the move amidst chaotic matter. Operations outside would require long voyages to the tag ends, starspace voyages measured in decades.

Did the Outsider humans understand that their masters were going to abandon them?

The existence of this place, and the planning behind it, said many things. One was that Turtle was caught in the jaws of another moral quandary.

To engineer the destruction of Starbase in a manner that insured that Canon had to change radically to survive was not the same as destroying it to guarantee the survival of a repugnant and predatory creed.

He glanced at the Valerena, at Blessed, at the Proviks, as though for inspiration—and found it. In what they were. In what they represented. One of Canon's great pestilences could become a blessing, through their greed.

There was unimaginable wealth in this waste space. Let the Houses battle the darkness for it.

"This may be our home for a long time," he said. "Let's hope it's not our last."

The Outsiders had an agenda more brisk than Turtle's. They barely gave him a chance to find his quarters before they put him to work.

The heart of the station was a major military headquarters. They presented it to him in its entirety. All its resources and personnel were assigned to his project. He was shown how things worked, given a team of translators, and was told to get busy.

They gave him access to everything worth knowing about their military and industrial capacity. They gave him technicians who could communicate with any Godspeaker anywhere on the Web, through Godspeakers here. He could check every fighting unit and what it faced. He could take charge if the whim hit.

His employers were determined to let him do his job.

It was a General's dream.

He had been created an all-powerful warlord, but even he could not believe this.

Turtle spent most of his time in that command center, learning, putting together what needed putting together, running models, reaching across the light years to experiment, even interfering where interference would save lives and forces or would avoid stupidities that offended him professionally. And all the while his employers studied him, feeling for the truths within.

The methane breathers watched every breath he took, humping and slithering through transparent pressurized tubes that meandered throughout the station.

Sometimes he could not resist temptation, used his power to twist Guardship noses. It was a trying year for the fleet.

Turtle found fewer and fewer occasions to consult his conscience. He had become too caught up doing what he had been designed to do.

The Outsiders even presented him with a command ship, of a type as yet uncommitted to combat, unsubtly named *Delicate Harmony.* It came complete with quarters for six Godspeakers, his long-range communicators. And keepers.

## - 116 -

WarAvocat quietly attended the business of a ruthless, efficient, merciless conquest. Deified criticism faded.

He shared his thoughts with no one but Aleas. Aleas did not criticize when she disagreed. She argued, but did not carp or collude or try to rally the opinions of others, as the Deified had become accustomed to do since Makarska Vis introduced the spirit of divisiveness.

He had thoughts he reserved from his best friend. Perhaps *Gemina* knew them. *Gemina* knew so much. But *Gemina* did not betray him.

Long months after *VII Gemina* crossed the Rim, during a quiet interval, he tested the waters. "Something dramatic has happened on the other side, Aleas. Have you noticed?"

"They're getting harder to find and it's harder to get them to stand still when we find them. And they're more clever than they were."

"Uhm?"

"Maybe they're adopting some of our tactics?"

He slipped a sheet of hard copy out of a stack. "Read this."

Three Guardship assault, Objective Sixty-Nine, sector capital, four orbital fortresses. Point Guardship, magnum launch, object, forcing fortresses to raise screens. Enemy fighters launched. Standard. Nonstandard, attack upon fighters rather than Guardships.

Present insystem, twelve methane breather heavies, at distance, never before seen in concentration. Remained passive till time to recover and rearm fighters.

Warship fighters launched. Guardships forced to raise screens. Guardship secondaries decimated. Fortress-based and ship-based fighters alternate waves. Outsiders gain total secondary supremacy.

Point Guardship surprised at point of attack, Hellspinner funnel flooded with counterbarrage of self-shielded CT projectiles. Point Guardship disabled. Support Guardships destroy fortresses. Outsider secondaries destroy disabled Guardship. Support Guardships attempt close engagement with methane breathers, which remain at distance, employing secondaries.

WarAvocats consult, elect to return to Starbase. Methane breathers block path to Web strand, intentionally collide with one Guardship. Remaining Guardship retires at speed through starspace, catching strand after shaking pursuit.

This warning four months old.

Aleas read it twice. WarAvocat said, "That's not out of my fevered imagination. *Gemina* analyzed the action at Objectives Sixty through Seventy-Five. There's been a shakeup in the enemy high command. Chicken or egg, dramatically different goals have been adopted. They're preserving their best and maximizing our losses. To me that says they're preparing something they think will rock Canon and galvanize its enemies. They're getting ready to bet everything on one pass of the dice."

"I can't contradict you." Aleas was troubled. She looked at him oddly, decided to speak her mind. "You think the Ku is directing them."

"That's possible. It's also possible they've learned how to run a war."

She did not bite at the disclaimer. "And you're sure he'll take a shot at Starbase."

"That's a possibility, too. But not the only one. There's the operation he was planning when he got the rug yanked by the Ku Surrender."

"I'm no student of the times. Illuminate me."

"He was going to try Capitola Primagenia."

Aleas frowned.

"It's an easier target. Imagine the impact Outside. Imagine the civil chaos. He might prefer Starbase but he's a realist. He doesn't try to do something when he doesn't have the resources."

"You might suggest that an attack on Capitola Primagenia could be coming, but don't mention the Ku. Some of the Deified think you're as screwy about him as Makarska Vis."

WarAvocat snorted. When the hour came, he would bet his immortality on his intuition. He would use all his power to do what had to be done.

Meantime, there were worlds to conquer.

## - 117 -

Lupo looked up as Two came in. "What did they think?" A fraction of the take from the Hemebuk Neutrality had arrived. T.W. and one of the Valerenas had introduced the Directors to the undistributed pile. Two had gone along disguised as one of T.W.'s assistants.

"They were impressed. T.W. told them there would be more. I didn't hear much grumbling about how we shut them out."

"Simpletons. As long as they can afford to indulge themselves, they don't care *what* we do. It was worth the investment for the little time we need."

Lupo Provik had embezzled the majority of the Outsider payoff. He'd already bought the shell and assets of a dying colonial corporation from artifacts who had hoped to establish their own closed society. He had gotten a bargain by agreeing to maintain their social goals.

Now he was shopping for independently held, financially troubled, potentially profitable star systems, preferably with the foundation infrastructures in place. Given those, he could put together a new House. With capital left over.

It would not be House Tregesser, but it would be safe.

It would be a veil behind which he and his could vanish. If the dam just held till he cobbled it together.

Two said, "There's something going on out there in the shadows."

"Uhm?"

"Somebody is going to try something. A couple of the Directors had that slinky feel. And there are tensions down below. Like people sense a storm gathering."

Lupo leaned back, frowned, wondered who and why. "Anything concrete?"

"No."

"Any ideas?"

"Not unless the Worgemuth faction thinks it's a good time to unforget and forgive about Myth."

"I can't buy that."

"I don't either, really."

"What's T.W. say?"

"She feels it but she hasn't found anything. I told her to keep an eye on everybody since there's no sane reason for anybody to try something."

"Tina too?"

"Even Tina. What the hell are you messing with? You've been at it for two days."

"Putting together specs for a star chart like we had in the end space. I figure if we're going into business on stolen money, we ought to buy at least one toy while we're at it."

# - 118 -

It took a week to get loose. The Pioyugovs had to do some fancy talking and, Jo suspected, had to grease a few palms. Station could get away with screwing aliens easier than humankind.

At P. Jaksonica 3 they collided with bureaucracy grinding its finest, for reasons not immediately clear. Station said that since Jo and AnyKaat had no documentation, they could not be permitted egress from the Traveler. But hundreds of people ought to be able to identify AnyKaat. And Station Master Magnahs and STASIS Director Otten should remember her. But Admin played the game as though what mattered was not people but papers. They wouldn't even let AnyKaat see her mother or son. Wouldn't notify them that someone claiming to be AnyKaat had arrived.

The people responsible bulwarked themselves behind a claim for need of a clearance from Sector General Secretariat.

Jo's patience cracked. She established herself in the Traveler's lounge, told a steward, "Tell Amber Soul I want to see her as soon as possible."

Amber Soul came immediately.

Jo had found she could communicate with her more completely than she could with Seeker. They had Merod Schene in common. Emotionally Jo shared little with Seeker but goals.

She told Amber Soul, "I've lost patience with these dinks. They're tearing AnyKaat apart. I want to go twist some arms. I want you to go along and scare the shit out of anybody who gives me any grief. Can you do that?"

*Yes.* As simple as that, understanding bridging the gulf.

"Let's go." The opposite of bureaucracy. Decide. Do it.

Jo did not see what Amber Soul showed the STASIS guards dockside. They took off howling. What if somebody got scared and did something stupid and lethal?

They had no trouble reaching the hub, and got there fast enough to catch Gitto Otten as he was sneaking away from his office. Amber Soul put a fear in him that welded his feet to the deckplates.

Jo said, "I came up to deliver a message. We're pulling out on the tenth. Headed for Starbase. I estimate a max thirty-two-day turnaround. You recall how Guardships get about respect? I think you'll see one here about the twelfth of next month. Unless something really upbeat happens here before the tenth. You get my drift?"

Otten gulped, looked over her shoulder, over his own, and found no help there. "Are you threatening me?"

"Damned straight."

Otten sputtered.

"Think about it. Get advice from Master Magnahs. You don't have much time." She headed back to the Traveler.

AnyKaat's son and mother reached the Traveler twelve hours after Jo visited Director Otten. The boy was pale and anxious, probably armed with only the vaguest memories of his mother. With them came a nervous Admin clerk who handed over "emergency" documentation for AnyKaat and Jo. He delivered a hasty, mumbled admonition about getting final approval from Sector General Secretariat, then fled.

Jo hung around as long as it took to be introduced, then withdrew. She took a lot of pain back to her cabin. After calling Otten and delivering a polite "Thank you," she lay down in the dark to stare at an overhead she could not see, wondering why that reunion filled her with hurt when she should be pleased for her friend.

Next day AnyKaat took advantage of her new mobility to go in search of friends. Jo watched her go. She looked troubled. Like she had not found what she wanted with her mother and son.

Jo knew. You could not go back. She had been through that time warp. A bad case of divergence shock awaited her now. She had evolved since last she was aboard *VII Gemina*.

The Guardship would not have changed.

That face of the future terrified her.

Amber Soul caught her at the exit hatch, in her dark musing.. *Seeker would consult with you, Jo Klass.*

Startled, Jo grunted, recovered. "Of course." He must be getting impatient.

It was her first visit to the suite the aliens shared. The smell hit her like a blow, made her eyes water. It was like a place overpopulated by untrained pets.

They had brought a little of home with them, murky lighting, odd furnishings, the smell that was mostly just of themselves, a chill to the air. Their only concession to her comfort was humanlike appearance. Jo realized she'd never seen them in their true shape.

*Those who carry wickedness across the Web, who have made themselves the enemies of my people, which has not known violence since before yours evolved, have begun to move in more dangerous directions. They have found new weapons.*

Jo pictured the Outsiders armed with Hellspinners. She did not take into account the imprecision with which her brain rendered what it received. She rubbed the tears away, tried to breathe shallowly. That did no good.

*Time is a luxury no more, Jo Klass. They are planning moves. They are sufficiently pressed that they are not discussing those moves across the Web. They are afraid. Those who fear are doubly dangerous, and those who serve them nurture their fears, for they have a broader investment in their philosophical symbiosis.*

"Wait a minute. Those methane breathers can read each other's thoughts clear across the Web?"

*Yes.*

"And your people can tap into that? And you never told us?"

Maybe Seeker had, she reflected, back when he'd had his first interview with WarAvocat. The implication had been there.

*We are old as a species and as individuals. Our young are rare and precious, as is our solitude. Once we had our hour on the galactic stage, our time of exploration and adventure, but ages ago we turned away and returned home to contemplate what we had learned. We knew the Web well. It continued to be a source of news. We let the players on the galactic stage be. Most have been perceptive enough not to trouble the aged. Till your kind sprang up here and there, inexplicably, like fungi, and as often as not faded as quickly.*

*You excited a small, renewed outward interest because you were so absurd.*

*You came from nowhere, headed nowhere. You do not have one unique quality but the qualities you do have exist in paradoxical juxtaposition. You are capable of rejecting the evidence of science and reason in order to believe the impossible, yet you are so curious about hows and whys that you keep picking at a scab concealing a secret even knowing that it will devour you. You are lawless, predatory, capable of eating your own young in the search for profit, yet you created something unprecedentedly lawful in the Guardship fleet. That is flawed, skewed, even internally aberrant, but it is evolving toward what it should be. At the moment the messengers of shadow believe the Guardships are invincible. But soon they will be shown the truth.*

*I must find your WarAvocat and make him see. Amber Soul and I must make available the wisdom of our kind while the Guardships remain capable of becoming what they should be.*

Jo did not know if something was getting lost or if she was just stupid. That had been Seeker's longest and most revelatory communication ever and, she suspected, his most carefully rehearsed, but she did not think she had gotten the true sense of what he wanted to convey. She sensed his disappointment. She said, "If it's that critical why waste time looking for *VII*

*Gemina?* Go to Starbase."

*The warning must be presented to someone with the capacity, even the inclination, to listen. Will I find such a person at Starbase?*

"Probably not."

*Then we must find the man who will listen. There is not much time. You must tell the other one.*

What she had expected. Telling them to get their butts in gear. "I will."


When AnyKaat came back, Jo figured it would be just to gather whatever she wanted to take with her. She went to the lounge to make up her mind if she would put herself through a farewell scene or just let it slide.

She had a drink. It did not help. She concocted another with twice the firepower, but then just sat there nursing it.

"There you are. I thought you'd disappeared."

The moment had come. But AnyKaat did not look like she was going anywhere. Looked ragged as hell, in fact. "Hi." Glumly. "Got a message for you from Seeker."

"He wants to get moving. Don't take much genius to guess that." She sat down.

"You got it. How'd it go?"

"It didn't. Jo, I can't talk to my own mother. She doesn't have the slightest idea what I'm telling her. The things she tells me all seem shallow and trivial after Merod Schene. And my son doesn't know who the hell I am and doesn't trust me enough to want to find out. My old friends are scared of me. Degas's people aren't the least bit shy about telling me it's all my fault he isn't here. Era's people aren't talking at all. The department is in a tizzy because the back pay they owe us, with the interest setup we had, will screw the budget for a couple of years. They wrote us off and stopped figuring us in. Not to mention what my accrued seniority might mean if I get plugged back into the system."

Jo mixed her one of her favorites. "Chew on this."

AnyKaat took a gulp. "I would've been better off if we hadn't gotten off V. Rothica 4. Hell. Everybody would have been better off. They wouldn't all hate me for turning up alive and making them feel guilty about how they feel."

Jo grunted. She could not think of anything to say to that.

"It hurts, Jo. Even when you understand what's going on. All that time hanging onto a thread, and here wasn't here anymore when I got here."

"I know. I've been through it. And it's all I have looking at me when I catch *VII Gemina*."

AnyKaat fiddled with things not there. "So how do you cope with it?"

"I don't know. After a while we just avoid attachments and commitments. We put everything into being a good soldier."

AnyKaat closed her eyes, expression momentarily surprised. Jo suspected she had realized that a certain Guardship soldier had formed an attachment despite herself. She hoped AnyKaat would not want to talk about it. That was when things got strange and scary and misinterpreted and turned into things they were not.

"I told Otten we were pulling out on the tenth. That's about as long as Seeker will be patient. He's real worried."

AnyKaat took the offered escape hatch. "How come?"

"I don't know. He don't always make sense even when Amber Soul helps him try."

"She's weird. She gives me the creeps."

"She gives herself the creeps. She's lived through what you're suffering right now, a hundred times worse."

"Yeah." AnyKaat reached across, touched the back of Jo's hand. "Thanks, Jo."

"Hunh? What?"

"Nothing. I got to check some things out."

Jo watched her leave, puzzled.

AnyKaat was aboard *Dawn Watch* when the Traveler undocked. Her face was puffy from crying. She could not forget all she had chosen to leave behind, though she had lost it long ago. Jo left her alone.

Jo did not think she could have walked away rather than cling to the edges of the once known....

Seeker had a vague notion where to start looking, almost two months of hard running beyond the Rim. The crew did not argue. However they were being paid, it was enough to make them bite down on their fear.

With unavoidable stops, misnavigations, and evasions, four months elapsed before *Dawn Watch* reached its destination. *VII Gemina* was not there. There was nothing in that system but the leavings of an old skirmish the defenders had not won. Seeker would have to continue spying on the methane breathers till he extracted a hint where to move next.

# - 119 -

Blessed gazed in apparent benignity on the hundreds gathered in the back courts of his Fuerogomenga Gorge castle. Most were watching an outstanding nighttime display in the canyon. The Directors were all there. All the senior managers had come. Only T.W. Trice had failed to appear. No excuses, no regrets, no nothing, just no show.

Nyo came to stand beside him. "Fantastic party so far. You figured out which one she is?" He indicated the Valerena holding court below.

"The one out of the inner office. Cable says the others are holed up in the old place in the High City, having a party with some men they scraped up out of DownTown. Cable can take care of it."

Nyo sighed, relieved. He was not handling the pressure well. "That puts a lock on it, doesn't it?"

"Except for T.W. We don't have her covered. But I can handle her."

"What about Tina?"

"Tina and Placidia are away from it and perfectly safe. Did you bring Rash Norym?"

"She's inside."

"Bring her out here. *I* want her seen with me."

Nyo shrugged, went inside, herded a flustered Rash Norym onto the balcony. "Is this wise?" she demanded.

"Probably not for you if we screw up. Which means you'd better give it all you've got to make sure we don't." He smiled. Rash Norym had been a big help, but he could not shake the feeling that she was holding back. "Tonight is the night."

"I... I don't think you should."

"Why not?"

"Uh... T.W. is sure there's something going on. She's doing things that look like she's getting ready for something." It had been a stroke of luck, finding Norym in Intelligence. Pity she could not have gotten closer to the center.

"Her people would have to be deaf and blind to miss all the signs, wouldn't they? The question is, does she know where it's coming from?"

"I don't think so. But I don't think you should count on that making any difference. She seems sure she can handle anything."

"Let's find out. Nyo, send out the word."

Bofokú gulped a mouthful of air, bobbed his head, went to push the thing past the point of no return.

Blessed leaned on the balcony rail, smiling and waving, and waited for his soldiers to move in.

Kez Maefele had left him with a useful little army. Be a

shame to waste it.

Cable Shike had left the High City house reworked to his own specifications when Blessed moved. Just in case, someday. Someday had come. He entered his codes. A prepped security system not only allowed him inside, it concluded that he was not there at all. He must be a ghost or glitch.

He asked how many people were in the house and where they were. Four men and three women, all in one upstairs suite.

He went.

They had the place to themselves. They did not need to close doors.

Cable glanced in from the darkened hallway. The Valerenas were in a NoGrav bubble with two men, preoccupied. A third man leaned against a sideboard, naked, dull-eyed, sipping something, watching like he had come along only because he had not had anything better to do. The fourth man was nowhere in sight. He would be behind the closed bathroom door.

The man at the sideboard glanced Cable's way when Shike released the safety on his hairsplitter. The man said, "Aw, shit!" and squealed when the pellet hit him.

Cable snapped quick shots at the others as they broke it up, to slow any running starts, then finished it carefully, without them getting off a yell loud enough to disturb the man using the toilet. The Valerenas went out looking at him like they could not believe what was happening.

He still had trouble getting a hold on it himself.

He laid his weapon down, left the house at a brisk walk, pausing only to tell the security system to start raising hell. That poor bastard in the john. He was in for some heavy shit.

Shike checked the time. Fifteen minutes ahead of schedule. He checked the time again as he walked in one of the ground-level entrances of the Tregesser Pylon. Still fifteen up. Right on track.

The Directors, separated from everyone else, got real attentive after Blessed splattered the Valerena's brains all over the wall. He settled atop a shaga wood desk that had belonged to his mother. He held his weapon negligently but pointed in their direction. "It's a long story. I'll only hit the high points."

He told them the last thing Provik had let them in on was his grandfather's death. He told them about the Simon Other trying to kill him, Valerena, and Provik. He told them about Valerena gaining control of *VI Adjutrix* and the fate that had befallen her. He told them about Provik making a deal with the surviving Valerenas, then about the campaign by the Outsiders to force Tregesser assistance. He told them about the hostages House Tregesser had been forced to give.

He slipped off the desk, walked across the room, walked back, slapping his hairsplitter into his palm. "With Provik gone there's only one man on Prime whose testimony would get any serious attention if a question about the identity of the Valerenas arose. They were about to correct that. With help from some of you. I was lucky. I had a friend in the other camp."

They would find that plausible. It fit the absurdities of House politics. Once they bought the whole, that could be transformed into a mandate for a housecleaning.

"I've moved first. A lesson I learned from Provik. The matter will be settled before dawn. You're all here. We have a quorum. Before I go into the city I want my succession formally accepted."

What choice did they have? Anyone who voted against him would set himself up to be purged.

Nyo settled into the skimmer beside Blessed, buckled in.

Blessed asked, "What's the matter?" He started the skimmer rolling, checked the time. "Cable will move soon. Trice will be all that's left."

Nyo glanced back at Rash Norym, squeezed into the luggage space behind them, and through the back light at vehicles carrying twenty nonhuman commandos. Norym was terrified. "I don't know, Blessed. Maybe I'm turning wimp. But I have a feeling we missed an angle."

Blessed was euphoric. He could not conceive of anything going wrong now. They would catch T.W. sleeping and that would be that.

Three and Five had sent an alarm to the family already when T.W. hustled in, still fuddled from sleep. "You got the flash from the High City?"

"Yes. This might be it."

"Cable Shike just walked in downstairs."

Shike's half-brother and two associates from the Black Ring watched the three vehicles dwindle into the distance. "Right on time."

"Let's go."

Two minutes later they were inside the castle, undetected by guards or security systems. Four minutes later still they reached the room where House Tregesser's Directors were confined. There were no guards outside. They burst into the room, shot everyone there, and were out of the castle within eight minutes more.

The assistant assassins, with no idea who their victims had been, met a similar fate within minutes.

Blessed and Nyo entered the Pylon and started the long trek to the lifter banks. Commandos came in various entrances and drifted toward the banks, too. Blessed and Nyo would disarm the security checkpoints ahead of them.

Blessed glanced around. The place was as quiet as it should be. Cable was sipping a drink at the island usually occupied by someone from Provik's office, security's outermost sentinel. Blessed was now sure he could move fast enough no matter what alarms he tripped. He had the people and the equipment to do the job.

It went perfectly at every checkpoint. And the more promising it looked, the darker Nyo's mood became, as if he was more afraid of success than he was of failure.

They reached the level where Trice lived, spread out. Rash Norym had provided a floor plan. They penetrated at four points, advanced on Trice's apartment, broke into that and headed for her bedroom.

It was empty.

Nyo said, "Oh, shit!"

Blessed was rattled but refused to show it. "So she broke routine. So we have to hunt her down. We've got the people."

"She was in bed. It's messed up. She's gone. And she has the people, too. A lot of them, trained by the Ku while he was building in the planetary defense stuff."

"These guys are veterans, Nyo. Come on. We'll get her."

The comm beside Trice's bed beeped. T.W. appeared on its viewscreen.

"I knew it," Nyo said. "She was laying for us."

"Norym is dead meat." Blessed covered the visual pickup, opened the circuit.

Trice said, "That level has been isolated, Blessed. Utilities and services are about to be withdrawn. If you want to talk your way out of this, send your people home. You and Nyo take the freight lift to Lupo's office." The screen went dead. The lights died a moment later.

"Better talk," Nyo said. "We'd be fighting shadows. She knows where we're at and what we've got. We don't know what she's got. We don't know these aliens will stick if the shit starts flying."

"Cable won't be happy." Shike wanted House security.

"He'll understand. Hell, maybe she'll give it up. She wants out alive, too."

"Maybe." Blessed wished he could see his soldiers to get a read on their attitudes. They knew what was happening. Nyo was right. They wouldn't stick for all or nothing. "Damn her. We don't have any choice."

He had gone from euphoria to despair in two minutes.

Lupo and Two stepped into the office a moment after Blessed and Nyo walked in. Nyo said, "Oh, *shit!*" This debacle had robbed him of his vocabulary.

Blessed looked like he was going to faint. "You?"

"Me, Blessed. Sit down." Lupo checked them for weapons. Two covered, smiling her little smile. "They're clean." T.W. glared at them, not pleased.

Cable Shike walked in.

Two's smile grew as Blessed worked it out.

"Cable?"

"I didn't want it this way."

"Why?"

"Placidia. Tina. Sooner or later you were going to realize you weren't Placidia's father. Sorry."

Blessed glanced at Provik. "Did you know?"

"I suspected. Don't be too broken up. He couldn't make up his mind till the last second. Not that you could have pulled it off anyway. Though you might have gotten to T.W. Which makes her real happy. She keeps muttering about how she used to change your diapers."

Nyo looked more desperate by the moment. He did not understand everything—especially not Lupo and his woman being here instead of off with the Ku—but he did see that he and Blessed had stumbled into a position where the others could not forgive and forget.

Blessed was slower. He didn't get it till Cable said, "I'm really sorry," and walked out.

"T.W? You want the honors?"

"Provik! You can't do this! I'm the Chair!"

"You're the Blessed Other. You just tried the biggest double-shuffle of all time. As Shike will explain to the Directors when he releases them. If the Ku comes home, Cable can discover a huge miscarriage of justice. I won't care. I won't be here."

Lupo secured the comm, grim. "That was Shike. It's not over. He found the Directors all shot to death when he got home. Five, Six, you go. Take forensic people. Find me something."

He was angry and depressed. He did not have time for this. Why couldn't Blessed have waited?

## - 120 -

*Delicate Harmony* let go its last hold on station. Station reciprocated. The mixed bridge gang backed off on steering jets, turned, sought the beacon range. Comm chattered with station, with two ships already in the range, with four that would come out behind *Delicate Harmony*.

Turtle's flag squadron was off to war.

Despite his circumstances, he was content. The restless warrior had sword in hand and a perspective too narrow to worry about anything but the dance toward battle with the dragon.

The wizard was not asleep. It rode observer, sardonically amused. This flagship was so bizarrely crewed. Turtle had his own followers, Ku and soldiers of four other species. He had six methane breathers in a sealed and pressurized environment at the heart of the ship. He had two hundred twelve Outsider humans, half of whom would have little to do unless he launched his two riders and four fighters. He had Blessed, Midnight, the Valerena, Provik and his woman, none of whom could contribute much but were, at least, where he had some chance to shape their destinies.

He'd had no trouble keeping them. The decision-makers over there believed their complement could control him and his twenty-four soldiers. They did not count the hostages as anything else.

Turtle was counting on them heavily.

His Outsiders laid the ship into the range the way they did everything, with humorless precision, keeping exact station on the ship ahead, a twin of *Delicate Harmony.* All the squadron were identical, drawn from a litter of thirty reserved for a debut during the operation.

Turtle looked at those Outsiders. They and the Guardship people would feel at home with each other. But for their ideals they were much alike.

His command. His first since the Dire Radiant. No fantasy now. Was he up to the task? Had everyone made too much of the legend?

His command. And every Outsider on three hundred ships would jump if he barked—so long as his methane breathers remained satisfied.

He went to his combat command center, which abutted the pressure hull of methane country. He scanned a display revealing last known dispositions of forces friendly and otherwise. The display was static now, several days behind realtime. Locations for the Guardships were guesswork. But that would change.

From the viewpoint of the Godspeakers, that simulated starscape had to be disheartening. There were just twelve worlds left where their kind held on. The number of subject worlds had begun to dwindle, too, as Guardships searched for forces they believed ought to be resisting them. At Turtle's suggestion those worlds were not defending themselves, Their mobile strength had been drawn off for his ever more complex operation.

Let them surrender, become a burden upon the enemy, and wait till they could be reclaimed.

The communication personas of the Godspeakers were susceptible to persuasion. Like their human aides, they believed what they wanted to be true.

The Outsiders were possessed of more strength than Turtle had expected. More than the Guardships suspected. So the grand plan had been expanded, his aims growing with his confidence in his power to manipulate those who wanted him to be their redeemer.

He would launch blows at both heads of the dragon. Capitola Primagenia would sustain the first strike.

Everyone went to stations as *Delicate Harmony* approached the tag end. In moments the Web would rattle with instructions for and communications from units throughout the Outsider empire and Canon. In moments the clock of the grand design would begin to run.

## - 121 -

The Pioyugov crew grew more sullen and fearful daily. Months had passed. They were sure they'd never get home. Jo was not sure she did not agree.

It was hard to sustain an allegiance to Seeker's obsessive search for a Guardship that was never there when they reached its last reported destination.

The Pioyugovs had come near rebelling twice. Seeker had charmed them. Signs were the storm was gathering again. Charm would not work a third time.

Jo told AnyKaat, "I've got to talk him into heading for

Starbase. Any bright ideas?"

"Lay it out and pound on the facts."

"Big help. We're going to run out of luck. We've had more than our share already. They know there's a Traveler loose out here. These Pioyugovs are sneaky, but nobody's good enough to get away from a whole fleet."

"Tell him."

Amber Soul answered her knock. She laid a finger to her mouth, a surprisingly human gesture. *He is listening. They have ended their silence.*

There was an undercurrent of excitement here. Whatever Seeker sensed, it was significant.

*I will let him know you are here when the moment is opportune. Unless I will serve. He will want to inform you.*

"We need to talk to him."

Amber Soul went to hover over Seeker, who had installed himself in a reclining chair of primitive manufacture. It was entirely mechanical.

Seeker distracted the eye from the chair, though. He was doing nothing to conceal his appearance. That, while bifurcate and bilateral, was as far from human as Jo could imagine. He looked like a snake that had tried to turn into a man and had gone down a blind alley toward albino, fishy horror built on birdlike feet. In places he was semitransparent.

Jo was not sure she ought to believe her eyes even now.

She turned her back so she could keep her mind on business. AnyKaat copied her. They spent twenty minutes rubbing water out of her eyes and wishing they were somewhere else.

*Lieutenant Jo?*

She turned. Seeker had on his public face. "Amber Soul says you've been listening in on the Outsiders."

*The Web is awash with their communications. So heavily it is impossible to follow everything. I will have to use Amber Soul as well if we are to keep abreast, if the deluge continues.*

"What's happened?"

*They have begun their counterattack, starting with great confidence that they will cause Canon and the Guardships much grief and force the Guardships to withdraw.*

"They won't do that. The Guardships don't defend Canon, they exterminate Canon's enemies. There's a difference."

*Their mission of vengeance is... different.*

*Their command force came onto the Web not long ago. It sent the order to begin, working against a count approximating one hundred of your days. There are many forces involved. One seems headed for Capitola Primagenia.*

"Shit! That would be a kick in the balls." Capitola Primagenia! That would set Canon's Rims afire. They might burn for centuries.

*Of interest to us is that ships have been sent to follow and report on Guardships. They may find VII Gemina for us. And a ship has been assigned to track us down.*

"That's about why I'm here. If we don't light out pretty soon the crew will kill us. They're too scared to reason with."

*Instruct the Chief Operating Officer to move toward friendly space. He is not to follow the direct strand. The hunter is coming that way. Go. We are in a race. Minutes may be critical. It is a long run to an anchor point where we can present the pursuit with more options than it can follow.*

Jo went, boggled and baffled, found the Pioyugov Chief, told him he could head for home and cautioned him that a hunter might be on their track.

Jo was in the galley when she felt Seeker's compelling summons. She dropped what she was doing and went. As Amber Soul beckoned her into the suite alarms sounded. "Proximity!" Jo cursed. "That sonofabitch took the direct strand."

*Yes.*

"Him and me are going to have a talk."

*Wait! Hope is not yet lost. It will take the hunter time to reach a turn node. We will have a fourteen-hour lead when it begins its chase. It will need several days to catch up. There is a Guardship we can reach first.*

"Which one?"

*I do not know. They are using a code for unhurried reports. Its identity matters less than its proximity.*

"To you, maybe. I'd as soon take my chances with the Outsiders as be saved by *IV Trajana* again."

*It is the only safe isle in a hostile sea.*

"I'm going to have my meeting of the minds with the Chief."

*I shall be along presently.*

Jo stopped off to consult her arsenal before visiting the bridge.

Jo or AnyKaat remained on the bridge every moment, armed and angry. They made sure the Pioyugovs held the heart of the strand and ran in the red.

They understood better a day later, when Seeker came onto the bridge. *The hunter is a new type. It has more power than expected. It is gaining faster than expected.*

"Catch that, genius?" Jo snapped at the Chief. "You wind this son out and stretch it or I'm personally going to make sure those bastards take *you* alive."

# - 122 -

Six Tregesser ships left P. Benetonica 3B together: three overstuffed Haulers, two crowded Travelers, and a Voyager carrying Lupo Provik, his family, and T.W. Trice. House Tregesser's fleet would limp for a while. Provik did not intend sending those ships home.

House Tregesser belonged to Tina Bofoku and Cable Shike

now. And Shike would have no trouble running it his way. It would be a long time before the Directorate recovered.

Lupo watched his homeworld dwindle. T.W. joined him. She was on the same wavelength. "Shike killed them, didn't he?"

"I think so."

"I checked every angle I could think of."

"He did it. Even if he and Tina can account for every second."

"Maybe if we knew what he planned before he walked into the Pylon and found out you weren't gone."

"It doesn't matter. He won't last. The Guardships or Outsiders will finish him before the year is up."

"I'm glad you finally took my advice." For years she had urged him to get out.

"We finally could afford to."

## - 123 -

WarAvocat rested his hands on the back of Aleas's seat. A black ship model floated before her. Its length-to-thickness ratio was the highest he'd ever seen. That indicated a high-powered linear-accelerator-type starspace drive. Ought to be a going sonofabitch running a straight course.

"New approximation?" The original had been watching them for two days.

"Yes. And *Gemina* doesn't like it. These bulges along here, all the way back, are riders." She tapped her board. Two lesser hulls separated from opposite sides of the main. "The riders' drives are always clear. They can output with the rider nested. These blisters between riders are fighters. They nest nose down thirty degrees with their drives clear."

"They can thrust to maneuver the main?"

"*Gemina* says the whole can outrun and outmaneuver most anything."

"Tractor vanes on the riders, too?"

"Light duty but mounted so they can supplement those on the main."

"A beautifully wicked piece of machinery."

"Probe has both oxygen and methane readings from inside."

"Let's see what it can do."

WarAvocat launched five riders and a dozen pursuit fighters on silent approaches. He and Aleas moved to WarCentral.

"WarAvocat. Target is moving."

Impossible. "No way could he have picked up our secondaries yet."

"*Gemina* concurs. Target action is independent of ours."

WarAvocat watched track data develop. Moving closer to the Web. And not sneaking. "Find its closest point of approach to the strand. Redirect the strike there."

The strand marked the apex of a triangle. The shortest leg ran to *VII Gemina*. Time passed. The Outsider spotted the secondaries. It accelerated.

"That bastard can move!"

"Attack speed," WarAvocat directed.

Minutes later, "WarAvocat, target has launched two riders and four fighters."

He asked Aleas, "Why? They can't handle what I sent." He studied the geometry. His secondaries would reach CPA moments behind the Outsiders.

A pinpoint of light appeared in the main action tank, waxed, waned, between converging forces. A breakaway.

On the time lag mark, *Gemina* piped, "... emergency. Guardship, this is Lieutenant Jo Klass TAD off Guardship *VII Gemina* aboard Pioyugov Traveler *Dawn Watch*. I have a bogie on my tail. Emergency. Emergency."

"Red One!" WarAvocat snapped. "Aleas. Missiles and

interceptors." Alarms wailed. "Access, OpsAvocat. Stand by to move ship."

A second breakaway came. The speaker added to her message, "The bogie is off the Web and launching. I have you fixed. I'm coming in hard."

Missile tracks moved toward the action at accelerations that would cause ordinary steel to creep like heated wax.

Aleas remarked, "She's cool."

"She's a good soldier." Jo Klass. Out here. With two top-tech Outsiders trying to keep her from getting home. What the hell?

They were shooting out there now.

His secondaries brushed the insystem group away from the Traveler. Others met the breakaway in a head-on firing pass. A fighter died on each side. The breakaway had not put out its riders. It was gaining on the Traveler fast. No way his secondaries could turn and catch up. The Traveler would live or die depending on Aleas's missiles.

The voice from the Traveler calmly announced, "Bogie is launching missiles."

WarAvocat watched his own streak closer, chased by lagging interceptors. He did not ask *Gemina* for the probabilities. He had a bad feeling and did not want it confirmed.

Klass must have had a bad feeling, too. "WarAvocat, we're getting a coded squirt from the Traveler."

"WarAvocat, the Outsider has done a rollover and is using full thrust to dump velocity."

They believed they had their kill.

He checked his secondaries. Most were maneuvering to face the Outsider's escape run. The other and its riders had climbed onto the Web, to safety, leaving its fighters to fend for themselves.

His first missiles streaked past the Traveler as the enemy's arrived. That fraction of the universe turned to fire.

"Guardship, we have damage aft. The ship is starting to break—" A roaring blast of static. Then nothing.

## - 124 -

Excluding *Delicate Harmony*, all ships of the new class had names like *Sword of Shadow*, *Fang of Darkness*, *Voice of Doom*. Turtle thought the Outsiders a real uplifting, cheerful bunch.

He had been summoned to combat because *Hunger of the Destroyer*, shadowing *VII Gemina*, and *Edge of Night*, chasing a mystery Traveler, had them a situation.

He entered combat, glanced at a display of that remote encounter. "What have we got?"

An Outsider brought him the brittle yellow paper they used for hard copy. "Transcript of in-clear messages from the Traveler to the Guardship. They transmitted more by coded squirt."

The Traveler had been fading when he arrived. Now a missile, making an appreciable percentage of the velocity of light, caught *Edge of Night*. End of that story.

*Hunger of the Destroyer* sat on the Web nearby, recovering its riders. It would resume shadowing *VII Gemina* once it had its riders aboard.

He scanned the intercepted messages. "Klass?" That did not seem possible. How much had she passed to the Guardship? Enough, probably.

"Who has seen these?" he asked.

One of his own said, "You and the tech who transcribed them."

Good. The tech would say nothing. He would not. No telling what the Tregesser hostages would do if they heard. Something suicidal, surely. This meant the game was up for House Tregesser.

What else it might mean remained to be seen. The wizard would have to chew on it.

*Delicate Harmony* continued its headlong plunge toward Canon space.

# - 125 -

WarAvocat let Klass's decrypted report scroll a few lines, stopped it. He glanced over to see how they were doing rounding up the chunks of the Pioyugov Traveler, to see if they were keeping that in the Guardship's shadow relative to the Outsider, which had broken off the Web again. Then he looked up.

The Deified had abandoned their screens. All but the Deified Kole Marmigus, who grinned a monster of a grin. Marmigus winked.

WarAvocat rolled the message back to start. "Aleas. Read this with me."

She did not look pleased but joined him. He let the message scroll. It ran a half-hour at his reading speed, hitting the high points of Klass's adventures.

Aleas had nothing to say.

If it stunned her, how much more impact on those Deified after his gonads? "Access, OpsAvocat. WarAvocat here. We'll be returning to Canon space as soon as we've completed recovery. Destination is P. Benetonica 3. Out."

Aleas said, "So. You win a big round with the Deified."

"I sure do. May take them weeks to start aggravating me again." He rose, confident that his power never had been greater or more secure, faced a ragged and badly aged Lieutenant Klass, who'd come into WarCentral with the other survivors from the Pioyugov Traveler.

Aleas asked, "What'll you do about the other Klass?"

Jo nearly lost it when she saw WarAvocat. AnyKaat caught her arm and steadied her. "Not yet, Jo. We're almost there."

Seeker touched her with a similar sentiment, though most of his attention was on Amber Soul, who was on her way to Hospital with several injured Pioyugovs.

Even the crew had been lucky, relatively. Only eight were missing.

Jo got hold of herself, advanced toward Strate, pleased that he was still in charge. Could she keep from smashing his face if he came up with some typical tight-ass officer's crap about her appearance?

He came to meet her. He wrapped his arms around her and held her. Must be shipwide cameras watching, she thought. "Welcome home, Colonel."

The bastard had her confused with Haget!

But she accepted his welcome, and enjoyed it till she collapsed.

## - 126 -

Turtle followed *VII Gemina*'s progress closely. The Guardship zigged, zagged, ducked in and out of starspace, doubled back, tried to ambush *Hunger of the Destroyer*. And could neither shake its shadow nor catch it. *Hunger* hung on like a tail.

Its commander deserved a commendation. Not only was he carrying out his assignment, he was causing *VII Gemina* to fall farther and farther behind by taunting it into wasting time on those maneuvers.

The wizard had reasoned it out. There had been a Meddinian aboard the Traveler. Probably one of the two he had talked Provik into sending home. Having concluded that, he studied the messages that had crossed the Web since the countdown began.

They might have gotten enough to anticipate the strike at

Capitola Primagenia.

If they'd just break off to vent their spleen on Tregesser Prime... He could advance the S. Alisonica attack. All units would be in position early. If *VII Gemina* could be drawn to Capitola Primagenia it would be too far away to interfere at Starbase.

This would be delicate.

*Delicate Harmony* crossed the Rim into Canon space. He shifted the countdown from a daily to an every-four-hour count on the chance the Meddinian had survived the destruction of its Traveler. He would not put that hope to the test till *VII Gemina* had paid its respects at Tregesser Prime. If it did.

It did.

Turtle gave the Guardship time to become preoccupied with the surprises he had bestowed upon P. Benetonica. Then he rattled the Web with a coded torrent.

His Godspeaker masters approved what he was trying to do.

Good. Their minds had to be adjusted to a specific set, too.

## - 127 -

WarAvocat had not mistaken Jo for Haget. He had promoted her. Hardly had she been cleared by Medical than she was chin deep in planning a chastisement operation against House Tregesser. Her assignment was War-Avocat's idea of a reward.

She was to lead the regimental combat team assigned to capture Tregesser Horata and the villains.

He made no mistake calling her Colonel. His mistake was failing to wonder what mischief Kez Maefele had been up to during his stay on Tregesser Prime.

*VII Gemina* broke off the Web and swooped in the grand Guardship style, attacking without warning, without explanation, to a system that went into a whining panic, wanting to know what they had done. They always did.

The change came when Jo's assault craft reached four thousand meters altitude, while riderships filled with invaders began forcing dockage all around station 3B.

Some unsuspected, undetected, automated system wakened.

A shaped blast gutted every docked rider. Soldiers already disembarked hurtled out of the ring, carried by the winds of decompression.

*VII Gemina* fighter patrols came under fire from a thousand small killer satellites.

Jo's assault craft encountered a barrage so accurate and intense forty percent did not reach the ground intact.

The survivors arrived scattered, disorganized, and without communications because a heavy jam blanket had spread over the whole region. Automatic strongpoints, indistinguishable from workaday structures, responded to the presence of unknown weapons. They were proof against all but the regiment's heaviest weapons.

It got worse when the city's shields went up. And worse still when Tregesser security forces counterattacked.

They were no untrained, disorganized rabble.

Jo survived the landing. She wondered if she would be as lucky with the inquiry certain to follow the fighting. This would not be an auspicious entry in her record.

WarAvocat had gone a sickly grey. He stood nose to nose with the worst moment of his life. WarCentral's wall display screamed debacle. Casualties already between forty-five hundred and six thousand. Those for the landing team were uncertain. *VII Gemina* had no contact with the ground.

Every station in the system had raised Guardship-quality screens. The 3A, an antique supposedly out of service, was spewing seeker mines that made fighter deployments suicidal.

Down below every significant population center had vanished behind a pearlescent screen.

WarAvocat had not encountered that before. He did not like it. He had the firepower to scorch Tregesser Prime several times over. If he tried, when he ran out of ammunition, those cities would be sitting there still. The atmosphere itself protected them from his most powerful arguments.

Aleas came. "Message just arrived via system traffic band. You'd better listen."

He accessed Communications. The shimmer behind his shoulder said, "Invader, your hostile behavior has triggered an automated doomsday defense which cannot be deactivated by anyone in this system. It will remain active till it is destroyed, you are destroyed, or its control is satisfied that you have withdrawn."

WarAvocat cursed. He accessed *Gemina* and discovered that he could not communicate with House authorities because of the jam blanket. He learned that those authorities had tried to warn *VII Gemina* before system defenses went active.

"Damn! We just shot ourself in the foot. I can hear the Ku laughing."

"You think he's responsible?"

"Yes. If we'd come in and said 'Please' and had taken Traffic direction, we wouldn't have run into anything. Only he would design a system triggered by our bad manners."

He asked *Gemina* for tactical suggestions. The choices were not exciting. He did not want to destroy Tregesser Prime. He wanted to punish House Tregesser's scheming masters. If he limited himself to that, he had to invade Tregesser Horata and the Tregesser Pylon. Which meant accepting heavy losses.

"We could pronounce a Ban," Aleas suggested.

"And have all Canon mock us." Aching inside, he issued orders. It would be the hard way.

What else had the Ku left him?

Jo gained control gradually. She used messengers till she discovered that the public comm service remained undisturbed by the jam blanket. After six hours she had communications with all her battalion and company commanders. She told them to avoid fighting, to find ways around the strong-points and under the screens.

Air support arrived. Reinforcements came. Armor and heavy artillery materialized. It still took another two days. And not once did she take one prisoner who had the slightest idea why a Guardship would attack Tregesser Prime. They thought *VII Gemina* had gone rogue.

The House security forces were embarrassingly good. They made the soldiers buy every meter with blood. Their only failing was inadequate numbers.

WarAvocat greeted Colonel Klass wearily. "Plant yourself. Relax." Pause. "This has been the most embarrassing incident of my life. Eighteen thousand casualties. Massive equipment losses. Their casualties were lighter than ours. And we did not catch one criminal."

"They had positional advantages." Klass sighed. "I'm confused. I was sure I killed Provik, Shike, and Provik's girlfriend on V. Rothica 4. Though AnyKaat didn't find their bodies when she got their stuff. You dealt with them here, later. Seeker says none of them went offworld while he was here."

"It is puzzling. It has been from the day we ran into a krekelen shapechanger centuries after the last one died. Aleas wonders if someone isn't framing House Tregesser."

"I don't believe that."

"Neither does she. She entered it as a hypothesis because it doesn't contradict the known facts. She's useful that way."

Klass nodded. He supposed she was too tired to care. "Colonel, we lack the critical witness. Lupo Provik. Everyone else seems to be dead."

"I really thought we'd get it from Cable Shike. But I and I only got the inside story on some nasty family politics. And the Ku. He admitted that. But the case is thin. He didn't know the Ku had been aboard a Guardship or to Starbase till you bombed them with the news. The Ku was a major public figure at the time—I confirmed that with a minute's research—and they couldn't believe you'd missed, but since you did and you'd increased his value a million times, they weren't going to help you overcome your ignorance."

WarAvocat muttered to himself.

"Shike says the Ku and artifact convinced them they'd never been anywhere near Starbase, that you weren't interested in him at all, you were after her."

None of it held together. But Shike could not have lied. What they got from him was the truth he knew. But... His comm buzzed. "What?"

Aleas appeared. "Is Colonel Klass there?"

"Yes."

"The alien Seeker has gotten something off the Web. I can't make sense of what he's trying to tell me. He's excited. Upset-excited."

"Bring him." He broke the connection. "Your Meddinian friend is in a lather." He paused to think. She said nothing. "It all comes back to the Ku. Always. Each time we trace him, his reported behavior makes him look apolitical or even sympathetic. He saved you.... But nothing happened to you in the universe where the Tregessers live. I'm confused, too, Colonel. You sure as hell got stuck on Merod Schene somehow."

"The Ku, sir?"

"Where does he stand? What's he doing? He knows me. He knows the Deified. He knows *VII Gemina*. If he's taken up arms again, *he* may be the reason we can't extract a reliable version of the past. He may be causing us to collide with realities reshaped to the workings of the Ku mind. The Ku wizard could believe two or three conflicting truths."

Seeker was troubled. That was not good. It made communication more difficult. Jo did not always understand when he was calm.

She was not looking forward to her next assignment. She and AnyKaat were to record the secrets and history of the Godspeakers as they were known to Seeker's people. If Seeker's race was half as old as he claimed, they would be a long time getting a story.

Jo worked with him while WarAvocat and Notable argued softly about something she was too distracted to catch. Once she grasped what Seeker wanted to convey, she had trouble remaining calm herself.

"WarAvocat?"

"Have you got it?"

"He intercepted a message from the Outsider supreme commander to the commander of the ship shadowing us." That ship was sitting out there now, barely off the strand, watching. "Which goes by the name *Hunger of the Destroyer*."

"That's cheerful."

"Isn't it? The message was a heavyweight commendation for the way *Hunger* has hung on to us and made us waste time trying to shake or catch him. Also, for doing a good job, teamed with a ship called *Edge of Night*, of letting a Traveler deliver a partial message before destroying it."

WarAvocat frowned. He glanced at his woman friend. She shrugged. He asked, "Was that rigged?"

Jo shrugged, too. "They were trying to kill me. I wasn't

watching to see if they were trying to time it."

"There were Godspeakers on both ships. They *could* have."

"In which case I'm luckier than I thought."

"What's the rest of it?"

"The end of the message ran, 'The dragon took the poisoned bait. Now it is too late. Success is assured.'"

WarAvocat grunted as though he had been kicked in the groin.

Strate did not trust his voice not to crack. Aleas asked the question for him. "You're sure the word was dragon?"

"Yes. I triple-checked it."

How long had the Ku belonged to the Outsiders? He had run from Starbase to a station controlled by Godspeakers. An Outsider-operated Traveler, apparently with Godspeaker aboard, delivered him to the Tregesser system M. Shrilica. Maybe he had been using House Tregesser since. Maybe he had been the grand choreographer, not Lupo Provik.

Hell. Maybe it went back further. Maybe the krekelen, the Concord risings, the Outsider on the Cholot Traveler, had been pawns in a grand design to bring *VII Gemina* and the Ku together....

He shuddered like a wet dog. A man could go goofy worrying about the ever-widening possibilities. That was then and this was now, and the most dangerous mind alive was active again, directing the most powerful war machine ever. There was no time for might-have-beens.

"Colonel, does he know where the supreme commander is now?"

Klass and the Meddinian huddled. WarAvocat cued *Gemina* to review what it had overheard.

Klass said, "He says the supreme commander is now sending frequent countdowns. If he listens long enough and has access to good charts, he can position the transmission point. He thinks it's on the M. Bullica–M. Tennica strand now, moving toward M. Tennica."

Deep inside Canon, in the region where the Sixth, Second, and Fourth Presidencies converged. From M. Tennica one dramatically elongated strand arrowed to M. Lakica, into the heart of Canon, directly toward S. Alisonica. "It *is* Capitola Primagenia! Access, *Gemina*. Is Kez Maefele correct in thinking it's too late for us to take him at S. Alisonica?"

Tension mounted. *Gemina* took a long time getting the data up on screen.

The air shuddered, cracked. "Yes. Can catch."

Klass fainted.

Aleas screamed.

WarAvocat sat there chewing air like a fish out of water.

Seeker observed, bewildered.

*VII Gemina* was almost four thousand years old. Never before had that great mind down in the Core, *Gemina*, spoken to anyone directly. Speech did not come till a Core mind developed an identity and ego and concluded that it was a singular entity with the Guardship itself as flesh. From that leapoff, it was only centuries before it decided it was not a machine but a demigod.

Speech was the first climbing onto the Web of madness. The end of the strand was the hollow, lonely insanity of a *IV Trajana* or *VI Adjutrix*.

It was not too late to stop that. If the news did not leave this compartment, did not get discussed, and the *Gemina* ego did not become alert to its peril, Starbase could rectify the trouble. But would not try, should the ego become integral to the Guardship's functioning.

He would head in to Starbase as soon as they finished the Ku.

WarAvocat regained his composure. He accessed OpsAvocat

and ordered a crash run straight through to S. Alisonica. The hell with Tregesser Prime.

## - 128 -

The real Cable Shike and the real Tina Bofoku stood hand in hand on the Isle of Ise, watching the nighttime sky. Shike said, "And that's that. Won't any of them have any more use for House Tregesser now that they know only the innocent stayed behind." He laughed and squeezed Tina's hand.

She said, "I hope Lupo hid himself good. They'll never stop looking for him, will they?"

"No. But the universe itself doesn't have enough years left for anybody to find Lupo Provik if he doesn't want to be found. Let's go in. It's getting chilly."

The emperor and empress of House Tregesser went in out of the cold, content, safe from the wrath of the stars.

## - 129 -

Turtle's squadron charged in toward M. Tennica anchor point. The lead vessel shot off down the M. Lakica strand, taking up the countdown transmission. *Delicate Harmony* and the others shot off along the strand to A. Tellurica, where the squadron then scattered. Two ships remained with *Delicate Harmony*, one running ahead, one behind. Just in case.

Turtle followed the progress of *VII Gemina* closely. The Guardship was running the most direct strands toward S. Alisonica. But that meant nothing yet. WarAvocat might be pretending. No telling what he would do if he shook *Hunger of the Destroyer*. Which he might. He was running so hard that even riding the red on the edge of disaster *Hunger* was falling back. The race might go to whichever ship lasted longest without a malfunction.

*Hunger*'s commander needed not taunt fortune forever. He needed to maintain contact only till pickets spotted the Guardship headed toward an operational region.

Maybe WarAvocat wanted it known he was coming. He had no reason to suspect that countdown was a lie and zero was the time when all opening phases were supposed to be complete.

The days fled. There was little to do but wait and watch and worry about how he would arrange matters so he and the hostages could get out alive.

*Delicate Harmony* and its companions broke off the Web and began the long starspace crawl to the loose strand connecting Gateway and Starbase, chasing the attack fleet, which had departed its assembly point three days earlier.

*VII Gemina* was running toward Capitola Primagenia still. The pieces were falling into place, smoothly and on time.

## - 130 -

WarAvocat grew uneasy as *VII Gemina* drove nearer and nearer Canon's heart. That Outsider watcher had dropped away, but watcher or no, his intention must be apparent.

If he was indeed too late... For what? That was the question.

For the Ku, too late could mean too late to abort his attack. But that was not the mission *VII Gemina* had assumed. He was going to get Kez Maefele and rob the Outsiders of their most potent weapon. He need not be too late for that.

But he remained uneasy in the way he did when he left his quarters sure he had forgotten something important but could not think what it might be.

Even putting *Gemina* onto it surfaced nothing to justify his uneasiness.

What sort of reception would be waiting? Material losses at P. Benetonica would restrict his options. He consulted *Gemina* and the Deified, put together a straightforward consensus plan of attack.

*VII Gemina* would go in screened, thrash around till the Ku was spotted, then would chase him till he was caught. Those new ships were nimble, but they had to put into a station sometime.

With slightly over eight days on the count, Seeker reported the Ku's arrival at the S. Alisonica anchor point. An hour later he reported a big burst of coded transmission throughout that region.

"Are they jumping off early?"

Seeker did not know.

Soon afterward the Meddinian stopped reading anything. The implication was that the Outsiders were all in starspace and communicating by normal means. Which in turn implied that the attack had begun.

WarAvocat became more uneasy.

Next day Seeker reported catching the tail of a brief signal from behind. It could have originated anywhere between *VII Gemina* and the nether face of the Outsider empire.

Forty-six hours later he reported a similar unrangeable signal.

The record passage for a Voyager running from T. Rogolica to the Barbican was forty-three hours and some minutes.

Moments later *VII Gemina* ripped past an Outsider sitting in a turn node. It blatted a signal. Seeker reported it as a number.

Little things. Little things. WarAvocat was tempted to cancel.

*VII Gemina* broke away from the Web expecting anything.

And found nothing.

Capitola Primagenia had been attacked but not destroyed. The Outsiders had pulled out. Losses on both sides had been heavy, those of the Outsiders apparently heavier than they had expected. But a triumph had been within their grasp.

And they had gone.

Everyone began pestering WarAvocat about tactical dispositions and relief efforts. He shut them out and brooded, sure he was one piece short of a complete puzzle.

The last Outsider, another damned watcher, handed him that piece. It sent a message. *The dragon has taken the poisoned bait. Now it is too late. Success is assured.*

"Aleas! Get over here. It's Starbase!" he roared. "Damn his black heart!"

Aleas stared. "What are you howling about?"

"What's been nagging me. What I'd forgotten. The Ku always used decoys. You never knew what was real and what wasn't. He led us here. He knew the Meddinian was reading his signals. Now we're too far away to get into his hair at Starbase. That watcher is mocking us because we can't do anything but go back and count the cost." He started stomping around War-Central, indifferent to the disapproval of the Deified.

"You're not going to charge back there after him?"

"Damned right I am!"

"Isn't that message supposed to make you do that? We go, the fleet jumps back in here?"

WarAvocat stopped stomping. She was right.

He grinned.

*VII Gemina* climbed onto the Web but moved only a short distance. Two minutes after Seeker reported a bleep of a signal from the watcher, the Guardship broke back off on top of the Outsider, unleashing a Hellspinner storm so intense not a thought escaped.

WarAvocat disposed his secondaries and waited.

Only two ships survived his ambush.

*VII Gemina* clambered onto the Web cursed by Capitola Primagenia's bureaucratic legions for leaving them to fend for themselves.

Now for the Ku.

## - 131 -

Turtle faced a display representing starspace from Starbase to Gateway. His lieutenants were with him, arguing about how best to deploy the fleet—not quite in the manner their employers would have approved. For safety's sake, the discussion took place in warrior *ghifu* dialect.

They reached agreement. Turtle moved to the Outsider commtechs, gave them orders to relay to group commanders.

*Delicate Harmony* climbed onto the strand, moved toward Starbase, broke away again before reaching the end of the strand, sneaked forward to watch for the projectile strike coming in from behind Starbase.

The Outsider crew, human and methane breather, were awed by their target. They had not believed before. Not really.

The Valerena wandered into the combat center while the gawking was going on. Nobody paid any attention. She had become a familiar haunt. When she got bored she went roaming, looking for an Outsider who could be led into temptation.

She paused behind the commtechs, peered at a screen. "Is *that* Starbase?"

One of the Ku told her it was. The Outsiders understood body language better than they did the speech of Canon. She toyed with a man's shoulder for a while. Then she just slipped past, hit a few keys, and started yelling at Starbase to look out.

She ended up restrained by two of Turtle's people. Everyone

stood around looking at one another. Turtle checked the board. "She missed the safety key. It didn't go out. You. You." He picked two of his own and four Outsiders. "Collect the hostages. Lock them in the mess of the number two rider. They will have what they need there and there will be no more of this nonsense."

They went.

"Get to work." Turtle assumed his station, apparently studying Starbase.

The Valerena had played that well. The rest would have to manage as cleverly if they were to survive.

There was a lot of comm chatter. Starbase was engaged with the backside force. Turtle beckoned the senior Outsider on duty. "Right on schedule. We have fourteen hours. I want as many men rested as possible."

Those Turtle had sent to confine the hostages returned. One Ku twitched, so. Provik had surrendered the toxin he had been carrying disguised as medicine, finally.

He felt a stir of remorse, but his bets were down. He had chosen a narrow path between light and shadow. He could not balk at the price.

More waiting. More trying hours as the backside force hurtled closer, as his human and nonhuman supporters ran cautious backup checks throughout *Delicate Harmony*, seeking a flaw in the plan.

The Outsider techs sounded an alarm when they had the backside force in detection. Turtle hurried into Combat. What he saw troubled him. Starbase had defended itself better than expected. "The fools," he grumbled. "Send the move order now."

Techs looked at him askance. They had trouble with fluid tactics. They made a plan, they stuck to the plan. "They've lost three of the four projectiles targeted on Starbase. They haven't redirected any of the others. It's probably too late, but we'll try to adjust."

He was not entirely displeased.

The Godspeakers sent the move order to the main fleet.

Turtle determined which projectiles had chances of warping course enough to impact Starbase. "Code this and send it to projectiles Three and Nine," he told a commtech.

"Sir, if I send this, they'll know we're here."

"If you don't, we'll have no chance of victory." He faced the senior Outsider. "Man the fighters and number one rider. When that message passes Starbase, they'll send someone to investigate."

The Outsider looked at him hard, but fearfully, not suspiciously.

"This is your chance to be heroes. You plan to live forever? Wessel, Staich, the rest of you," he told his own people, "clear away as the combat crew comes on."

He got arguments. He snapped, "I want the best people at every post. That isn't you. Wait in your quarters till I need you. Comm. Has that order gone out?"

"Yes, sir."

"Alarm given? Secondaries manning?"

"Yes, sir."

"Good." The battle crew began replacing the watch. "Tell the secondaries they may separate at their discretion, but they're to stay close so we cast one shadow."

Twelve men aboard the fighters. Forty-two aboard the rider. That improved the odds. Not enough if the toxin failed, but some.

Detection reported, "Two ships headed this way, sir."

Turtle watched the data develop till he was sure they faced a standard Guardship rider and a courier that would be fast but lightly armed and screened. He ran simulations, chose his method of attack.

The Godspeakers reported the fleet on the strand, coming.

Time passed. Detection found two more riders outbound, running in the red. The first two had begun decelerating. Turtle said, "They see we're like nothing they've faced before. They're probably everything Starbase has left. We'll take the first two before we have to fight all four."

His attack was straightforward, the fighters going for the messenger, *Delicate Harmony* and its rider bracketing the enemy ridership. The fighters finished the courier immediately. The rider was more stubborn. It got in one lucky hit before retiring with heavy damage.

The second pair closed fast.

Turtle checked the time. His own people should be in place. "Man the number two rider."

He got no arguments.

He prepped detailed orders for the battle groups when the fleet came sleeting in.

The backside force was closing fast.

The second rider launched.

For a moment he felt lonely. Now he was the only non-Outsider on the main. How long till they figured it out? "Are those orders loaded?"

"Yes sir."

"Key them as soon as they break away. Don't wait for my order." He disposed his riders and fighters for attack passes meant to look innovative but designed to let the number two rider behave oddly.

He asked for time marks. Just over six minutes till the projectiles arrived. "Anyone has personal business, now is the time." He left them smirking. Strange people.

He hurried along a passageway, brushed the timer arm on a device his people had installed where the Godspeakers were blind. There was a lot they could not see. They had concentrated on obvious areas, like the bridge.

He had to pass the hatches that led to the number two rider bay. *That* was an area the Godspeakers did not monitor. Odd, their tapestry of concerns and fears.

He collected a sidearm his people had left, taken from one of the ridership crew, whom they had overcome as they had reported aboard.

Lot of good the weapon would do him, alone with one hundred sixteen Outsiders and six Godspeakers. But great raw material for the Ku legend weavers, the lone hero staying to buy time for his comrades.

Great stuff in stories. Not so great when you were there. But certainly an appropriate end for a dragonslayer who had stepped out of the obscurity of ages to raise the sword of honor one last time and script a cataclysm that would devour empires....

Whoa!

He was amused with himself. Had he developed a mild megalomania?

He returned to Combat. Things had gone predictably outside. Crew concentrated on their jobs. They were not yet suspicious.

In a few minutes it would not matter who suspected what. In a few minutes he would have won.

One of Starbase's satellite fortresses shed a blast of light.

First projectile was in.

*Delicate Harmony* went into its attack run. "Stand by. Fire as you bear."

Another orbital fortress vanished in fire. The first was a hulk with a hole punched through.

The lighting dimmed as *Delicate Harmony* fired.

"Breakaway! Breakaway!" someone shouted, excited as a child. "The fleet is coming in!"

They all grinned. For a moment some humanity shone through.

*Delicate Harmony* lurched. Turtle felt a touch of sadness.

Such a beautiful machine to waste. "What was that?" he demanded.

Techs looked puzzled. "Were we hit?" one asked.

"I can't get through to the bridge."

Turtle said, "Look at the hull. See where we're hit."

A man screamed. Others yelled. The techs who talked to the Godspeakers went crazy. Turtle yelled, "Help those men!" Provik's toxin worked! "What's happening?"

The ship lurched. A real hit. Panic shone in nearby faces.

"Calm down. Do your jobs. Get those men out of here if they're injured." One of the fighters did a suicide smash into an enemy ship. Another fighter had vanished. Turtle's number one rider limped badly.

A third orbital fortress took a hit. A projectile streaked through, hitting nothing. A fifth smashed into Starbase itself, with so much energy it started a slow rotation.

Turtle asked, "Comm, did you get that squirt off to the fleet?"

"Yes, sir."

"Good." That damned number two rider was not cutting around the action to head for the tag end. Were those fools going to try to get him out? "I want a message run to Damage Control. We need communications back."

One officer frowned. The first hint of suspicion. He wondered why the Godspeakers had become the first casualties.

Why didn't those halfwits get out? Soon it would be too late to slide around the fleet. If the Outsider crew figured it out... He made sure his back was clear.

Two more orbital fortresses went. A badly diminuated projectile hit Starbase. *Delicate Harmony* stood toe to toe with the remaining enemy. Armaments exhausted, the surviving fighters watched. The number two rider drifted closer but remained silent.

A tech gobbled, "All dying! Poison."

Turtle shot the three ranking officers before they finished turning. "Get to work." The crewman stared. "Work! Or none of us get out alive."

*Delicate Harmony* staggered.

# - 132 -

WarAvocat tried to think like Kez Maefele. Starbase was vulnerable, obviously. Else the Ku would not have engineered an all-out assault... Or would he? Or would he?

Breath of a suspicion.

"Alert! Red One! Prepare for magnum launch!"

Now. He would see if he *could* think like the Ku.

*VII Gemina* broke away at T. Rogolica.

"Damn me! I was right!" The system swarmed with the weakest and oldest units of the Outsider fleet.

In minutes he knew. The fleet had attacked, drawn off the Guardship covering the Barbican, and had fled just before that Guardship arrived. And had come back after the Guardship departed.

The Outsiders had no pickets watching for trouble from deeper inside Canon.

Only a few Outsiders escaped the Guardship's fury. Afterward, WarAvocat said, "Aleas, the Ku isn't quite the monster I supposed. Unless he's something worse."

"What?"

"I was gloating because I'd screwed up his schemes. But what if I *am* his scheme?"

"He sent those ships here hoping you'd destroy them?"

"I'm beginning to think so."

The Barbican was scrap and gas. Outsiders had not destroyed it.

They had captured it somehow. The Guardship returning

from T. Rogolica had destroyed it—and it had destroyed the Guardship. Local space was empty. No defenders. No attackers. No watchers. No Horigawas. Nothing but silence.

WarAvocat told Aleas, "I'm not sure I want to see what comes next."

"We have to go. *VII Gemina* needs repairs."

Not just because *Gemina* had spoken. Seventy percent of the secondaries were gone. The Guardship's skin was an encyclopedia of battle damage. *VII Gemina* ought not to risk another engagement before undergoing repairs.

There was life at Gateway. Of a sort. Gateway's orbitals had been destroyed. Gateway was beyond recognition. But its Core had survived.

It did not know the fate of Starbase. Nothing friendly had come out. Very little unfriendly had.

Tight-lipped, WarAvocat ordered the Guardship onward.

# - 133 -

The number two rider drifted as though it had been crippled, ignored. Then it blew the main drive off *Delicate Harmony*'s opponent. "Tricky," Turtle said. "Keep working. They haven't quit."

He saw what his people planned. Stupid. A bet against long odds. But they were going to try. He had to cooperate.

He backed to the nearest hatch, jammed it with a shot, did the same with a second, then stepped through a third, jammed it from the outside, headed toward the rider locks.

He ran headlong into the damage control party he had summoned. There was a tense moment. A shot sent them scurrying.

In minutes the whole ship would be alert.

Even if they took him off, how did they figure to pull out again under fire?

He knocked out spy eyes, welded hatchways shut. He created a zone where he could not be pinpointed. Then he examined the rider hatches. They could not be sealed by remote.

*Delicate Harmony* shuddered. Lighting faded, came back. A mechanical clanging started aft, hysterical in intensity. The ship lurched, lurched again. What the devil? It was hell being blind to everything but that passage.

He picked a spot near the middle hatch and prepared to make the stand so likely to get puffed in legend.

New noises started up forward. They had begun breaking through the sealed hatches.

*Delicate Harmony* continued to stumble and lurch and clatter.

The passageway was full of fire. On the deck were six Outsiders who had tried to be heroes. Turtle did not miss.

They could not get a clear shot without exposing themselves. Stalemate. Till the bunch working their way forward set up a crossfire.

Turtle had maybe three shots left. He was considering saving the last for himself. Or should he go out hand to hand, risking capture, torture, sacrifice?

*Zap!* A running Outsider pitched headlong. Two shots left. Or one and the easy way out.

He had refused that option when they ground the Dire Radiant down.

*Boom! Boom! Boom!* The outboard hatches blew inward. Grenades tumbled through with Ku warriors right behind.

The shooting was over in seconds. An assault team headed forward. Ah! They meant to hit Combat so there could be no shooting when the rider pulled away.

He reeled as Midnight smashed into him. "Oh! You're all right. I was so worried."

"You'd better get back..."

The Outsiders from back aft arrived. Turtle shoved Midnight

through the hatchway. A wild beam gnawed at his back. He grunted, shoved her at Provik. "Hang onto her!" He raced to the rider's Combat Center, ignoring pain.

Only one soldier was on duty. "Any comm off ship?"

"No, sir."

"Damn." But he had expected it. He tried to estimate how long to reach Combat, how much resistance, while catching up on the situation outside.

That was going exactly as choreographed.

He went to the nearest outboard lock. It was quiet out there now. They were waiting to cover the assault team. He asked one of his people, "You arrange to unload the rider crew?"

"They go out fore and aft, shielding us as we fall back through the midships hatchway. They've been told they have forty seconds before we disconnect and decompress the passageway."

"Good. Carry on. I'll be in Combat."

He did not make it. His wound was worse than he thought. Blessed, Midnight, and the Valerena dragged him to the rider's rudimentary dispensary.

The rider had been away two hours, tumbling like a derelict, when Turtle did reach Combat. "I ought to court-martial you all. But where would I find an unbiased court?"

They were drifting away from the action. The attack was nearing its peak. It would continue a long time unless the Godspeakers had an uncharacteristic attack of strategic sense.

"We pulled it off," he said. "And have a chance of getting out." Six hours and the rider would be outside detection range. There would be futures to consider, probably in the guest colonies Outside.

# - 134 -

WarAvocat watched the minutes drag. The suspense was worse than it had been going into that end-space ambush. "I want to break away moving dead slow, screen up."

"You think we'll find…?" Aleas's voice caught.

"We'll find Starbase beat all to hell and the Outsider fleet wiped out."

"Why?"

"Or I could be wrong. He could have fooled me again."

*VII Gemina* broke away into a warships' graveyard. Nothing moved, except as it had died. The heat had fled most of the wreckage. It had been over a long time.

"Prophylactic screening," WarAvocat ordered. "Ahead slow. Anything from Starbase?"

"Negative, sir."

"Scan." Most of the wreckage would have drifted out of detection already. He was awed by what the Ku had brought to the slaughter.

"We have a signal from Orbital Six, sir. Starbase Core survived but lost ninety percent-plus out-ports. It's using that capacity to seek breaches in its environmental armor."

He exchanged glances with Aleas. Starbase would be no help taming *Gemina*. She said, "You were going to vent a theory about the Ku."

"About how he used us. He stepped into the middle and manipulated everything so it came out to his specs."

She thought he was mad.

"How many got away at S. Alisonica? At T. Rogolica? How many here? He planted them where he could squash them. Without killing any bystanders."

She scowled. She could not believe the Ku had put them through hoops.

The next few decades would be difficult for some Guardship people.

Aleas said, "What I see is the death of the myth of our invincibility. He engineered this, and he failed. Another triumph for us. And that's all. But if news of this gets around, we'll have fires on all the Rims."

She was right. The rest of the universe should hear only of another crushing defeat for Canon's enemies.

How long till Starbase repaired itself? Centuries?

She had made a point within her point. The fleet could not brag about what had happened. The Outsiders would not admit their forces had been crushed. But if the Ku remained at large...

He was at twenty-eight percent of strength with no hope for replacements short of getting in line at Starbase Dengaida. He could not go there till he knew about the Ku.

He cued a conference of rider commanders and fighter pilots, told them he needed Outsider ships with surviving personnel or data systems capable of yielding information. He sent them out. Then he asked Orbital Six for everything about the fighting. When the data was in, he settled to watch the replay.

Simple little thing like history, Jo thought. This happened. So and so did that. Whatchamacallit reacted thus. Facts and dates in serial, maybe with a body count if that shed any light: History.

Seeker did not see it that way. Specific events, times, persons had little meaning. History was process and context and slowly oscillating emotion in a psychically unified, intimately interconnected milieu where the players never changed. History was a sluggish, silty river, and he was a fish in a school. The river could not be sliced.

It had looked like a straightforward job of translating, slow but not insurmountable. It had turned into a nightmare of misinterpretations, misapprehensions, mistakes, and miseries. She could not have sustained the task without AnyKaat. Seeker could not have survived without Amber Soul.

"AnyKaat. You ever get nostalgic about Merod Schene?"

"No. That wasn't a good time."

"Life was simpler."

"Too damned simple." AnyKaat snorted. "This loafing is too much for you; why don't you blow yourself away?"

"I wouldn't wish it on another me. Strate would have another Jo out in three days. Hell. I'm about done. If I can just get straight what he's saying about the Web and the Presence."

WarAvocat ran the encounter with the Outsider forerunner five times, speed up, slow down, trying to find a clue to why the ship tripped alarms. Aleas finally took pity. She froze the scene, blew up the nose of the Outsider, scribed a circle. "Those characters are Ku. They translate 'Delicate Harmony.' The characters on the vanes translate 'Dire Radiant, One.' The characters between the fighter nests are the Ku date for their surrender and a word that comes through as dishonor but means more."

He disappointed her expectations of gratitude. "He wouldn't advertise himself like that."

"How often would he see the outside of his ship?"

"Not often." Did the Outsiders have their politics, too?

No matter. It was evidence the Ku had been here. "Access, *Gemina*. Isolate the battle data pertaining to this vessel." It could be another of the Ku's diversions. "I want it temporal, regardless of source. Run at one hundred times realtime. Sit down, Colonel Klass. Where have you been hiding?"

"With our aliens, sir."

"Uhm." Strange, that maneuvering with the riderships... There it was. "But you've got something?"

"It may not be important but it's got to be interesting to

anybody who believes the fleet is the pinnacle of technological possibility."

"That sounds ominous. One minute." He watched the tumbling rider till it vanished. He launched a blossom of nine probes down its track, ran up views of Web strands, launched more probes, then faced Klass. "Tell me about it."

She went at it directly. "The Web is an artifact. The Presence—there are three in our part of the galaxy—is an automated repair device."

"Well," he said. And was so stunned he could only repeat himself. "Well." Nowhere in any hypothesis was there a suggestion that the Web was a construct—except in the theological sense. Starbase was the ultimate macroengineering concept.

Klass said, "Seeker says his people have been on the Web six million years. They met one race that had been around an eon. *They* didn't know who built the Web, they just had legends from older races. The Builders probably were the first intelligence to evolve, and were functionally immortal. They laid out the pattern in starspace at low sublight velocities, taking eons. When they finished this galaxy, they supposedly were going to connect the nearer galaxies. Maybe they're out there spinning the Web right now."

He said nothing. He was in shock.

"The Web wasn't meant for travel, it was a means of communications, like a fiber-optic network. Of course, all that's hearsay now."

"These Builders sure built for the ages if their 'machines' are still operating."

"Seeker says the Web is deteriorating. Traffic wears it out. In the past billion years a thousand races have found it. The Presences can't keep up. They've stopped trying in some regions."

"Whoa. This is too much right now, with everything else." He had waiting calls nagging. "Get it prepared for review. Sounds like a first-rate job."

"Thank you, sir. It hasn't been easy. I thought you'd want the key information. I wouldn't have interrupted had I realized we were operationally engaged." She departed.

He muttered, "She *has* been preoccupied."

Aleas said, "An interesting revelation. Consider the consequences of that becoming general knowledge."

"Eh?"

"We've spent millennia claiming Guardships represent the limit to technology. We believed it. Now suppose this gets out."

"Why worry? The information hasn't exactly been secret." He turned to his calls waiting.

The third was interesting. A fighter had located the main of the Outsider forerunner. It was damaged but functioning.

He ordered the derelict collected.

# - 135 -

The starspace journey became dreary fast. There was only so much planning possible. Once everyone had added to the wishlist, there was nothing left but routine duty and watching stores dwindle. Turtle spent his time with Midnight, trying to know her while he could.

Time's gnawing had become obvious. Blessed was troubled. Then Midnight herself caught on, at least unconsciously. She suffered mild depressions. They would get worse.

Turtle was nursing her through a spate of tears when Provik appeared. "Better come forward." His tone was grim.

A crowd had gathered. One of his people had held his seat. "It's set to run."

He ran the tape.

A recon probe ripped past. "Twenty minutes ago." Two more followed, barely detectable. Calculation indicated they had come from the vicinity of Starbase.

"*VII Gemina.* WarAvocat figured it out."

His people had run the options. They had found what he expected. There were no options.

The rider did not carry foodstuffs enough and could recycle nothing but air and water. It had not been designed for protracted independent operation.

They were committed to the shortest possible starspace run.

One of his people said, "If ten of us were to—"

"No."

"It would give the rest more time."

"No."

"Better ten dead than all dead."

"Better no dead than ten."

"Sir—"

"The subject is closed. And I will not tolerate disobedience. Find out what resources we have. Hospital, chemicals normally used for other purposes, vermin, whatever." He had a despicable idea. "Anyone kills himself, the rest of us will eat him." His gorge rose but he meant it. They knew that. None would subject his comrades to that.

"We begin strict rationing. We avoid activity as much as possible."

Turtle made a course adjustment. It would take two days longer to reach the strand, away from where it had intersected his earlier course. It was the best he could do.

All systems went down to minimal. He ran Stealth and SCAM patterns to blind active scans, launched an ECM probe programmed to look like a ridership trying to do a sneak down his former course. He sent a second probe off on a likely alternate course. He reviewed the tricks they had used in the old days. Some should be good still.

He hoped Hanaver Strate was WarAvocat *VII Gemina* still.

# - 136 -

**VII** *Gemina* broke away running dead slow relative. Ops took sights and moved ship to a position astride the quarry's last known course. No scan, passive or active, detected anything.

That was to be expected. The Guardship was days early.

WarAvocat was in Hall of the Watchers. The display wall showed nothing but the starfield. Outwardly he appeared calm, confident. But that was half his job. Inwardly, he was paralyzed by a conviction that whatever he did the Ku would anticipate. Like they were tied into a knot of predestination.

He could not see beyond the Ku's prime objective, the strand, which he would use for all it was worth, on and off, to shake the Guardship.

Aleas said, "He'll see our corona soon, Hanaver."

"I know." He moved closer, whispered, "My mind has turned to gelatin. I don't know what to do besides wait. Unless I make him go against an unknown."

Aleas looked quizzical.

"You take him. He doesn't know you."

"Are you serious?"

"Yes."

Aleas reflected, examined the estimated situation, ran some calculations. She saw her intent, was surprised he had not thought of it himself, and worried. If the Ku did slip past, it was all over. He would vanish before they could recover riders. Secondaries had become too precious to abandon.

Aleas took *VII Gemina* onto the Web, moved twelve light minutes, broke away, launched a fourth of the secondaries and a decoy that would look like a Guardship. Then she moved twenty-four minutes the other way, made an identical launch. Then she returned *VII Gemina* to its starting point, through starspace. She launched the remaining secondaries and another decoy construct.

WarAvocat wanted to ask questions. He refrained. He had put it into her hands. He had to let her run it. Even though he would answer for any failure.

Aleas ordered all secondaries to assemble on the central construct if *VII Gemina* went onto the Web in pursuit.

A perfect solution.

It took her thirty-five hours to make her dispositions.

She had one more surprise. She ordered the whole sprawl to advance toward Starbase.

# - 137 -

Turtle was not surprised by the third corona.

Provik said, "They want us bad, don't they?"

"Kez Maefele, we will pass within a million kilometers of the one on the right," a watchstander reported.

"Feed me the data." He retreated inside himself, put everything to the wizard. The way they had done in the old days, never depending on the infallibility of computation systems. Let intuition bear the load.

It took an hour to fall into place.

"There is only one Guardship. They could not have gotten three together. The one in the middle will be real. We will maintain our present heading."

He wished he had not launched those decoys.

He ran calculations. He could reach them with a carefully aimed tight-beam pulse without betraying himself.

"Use the docking jets to put the tumble back on," he directed. "We'll take our radiation profile down till we can barely stand the cold. We'll try sliding through as a wreck."

Watchers reported an intercepter had a contact, on the

time mark and not far off the Ku's projected track. Riders converged.

"A missile," Aleas grumped. "Hell. All that excitement for nothing."

WarAvocat double-checked. It was enemy. Seemed unlikely that the Ku would have used so passive a decoy. He went back to *Gemina*'s visuals of the fighting. He could find nothing that argued one way or another. The resolution was not fine enough to discriminate missiles and projectiles.

Next contact came fourteen hours later. Another loose missile.

WarAvocat frowned. That seemed a long coincidence, but they did not fit the Ku's style. They should have come in a hurry, making a racket. Serials and other markings might show from which ship they had launched. But there was no reason to expect their proximity fuses to have failed.

Twenty hours after the second contact Aleas asked, "Could he have turned back?"

"I don't know. He might have headed for the strand behind Starbase. He might have shifted course up, down, or sideways. He might have stopped to wait us out."

Came word of a contact way off to the left, followed by word that it was just a piece of cold matter. Then to the right, before the nerves settled, a pursuit ship caught a ghost of an echo of something moving behind it.

Some secondaries had been out over three days. That was hard on fighter crews. Discipline flagged with endurance. Each contact drew some fighters out of position.

The ghost proved to be another missile. One that had gotten through, undetected till the last instant.

"And there's our problem," Strate told Aleas. "Even though we're not covering a large region, we're not covering it completely. He could fall through the cracks."

They had two riderships and a fighter on passive scan. Turtle kept making minute adjustments with the undetectable docking jets, holding a groove through the heart of the triangle.

Provik said, "They don't care who sees them, do they? They've got everything cranked up enough to cook eggs at a thousand kilometers."

Turtle grunted, bled a little more power into the Stealth, SCAM, and ECM systems. He gestured for quiet. He wanted to keep an ear on intercepted inter-ship chatter. Most was military gabble but he spoke gabble well.

"Passing the plane, Kez Maefele. Sixteen hours to the strand. Shall we take off the tumble?"

"Not yet." Ghosts off tumbling Stealth surfaces were more likely to filter out of a detection system than those off a steady surface.

One of his people said, "Been a long time, hasn't it? I forgot how tense it gets."

Turtle nodded. They had done this often in the old days, mostly going in to attack, usually against watchers less alert.

He tried to calculate the position of the rock causing the excitement. Not that far away. That was not good.

Course adjustments had the rider running straight at the false Guardship. What detection and comm capacity were mounted there? He would not have bothered, himself.

He would know soon enough.

He was tempted to take it out as he passed, as a rude farewell, but that was not a Ku sort of gesture.

Thirteen hours. The fighter had faded from detection and had become one probability point among dozens deduced from comm transmissions. The riderships were fading. Nothing lay between them and the strand but the decoy, four hours away.

Eleven hours. Nothing but probability points on screen. They were through. He gave permission to stabilize ship.

"Twenty minutes to drive on line. Five percent." That would not generate enough emissions to stand out against the background of the universe. He would kick it up gradually....

"Kez Maefele!"

"I have it."

The interceptor had come out of nowhere, burning a hole through vacuum, headed toward *VII Gemina*, running with nothing but nav scan extended.

*Crack!* It was gone.

"The IFF steal worked." Turtle sighed. "I was afraid we hadn't gotten enough data." It was another old trick, stealing the enemy's mutual identification signals. "They must have an emergency aboard."

WarAvocat was exhausted. It remained only for Aleas to cry uncle....

"Anomaly, WarAvocat."

"Hunh?" The air had spoken.

Everyone in Hall of the Watchers froze, stared with wide, terrified eyes.

Damn! What a time for it to happen. "Explain, please."

Inbound interceptor DZ539, with a medical emergency, nearly collided with a rider. IFF exchange went normally but rider JV47 is supposed to be on station several hours away. Comm check shows JV47 maintaining station properly."

"Goma Maradak!" WarAvocat swore.

"What?" Aleas asked.

"The Goma Maradak waste space. We used it for training during the Ku Wars. It resembled places the Ku liked to hide. When *XXV Iberica* went in, the Dire Radiant was hiding *there*. They stole IFF signals, took a dozen ships into rider bays.... They stole IFF throughout the war. And now he's pulled it again, walking right through pretending to be one of us."

But when he ran data from the region, he could not find a

hint of anything to support his suspicion. If Kez Maefele had come through, he had done so like a ghost.

Aleas thought, attacked the problem from a different perspective. She input the tumbling rider exiting the Starbase end space, the probe blossom, the missiles that had been detected at this end, and told *Gemina* to see if the known data forbade them being linked or made it impossible for that anomalous contact to be the Ku.

## - 138 -

The rise in comm chatter was ominous. Turtle altered course a hair. "Get me a pod of missiles ready." His people knew what to do. It would be a twist on another old trick. Several began the complicated programming.

Before they finished, the probability points on screen had shown drive sign. "That IFF didn't fool them," Turtle said. "Though they had to think about it for a while."

"What're you going to do?" Provik asked.

"Put a pod of missiles out running the vectors we were making when the interceptor spotted us. On scan they'll echo like a rider. They'll provide an IFF feedback. Another old trick."

"What about us?"

"We'll vanish. If the pod does its job, they'll think we're dead."

Aleas had called in the secondaries to *VII Gemina*'s right and had sent riders from the center to the left. It would be hours before recovery was complete and the Guardship could move to the center of action.

"Contact report came. Right where it ought to be. IFF responder IDing ridership JV47."

"That isn't a *VII Gemina* rider," WarAvocat said.

"Could the interceptor have made a mistake?"

"Of course. They were preoccupied. But I'll bet they didn't."

Aleas moved ships to close a pocket around the contact. "You want them alive?" She knew he did.

He was troubled. This had developed too passively.

Aleas ordered a fighter closer to the target. There was a chance the Outsider really was crippled.

It did not respond to comm attempts, except for the automated IFF. It looked too cold to support life. "You think they might be dead?"

"No." Because he did not want the Ku to evade him that way, either. Nor any of the others... He tried not to think about the artifact.

"We'll know once Probe takes a look."

The fighter drifted closer, ignored. Then, "I'm getting weird drive readings. Like they're in bad shape. Starting to move. Turning toward the Web."

WarAvocat was acutely aware that he was hearing news twelve minutes old. Neither he nor Aleas could control what was happening.

The fighter reported the rider's drives behaving increasingly erratically. The senior officer present ordered the fighter to fire across the rider's nose. The fighter closed in. "Can't see them yet. Must be running high SCAM. Wait. There's a drive glow...."

A static blast overrode the signal.

Turtle eased the rider up to the array proclaiming itself a Guardship. It was bigger than he had hoped.

Provik and his girlfriend, Blessed and the Valerena, were EVA. Only they could squeeze into Outsider suits. They floated ahead, on tethers, opened a passage through the decoy's titanium and filament frame. Turtle nudged the rider through. The people outside closed up behind.

Provik and his woman anchored the array to the rider. Blessed and the Valerena made connections so its broadcast output could be controlled from the ship. Both tasks took hours.

Turtle greeted them when they returned. "Good job. The pod just blew. From all the cursing it looks like they bought it."

He went to the bridge, gently nudged the array toward the strand. He programmed the decoy's output to decline gradually.

It would take longer to escape this way, but he felt good about his chances. Hell. They might even pull out now.

He settled down to rest, tried not to think about hunger.

WarAvocat retreated to his quarters to sulk. He slept for twelve hours. And awakened with the conviction that the Ku was not dead. But he could produce no rational support for the feeling.

"Access, Colonel Jo Klass. Klass, WarAvocat. Meet me in the aliens' quarters."

He stepped into the passageway—and found himself face to face with a naked woman, the most beautiful, erotically stimulating women he'd ever seen. She smiled as she passed.

He stared. No woman aboard *VII Gemina* looked that good. None ever had.

His voice squeaked. "Tawn?"

She smiled over her shoulder, turned into a cross corridor. He ran after her. When he turned the corner he saw no one.

Aleas would shit.

He wandered off to keep his appointment, bemused. That was enough to make you forget other women existed.

For a few minutes, anyway.

WarAvocat tightened his nostrils. He'd never get used to the smell. He told Klass, "There were several people on that rider we both knew. I want to know if they can be found the way Seeker found you."

Klass was puzzled. "But they're dead. I heard they tried to run on a bad drive and blew their Q."

"Indulge me, Colonel."

# - 139 -

Turtle glared at the screen. *VII Gemina* had no reason to hang around but it was, still running random rider patrols. He could not get enough from their comm chatter to understand why.

Their presence kept him moving at a crawl. He was two hours from the strand. He would take this for one more, then he would run.

He had been telling himself that for eight hours. Gut it out another hour before making the run.

One of his non-Ku said, "Kez Maefele, I'm getting a ghost. Not like anything I've ever seen."

Turtle's stomach grumbled as he bestirred himself.... "That's a Guardship trying to run silent. They know we're here. Stand by for violent maneuvers." He surveyed screens. They had put out another decoy, then had sneaked around to get between him and the strand. Only you could not sneak with something that big.

The drives were warm. All go. "Ready?" He slammed it into the red. The rider ripped the decoy apart.

Immediately the screens sparkled with radiation from drives. He was not surprised. He would have sneaked up from behind, too. They would be decelerating to match his pace.

"Head straight for the strand. They won't shoot right away." He eased back on the acceleration. Had to hold something back. He would need it soon.

Jo stood on the operating bridge of a ridership clad in lightweight EVA armor used for boarding operations. She shared her post with Group Commander Colonel Haget. He had reverted to the Haget of old. They might never have met.

His task was to catch the Ku's rider. Hers was to capture the Ku.

She said, "WarAvocat guessed right again."

Haget grunted..

"That bastard can *move*."

"We had a running start."

No point being there with him. She joined AnyKaat and her troops, real soldiers who understood what it meant to be soldiers. AnyKaat was sweating. "Relax. Pretend it's Merod Schene."

"But it isn't Merod Schene. And we aren't up against retarded bastards."

"True." There were Ku aboard that rider.

"Boarders, stand by," came by overhead.

Why the hell did WarAvocat want them alive?

Twenty riders in the pack, too close to escape. But not shooting. WarAvocat wanted prisoners.

Turtle felt he had no right to make a decision for everyone. "Listen up, please. We're trapped. We're one hour thirty-nine minutes from the strand with *VII Gemina* moving into our path. We have a slim chance because they want to capture us. If we go for that chance, we'll have to fight. If we fight, the odds are they'll kill us. Our deaths would have only symbolic value. Do we fight or surrender?"

His Ku did not hesitate. "We fight. They will kill us anyway." The other soldiers agreed, as did Provik and his woman. Midnight and the Valerena disagreed. Which left Blessed.

"Put the women into an escape pod. Blessed, you have till it releases."

Three minutes later the pod was away. Blessed Tregesser

was not aboard it.

"First bunch closing."

Four of them, in from each quarter. He had not yet fired. Neither had they. Why hadn't they hit his vanes?

He waited till they were too close to raise screens.

He hit the two nearest with missiles, slammed on maximum dump, shot the other two in their drives, rotated ship violently and pushed it into the red, headed out the side of the pocket.

Metal shrieked. The rider staggered. Some rider commander with more guts than brains had permitted a collision and had grappled. Turtle could not break free. He put on violent pitch, roll, and yaw to keep another from grappling. The other ship fought him, but he had the more potent drives.

His soldiers went to greet the boarders.

That damned Haget was a madman. But he'd sure done his part.

The sucker was in place. Jo blew the charges, sliced a hole through the other hull. The assault squads charged. She and AnyKaat went over behind the first platoon.

There was a dramatic shift in gravitational attitude.

The Ku had exploited that moment of disorientation thoroughly. The first two squads had been slaughtered. Would a hundred soldiers be enough?

"AnyKaat. Move out aft. Come on, people! Move!"

The woman nearest her shed flesh and fire.

"Colonel Klass is aboard," the air said. "JV83 is collecting the escape pod."

"Very well." WarAvocat was confident the artifact would be aboard. He knew the Ku that well.

Where the hell was Aleas? No one had seen her for hours. Never had his people been so distracted and grim. They could not keep their minds on business. Damn *Gemina!* Why now?

There was no way to still their fears.

Four Ku stepped out of nowhere and killed the six Guard-ship soldiers guarding the connection with their rider. The four went across and killed their way toward the rider's bridge.

AnyKaat was lost. Her helmet had gone out. She had dumped it. She had no way of knowing how Jo was doing.

Two-thirds of her force had been killed, mainly in hand-to-hand fighting. They had taken no prisoners. She had seen only two enemy dead.

The drive aft had stalled at a cross passage. Someone around there had killed three soldiers already, hitting them with inhu-man quickness and accuracy when they tried the corner.

A soldier signed that he would throw a grenade and they should all charge. She nodded. He threw.

The grenade came back as they moved.

The mass of bodies shielded her from the worst, but concus-sion stunned her. She wobbled into the cross corridor, found herself face to face with Blessed Tregesser, Lupo Provik, and Provik's girlfriend. The girlfriend's eyes got big. She smiled. "This is for Merod Schene."

AnyKaat joined Degas in the shadows.

Turtle continued wriggling the ship so no other rider could grapple. He hit another two with his last two missiles. He got the drives of three more with his cannon. He dodged attacks on his own drives and vanes.

He was better than they, yes, but still their efforts seemed half-hearted. Why?

Comm. The team he had sent aboard the ridership. "We have the bridge, Kez Maefele."

"Sabotage it and come back."

"I can't. Too badly hurt. The others are on their way. Stand by to seal the breach."

"Right." It was a warrior's choice.

A red pinlight lighted. The patch was on. The light turned green. The patch was airtight.

The ridership turned loose.

Turtle slammed it into the red, raised screen, shot out of the crowd. The Ku who controlled the other rider hurled it between two others and blew the Q.

Twenty-six minutes to the strand. He was ahead of the pack and gaining. He put on all the ECM, SCAM, and Stealth he had.

*VII Gemina* sat squarely astride his path.

The hatchway ripped open. A squat, ragged Guardship soldier stumbled through. He moved. She shot his seat. "Told you I'd come, Ku."

He slid around, darted in, knocked the weapon from her hand, kicked. "And I cautioned you that that would be fatal."

The light went out of her eyes.

WarAvocat watched the Outsider rider hurtle closer. A report came saying the escape pod had contained the artifact and a second woman. "Ready the Hellspinners," he ordered. Why the hell wouldn't the Ku give up?

Twelve riders lost or damaged. A hundred boarders wiped out, probably. To what purpose?

He did not comprehend. Though now he knew he could have gone shitstorm in that end space.

Enough was enough. If the Ku insisted, then die he would.

"Access, the Deified Aleas Notable."

After a long pause, a strained, "Yes?"

"Where the hell are you?"

"Here." From one of the screens reserved for the Deified.

"What have you done?"

"I nearly lost my objectivity, Hanaver. I had to come back."

"But..."

"Don't argue. There's no point. You have a task to complete. Complete it." She vanished.

He faced the wall display, sliced off the pain.

The Ku was coming like he meant to smash through *VII Gemina.*

He suffered an epiphany. He would not long survive the Ku. That was there in the way Aleas told him he had a job to finish.

The incoming rider adjusted course. The Ku would have to do more if he was not to overshoot the strand....

He laughed. "You bastard! I've seen this trick before." The Ku would threaten collision till he raised screen, then would slide past without a shot being fired, too fast for the Hellspinners. Or, if the screen stayed down, he would run in on the skin of the Guardship, too close and fast to track accurately, holding himself in with strands of artificial gravity—till he decided to let loose and whipped off at some unpredictable angle.

WarAvocat gave orders.

Beams licked out. Shells ricocheted off the rider's screen. A few Hellspinners rolled, just for effect. The rider came in like a Lock Runner.

It passed inside screen limit.

WarAvocat raised screen.

The Ku was trapped inside.


Provik said, "It didn't work."

"Not this time." Turtle dumped velocity as violently as possible. He kept an eye on the surface of the Guardship. It took four orbits to shed speed. He put the rider down in a wasteland of battle damage, set SCAM to blend, cycled down as far as he could. "They can't detect us here from inside or out. They'll have to send searchers. Let's hope they make a mistake before they find us." He fought off weariness. "We have work to do. Those bodies have to go. Their equipment and weapons and rations have to be collected."

WarAvocat watched the riders straggle in, ignoring the scrutiny of the Deified and live crew, wondering what next.

What next was the Ku would wait for him to screw up while he waited for them to get hungry and make their own mistake.

He issued general orders, said, "Bring the prisoners to my quarters when they arrive." The hell with what anybody thought.

# - 140 -

Lupo Provik disentangled himself from Two. He went to a window. Beyond lay the world he had chosen as the seat of his stolen empire. It was a beautiful world, still untarnished. He meant to keep it that way.

"You're brooding again."

"I suppose."

"One and Four again?"

"Yes." The news dribbled in. The Ku seemed to have done everything but get the hostages away.

"It was a thin hope."

"I know. I know. It had to be done. And they volunteered. But knowing that doesn't fill the hole in here." He studied the forest that swept up his mountain. "Now we're safely out, I can't help wondering if it was worth it."

Two understood. "It was. This isn't Tregesser Horata Down-Town, where you'd be dead by now if you hadn't reached up and grabbed. And none of the rest of us would have lived."

"I suppose."

"If you have to brood, worry about how we're going to keep the Guardships from finding us."

. "They'll be too busy picking up the pieces and holding the Rims."

"If you can't do anything constructive with your mind, come do something useful with the rest of you."

## - 141 -

WarAvocat was wounded. Lady Midnight did not remember him. And she had aged. It was terrible to look at her and recall the beauty that had faded. So he looked at the other woman, who had come aboard as haughty as a queen, unafraid, contemptuous.

He could not fathom her attitude. It seemed misplaced. "You're not in the Tregesser Pylon," he told her.

"Which renders me vulnerable to maltreatment. It doesn't change who's quality and who isn't."

Ouch. He lifted an eyebrow. "Why did you leave your companions? Why should you expect any mercy?" She radiated something intensely sexual. He wondered how she would be.

"The Ku and his bullies are determined to go out in high Ku style. They *want* to die. But they also want to make a fool of you for as long as they can."

"They haven't done a bad job."

"They've forgotten something in the heat of their game. Getting the Outsider fleets to suicide only gets rid of the fleets. The point of the war for the methane breathers is to buy time while they ready a place to hide."

WarAvocat frowned. "There is no safe place."

"Wrong. We spent a year there. But I can't tell you where.

Only the Ku knows. And he has no reason to tell you."

He quizzed her. She was forthright. But why? He asked.

"I have people on that rider, including a son."

There it was. She wanted to cut a deal. "I'll think about this." Long enough for them to get real hungry out there. If shipboard politics permitted.

Three days. He had not made a dent in Midnight. The Tregesser woman had been easy, and interesting, but inclined to manipulate. She overvalued her skills.

She was strange. In the usual loose confinement, she roamed around muttering like a madwoman.

He did not think she was crazy. She was up to something. She got around too well, too, like she knew where she was going....

Ku wearing captured combat gear invaded a rider bay and carried off shipboard rations. WarAdvocat had not anticipated that. They were daring. They could become lice on the body of the Guardship.

Were they trying to force something? More likely they had no choice. Midnight and the Tregesser woman had come aboard gaunt.

They were vulnerable out there, even if they were undetectable. He had options. He sent fighters to pepper the area with 40mm CT. Afterward, he sent a message. He wanted the methane breathers' final redoubt.

Instant uproar. The Deified did not want deals. They wanted revenge. Living crew did not want campaigns, they wanted Starbase Dengaida, to get *Gemina* into therapy.

The Valerena's muttering paid off sooner than she expected. She took a turn in a remote corridor and there was Tawn. Had to be, though it was female. It had that look.

Its being female was a surprise. That would make seduction

more difficult. And this Tawn, on a Guardship filled with the Living, would be less naive.

WarAvocat waited uneasily for the Ku's representative. Provik appeared to need no guide. Disturbing. "Do you have yourself under control, Colonel?"

Klass nodded. She knew she was a psychological counter. She was tough. She had come out of the tank knowing she had been killed and had gone to find out how and why. She was ready to hunt the Ku. Maybe too ready.

Why was Provik with the Ku? They had lied skillfully at P. Benetonica....

The air asked his attention, communication for his ears only. He listened, accessed the surveillance on the Tregesser woman's quarters. She was having a conversation with someone who was not there. Bizarre. He would have to give that more attention.

Provik arrived. He was direct. "The Ku says he'll give you the location and a method of attack if you'll give him Midnight and Valerena Tregesser and turn your back while he disappears."

"Maybe he'd like another shower of CT."

"He might worry if your gunners could hit the broad side of a Guardship."

"I see. So. You once said, 'We have our own politics to survive.' I have my own politics to survive."

Provik shrugged. "All the same to them. They've made up their minds to die. They won't bargain."

He had feared that. Damned Ku style. "And you Tregessers?"

"We wrote ourselves off way back. We have nothing to gain from you."

Too true. Life was the only chip he had on his side of the table. And they would not play for that stake. He glanced at

Klass. Provik seemed untroubled by her presence.

"We have an impasse. I don't know how to break it."

"Ask *Gemina*."

Crew were troubled enough. If *Gemina* offered an unpopular suggestion... Even so. "Access, *Gemina*. You have been monitoring. Respond to Mr. Provik's suggestion, please."

It was a long wait. Bad. It might mean.... It did.

"Enlist the Ku according to recent fleet directives. Assign them detached duty with orders to report at an unspecified date."

Impractical. "The Directive disallows anyone who has stood in arms against Canon."

"Hire him as a special operative, independently assigned, under suspended death sentence."

Interesting. *Gemina* understood Ku warrior psychology. Enlisted, their concepts of faith and honor would compel them to fulfill whatever obligation they undertook. It would lay a fat temptation before Kez Maefele, who wanted to get his people out. The unspoken agreement would be no commentary ever about what had happened to Starbase.

"Do you understand the undertaking there, Provik?"

It would not be politically acceptable, but he could order it. If he did not mind putting his Deification more at risk than it was.

Once he had been ready to risk it to get the Ku. Must he now risk it to silence an enemy more terrible and repugnant?

"Tell the Ku I'm considering dealing. On about those terms. If he convinces me totally that this Outsider hideout is dangerous."

"I see the angles, Strate." Provik walked out.

WarAvocat looked at Klass. "Well?"

"You haven't kept up on my work with the Meddinians."

"I haven't had time. What have I missed?"

"Seeker claims it's critical that we beat the Godspeakers

now, before they dig in. If we don't, we'll never beat them completely. They'll devour us in the long run. He says. In fact, he goes on like we may have missed our chance already."

"I'll review the material. See what you'll need if we have to deal with the Ku the hard way."

"Yes, sir." She went.

He reviewed the material though he was too tired to concentrate.


Turtle said, "Let me think," after hearing Provik's report. The snare was patent. They would turn him into a living endorsement for the fleet.

He should not have survived Starbase. If his people had followed orders, they would be safely away. He would not be eyeball to eyeball with another moral monster.

They would insist on keeping the attack secret. But the Ku needed to know that their ignominy had been redeemed. But the news running free might hamstring the Guardships when they needed everything to end the Godspeakers' threat.

Had he hurt them too much? Had he made it impossible for them to compromise?


Jo eased into the darkness outside *VII Gemina*. It had been a long time since EVA school. She had to be careful. She was wearing a field combat suit for the sake of its detection capacity. It would be clumsy in free fall and had no maneuvering jets. She attached a safety line and jumped.

She stopped paying out after two hundred meters, studied the damage, looked for sentinels. She could find none.

The motion vectors of her jump, the unyielding safety line, and the slow rotation of the Guardship swung her out over the damage. When she was headed for the horizon, she began paying out again. There were twenty kilometers of monofilament on the reel, more than enough.

Hey! Didn't that look like a tractor vane, that trapezoidal regularity in the wilderness of twisted metal? Hard to be sure. No way to make sure without getting too close.

What the hell? She worked the rocket launcher around, sighted, launched, hit rewind. The takeup reeled her in so fast she did not see the rocket strike.

WarAvocat needed no convincing when Provik returned. He believed the Meddinians. The Godspeakers would constitute a deadly threat while they maintained belief in a Destroyer deity.

The Godspeakers understood the Web less than did any other race.

The Presence radiated dread as a defense, as a tool with which it frightened away destructive vermin. Only a pest encountered repeatedly risked destruction. Predisposed by evolution to dark interpretations, the Godspeakers had seen the Presence as a manifest avatar of a greater power, a child sent by the Darkness to demonstrate Truth.

They had stumbled onto a way of summoning the Presence. Announcements attributed to it were fancies or wishful thinking. They lied to their human allies, who lied in turn to the subject races.

WarAvocat entered a directive: Obtain that summons. Web maintenance could be concentrated in Canon space.

The murder rites did affect the Presence. Seeker suggested that was because it misread the sacrifices.

Provik presented a crude star chart. "There's what you'll have to dig them out of if you let them get ready."

WarAvocat plugged it in, let *Gemina* translate, stared.

Grim.

"They're providing themselves with habitats capable of surviving there?"

"Construction was ahead of schedule when we left."

WarAvocat glared at the chart. "I can find it now."

"But how long will that take?"

WarAvocat accessed the data from *VI Adjutrix*. What he needed still was not there. He glanced up. Provik grinned.

Had they gotten aboard *VI Adjutrix* during its stay at P. Benetonica? That would explain a lot. "I'll need a face-to-face on this."

No protest. No argument. "I'll tell him. I'd like to see Midnight and Valerena before I go. I have messages for them."

That hurt. He had made no headway with the artifact. "I'll have someone take you. Don't dally."

Provik grinned again. "We're not in any hurry. There's no time pressure on us."

The *clang* rang through the rider. "What was that?"

Turtle had it in a minute. "Something hit one of the vanes." He could not get a good look. "Someone will have to go look."

One of his people went out. His report was not good. "There is an anti-armor rocket embedded in the vane. It did not detonate."

"A dud? Or intentional?" Turtle worried. They knew where he was now.

"That will be the big question."

Turtle accessed the ship's schematics. They went to work figuring out how much damage the warhead could do and what options existed.

Turtle muttered the whole time. He had a damned good idea who had put the rocket there.

Blessed told the women, "I'm here because we're negotiating. We've almost closed a deal."

The Valerena was not excited. "Oh."

"We have something they want."

"The Outsider hideout?"

"Yes."

"I don't want to go back, Lupo. I like it here."

One raised an eyebrow. He did not tax her, though. "Midnight?"

"I go with Blessed. Wherever he goes."

One nodded. He saw the weariness the Ku had mentioned, the encroachments of time. "It shouldn't be long. WarAvocat is pressed for time."

WarAvocat was pressed politically. He had presented the available evidence to Kole Marmigus, the Dictats, and the Avocats. Marmigus and the Deified Pursole Styles, dct. 3 and former WarAvocat, agreed immediate action was indicated. Hereo Jaspyon, dct. 7, and the Avocats wanted to head for Starbase Dengaida. Now! They refused to believe a beaten species could pose a continued threat—despite the Ku's example.

They did not want to believe.

Aleas had broken her silence to warn him that Makarska Vis had come out of seclusion. She led a cabal dead set against handing the Ku anything but his head.

"Damn! I thought we were a sensible, pragmatic people." He was talking to himself, thinking about resigning again.

There would be no easy way out. The options were fading. He would be forced to put his immortality on the line one way or another.

Someone tapped on his door, uncertainly, then with resolution. "Enter." He was startled. "Midnight!"

"Hello, Hanaver," she said in a tiny, frightened voice.

Turtle supervised the dismantling of the vane personally. That was not difficult. The rider had been designed for easy repairs under poor conditions, in expectation the work would be done by inexperienced people with common tools.

They had the dud out within the hour. Turtle prepared a timer and destructor charge and hurled it toward the Guardship's horizon. It flew on till it encountered the screen, slid around the curve, finally blew.

Under cover of that distraction, Turtle moved ship five hundred meters, to a better hiding place.

# - 142 -

WarAvocat met Provik in an empty fighter nest. Klass and Midnight accompanied him. Blessed Tregesser and Provik's girlfriend completed the other party. Midnight bustled off to Tregesser. WarAvocat maintained a face of stone, his suspicion that she had visited him to soften his heart confirmed.

Provik said, "He didn't expect you to come to him."

"The political situation has devolved into the grotesque. I have to do something quickly."

Provik's girlfriend muttered, "How many times do we have to kill her before she stays dead?" She and Klass glowered at one another.

WarAvocat finally understood. The Tregessers had replication technology. Nothing else explained the mysteries so neatly. He had not seen the obvious because it was not supposed to be there.

The fleet desperately needed newer, more flexible minds. His own generation had brains set in concrete.

"Klass. Compose yourself. We're not animals. There's more at stake than your outrage. Provik, take me to him." He had come prepared to go outside, though he had not known what to do about Midnight. There were no EVA suits for winged people.

Provik solved that with a fighter pilot's blow bag, a poor man's escape pod. They closed her into one, inflated it, and ssed Tregesser towed it like a child's balloon once they were outside.

WarAvocat's heartbeat rose. His blood coursed as it had not in millennia. Going to meet the enemy... This was not the same as standing in WarCentral moving pawns who actually did meet the enemy eyeball to eyeball.

"WarAvocat is coming himself."

Turtle was astonished. Then suspicious. Why would the man do that? "Watch him every second."

"The female soldier is with him, Kez Maefele."

"Watch her twice as close. She's twice as dangerous."

They came to the rider's bridge. WarAvocat glanced around. "Are we this much trouble?" He was a tired old man, moving slowly.

"You are."

"To be honored by the enemy is a greater accomplishment than to be honored by one's own, I suppose. It's been an interesting few years. I'm glad you didn't want it all."

"The alternatives were less appealing. Lupo says you had great success at S. Alisonica and T. Rogolica."

"Few got away."

"Excellent. I hope the blow to your pride wasn't insupportable."

"My pride is fine. It couldn't have been managed on a cooperative basis. But I have to live with the political consequences."

"I imagine Makarska Vis is exercised."

"You imagine right. And there are others after my blood. There have been changes since you left."

"Yes? So. I gather you see a way to break our deadlock."

"A basic approach. Providing you have a functional escape pod."

"I do." Turtle was intrigued. His gut feeling was that Strate did mean to let them go. Why? Some political angle?

"At fifteen hundred hours my chief of staff will open a port in the screen. You will shoot through and head for the strand. When you're convinced you'll make it, you'll eject me, the Colonel, and the data."

"And we're quits?"

Klass said, "No. I'll find you someday." She moved slightly. Provik's woman had the mouth of a weapon in her face almost before she started.

"How many times you have to die?"

"I only have to get through once."

"Colonel! No immunity, Kez Maefele. Just a head start. In exchange for that information."

Turtle nodded. "And if I don't come through?"

"Colonel Klass is carrying an explosive device. She won't hesitate to use it."

WarAvocat probably had his own, Turtle reflected. "I'll take a chance. It may be the only chance." He produced a cassette. "Everything I can give you is on this. You may review it if you like."

"I like."

The rider powered up cautiously, lifted off the Guardship, pointed its nose toward where WarAvocat claimed a port would open.

It opened on the mark, a black mouth in the pearly shimmer.

Turtle shoved it deep into the red. The rider plunged forward.

"Hellspinners, Kez Maefele."

"Raise screen."

"Miss. Another miss."

"Someone must not care if they get WarAvocat along with us."

"Missiles launching, Kez Maefele."

Turtle's human companions cursed and blustered. His Ku stuck to business. He put the rider through the port. It popped shut behind them. The missiles exploded against the inner face of the screen. "Politics," Turtle said. "They must be on the verge of civil war. Launch the pod as soon as they're ready. Let them chase that."

The sudden acceleration caught Strate unprepared. "Can't he do anything gently?"

Three minutes later there was a violent thrust at right angles to the first. The Ku had launched the pod.

It revolved. WarAvocat saw missiles banging off the inside of *VII Gemina*'s screen, saw Hellspinners seeping through. He became so angry he almost had a stroke.

*VII Gemina*, operationally in control of OpsCrew rebels, accelerated toward the strand but arrived too late. Three days of hurtling back and forth produced no sign of the rider.

WarCrew backed by *Gemina* regained control, went back, collected War-Avocat. He was hale enough to vent his rage. Within an hour there was a new OpsAvocat, and a dozen Deified had gone to the electronic equivalent of purgatory. One was a Dictat. WarAvocat exceeded his legitimate powers dramatically. WarCrew who had cooperated, even unwittingly, he had recycled.

In hours living WarCrew were in control, totally and absolutely. Soon the Guardship was on the Web, headed Outside.

Strate formally informed crew of his intentions. "We will finalize the matter of the Godspeakers. Then we will visit Starbase Dengaida for what help may be available. Then we will travel to P. Benetonica to pick up our unfinished business there."

Privately, he told Colonel Klass, "I think the Ku will try to rejoin the original Lupo Provik, wherever he's gone. Somewhere on P. Benetonica 3 there'll be someone who knows some truth and someone who's in contact with Provik, however indirectly, who'll serve as the first stepping-stone in the chain."

The Valerena Tregesser heard the public announcement. From that she reasoned forward to WarAvocat's private thoughts.

# - 143 -

VII *Gemina* limped across the Rim, a determined cripple, much slower than during the crashing inward run. In private WarAvocat was as concerned as anyone else. *Gemina* had no recollection of a time so desperate the Guardship had carried on with this much damage.

He hoped for the best.

A long, slow passage, without political complications, allowed time to look into what he had shelved or missed. He spent a lot with Klass and her Meddinians, trying to integrate their knowledge into what *Gemina* already had. Which meant frequent collisions with the unpleasant fact of *Gemina*'s burgeoning ego.

He spent some time in damaged areas where *Gemina* could not eavesdrop, too, discussing that with senior live crew. The meetings did not produce much. He did learn that there were no breaches in the Core's armor or seals. The problem was not organic. It would develop slowly—but could not be treated medically.

Klass had a suggestion: resurrect her sidekick. "She's the only one aboard who's had a kid or has had to deal with one. Right now *Gemina* is a real bright baby. We could make some breaks for ourselves if we started from the beginning trying to bring it up right."

He chuckled, not taking her seriously.

"You start right now teaching it 'I Am A Soldier.' That it's got specific duties and responsibilities and honors and privileges. Teach it that it's an important part of the crew but only a member of the crew. That's in the programme already. Reinforce it whenever you deal with the personality. Treat it that way and demand that it behave that way."

An amusingly flaky idea—that grew on him. He adopted it. It might buy needed time. He authorized AnyKaat's restoration.

He permitted the Tregesser woman to insinuate herself into his bed. It was a way to keep an eye on her. She had some private agenda. What it was he could not fathom.

He suspected she was in regular contact with Tawn, and they might even have a physical relationship, but he could worm nothing out of her. Nor could he learn much through surveillance. *Gemina* still insisted Tawn was mythical and would not see her though crew sightings were a commonplace.

He took *VII Gemina* off the Web at a system already designated B. Alenica, nicknamed Chatterpoint, deep within the methane-breather empire. Chatterpoint was the place to leave data packages whenever one Guardship had something worth sharing with others.

There were recent optimistic packages from old confederates *IV Trajana* and *XII Fulminata*. According to them, it was almost over. A couple more gas giants to hit, some mopping up, putting quits to roving warships without bases to support them anymore.

Simpletons.

WarAvocat set out a package containing *VII Gemina*'s news, with requests for support in the waste space.

Valerena came early the day *VII Gemina* departed Chatterpoint. She was troubled. He asked, "What is it?"

"Guardship politics. I made a mistake, staying. I don't fit this reality at all. Some of the Deified are going to try to kill yo

But I don't see how they could."

# - 144 -

Lupo hugged everybody, including Turtle, then hugged everybody again. For hours everybody told everyone what had happened for a year and a half. "You pulled it off!" Provik enthused. "I don't believe it. But why did you come back, Kez Maefele? I thought you'd do another long disappearance."

"I hope I have." The Ku looked around. "And there was nowhere else where I had more friends."

Lupo was startled. He heard truth there, if not the whole truth. "There's more."

"Yes. When I gave WarAvocat the data, all I gave him was what he needed to silence the methane breathers. I reserved information about several tag ends with no military significance. If I could find a partner willing to share the wealth of that waste space with the Ku people..."

Lupo burst out laughing. "You never stop scheming, do you?"

"Do you? I have to be what I was made to be."

"You have a deal. Down the middle. I'll put up equipment and capital. You come up with the manpower and keep the Guardships out of our hair. They haven't given up on us."

"No. But *VII Gemina* will be occupied with internal problems perhaps long enough for us to become a matter of no consequence."

"I hope so. Come on, we have to have an all-Canon blowout to celebrate the most bizarre passage in modern history."

# - 145 -

Jo caught AnyKaat's signal, cocked the hairsplitter she had kept as a souvenir. Two furtive OpsCrew types came along an aisle between vats, supporting a limber-limbed replica of Makarska Vis.

WarAvocat had anticipated his enemies correctly.

The OpsCrew conspirators were headed for Personnel Recording. While the replica was in the vat, and in transit to Recording afterward, it was the only record of the Deified.

Jo stepped into their path, aimed at Vis's forehead, blew her brains out. After the woman fell, Jo shot her through the head twice more, walked away.

The Deified Makarska Vis was dead forever. There was no way she could be restored.

Jo figured the Deified would get WarAvocat's message.

# - 146 -

Seeker and Amber Soul were beside Strate when he took *VII Gemina* into the waste space. Colonel Klass and AnyKaat were there to help communicate. WarAvocat was awed by the stellar display, which had been invisible from Web-space. "I wasn't convinced," he said. "Until now. You could hide anything in that."

The Godspeakers had plenty of warning, though WarAvocat used Hellspinners liberally to burrow a channel so he could reach his objective more quickly. He sent a rider force ahead to strike at two incomplete habitats Seeker feared would flee before they could be destroyed.

Strate told Klass, "Tell him to concentrate on tracking those things." Minutes after *VII Gemina*'s breakaway Seeker had announced that each habitat contained a "brood mass," a mindless superGodspeaker colony serving a reproductive function resembling that of a queen ant and the data storage function of a Starbase Core—though the brood mass could not manipulate that data itself.

"It's a repository for genes and knowledge," Klass sa'

"Without one there could be no more Godspeakers."

"Why hasn't he mentioned it before? He's been holding out."

"We destroyed the original when we hit their homeworld. He says he didn't think they could put another one together. They've never had two at once, ever."

WarAvocat knew little about the biology of the methane breathers. He did not care. They were the enemy. Their biology signified only when it could be used against them.

He did not accept Seeker's claim. He had known. Brood masses had to be the reason he'd been so keen to get a Guardship out here....

Dammit! He'd turned the Ku loose for nothing. Seeker could have gotten them here if only they had had sense enough to ask the right questions.

The Meddinians had high moral pretensions. No matter the pragmatic necessity they'd never admit a desire for genocide. They would not want to take the guilt back home.

His rider force was too weak. The Outsiders forced it back, launched a counterattack *VII Gemina* repelled with difficulty.

WarAvocat feared he had been too optimistic. Or maybe he had been suckered again, if Kez Maefele had sent the Guardship to its destruction.

That would be the perfect solution from his point of view, wouldn't it? Let *VII Gemina* be destroyed finishing the Godspeaker threat so he would have no enemies left over.

Klass reported Seeker sensing one of the habitats beginning to move deeper into the waste space.

A second attack came in. He rode this one out behind his screen, using Hellspinners sparingly. Let them spend themselves now and be in for rearming when he reached their base.

He noticed an interesting phenomenon: Every ship capable

of climbing onto the Web, which had neither methane breather nor human aboard, expended its munitions and ran for the tag end.

The glue of loyalty had come unstuck. They would make no last stand for masters who would abandon them.

Klass reported the second habitat moving, but slowly. Seeker said it was less finished than the first.

The fight at the station was no epic to be recalled for a thousand years. WarAvocat took *VII Gemina* into the cleared space, screen maxed, ignored the two methane-breather heavies and a dozen human warships, picked an angle from which the station could not defend itself, ran out the funnel, poured in fire till Probe said there was nothing left alive. Then he went after the slower habitat. It had only a four-hour start.

The Outsiders attacked continuously, desperately. WarAvocat heard grumbling because he would not fight back. He ignored it.

The habitat scurried into a swarm of cold matter. That suited WarAvocat fine. There was so much garbage flying around, the Outsiders could not bring but a fraction of their strength to bear. He went to prophylactic screening and began picking them off—never slowing in his pursuit of the habitat.

Catching up took more than a day.

The moment the inevitable became obvious, the Outsiders gave up trying to prevent it.

WarAvocat shouted, "Colonel Klass! Ask Seeker if they can form another brood mass if we destroy both habitats."

She did so. "Negative, sir."

"They've decided to concentrate on saving the other one, then. Do we have contact still?"

"Yes, sir."

"If he loses it, I'll slice off his ears. Understood?"

"Yes, sir."

The habitat, once caught, was easy. It had no defenses and

could not maneuver.

WarAvocat was in his element now, dealing with an enemy of known strength and capability who was locked into a mission with absolute parameters.

The Outsiders left one watcher—which he deluded with the guile of a Ku and waylaid before he finished the habitat.

Then the real chase was on. It was apparent quickly that it would not be over soon. They knew the waste space. He did not. But he knew where they were and, for the moment, he was invisible to them.

## - 147 -

The Valerena tracked events through Tawn. That relationship was nearing its peak heat, where Tawn would be at her most pliable. The Valerena was concerned that WarAvocat would stretch it out so long her influence would wane.

She experimented.

Tawn was invisible to *Gemina*. *Gemina* refused to believe she existed. Invisibility would be handy as hell for an interloper with ambitions. She asked Tawn to try to fix it.

Tawn tried. It worked. As long as the Valerena was not in the presence of someone *Gemina* did accept and recognize.

Perfect.

The Valerena went to work nagging about getting a replica of herself made. Better than being invisible would be being invisible and being able to be two places at once.

## - 148 -

Eighteen days since the destruction of the first habitat. The Outsiders had not regained contact with the Guardship, grace of Seeker and Amber Soul. WarAvocat had gotten ahead of the habitat and its convoy. He placed a decoy inside a swarm of cold matter, moved on to another swarm within a stream of very active gas.

He launched secondaries, had them pair with rocks, vanishing in their shadows. "One from your book, Kez Maefele," he muttered.

*VII Gemina* waited.

The Outsider scouts spotted the decoy, darted back. The convoy stole into the hyperactive gas stream. It would be harder to detect there.

It was not the perfect ambush. The Outsiders' leading vessels tripped it too soon.

For those it was thorough and final.

The Outsiders did what they had to do.

When the shooting stopped, one of their heavies was out and the other was crippled. Their secondaries had spent themselves in suicide attacks so effective WarAvocat elected to slough the Guardship's two outermost layers. The smaller Outsider ships all suffered. Three more perished. But the habitat made its getaway, sustaining minimal damage.

It hurried toward the neutron star whose gravity had helped create the river of hyperactive gas.

Plodding and implacable, Hanaver Strate went after it.

The habitat was down close to the neutron star. *VII Gemina* could not get into decent range. Neither Guardship nor personnel could withstand the tidal forces that seemed no inconvenience to the methane breathers. Their habitat was nimble enough and shielded well enough to survive everything WarAvocat threw down there.

Forty-two days passed. WarAvocat occasionally pestered the Godspeakers with a shower of missiles and shells. Sometimes the bombardment went on for hours. It did no good.

# - 149 -

The Valerena was in her quarters with her replica when the alarm sounded. "That's Red One. They're going to do it. Head for WarCentral so you can be seen with WarAvocat while it's happening."

She turned to her small info screen, glad Tawn was elsewhere and did not have to be managed.

*VII Gemina* hit the habitat with the heaviest and most prolonged bombardment yet. It did no harm. That was not expected. The flash and crash was meant to keep the Godspeakers blind to what was really happening.

WarAvocat had borrowed from Kez Maefele again.

The chunk of cold matter inbound was eight kilometers by three and was moving one hundred twelve thousand meters per second when the Godspeakers detected it. It was too late for the habitat to prance aside.

Asteroid and habitat met head-on.

The Valerena loped passageways as naked of life as any of *VI Adjutrix*'s had been. They were identically constructed. She located the nexus of nutrient delivery for the Core. It took two minutes to inject ten cubic centimeters of sterile freon into each of two feed lines.

She raced back to her quarters, invisible to the eyes of the thing she had attacked.

The physical effects of the embolisms were trivial. But *Gemina* forgot how to burn starspace drives and lost track of the critical function in calculations of how to climb onto the Web.

The door to the Valerena's quarters smashed inward. WarAvocat entered behind his living shadow, Colonel Klass, and her permanent sidekick. The Valerena queried, "Hanaver?"

"You overlooked one trivial technical detail when you sent your replica to distract me. She was a virgin. All else could be reasoned back from that."

The Valerena shrugged. "So I've failed to achieve my personal goal. The House is safe." The Guardship had started moving just before the embolisms struck. Helpless, *VII Gemina* was drifting deeper into the waste space.

"I wouldn't count on that," Strate said. "We hold grudges forever. Colonel."

Klass fired one shot, through the Valerena's brain.

## - 150 -

Provik found him tending Midnight's grave, which he still did after all these years. "Kez Maefele, this just came in on one of our Haulers out of the New Presidencies."

Turtle glanced at the brief document. "We were overly optimistic again."

"The strong survive."

Turtle read the document again.

> *FLEET DIRECTIVE*
> The Dragon Never Sleeps
> —*WarAvocat* VII Gemina *Jo Klass*

"They do, don't they?"

## - 151 -

**Guardship: VII Gemina**
**Off tag end 27P29Z6 awaiting Core restructure**
**assistance 2/17 shipsyear 3751; year 66 of the**

Deified
Hanaver Strate
Dictats: The Deified Hanaver Strate, dct. 7
    WarAvocat/OpsAvocat Jo Klass, dct. 3
Alert Status: Yellow One
    WarCrew sleeping [.18 duty section]
Surveillance Mode: Active